THE DREAMWALKER

Praise for *The Hiding*

"On its face, *The Hiding* is an enthralling adventure of demons, spirits, witches and their hunters. Within its secret rooms, it's an examination of identity and community and the very real magic therein."
—Rae Knowles, author of *The Stradivarius* & *Merciless Waters*

"A delightful weave of supernatural mystery and family drama, balanced against a tale of found family and pain."
—Alexander James, author of *The Woodkin*

"A surreal supernatural murder mystery through the streets of an alternate York, woven with chilling prose, throat-rending creatures, and a found family to triumph over all."
—S. A. MacLean author of *The Phoenix Keeper*

Praise for *The Somnia*

"With prose as lyrical as it is sinister, supernatural found-family vibes and an atmosphere so thick you'll be wearing it for days, *The Somnia* is a superb sequel with a chilling mystery at its heart. I simply cannot get enough of Lyons' dark, magical York and the hauntingly brilliant characters who inhabit it."

—Ed Crocker, author of *Lightfall*

"Lyons beckons you deeper into her storytelling's snickleways and alleys, and I promise you'll want to follow. A captivating tale pulling together the best of sisterhood, friendship, and the power of self-determination and magic, *The Somnia* weaves its melody into your very heart. Lyons's fans will be delighted to see this beautifully rendered story alongside the triumph of *The Hiding*. I loved every second reading this harrowing and delightful book."

—Taylor Grothe, author of *Hollow*

Praise for *The Dreamwalker*

"A mysterious new enemy is preying on the minds of artists, trapping them in a dangerous spell, and Harper and her crew must stop them before they destroy everything. From the streets of a dark, alternate York to the misty canals of Venice, Lyons weaves an enchanting urban fantasy about dreams, art and dangerous magic that will pull you deep into its vivid, nightmarish world."
—Jelena Dunato, author of *Dark Woods, Deep Water*

"A love letter to dreams, music and art, composed with passion and coloured with patience. An absolute pleasure to read."
—Jade Black, author of *The Determined Ones*

"Both beautifully tender and fraught with action, Lyons' epic continuation in *The Seer of York* is an ode to magic, the uncanny, and the ties that bind us all. Wrought with a masterful hand, the gothic prose and deep relationships in *The Dreamwalker* will not disappoint—and through it all, you'll be absorbed by the mystery at the heart of these pages. *The Dreamwalker* is a book to keep in your heart forever."
—Taylor Grothe, author of *Hollow* and *Lethal Kiss*

"A mysterious new enemy is preying on the minds of artists, trapping them in a dangerous spell, and Harper and her crew must stop them before they destroy everything. From the streets of a dark, alternate York to the misty canals of Venice, Lyons weaves an enchanting urban fantasy about dreams, art and dangerous magic that will pull you deep into its vivid, nightmarish world."
—Jelena Dunato, author of *Dark Woods, Deep Water*

"This book doesn't pull its punches - whether that's with characters, plot or how proudly it proclaims diversity as strength. Another stunning look at the murky morally grey spaces that exist when people and systems are the real monsters. You will want to befriend the whole team, and fight for their causes."

—P. S. C. Willis, author of *Crying Out for Magic*

"Lyons' third instalment of *The Seer of York* series masterfully blends Gothic fiction and English folklore into a dark fantasy mystery adventure that will keep readers turning pages until well after midnight. With a magical and deliciously grey cast of characters, *The Dreamwalker* is one of those novels that will stay with you long after you've closed the book."

—MJ Pankey, author of *Epic of Helinthia*

THE DREAMWALKER

Book Three of the Seer of York

by Alethea Lyons

The Dreamwalker

Copyright 2025 © Alethea Lyons

This book is a work of fiction. All of the characters, organizations, and events portrayed in this story are either products of the author's imagination or are used fictitiously. Any resemblance to actual events or locales or persons, living or dead, is entirely coincidental.

All rights reserved. No part of this publication may be reproduced in any form or by any means without the express written permission of the publisher, except in the case of brief excerpts in critical reviews or articles.

All opinions expressed by characters in relation to magic and religion are their personal opinions and are subject to the rules of their universe, which are different from the rules of ours. No characters are scholars in this area, and all are simply coming from a place of trying to do good.

Edited by: M. J. Pankey
Proofed and formatted by: Stephanie Ellis
Cover illustration and design by: Alison Flannery

Chapter header adapted from photo by Kaihsu Tai - Own work, CC BY-SA 3.0, https://commons.wikimedia.org/w/index.php?curid=5694404

First Edition: March 2026

ISBN (paperback): 978-1-963355-47-5

ISBN (hardback): 978-1-963355-48-2

ISBN (ebook): 978-1-963355-46-8

Library of Congress Control Number: 202693144

BRIGIDS GATE PRESS

Overland Park, Kansas

www.brigidsgatepress.com

Printed in the United States of America

Also by Alethea Lyons

The Seer of York Series

The Hiding

Reawakening: A Collection of Short Stories

The Somnia

The Dreamwalker

The Mistlings (*Coming March 2027*)

Content warnings are provided at the end of this book

*To those who are still discovering their own secrets,
to those who have to hide who they are,
and to those who can't hide but live in fear.*

*Your differences are beautiful.
Society can only blossom when it embraces diversity.*

Twixt life and death, 'tis but a moment,
As 'twixt wakening and sleep.
Within them all there is one constant,
In the dreams our soul does keep.

Magic dreams, a prayer most potent,
Beneath the Earth in slumber deep.
And while it dreams, it passes judgement,
On all the reasons we should weep.

Its birthing comes, no longer dormant,
Magic waken, dance, and leap.
It will roar up, its power rampant,
And what we sowed, we soon shall reap.

Previously On ...

After experiencing visceral visions of death, Harper Ashbury searches for the killer. With help from her demonhunter foster sister, Grace De Santos, she uses illegal magic and her position as arcane archivist at the cathedral. During their investigation, they meet Saqib Siddique, forensic supernaturalist, and AJ Tailor, techno-witch, both of whom eventually join them. Harper also accidentally summons a deception spirit who decides to call himself 'Heresy.'

They discover the spirit of the River Ouse is enacting a ritual to hide England's magic folk—creatures most humans think were banished or exterminated long ago but who have been hiding in plain sight all along. As a witch, Harper is torn between wanting to protect magic users and wanting to stop the murder of innocent humans whose body parts are needed for the ritual.

She attempts to talk the Ouse out of completing the ritual. Frozen by magic, the spirit disintegrates during their conversation leaving Harper guilt-stricken at what she believes to be her accidental death.

Because the Hiding was never completed, and because the Ouse was killed, the amount of dark magic and dangerous creatures in York increases. Harper and the team make a pact to protect innocents on both sides. They have various (mis)adventures including releasing disembodied voices from a book, tracking missing people, and working with the secret police.

When some of the vanished people reappear with their eyes gouged out, Harper investigates. She discovers the new killer, the Somnia, is linked to Harper's forgotten past. Thanks to Heresy trying to possess a stray cat in the garden, they find a shifter, Fionn, spying on them. He's also connected to Harper's childhood, though neither of them remember how.

Fionn was set to watch Harper after an omen linked her death to his master's, the most powerful magician in England who plays both sides of the fence in a much darker way than Harper. In addition to this, Fionn helps his master with blood rites, alchemical experiments, and collects dreams to use as power sources. He's become attached to one dreamer in particular while doing this.

Harper confronts the Somnia and fails with disastrous consequences for everyone else in the household. In return for helping Harper learn violin magic to defeat the Protector, the River Foss demands Harper either find a new river spirit for the Ouse or become the spirit herself. The deadline is the vernal equinox.

With the help of Fionn, she faces the Somnia again and eventually defeats him. Believing she banished their Protector, Harper's newly discovered birth family casts her out. They remained hidden in a tiny bubble realm.

Chapter One

Finding a Dream Home

Harper Saw through the eyes of another as history repeated. Her mistakes would become their mistakes, just as she had taken on the burden of her mother's and grandmother's. Generations of seers, all blinded by fear.

Fire blazed, contained in this reality while raging unbound in another. Light and shadow flitted over the sides of a large tent. Figures in tapestry rugs danced to the tune of a violin only she could Hear. They played out the tales of her people. For so long, they'd been trapped in this place, yet their stories endured, passed down from parent to child for over four hundred years.

Her outstretched hands were almost in the fire, yet it didn't burn her. Magic flowed between her fingers and the hypnotic flames. They danced left, then right as she waved her hands.

"Well done, sweet girl." An arthritic hand patted her shoulder and she released her grip on the fire. It settled back to a low crackle, grumbling at having been forced outside its chaotic nature.

Harper recognised the voice. Though she'd heard it only briefly at dawn in her village, memories were trickling back. There was no mistaking the matriarch of the clan. Her grandmother. She clung to the dream, desperate to know more and wondering if she'd See something of her own past through this other child's memory.

"Thank you, Grandmama." Though her lips formed the words, it was not Harper's voice but the child's. Not just any child. Her little sister. "Will the Protector be happy with me next time he visits?"

Disappointment soured in Harper's stomach, both at the way her sister sucked up to their jailer and at the fact this memory couldn't be old enough to show her own past. Her sister had not yet been conceived when she fled home. The twinge twitched the dreaming and the child scowled at the ruffled feelings not her own.

"He'll be proud of you, little Seer." Their grandmama bestowed a gentle smile of approval, though her eyes were tight with sorrow. Not for her lost grandchildren. For the entity who'd hurt and manipulated them.

Harper drank in every feature. Eyes so like her own. Hair greyer than in the memories that were trickling back to her. An aura of power not to be trifled with.

"I'll find him, as you ask, Grandmama," the child said.

No. Harper wanted to shout, but she was stuck behind the glass of the girl's eyes. *I banished him. He'll hurt you!*

"You will, little one. You're a good girl. Not like your sister."

"Why did she send the Protector away?"

Their grandmama looked the little girl straight in the eyes. The fierceness of her gaze struck Harper like an arrow. "She was always unnatural, a blight to this family. You, my dearest, are pure, true, and loyal. You will See a way to bring our Protector back to us. And as for *you* …" Her tone sharpened. "Get out of my grandchild. Keep your treachery away from us."

The old woman's hand jangled with bracelets as she raised it. A sharp tap to the girl's forehead shoved Harper out of her body. For a moment, her consciousness hung in blank nothingness. Then she woke up with a curse.

Harper lay in bed, staring at the stucco ceiling and panting. Her head ached as though her grandmother had opened her skull and jammed her pointed nails into Harper's brain.

"Heresy?" Harper groaned and rolled over. There was no pile of ash on her pillow nor any obvious dark corners of extra shadow around the room. He often slept, or at least rested, beside her. She wasn't actually sure if he slept or not. It was difficult to tell with an eyeless soot ball who lied incessantly. "Heresy? Are you up here?"

"My dearest Harper. Pray tell me all your wishes and desires. I have nothing better to do than to wait around this dull room while you sleep." Heresy materialised from under the bed.

Harper shot him a suspicious look. "What were you doing down there?"

"Playing."

"With?" She swung her feet out of bed, nudged him aside with her toes, and got down to peer into the shadows. The loose floorboard under which she hid all her magical paraphernalia appeared undisturbed. As Heresy could pass through solid matter, it wasn't a reassuring fact.

"Poking things to see what would happen." Heresy's wide, Cheshire Cat grin split his body and he waved an ashen tentacle at her.

"If I told you not to, would it make any difference?" Harper asked wearily.

"It would not," Heresy chirped. "For what purpose did you request my presence?"

"I had a dream. A vision, I guess? I Saw my family. I thought you were supposed to keep my dreams safe. That *is* why I let you stay."

"And so I could teach you magic," Heresy added with unaccustomed haste.

"I'm not banishing you." Harper sat on the floor, head back against the bed. "Though I think Fionn is happier teaching me than you are." *If he ever comes back.* Harper told herself it was only two days since they banished the Somnia. He'd returned home with her afterwards, though he kept to himself and sat by the back door rather than join them at the table. Then he'd pulled on his collar, pain in his eyes, shifted back to cat-shape and disappeared into a silver swirling portal. Most of the time, his portals were black, and she was worried what the change portended. Maybe she'd try scrying for him, not that she was very good at it even with Heresy's tutelage.

"The not-a-cat does not do good magic," Heresy said primly. "I am a much better teacher."

"You haven't answered my question," Harper pointed out. "Why didn't you hide me from them?"

"Was not the purpose of all of this for you to find them? I was unaware you now wished to avoid. Your mind seeks them. As with the creature, that Somnia, who hunted you, I cannot hide you from something you deliberately invite."

"I didn't …" Harper trailed off. *Did I?* For years she'd longed to go home. Then she found the way, only to be denied entry.

Rubbing her temples, Harper hauled herself to her feet. Her birth family didn't want her, her birth brother was missing, but her foster sister, the woman closer to her than blood, was right next door. Grace would never turn Harper away. She stayed at her sister's side even though Harper's magic was the anathema of everything Grace's family stood for.

Harper slipped into Grace's room through the adjoining Jack-and-Jill bathroom. Her sister was exhausted from her ordeal in the Somnia's cave and very grumpy about admitting that, so Harper didn't want to wake her. Instead, she crawled into the single bed and snuggled against Grace's back. The deep coffee and sweet vanilla of Grace's perfume comforted her with every breath.

Home wasn't out in the Swaledale hills with folk who never really understood her.

Home was here, with her sister, and it always would be.

Even if saving Grace meant leaving her to become the new guardian of the vacant River Ouse.

Chapter Two

An Unhelpful Chat

The next morning, bleary-eyed from lack of sleep, Harper stood at the end of the thin strip of land that jutted between the River Foss and the River Ouse. Thoughts and memories scratched inside her brain, half-formed and panicked. Her grandmama would never let her come home. The Somnia would return. She'd be unable to save them a second time. Instead, she'd be here, trapped as guardian to the Ouse. She would keep her word—find a river spirit to take the role by the vernal equinox or fill it herself—but she fervently prayed a better candidate would come along.

As always, the twin calls of the cathedral bells and the muezzin reciting the adhan brought a sense of peace. She turned her face into the fine mist of rain that dampened her skin. It reduced the world to grey beyond a few metres and muffled the nearby traffic. No one walked on days like today. *Except me, it seems.*

Confident no human was around, Harper summoned her Sight. Magic flowed easily to her retinae as though it desired to be there always. It was almost a reversal: harder to banish than to summon the more she used it. Heresy smugly told her it was as it should be. She worried whether a day would come where the magic wouldn't hide. *What if my true nature refuses to be repressed?*

Shaking off her concerns, Harper drew the moist February air into her lungs. It clarified her racing thoughts and cooled the burn of magic. Her Sight brought the dreary day into focus.

No longer a miasma of droplets, wraiths moved through the haze. She'd Seen them before—at the Shambles Market, outside her house the day AJ's coven visited, near the cathedral—never quite sure if they were real or shadows of visions.

Harper…

We're still waiting…

Still hungry…

Harper…

Overlapping myriad whispers. They'd followed her out of a book, out of the cathedral archives, and tried to lure her to God-knew-what fate in the Museum Gardens.

"Heresy? Can you see them?" Harper whispered. The figures roamed aimlessly along the riverbank, fading in and out of view. Every time she'd encountered them, they turned nasty fast.

"The mistlings?" The spirit on her shoulder huffed. "They are always there. Ignore them."

We want to play…

Come play with us, Harper…

Let us consume you…

Despite Heresy's nonchalance, Harper's nerves screamed at her to back away, run, but like a rabbit in a snare she was tethered to the spot.

"I told you, they are always there." Heresy huffed his impatience. "You simply do not bother to perceive them. Pesky creatures. Get on with why we are here and they will go away. Would I allow harm to come to you and spoil my fun?"

Holding her breath, Harper forced herself to turn back to the joining of the rivers. Her shoulder blades hunched in fear of frozen fingers that would undoubtedly be thrust between them, just as Usa had plunged her hand through the ghostwalker's neck on this very spot. Her fingers itched for a blade, even though it would be useless against such ephemeral supernaturals.

While Heresy wouldn't let her die, probably, or even be maimed, he would find a minor injury pretty funny. She flinched, expecting sharp teeth or bitter cold magic. Nothing happened. Without turning her head more than necessary, Harper glanced over her shoulder. The mistlings had vanished. *Which isn't actually comforting at all.*

"You waste time," an almost friendly voice chastised.

She spun, heart in her mouth. The fossegrim, adopted spirit of the River Foss, looked as she'd last seen him. Dressed with no care as to the season. Bright blue hair framing an artistically perfect face. A cocky smirk playing about his lips.

Harper suppressed a scowl at the mockery in his eyes. "I'll get straight to the point. Do you know where we might find a suitable candidate to look after the river?" The Foss took the oath from her as payment for his help defeating the Somnia; he must have some idea of how she could fulfil it. "At the Soul Traders' Market, maybe? Or is there a water-based community I can reach out to?"

"Taking the mantle of the Ouse is a big responsibility. Contrary to human belief, not all the folk are power-hungry. Most of us wish to continue our existence as is, without further entanglement with humans. You may have to seek farther afield. There are places where the folk of England fled. They may be willing to accept the risk if it means they can return home, or their children may be willing to reclaim an old heritage."

"I'd need a good reason to leave the country and I've no idea how to sneak a supe—I mean one of the folk—back in."

"Whatever happens, the Ouse will have its guardian." The Foss remained frustratingly calm. "So it matters little to me."

"It should. You have to live with whomever it is, right?" Harper waved a hand to where the two rivers met.

"Less so than you think, and I don't object to you. Certainly not enough to leave the river empty and soulless. You play passably well. Staying here was not without sacrifice for me, but I believe it worthwhile. I hope you, too, will one day understand the cost of duty is a minor thing when the need is great."

"Like I don't already know," Harper snapped, fed up with his condescending attitude. At the mention of the violin, she thought of the bone instrument lying under her bed. "If I bring you a different violin, would you be able to tell me about it? What magic is in it, maybe?"

"The one you conquered?"

"How much exactly do you know?" Harper challenged, tired of semi-cryptic supes.

"Only what I told you then. That your music would be the key. 'Twas an assumption, a true one it seems, that whomever you fought also possessed an instrument of power."

"Tell me what you know about my brother. He's the one you taught years ago, the one you told me about, isn't he?"

"I never knew his name for he didn't know it, but yes, he was your kin."

"You said before he wanted to use music to free our people. He must've remembered something of where he came from."

"If indeed it was him, then he remembered little. No specifics, no names, yet he was certain he had family back in the mists of Swaledale and that something terrible must have happened to him. He was haunted by the music he believed to be the key. Usa knew a little of what lurked on the banks of the Swale, for it was her tributary. She warned him that he did not have the power. Only a seer and a dreamwalker had the potential. At the point he dwelt with us, he was neither."

"And when he left you? Did he follow the river?" Harper pressed.

"For a ways, at least such was his plan. Past this point, my vision is no more than a human's. Usa would have known. Alas, she cannot tell you."

Harper glared, but his comment gave her an idea. Her brother had passed through here. It was possible she could See him just as she Saw the ghostwalker's demise. If her ability was capable of Seeing back so far, that was. He might not be dead, or so she fervently prayed, willing to give God the benefit of the doubt if it helped.

"If we are quite done, I am sure you have things to be getting on with," the Foss said in his haughty tone. "Look farther afield for a replacement if you do not wish to become that which you vanquished." With that helpful advice, the river guardian disappeared into his waters without a ripple.

Harper scanned the fog in case the mistlings had returned. Nothing but chaotic swirls. Still nervous about turning her back, Harper crouched at the end of the pier.

Heresy counselled, "Think of the connection of your blood, not any snippets of dream memories. Dreams are illusions, and you would not know if inaccuracies crept in."

The scene before her remained unchanged, the rain-swollen rivers blending and rushing away to the Humber and the North Sea. Then she Saw him. A boy with the gangly limbs of a growth spurt and hazy stubble on his cheeks. Dark brown eyes swept the scene, oblivious to the sister who watched from over fifteen years in the future. Roses adorned the acoustic violin clutched to his chest, almost the duplicate of the ones Harper had painted on her own instrument.

Next to him, the Foss stared over the twilight-clad Ouse. Harper's breath caught when the water rose up. It didn't take the form of the woman she'd met. Rather, it remained as rippling liquid, though it flowed up and over the path in a conscious choice. It rose around the ankles of the boy, then receded. The boy set the violin under his chin and played. He played the world around him, just as the Foss taught her, with the breathtakingly beautiful skill of intense practice. It was pure, with no battle in it. Lapping waves beckoned him into the river's embrace.

He stepped into the Ouse and was borne away. As he rushed past Harper, he was neither human nor a creature of the water, rather something in between. He'd learnt more than music from the Foss: he learnt how to truly become one with nature. Harper had joined with the hill of her blood and bones, where her ancestors dwelt for hundreds of years, where magic tied her to the land. He played a new realm with no knowledge of him, and it welcomed him.

Long after he washed out of Sight beyond the bend of the river, Harper sat and stared with tears in her eyes.

"It may not be wise to linger." Heresy's static buzz in her ear set her teeth on edge. "But then, you are rarely wise."

"Yeah." Harper took a deep breath and forced the magic back to its hiding place. "'Rarely,' huh? Which means I have done at least one thing you think was wise."

She itched to follow the vision down the river until she found him. But fifteen years had passed. She couldn't track him purely by following in his footsteps. Even if she could catch a glimpse of him downriver, or find where he came ashore, she couldn't follow on foot. He'd waited this long; he would wait a while longer. The empty Ouse would not.

As she turned away, an image flashed through Harper's mind. *A different river, one high up in the hills where no river ran in the wakening, human realm. On it, a raft bearing a boy. His face twisted in shock and panic. Fingers outstretched to her.*

"Harper!"

Then he was gone.

"Harper?"

She shuddered as all the hairs on the back of her neck rose in response to Heresy draping himself around her shoulders. Her legs trembled, her joints ached, and her head swam as though deeply submerged and rising too fast. "Yeah. I'm going. It was only a memory." *The last time I saw him.*

As she meandered to the cathedral, Harper tried again to summon to mind the events leading up to Dorian's banishment, but her memories remained stubbornly blank.

Chapter Three

Haunted by the Past

Fionn lay with his face buried in the plump pillows of his master's bed even though it squished his whiskers. Sleep wanted him but he didn't want it. Dreams brought memories. He was content not knowing his past. He had a home. His master wanted him. He was important. Loved.

But he *did* want to remember Harper. He'd been loved there too. By her. Remembering might help her reclaim the past she wanted so badly. The snippets that ambushed him in the wakening weren't enough. Yet he shied away from the dreamscape. The memories were dark and wet.

"Merow." He fluffed himself, then licked his fur to smooth it.

"You can forget again, Zero." His master's fingers took over. "If I order it, your mind would repel the memories. It pains me to see you hurting, my pet."

Fionn shook his head and patted his master's robed leg with his left paw to indicate 'no.' Much as the memories hurt, he needed to experience them, to help Harper.

"Very well, Zero. *For now*. It aids to have that blight removed from our land, and we must give thought to how to reintegrate that realm and its people, but it also distracts from our already busy schedule. You will pursue these memories and resolve this matter swiftly. Search for an answer to bringing these folk back into our realm. Keep an eye on the witch and seek an answer as to why her fetch was tied to mine. Remain in this form and limit your exposure to the other humans. Return to me each morning two hours before dawn."

Fionn recognised a dismissal when he heard it. Of course, he wouldn't be allowed the luxury of his place in his master's bed. He was a troublesome, selfish cat whose dreams would cause bother. He hoped the kitchen would welcome him and let him sleep by the fire. It was too late to go to Harper's house, and he had nothing to offer her. At least the castle's presence and the bustle of work would mean he wasn't completely alone.

Buoyed by this, he made his way through dark passages deeper within the underground maze of the castle. Though it changed its corridors sometimes, they were friends, and it never let him get lost unless they were playing. He kept an ear cocked for One, his master's hare familiar. He hadn't seen her since their confrontation three ... *four?* ... days ago. Probably about their master's business. She'd always been more diligent than he was.

Unassailed by the hare, the castle led him to the kitchen where he was greeted by a roaring fire that warmed the otherwise chilly flagstones. Various whisks, spoons, and bowls clattered around the sink and island table as the castle readied his master's evening meal. The open oven poured out heat, and an enticing aroma of meat made Fionn's stomach growl. *When was the last time I was fed? Long enough ago that I might be permitted to eat?*

As the casserole dish took itself out of the oven and placed itself on the counter, Fionn paced under it. He paused to raise his front paws and mew in question, even though he knew the answer. A wooden spoon bapped his nose and he yelped, drawing back. Not for him. Not good for a cat tummy or mind to indulge too much.

A shallow dish filled itself with water and settled by the fire. He lapped at it with a grateful meow of thanks to the castle. A bowl of dry kibble joined it a moment later. He chomped it down too fast to taste it. It wasn't bad, but his mind whined for turkey bacon and chicken sausages accompanied by a glass of milk. *Spoilt, ungrateful cat.*

The steady buzz emanating from his collar didn't let him forget his task. Fionn lay next to the fire and tried to sleep. To enter the dreamscape required a fine balance of dreaming and wakefulness. To dream himself was something different: a deeper submersion that surrendered his conscious mind. Once he slowed enough to let it, the exhaustion of multiple healings and great magics caught up fast and he was soon asleep, curled in a tight knot of anxiety.

Fionn sat atop the tower just as he and Harper had when she battled the Somnia, only this time, no malevolent presence swooped down on them. The Protector's star watched them. It always did. No matter where they were, it was there, its piercing gaze flickering through trees. In the village, they said that so long as it glowed, the nights were safe from mares and other predators, though they still hid inside when the sun went down. They counted Fionn as such a predator, suspicious of the 'ghost cat' and confused as to why their protector didn't cast him out.

New memories flickered around him like Saqib changing images on the big, black rectangle, yet none of them went back further than his first shapeshift. There was no mama cat, no litter of siblings, nothing before he met Harper. *Because I was too small or something else?* He couldn't remember remembering. Nor could he remember being puzzled about not remembering. Even in a dream it gave him a headache. Fionn concentrated on the tower, the tiles beneath his fingers, the cold wind flushing furless cheeks. The flashing memories calmed to an aurora of distant lights threading between the stars.

It let him draw them out and examine them. The Protector's star couldn't really see everything under its domain. It didn't know he could be a boy as well as a cat. If it did, he would've been cast out long ago. The Protector found his magic a useful supplement to Harper's, though the demi-god found his intelligence suspect. If he knew Fionn could talk to her in ideas and not just pleas for food, if he knew the cat was a boy and could potentially pollute the carefully plotted bloodline by making kittens with her, it would cast him out for sure, possibly even kill him.

Not that he and Harper wanted to make kittens. The very idea was repulsive to him. He was too young to even think about that, at least by human standards. Though she was a couple of years older than he was, she was too young as well. Old enough for families to parade their sons before her parents. Too young for a commitment, let alone another generation of seers. Old enough to have shooed him away and slipped off with Dawn. He wasn't sure why she'd done that with smells of excitement and fear equally balanced. She hadn't wanted to talk about it.

He teased out a memory at random. A celebration of some sort. He hunkered under a tree, not quite part of things as usual. Harper's grandmama mistrusted him, though she tolerated him for some reason. Fionn suspected the old seer had some inkling of what he was. Though she looked at him with open contempt, she must have also Seen something which caused her to let him stay.

Harper sat by a bonfire, head on her grandmama's shoulder, watching her brother and mother dance to the twinkling tune of her father's violin. Others danced with them and a small band played with her father. Every full moon, month in month out, they celebrated the vanquishing of the mare and the night they came to this sanctuary. He'd been too young to doubt the narrative, though Harper's brother was already questioning.

A soft smile touched Harper's face. The lilac glow in her eyes implied she Saw an augmented reality.

The memory juddered and shifted. Another full moon. Harper older but in the same place. Her hair hung limp as a weeping willow in a rainstorm, and her eyes sunk in shadows as dark as shale. A shaking hand clutched her grandmother's skirts. Then, as now, Fionn was overcome with a need to comfort her, and he trotted past the fire to mew at her feet. Her grandmama kicked him away. Stinging ribs. A minor pain to a kitten used to cuts and broken bones. He slunk away, afraid of upsetting the matriarch further.

Grass under his paws became rock, wet and slippery, and limestone closed over their heads. Fionn hissed each time a stalactite dripped on him. Next to him, Harper's feet dragged over the uneven surface. They'd done this many times, hundreds even, yet he knew with the certainty one did in dreams that this time was different. This time, her brother wouldn't be waiting for them when they returned.

They faced the one who banished him with hollow looks. The Protector's poppy red eyes were haughty with unconcealed gloat. He held a violin of bone—one with no strings—and a knife, both of which he laid on a dais surrounded by sanguine petals.

"Place the cat next to the violin."

Fionn cowered. He didn't like it when the Protector involved him in their spells. He wanted to use his magic to help Harper of his own accord, not with threats and force. She clutched him to her chest, fingers deep in his fur.

"Please. I can do it on my own. We don't need to use his magic," Harper pleaded with the ancient personification of dreams and music.

"To truly wield a weapon, you must understand every part of its making. I have shown you from whence came the body, the pegs, the bridge, the bow strings, and how they were formed of magic and DNA. Now you must string your instrument. For while the body endures back to the first of your line to pledge herself to our cause, strings break and must be made anew. Your blood is in this creature. His strings will be stronger than those it held before."

Sharp claws ripped Fionn from Harper's grasp even as she cried and reached for him. Cold stone sucked at his paws, preventing his escape. He was tired. So tired. A lullaby drifted by and swept his consciousness with it. There was no pain. Not while he was as unconscious as if drugged. Later, scar on his belly itching, there was pain until Harper recovered enough strength to safely share her blood. Even then, she could only heal him of the physical ill, and that in limited amounts. The pain of the magic that allowed the Somnia to take his gut and stretch it across the violin without killing him lasted far longer.

Fionn awoke with a howl. Back arched, fur frizzled, he bolted under the kitchen table, to the surprise of a broom sweeping up flour. There was no attack here, nothing to hide from nor fight against, though every instinct screamed to scratch and bite. It was memory. Only memory. His collar prickled at him to return to sleep and find more.

The cycle repeated. Nice dreams. Nightmares. Nice dreams. Nightmares. Memories blended together in confusion or stood out like neon signs in the Soul Traders' Market. Eventually, the zing of the collar faded to a barely registered gritch through the exhaustion of cycling adrenaline, fear, and magic. Fionn limped through the dreamscape, fleeing rather than seeking his memories. He'd had enough. No more. That life was gone and he didn't want it.

The dreamscape was full of minds, meaning curfew had passed and humans slumbered. It wasn't hard to find the one he wanted. Bright and energetic as always, the dreamer splashed colours so vivid they breached the confines of their own dream and swirled into the void of the dreamscape behind.

Fionn sank into the arty dream with a sigh of relief. Here he was safe.

Kitty, kitty? Here, kitty, kitty?

They did this so often, the dreamer's mind sensed his approach and welcomed him.

When the dreamer passed beyond REM sleep, Fionn slept, too, until he was jolted awake by a sharp zap at the top of his spine.

"Zero." His master's voice echoed through the kitchen. Every utensil and piece of equipment froze, before going into overdrive at whatever cooking or cleaning they were doing.

Fionn leapt to his feet and dashed through the castle until he reached his master in the Great Hall.

"I warned you that your distraction with this unnecessary past could not be allowed to interfere with our work. You were to check in with me two hours before dawn."

Ze wore the mask of fiery red and swirling gold ze usually reserved for sanguimancy. Fionn raised a paw to pre-emptively lick a wound that didn't exist yet. He dropped it again, tongue blepped out.

"You will need human words for this." Ze spoke with disdain towards Fionn's human form. It was unpleasant and only to be brought out when necessary. His master had long since stopped needing to explain that to him. It wasn't that the process of changing his body was repulsive. As far as he understood it, the physical conversion to change his mass by either taking from or adding to atoms around him meant a by-product of wasted energy in the form of brilliant light. No one could see the shift itself. It was the end product that was a source of disgust.

He shifted and stood naked, save his collar, head bowed, hands clasped behind his back. If he was being sent out into the world, his master would've provided clothing. Here, in his home, such unnatural deceptions weren't necessary. He didn't need to hide his ugly form from someone who truly loved him.

Tears gathered in the corners of Fionn's eyes, but he knew better than to let them fall. "I was a selfish, bad cat. I'm sorry. I will do better."

"I should hope so, Zero. Many are relying on you. You have great things in you, if you can put aside the selfishness and laziness nature saddled you with."

Fionn flinched as his master's hand fell on his shoulder, but ze merely gave him a gentle pat.

"We have been asked to perform a protection for an expected bairn and been given a focus upon which to cast it. I have drawn the spell. I wish you to add pleasant dreams and protection from nightmares, then read the actual casting while I perform the magic."

It was a relatively common request, although granted to only a few. His master confirmed his suspicions as ze explained further.

"It is for the Queen's nephew, who is heavy with child. The stars are auspicious for the birth, but with all the unrest, I wish to make the spell as strong as possible to be safe."

"Master?" Fionn ventured a question. His master was in a lenient mood and he received a nod to continue. "Aren't you worried the spell might reverse and harm the baby?" The thought froze his insides. *I'd never risk harming a kitten.* His gut ached from the memory in the dream.

"That problem has not yet gained the power needed to disrupt my magic, nor have there been any instances of it attacking the folk yet."

"It's only attacking human magic?" Fionn extrapolated. "Why do you speak like you're—"

His head snapped to the side with the force of the interrupting slap.

"Do not question me, Zero." All his master's voices were dangerously low, each tone crackling with uncontained fury. "We don't have time for your insolence. Begin the ritual. I'll teach you how to be more grateful later."

"Mau." Fionn scrunched his eyes closed. "Thank you for teaching me, Master. I will do my duty." He recognised the spell, didn't need the tome open by his master's throne, so he took the knife, wet it with his blood, and began to draw his part.

Chapter Four

An Afternoon at the Opera

When Harper returned home from work, Heresy greeted her with a huff of soot from his hiding place in the front door peephole. Harper stepped in with some trepidation and was surprised to see AJ's door ajar and hear him talking. Saqib should've been at work and AJ usually forbade Grace entry.

"Occult programming isn't so different to any other high-level language in terms of how you integrate it. It has its own syntax and symbols. Once you know them, anyone with magic can use it. I've imported these libraries so the two subroutines will function in tandem so long as the identifiers stay within given parameters. Should they go outside those parameters, i.e. the output is no longer true, then it triggers a different script which alerts us to the breach."

"Mrow meow?"

"Fionn!" Harper burst into AJ's room without knocking and gathered the white-fluff kitty into a hug. He gave a *mau* of surprise and dug his claws into her shirt. "Sorry, I didn't mean to startle you."

"Merow." Fionn purred and rubbed his head under her chin, eyes closed.

There was no direct English translation in Harper's head. Her magic Heard it as a cross between *It's okay, I'm happy to see you*, and a somewhat untrue statement of *Who, me? You didn't startle me*.

"I was afraid you wouldn't come back." She buried her face in his fur.

"I was afraid you wouldn't come back," her younger voice echoed in her head as she clutched a smaller Fionn in the same way she held him now. There was an argument. Someone threw a pan at him. He fled into the woods. She'd thought he'd never return, that she'd have to go to the Protector without him.

I should've let him go, adult Harper thought with a jolt of remorse. *I was a coward because it comforted me to have a friend. I should've driven him away, even if it made him hate me.*

"Mau?" A paw dabbed the tear trickling down her cheek, then Fionn pulled a face and licked it. "Mau mau," he grumbled.

"Sorry about the nasty wet on you," Harper kissed his nose, before setting him gently back on AJ's desk, where he promptly sat on one of the many keyboards. To her surprise, AJ didn't shoo him off, just switched to a different keyboard.

Harper had a hundred questions to ask Fionn: about home, about where he'd been, about his memories. She'd been so tired and grateful to be home that none of them got asked the night they returned after defeating the Somnia.

She settled for, "How are you?"

"Mrow." Fionn sat licking a paw.

Harper raised a sceptical eyebrow. *"I'm fine* usually means someone isn't."

The cat flicked his tail.

"I fed him," AJ said without looking up. "He's stayed this shape though. Keeps no-pawing me."

"You can't shift?" Harper asked the cat. "Or you don't want to."

The tip of his tail twitched and he scratched at his collar.

Or you're not allowed to? Harper scritched behind his ear and down his back, cautiously probing the collar as she did. There was no visible clasp and she couldn't feel one either. Magic might be the only way to remove it, but she was scared to try even her Sight lest it trigger some kind of alarm or hurt Fionn.

"I'm going to grab some food, then get dressed to go out with Grace. We have free opera tickets, courtesy of AJ avoiding his mum. She's on the board and sent them to him. Unless you've changed your mind, AJ?"

"Pfft."

Harper smiled behind AJ's back. She suspected seeing his mother and sitting through an opera were vying for bottom place on his wish list of things to do.

"Do you want to come with me for food or stay here?" she asked Fionn.

"Meow." Fionn held up his front paws so Harper could lift him again.

"Yes, you may sit in your box in the kitchen, but it's not sunny."

Harper carried him through and set him in a box lined with her clothes. She was making a sandwich when a beam of sun came through the window and fell directly on the box. Considering the rain minutes earlier, it seemed suspect and she raised an eyebrow at the cat.

"Did you …?"

"Mrow."

"I know sunshine is good, but this is northern England and … you know what? It's fine. Just don't cause a storm somewhere else."

She sat at the table with her sandwich and set a bowl of tuna at Grace's usual place. It didn't take long for a pink nose and quivering whiskers to appear over the edge of the box. A swirling black vortex opened above the table.

"Fionn? There's a—" Harper barely had time to be alarmed before Fionn stepped through it, gave her a reproachful look, and tucked into the fish. Harper huffed, the burst of adrenaline not so easy to quiet. "Little lazy, isn't it?"

Fionn shrank, shoulders hunched, tail curled in, head lowered as he mewed sadly at her.

"Sorry." Harper patted his head. "I was only teasing. You're not a lazy cat. Eat your tuna."

But he batted it away, almost knocking the bowl to the floor.

"Fionn. Please eat. I'm sorry."

"Mrow." He turned himself into a loaf on the far corner of the table. "Merow mau."

Harper started to sigh as he dismissed her apology, then her breath caught at the rest of what he said. "You dreamt about my family? About where we used to live? Do you know what happened to my brother?"

"Merow."

Her eyes widened. "Please Fionn, please can you shift and tell me properly?"

He shook his head, briefly stretching out his left paw, the one for 'no,' and spreading his toes at her. "Meow."

"As if you recorded your dream and replayed it for me?"

He yawned and stretched again, then hopped off the table and returned to his sunny patch. "Mrow."

"Thank you, Fionn." Harper knelt next to the box to stroke the cat. Eventually, a low purr rumbled from him. "You know you have a home here regardless of being useful, right? I'll look after you. There's always food for you and a place to sleep."

"Mau." He gave her fingertips a drowsy lick as he closed his eyes.

"You're welcome. I'm going to get changed now. You can use my bed while I'm out if you want a nap. Or the attic if you want to do any magic stuff."

She left the dozing cat with a heavy heart. A bit of tuna and a patch of sun were all she could offer him. It wasn't enough.

As she navigated the steep stairs back down, Harper was glad she'd opted for a looser-fit formal dress. While she and her sister were able to agree, or compromise, on most things, fashion was something they never saw eye-to-eye on. Where Harper favoured bright colours and ease of movement, Grace liked dark and tight.

This afternoon was no exception. There was a regal beauty in Grace's sleek carmine satin dress and the way her loose hair tumbled over her shoulders. No doubt Grace could turn heads; the problem was keeping their interest once they heard the name of the famous demonhunter family.

"Ready to go?" Harper asked as she entered the kitchen to find Grace reading at the table, feet on a chair despite her elegant gown.

"Almost." Grace tweaked Harper's ribbon-braided hair and smoothed out her blush. "Okay, now we're ready to go."

A huffy Heresy waited for them in the front door peephole. "Are you sure it is wise to go out for such a frivolous reason?"

"Jealous you aren't coming?" Grace yanked the door open.

Heresy sniffed. "As if I would ever be jealous of you, Graceless. Although it would be pleasant to leave the house for a while."

Harper opened her handbag. "Heresy, you may come if you stay quiet and keep my magic hidden from any witches in the audience."

"Deal." The deception demon floated out of the door and into Harper's purse. The small porch shielded the vaporous spirit from the neighbours' curtain-twitching view. Across the street there were no houses, only York's ancient wall. Grace glared but said nothing.

It was odd to walk through the streets dressed up so glamorously. With curfew strictly enforced and the city centre no longer night-safe, the Grand Opera House and other event venues had moved their evening performances to mid-afternoon. As the days got longer, they might move back to evening, but the equinox was still some weeks away. *Not enough weeks.* Harper squeezed Grace's arm as they walked, linked together. For her sister's freedom, giving up her own was a sacrifice she would not regret. Still, if there was a way to avoid it, she'd find it. She didn't *want* to become a river.

The Opera House was abustle with long skirts and sharp suits. Despite the mask of fanciness, Harper felt like a parasite hiding in a stranger's body. Grace fitted. Her easy authority parted crowds, and Harper trailed in her wake.

Grace led her to the side and spoke in a low voice. "Harp. You are as much a De Santos as I am. You don't need a piece of paper or a DNA test to be family. Chin up, relax your posture, meet their eyes, move on. Own your space and don't let anyone push into it. If they decide to be snobs about us not being regulars here, that's to their detriment, not ours."

"Yes, General." Harper did her best to walk confidently in the unfamiliar shoes, wondering how Grace managed to fight in heels.

She fidgeted with her hair as they waited for the opera to begin. While less imposing than the Gothic cathedral and its hidden archives, the gold-gilt opulence unsettled her. The wonky sign outside, squished between a florist and a sofa shop, belied the name 'Grand Opera House.' Inside was a gem hidden in a tatty old jewellery case. Each theatre box housed its swanky occupants in arches of plaster garlands, cherub faces, and sweeping curtains. Even the seats of the stalls were a plush crimson velvet. The domed ceiling was circled by gold leaves and wreaths.

The great chandelier dimmed and the orchestra struck up the jovial opening piece of *Orlando Furioso*. Harper relaxed into the anonymity of being a single particle in a sea of watchers. They were about halfway up the top circle, with a clear, if distant, view as the heavy red-and-gold curtains rose and revealed a stage flanked by giant marble colonnades in the style of ancient Rome. A woman strode confidently forward. She bore a shield with a gorgon head on it and wore a plumed helmet that had to be quite uncomfortable and impractical.

"Who's that?" Grace whispered in her ear.

"Orlando," Harper muttered back, having done her homework on the opera. "He's always been played by a contralto. There's a lot of gender ambiguity in this."

"Like the Virginia Woolf novel?"

"Kind of." Studying it in school seemed an age ago.

As a second singer glided onto stage in a white boat, Grace muttered, "Now there's a ridiculous dress."

"*Shh.*" Harper nudged her sister with her knee. For once, she and Grace agreed. The poofy white costume was impractical for anything, especially sailing.

During the performance, Heresy snuck up to sit on Harper's shoulder, providing commentary too quiet for any others to hear that made it very hard for her to keep a straight face.

The first intermission went smoothly. They stayed in their seats, Heresy safe in Harper's bag again.

When Orlando became trapped in the sorcerer Alcina's cave, Harper folded Grace's hand inside hers. It was so nearly a fate they'd shared.

As the second act closed, Harper decided to try to beat the bathroom queue and jumped up, but at the end of the aisle, a woman blocked her path.

"Ms. Ashbury. I'm so pleased you decided to join us this evening. I suspected my son would pass on the tickets. Ethel Tailor, she/her."

AJ's mother's imperious tone and posture was a match for Grace's even at her most commanding. Harper cursed her own brain for forgetting that of course AJ's mum would find them. She didn't need to know what they looked like; she knew the seat numbers. Harper tried to keep the dismay off her face as she shook the other woman's offered hand.

"Pleased to meet you." She managed to stop herself calling the older woman 'ma'am.' "I hope it's okay we took the tickets. I assume AJ cleared it with you."

A pinched smile didn't quite meet Mrs. Tailor's eyes. "My son very rarely informs me of anything. However, I suspected that would be their fate. As a member of the board, it is a pleasurable duty to introduce new people to the delights the Opera House can offer."

Harper wasn't entirely sure that wasn't a snub. "It is most appreciated. It's not often we have the time and resource given our own duties as patrons of the cathedral symphony, what with me working there and Grace being the archbishop's goddaughter."

"I heard my name." Grace appeared at her shoulder. Sparks flew as the two women locked eyes.

Stuck between a demonhunter and a witch. Great, a metaphor for my life. Harper took a deep breath. "We're going to get drinks. Can I bring you anything?" Somehow the word 'bathroom' seemed dirty in the hearing of this pristine personage, so now they had to get drinks.

"No, thank you." This enigmatic smile did reach the other witch's eyes. Harper wasn't sure if that was better or worse. "I hope you enjoy the third act."

"Thank you, I'm looking forward to it." Given that act three included the murder of an enchanter, Harper wondered if there was supposed to be some hidden threat in that statement.

After Mrs. Tailor left them, no one else approached, but Harper was distinctly more nervous as they returned to their seats with drinks in hand. She held her breath as the third act began. The static buzz of Heresy's curiosity prickling the hairs on her neck didn't help.

CHAPTER FIVE

What is Theatre but a Dream Played Out?

The enchanter, Alcina, stormed through an angry aria with lightning bursts of strings. Knowing what was coming, Harper caught the words 'Merlin' and 'spirto' as Alcina turned and raised her hands to the back wall. A flurry from the orchestra swept the columns of the set aside.

Heresy hissed, "Harper. See." A faint buzz settled around her head like a cloud of gnats as his magic worked to conceal hers.

Magic glimmered in the air around the singer. It gathered at her hands and pooled at her feet. Brilliant violet, so like Harper's own ability. And in front of her, framed by the emerging set of Hekate's temple, a wraith-like old man hovered. Harper blinked her Sight away and he disappeared.

Although Harper knew what she was Seeing, she refused to believe it. The tale said Merlin's ashes guarded Alcina's power and immortality within the temple of the ancient deity. Even if Merlin had existed—sources in the cathedral archives varied on this point—ghosts most certainly did not. She risked a peek with her Sight again and the apparition reappeared. *Not possible* ...

The song built to a pinnacle of power. Thick ropes of violet light, radiant to Harper's Sight, tore down what remained of the set to reveal Hekate's temple in its full glory. The violence of it juddered through the audience and the other singers all stared agape. The orchestra played with the frenzy of people possessed. They were the only ones not staring at Alcina. Fine threads of lavender wrenched their fingers and circled their throats. They were no longer the musicians but the instruments.

"That's not how it goes." A monospectacled man in front of Harper murmured, rigid in his fold down chair. "It's ..."

His voiced faded and his head drooped. The woman on his left slurred a query as her head knocked against his. As though Alcina were a stone dropped into a tranquil pond, a ripple of people crumpled in their seats.

"Grace?" Harper turned to her sister. Grace's stare was as vacant as everyone else's. Harper pinched her arm hard.

Grace blinked and lurched. "Wha? Did I fall asleep?"

"Gormless slumber." Heresy drifted from Harper's shoulder over to Grace's. She slapped him away and he chuckled. "Just making sure you are awake, dear."

"Alcina's doing actual magic," Harper hissed, pointing.

"Tut tut, silly girl." Heresy poked her with a tentacle. "The singer is simply that, a singer. She, too, is the instrument of someone else. Can you not See the magic comes from without?"

"Looks like it's coming from inside her to me." Harper stared harder. Much as she hated to admit it, Heresy was usually right when it came to magic. The lights flowed from inside Alcina, pouring out of her hands and between her lips. The glow of it suffused the stage and wormed out from the enchanter into the audience and pit.

The sleepiness of the magic battled against Harper's own magical wakefulness, trying to tip her into the dreamscape. Then she Saw it. The finest of threads where the pulsing light travelled into the singer to touch her heart. Once she Saw one, more became apparent in the woman's eyes, her brain, her throat.

The surprise of it jolted Harper fully awake and the threads vanished. "She's being controlled from the dreamscape."

They were rocked to sleep by the gentle waves of the Aegean. Scents mingled and limbs tangled as they lay in each other's arms, skin on skin making them one. Two dreams merged into a single consciousness of shared magic and memory. One of them to control the dreamscape. One of them to complete the magic. A perfect partnership.

For many years, they'd lain together in this way, but no previous iteration of the spell carried such weight. The world was out of balance.

Darkness tainted magic and caused its science to run awry. The places where little magic existed sucked on the rest with the inevitability of a black hole. They'd patched dead spots before, but never an entire country. The centuries-long blight that was England had to be cured.

They sniffed out their quarry like smooth-hound sharks. Darting in and out of deep slumber and skimming the surface of daydreams, they hunted for specific prey and found her exactly as they promised. In a place where the protections between magic and humans were thinning, it was easy to glide, unnoticed, through the cracks.

To do the magics to seal the infection, they needed more than an open dreamer. They needed one with potential for magic, dormant but woven into the fibre of their being, and a story through which to weave it. The dreamscape sparkled prismatic with potential as they dived into an imagination so vivid it became a waking dream.

The song enveloping them wove a story both familiar and alien. Humans had distorted a tale of magic, romance, and liminality into a fable against witchcraft.

They mourned the purity of Vivaldi's tragic legend, now warped by bigotry. Though Alcina had been manipulative in love, her magic hadn't been used for ill. Rather, it was part of her salvation.

The music drifted their minds to a simpler time. Teatro La Fenice. The Ten all in attendance out of joint deference to them and to the maestro. A city which was not yet ostracised from the world but a leader in art, music, and faith. Afterwards, Lucia and Anna, the singers of Alcina and Orlando, knelt before them. Pretty fruits ripe to be plucked.

The audience watched, mesmerised, tied by magic to the memory of those who first heard this song. So many minds on the edge of dreaming.

The singer playing the part of the enchanter was exquisite. She had within her the potential for magic deeply submerged, like the foundations of home. They could draw on it and amplify it. The contralto channelled the passions and fears of her character as if they were one person. The dreamwalkers would honour her by making that true.

They straddled the dreamscape and the wakening, one of them a tethering rope so the other's consciousness would not be drowned by the singer's mind. They reached into her magic and magnified it again and again and again, giving her all the power of the folk of La Serenissima. They twisted the magic and the story together.

Alcina raised her hands and magic poured forth. It tore down the walls and raised the temple of Hekate. It summoned the spirit of Merlin from his dormant, sleeping body. Spectres of reality, but not without power.

The magic spread, like an infection itself. The only way to create a cure. It touched the minds of everyone who watched and pulled them further into the dreaming. The ground was fertile. The seeds were scattered. Some might fall in rocky or thorny places, but enough would take root for a fruitful crop. The dreams of those where the fruits of their labour ripened would be magic-blessed until the final spell was enacted.

Then a voice. From the wakening. Not part of the story. It hurt. Like someone shaking them awake. Sharp pain stabbed through the dreamer and their connection shattered.

"We need to wake everyone up." Grace hiked up her split skirt to clamber over the backs of chairs and shove through hypnotised people until she reached an empty row. She sprinted toward the nearest exit and slammed down the fire alarm lever.

The wail sliced through the dreaming like a ruby-hot blade, severing threads of magic. People jumped up, shouting, spinning. A cacophony of questions thundered through the hall. Grace flattened herself against the wall to avoid being crushed as people scrambled for the exits. Kicking off her shoes and lifting her skirt over her knees, Harper fought through the throng to See the stage.

Alcina still sang. The singer playing Bradamante tugged her arm, her voice lost in the uproar. Her expression pleaded. Alcina's eyes glowed and Bradamante dropped her hand and fled.

Harper and Grace were swept along by the flow of people until they reached the ground floor, then they grabbed hands and fought past those fleeing the stalls. The orchestra was already gone. The fragments of broken instruments hurt Harper, but there was no time to mourn inanimate loss.

They each took a different side of the stage. The ghostly Merlin was nowhere to be Seen. Something was growing in the heart of the temple. *Hekate? Is she even real?* Harper didn't want to find out, not this way at least.

Grace reached Alcina first and, with a practised hand, clocked her in the temple. The magic blinked out, the dark presence vanished. Alcina dropped to the floor to be caught by Harper who checked her pulse and breathing, and loosened her clothes.

The only sound left was the scream of the alarm. When that cut off a couple of minutes later, silence buffeted them. It didn't last long. Alerted by the fleeing audience, the Guard and police rushed in and fanned out to cover all exits. Two hurried up to the stage, guns drawn. Heresy hid under the rubble of Hekate's temple. Sweat beaded on Harper's brow and she wiped moist hands on the back of her dress. She didn't want to look guilty, but the muzzles pointed towards her and Grace stole her breath away. Before she could move to shield her sister, Grace was already there, between Harper, Alcina, and the guns.

"It's under control." Grace met the Guards' eyes with a haughty confidence. "There's no fire. I set the alarm off to clear the Opera House. There was magic here, but it wasn't the singer." She crossed her arms over her chest and her chin jutted out as if daring them to try and arrest the unconscious woman.

"And you are?" the Guardsperson challenged. Their eyes flicked from Grace to Harper to Alcina on the floor and back again.

"Grace De Santos, she/her, and this is my sister Harper, she/her." Grace pulled out her official pass with the archbishop's seal for them to examine, but they waved it away upon hearing the names. Notoriety had never been on Harper's to-do list. It seemed like she could tick it off anyway.

"If the perpetrator wasn't this woman, you gave them the perfect escape," the other Guardsperson growled. "We should arrest you for aiding and abetting."

Grace's confidence guttered, just for a second, like a candle caught by the stray draught as a door closes. When the Guard suggested arresting her, she laughed. "Good luck explaining to my godfather. We'll come in and talk to Lieutenant Albrecht. That's it. She's our usual person. I'm sure you've detained everyone who was leaving and have already looked up the attendance register. Since the performance finishes a little after dark, we all showed ID. I claim this scene in the name of the Council of Faiths. In the interest of our recent partnership, I'll allow you to assist. I want this scene secured for forensics."

Taking her cue, Harper texted Saqib, telling him to grab his kit and get down there but absolutely not to let Fionn help as the place was crawling with Guard.

"And call an ambulance." Grace gestured to the singer. "She'll have a hell of a headache when she wakes up."

Despite their doubts about chain of command, several people nearby snapped to obey Grace. By the time an ambulance crew arrived and Saqib stumbled in, weighed down by several bags of gear, Grace was in complete charge of the scene. Even the higher-ranking Guard were low on the ladder and lacked the spine to stare her down.

Two accompanied the singer to hospital, with stern warnings from Grace that she better get there and that she would arrange for someone to meet them. The archbishop was only too happy to send people down rather than risk another citizen going missing. He promised to coordinate with other leaders in the Council and send people to help with the chaos outside the Opera House to ensure no disappearances from there, either.

Harper briefly wondered what had become of AJ's mother, and hoped she and any other family around weren't in trouble. They'd hidden their magic for centuries. They knew how to evade the Guard's gaze.

"Let's see what we can find." Harper helped Saqib onto the stage. While he set up various tests, she explained the non-witchy version of what happened, conscious of the Guard on the scene. It was awkward for him to test when she couldn't tell him what to test for. Then again, he had no way to test the dreamscape. She'd be stunned if he found anything.

Chapter Six

Dreaming of Home

They got home well after curfew, tired and ready to fall straight into bed, formal wear or not. It had almost been enough to make Harper forget Fionn promised to share dreams of family with her that night. Arriving home and thoughts of bed brought the memory flooding back.

"Fionn? We're home." Harper called.

Saqib stopped to debrief AJ and check whether he'd heard from his mum while Harper and Grace headed to the kitchen.

A thudding boom quaked the house.

The Somnia's back?

Grace sprinted for the attic. "It came from up there."

"Stay here," Harper shouted back to the two men as she raced after her. If Grace heard it and pinpointed it, the attack wasn't from the dreamscape. She almost tripped over her skirt as she took the stairs two at a time.

Grace was pulling down the ladder when a voice echoed from the attic. "Sorry."

Heresy, who was watching from Harper's shoulder with mild amusement, snorted. "The stupid not-a-cat is up to its tricks again, I see. Please make it a stray?"

"Fionn? What are you doing?" Harper pushed past Grace up the ladder and stuck her head through the hatch. The floor and beams of the attic were blackened and charred. Only Fionn's fluffy tail was still star-white, his cat ears now a charcoal grey.

You're human-shaped again. She glanced at his collar, but the soot hid whether it was too tight.

"I'm making you a nightlight." Fionn gave her a tentative smile. His ears were back and he cringed away from her.

"That *exploded*?" Grace's head popped up next to Harper's, both of them squished on the ladder together.

"Out of what?" Harper couldn't keep the incredulity out of her voice.

"Mostly hydrogen," Fionn answered. "Some helium. Those are easy. The smaller balances are harder and controlling the gravitational effects and heat is tricky."

"You're making ... for ... for a nightlight?" Harper's thoughts stalled at the impossibility. "Just ... clean this up before the landlady sees, okay? And try not to blow anything else up while you're here."

He bowed his head. "Sorry, Harper, Grace."

Harper sighed and cautiously ascended the rest of the way so she could pat his head. "It's not that I don't appreciate the gesture. It's ..." *Too much? Insane? Could destroy half the city with terrifying ease?* "You being here is enough help. You don't need to do anything extra."

"Me?" Fionn looked up, his turn for incredulity.

"Yes. You." Harper scritched behind his ear and he purred. Grace scooped up a grumbling Heresy and left. "Especially with memories starting to return. The feelings come first, then images, then sounds and other sensations. I remember us together, the feel of your fur. That's comforting. Will you stay here tonight? You can sleep in your box or on the couch and we'll sort something better tomorrow."

"I don't like sleeping alone." Fionn squirmed. "It means I've been bad."

"Not here it doesn't. If you want, I'll put your box in my room. Then you're not alone. Is that okay?"

He cuddled his tail, shoulders hunched. "Thank you."

She brushed his hair back, the older sibling feelings he often evoked rising. "You know you can stay? You don't *have* to go back."

A self-conscious hand jerked to the black collar tight around his neck, the one thing that stayed on in both his shapes. "I do."

"Fionn ..." The bruise on his cheek from his first night there had faded, but Harper's Sight showed the silvery scars of old pain and he flinched as though he still hurt. "You—"

"Need to keep working." He gave her a too-bright smile.

"Okay." Harper wanted to argue more, but she didn't know how. All she could do was to keep offering him the option of a safer place. "I'm going to bed. Join me when you're ready. In your box. And knock before coming in."

He nodded slightly. "You sleep in pretty clothes."

"They're not for sleeping. They were for the opera. Thanks anyway."

"Very pretty. Like your colours." He almost touched a finger to her gold-dusted eyelids.

He'd mostly seen her harrowed from lack of sleep or damp and bloody from fighting, so it didn't take much to look better. She'd take what little she could get. "If you want to learn how to do it, ask Grace. She's better at it than I am."

"I can't be pretty."

"Fionn ..."

But he'd already turned back to his work, sparks of flame swirling between his outstretched hands. Harper brushed a hand through his hair again and whispered, "You are pretty," but he ignored her. "Good night, Fionn. You come into my dreams whenever. If you don't feel up to showing me the family ones, that's okay. Don't hurt yourself." Saying it tightened her stomach. Impatience strained to demand he show her everything, yet the little cat looked so sad and defeated, it reined in her need and quietened her questions about the evening's opera mystery.

"Oh, I made you this." The fire vanished and Fionn offered her a large marble. "Put it under your pillow, and you'll see what I dreamt. It's a dream, not a memory, so it's not set in stone. Since you were there, any influence from your mind should enhance rather than change it."

Harper took the cold, pulsing crystal. "Thank you, Fionn." She kissed his forehead and left him scribbling in his notebook.

The marble made a uncomfortable bump under her pillow and anticipation of dreaming kept sleep at bay for a long time. Eventually, Harper fell into an uneasy slumber full of collapsing theatres, opera, and sad cat eyes.

A memory slid in of being snuggled in a fleecy blanket on her mother's lap while her father played a low melody on the violin. The arms around her become more real as memory blended into dream.

She was too old to sit on her mother's lap like this, but she did it every time she came home. Despite her mother and grandmother's insistence that the other place was home, the dank cave never felt like it. Home was this tent with her parents and her brother. Heavy eyelids rasped open to check everything was as it should be. Fionn crouched near the edge of the tent, tip of his tail twitching. The light in his eyes was brighter than the soft fuzziness of the rest of the scene: the real Fionn, resting behind his kitten self just as Harper watched from her child form.

In the memory, she fell asleep, exhausted from magic and grateful to be home. Adult Harper knew with certainty this was one of the last times this homecoming would play out. The dream shuddered. Stalactites thrust through the tent and cave walls ripped the double insulation of hanging rugs and blankets. A child screamed for her mama as she was dragged underground.

Fionn mewed—part cry, part command—and the scene returned to the dream. It skipped forward, playing out as near to his memory as a dream could. The sound of raised voices startled Harper from her dreamless sleep just as they had then. She crept to the edge of a hanging divider and peered through the gap into the family area around the fire. Her brother stood on one side, arms crossed and a frown on his face. Her parents' backs were to her, stiff and tense.

"How can you even consider sending her back there?" Her brother gestured toward Harper's sleeping mat and she shrank back. "Mama, he's hurting her. How can he be a protector if he's *hurting* her?"

"Dorian, there's a great deal of sacrifice involved in protection. Magic has a price. You know this. It is an honour for her—"

"It is *not*, Papa. Her fingertips are scabbed and she was struggling to breathe. Look at her cat. Something cut his paws. What kind of protector hurts someone's pet like that? The poor thing could hardly walk. Our 'Protector' is a sadist."

"*Dorian*." Their mother's hand flew to her mouth as though she could stop the blasphemy that came from her son's. "Never speak like that again. The Protector saved our people from death and torture at the hands of the humans outside. If the price is a bit of animal blood, so be it. We made sacrifices when I was Seer too. Blood magic is stronger and we need to be stronger. There are enemies, in the midnight world and the daylight one. Enemies who would torture our dreams again without the Seer to capture them when they invade. Don't think I send Harper into something blindly. I was the Seer. I know the cost. I paid it gladly and so does she."

"No, she doesn't. Harper hates being trapped here. So do I. It's a prison, Mama. Can't you see that? If you can't see how he hurt you and Grandmama, can't you see how he's hurting your child? She cries every time he summons her. She's scared. You're supposed to protect her. You're supposed to protect *us*."

"We do protect you." Her father's growl came to her mother's defence. "We must also think of the village. It is an honour for the power to pass to our daughter. She's a hero. Without her, everyone here, from the eldest to the newborn baby, *everyone* would be at risk. She would suffer far more at the hands of the humans outside or in an eternal nightmare as our people were before the Protector saved us."

"That was hundreds of years ago, Mama. Things must be different now. Surely, there's a way to—"

"*Enough.* Go to your bed, Dorian. Now. You will disrespect your ancestors and our Protector no longer. If you continue with your threats to our people, you will be re-educated."

Dorian opened his mouth, thought better of it, and snapped it shut. He turned on his heel, shoving rugs aside with more force than necessary.

"It's dark out. You will not leave—"

He'd already gone. Harper slipped her shoes on and stole out after him, not stopping to listen to her father's whispers and her mother's tears. Then, she'd sided with her parents. She'd been foolish not to listen to her brother.

Fionn trotted along with her. None of them, not even Dorian, knew the cat was also a boy. Dorian thought him a very intelligent pet. Everyone else thought him contaminated—a strange find from the outside world that should've been left to die in the snow. The couple of times Harper considered telling her parents what he really was, they were so disbelieving and hostile at the idea of a shapeshifter that she kept it secret.

"Dorian?" She caught up with her brother at the edge of the river. In the distance, the human world shimmered through surface of the barrier shielding her village. A small, quiet world where the river became a stream and the towering hill became a gently sloping mound. The taming of the world made humans seem benign and peaceful, but they shouldn't claim such mastery over the earth. They were a hate-filled race.

"Dor?" When he didn't respond, she tried again, tugging on his sleeve.

"You shouldn't be out here, Harp. You'll get in trouble."

"Already in trouble and no more than you will be."

"Less than I will be *and* more." He turned to face her, dried tears streaking his cheeks. "They'll always forgive you, because you're the Seer. You're important. They'll hurt you if they think you're questioning them. That's why I must do it. Someone unimportant."

"You're important." Harper lay her head against his shoulder.

"Only to you." He sighed and wrapped his arm around her. "Next time, Harp, I swear, I will do everything I can to stop him. If our parents won't protect you, I will. We could leave. Just you and me. Cat too. Poor little thing."

"We can't." There was no threat in the dale, but she'd Seen through the eyes of her ancestors and witnessed the persecution they fled. Human fires and the mare's torment in their dreams. She Saw the world as it was now. "There's nowhere in this country where our magic would be welcomed and there's no way out of this country."

"That's what he wants you to think," Dorian said bitterly.

"That's what I've Seen," Harper corrected.

"Are you staying because of the girl?"

"Huh?" Harper looked up with a frown. "What girl?"

"Grandmama saw you. Bit young for a first kiss, aren't you?"

"Beat you to it?" Harper giggled as Dorian scowled. It was the look of a bested older sibling, not the world-weary fear of moments before.

"You know they won't allow it," he said gently as the scowl faded. "The bloodline must be preserved. Our magic must be strong. Yours especially. Your children will be the future Seers. They'll pick you a mate. A boy with strong magic. Like I'm betrothed because of mine, because my mother was the Seer. They think it's an honour to welcome me to their family never considering whether I want it or not."

"Dor … if I leave, what becomes of them? Not just Dawn. All of them. Mama's right about that. What's a few cuts on my fingers compared to what I've Seen could happen if the barrier ever falls or if the nightmares get through again?"

"Harper …"

"You could go. Take Fionn with you. I'd rather give my blood than his."

Fionn mewed and pawed at her ankle. She knelt to lift him and he rubbed his head against her cheek. Fine silver scars marked his paws where she'd healed him. It didn't matter that her blood could heal him. What mattered was that he'd been hurt.

"I don't think he'll leave you. I don't want to, either. Please, Harp. Come with me. I won't stop fighting for you. They talk about sending you to live there when you're old enough, like Mama did until you were born. You'll be gone from our family whatever happens. At least you and I can be together."

A cold presence caused Harper to spin around. From the treeline, poppy red eyes watched them, emanating anger.

"Dor. We need to go back. Please." Harper tugged her brother's arm, Fionn draped over her shoulders.

Dorian stared down at the misty dale. "What if we just went? Now."

"We don't have any food or clothes or anything." Fear made it hard to breathe, then and now. She was going to lose him. The Protector was watching.

"There's stuff down there. We'll be fine." Dorian tugged her in turn. Her feet slid on the wet grass and she lost her grip on him. He jumped onto their raft, a fishing platform they unmoored and took outside the protections of the village too often for their parents' liking. The Protector's star watched them, and they remained within his influence. Their parents still thought it risky behaviour. "Better than staying here and getting cut up."

"We can't go. Who will protect Mama and Papa?"

"Who will protect *you*?"

"I will," the Somnia's cold voice cut deep.

Both children spun to meet the Protector's bloody gaze. Harper bowed her head immediately, eyes locked on a white pebble next to her toes. Fionn hissed from his perch on her shoulders.

Dorian squared his and glared. "You're not protecting anyone."

"*Dorian!*" Harper gasped.

Energy crackled around the Protector. It shot at her brother. Harper leapt in front of him, shielding Fionn behind a raised arm. The energy arched to strike the mooring pole for the raft. The rope snapped.

"No!" Harper screamed and snatched at Dorian's shirt. Her fingertips brushed it. Too late. The river had already washed him away.

"Harper!"

The last thing she saw was his stunned face, a vision older Harper remembered from dreams gone by. Her brother hadn't deserted her. She spun to face the Protector. "Please bring him back."

"He chose his path. He chose to leave. I do not force my goodwill upon those who scorn it."

"He'll steer back. He will." But through the tears, little Harper could see the poles on the grass. Her brother had no way to force the raft to return upstream. "He'll walk back."

"He has already passed the barrier." The Protector's grip on Harper's shoulder was steel. "All who leave forget. He cannot tell others about us, whether on purpose or by accident."

"Let me bring him back. Please. While he's close to the barrier. I can reach over and drag him back, can't I?" Harper turned beseeching eyes on the soul she'd put her faith in. He had to protect Dor too. Dor had left before, but he always came back quickly. He said the longer he was away, the fuzzier his mind became. But it was never this fast. "Please."

"*Shush*, child. He has made his choice to abandon his people, to abandon you. No longer shall my star watch over him, nor shall his name be spoken here."

A vision gripped Harper. It was invisible to her in a dream based on Fionn's memory, but she recalled what it taught her.

"Nor shall his name be spoken here," she repeated. A promise of different intent.

She would make the Protector forget, caution everyone not to speak it. She remembered things that were the future to her dream self. She remembered Fionn taking her into the dreamscape. They couldn't find Dorian, but they found the Somnia hunting him with intent to kill.

They'd snuck in at the back of his dreams, a magic of Fionn's that was unknown to the Somnia who was very careful only to let Harper into dreams under his magic and never let her try with her own. Fionn thought all cats were natural dreamwalkers. Because the Somnia thought him an ordinary cat, he hadn't guarded against the threat. Harper had removed Dorian's name from the Somnia's memory, a magic adapted from one they found in a book he made them study. Without it, he would never find her brother.

Harper woke up with a start. Blue eyes stared at her from a moonlight puddle of fluff on her pillow.

"I'm okay. Thanks for showing me." Harper kissed Fionn's nose and scratched behind his ears, delighted to hear a purr. Focussing on the white cat snuggled with her was easier than pinning down her whirling thoughts. Like her, her brother entered this world with no memories. Possibly even fewer than she'd had. She at least had known her name. She and Fionn had done so much research to try and find a safe way out. It hadn't worked. It took a long time to go back to sleep, but she eventually drifted off into dreamless slumber.

Fionn lay awake a long time after Harper fell asleep. Like her brother, he'd been washed down the river and breached the barrier. He was almost certain of it, his first memory of this world being one of a damp wooden crate bobbing along the rain-swollen Swale. Passed from hand to hand, river spirit to river spirit, until he reached the one for whom the tithe was intended—his master. Like Dorian before him, once away from the Protector's watchful star, Fionn's past vanished from his memory.

His master was expecting him back. Sadness lay heavy on him and he couldn't present such a selfish emotion. Would his life have been different if Harper had gone with Dorian that night? Or if he'd left her as she always urged him to do? Maybe there would've been less pain. He could've become a farm cat, hunted mice, and slept in front of a fire every night. He could've pretended he was nothing more than his outer form suggested, and he would've had a peaceful life. But he wouldn't have done anything useful. Not really. Not like he did now. His master's rules were strict because he was undisciplined and lazy. His master helped him be more than those selfish wants.

But for now, he would be a little selfish. If he'd been a regular pet, he would've visited the world of dreams. He would've looked in from the outside with a soul-deep longing that ached in his bones. Would he have left his farming family in search of the dream that felt like home? Maybe not. He was weak-willed and frightened of many things. His master protected him from that. Besides, what could he offer his dreamer that a regular cat couldn't do better?

Despite these thoughts, Fionn prowled the dreamscape like he was addicted to the sugar-high-esque euphoria of this one being. Maybe he was. But he was reckless and he didn't care.

With joy, he noted his arty dreamer was asleep and dreaming. As he neared, the dream's tattered edges and overall transparency became apparent. Not asleep but deep in a dream-like trance. Fionn had observed it before, though not from anyone else except Harper. He could understand why he could see her in the dreamscape during deep daydreams, however he was unsure why this one normal human stood out so. Possibly, it was the simple fact that Fionn spent so much time in their dreams.

There was a frantic energy beneath the haze of this dream. Colours danced, struck each other, and wheeled away. Music with garbled lyrics blared. Brush strokes swept the landscape. Unlike a real brush, they didn't leave a smear of one or two colours, they changed the whole image, as though the painting was evolving in the dreamer's mind even while they created it.

Fionn sank a paw into the dream and was swept away. Though the dreamer didn't directly acknowledge him, some of the frenetic energy changed state to contentment. It held no less momentum, yet Fionn thought it was happier. *Wishful thinking*. Though he wasn't truly there, not in human definitions, he hoped his friend could sense him a little and know they weren't alone.

He giggled as his tail became the paintbrush. The dreamer never really dreamt of themselves. They stared at the dreamscape through eyes that couldn't be seen and shaped it with invisible hands. Their energy wrapped around Fionn's, and he was at peace in the noise and chaos.

Chapter Seven

A Cat About Town

"Harrrpurr?"

A cold but human nose nuzzling against her ear bolted Harper awake the next morning.

"Fionn. What have I said about being human in my bed?"

It came out sharper than she intended, and he pulled back, hurt tears in his eyes. He hadn't shifted in his sleep; he was dressed and kneeling next to her bed rather than in it. Now he was no longer soot-stained, the redness around his neck and the paleness of his face stood out clearly.

"Too tight." Harper stretched a hand to his collar. He jerked back so fast and with such a look of horror that she withdrew. "Sorry. You startled me. Most people knock on the door."

"Oh. Okay. Sorry."

She ruffled his hair. "It's okay. I know it's all new to you. Been up for a while?"

He purred and pressed against her fingers. "Checked in at home first thing. Did some of the work I've been neglecting while I'm here." He winced as he pulled the sleeves of his hoodie down over his hands. "Breakfast time? I eat here and do work for you for foods?"

"Fionn, it's okay to have breakfast. You can help clean up. Are you hurt—"

But he'd already run out and clattered downstairs with an enthusiastic cry of, "Grace! Sausages?"

"Veggie sausages mostly. I've bought some chicken ones just for you."

"You're the best!"

"Gah. Get your nose off my cheek and sit down."

Harper sighed and swung her legs out of bed. Her toes curled at meeting the cold floor and she hastily yanked on slippers and a fluffy dressing gown.

When she got downstairs, Grace was dishing up breakfast to a surprisingly full kitchen.

"Eating breakfast with us, AJ?" Harper raised an eyebrow. "Or is this dinner for you?"

"AJ is helping me learn computers, and I'm helping him remember foods." Fionn beamed at her. "See. I helpful."

"You're very helpful." She scruffed his hair again as she took a seat next to him. "Glad you're here, both generally and specifically. I'm hoping your dreamwalking magic knows something about what happened at the Opera House." Guilt rattled in her chest that she hadn't told him last night.

"I wondered what you couldn't tell me," Saqib said between mouthfuls. "You better have a good reason for not suspecting the singer before you meet with Albrecht today."

Harper pulled a face. "Yeah, I know." As they ate, she filled them in, finishing with, "What do you think, Fionn? Fionn?"

He'd polished off everything on his plate and was staring at Grace with moist kitty eyes. Harper nudged him with her elbow.

"Bacon? Huh? Pardon?"

"All the turkey bacon's gone," Grace informed him, and his face fell. "You can have another glass of milk so long as you don't shift too soon afterwards. Not sure what your cat tummy can handle."

"Thanks, Grace!" Fionn hugged her and jumped up to pour more milk. It slopped a little as he filled it right to the rim. He conscientiously cleaned it up by magicking the spilt milk into a ball and popping it in his mouth.

"Fionn? Did you hear anything I said about what happened at the Opera House?" Harper asked, torn between amusement and impatience.

"Magic from dreamscape into singer, stage fell down, people entranced, I listen." Fionn's ears went back and he flinched away. "I always listen. Not used to having to talk."

"We would like your opinion." Harper scratched the chair, coaxing him back.

He sat down with his carefully balanced glass and took a sip that was a third of the cup. "I connected to Harper once while she was awake. She was in a daydream state where she was touching the edges of the dreamscape. But we already have a blood link. I couldn't connect to a random person unless they were asleep and dreaming properly. Which isn't to say it's impossible."

"Just really difficult and probably needs a powerful practitioner, or it's someone with a blood link to the singer?" Harper asked.

"Powerful, regardless. To channel magic through the song into the audience." Fionn's tone changed as though he was reciting a lesson. "Most people will peripherally touch the dreamscape at the theatre, in an art gallery, while reading, things like that. Things of imagination. That's not accessible by any dreamwalker I've read about." Fionn hesitated, his eyes sliding away from Harper. "We might find answers in the cathedral archives. Other than my master's library, that's the best resource."

"You visited the archives before. Come with me?" Harper ignored the twinge of conscience at asking him to break into the vaults. "They've moved some books elsewhere, but hopefully none we'll need. They're above my clearance."

"I know where they moved them." Fionn dipped a finger in and out of his milk then licked it. "I can't tell you where, but I've seen them. *The Hiding* book and others I know used to be in the vaults. So if … if it turns out you need one … I …" He shuddered and pawed his collar. The silver disk dangling from it jangled against his jugular notch.

Harper stuffed a too-large piece of sausage on toast in her mouth to make herself think before replying. His reaction implied the books were with his master, something that should be impossible. It would mean either the archbishop gave them to a magical entity or he didn't really know to whom he'd given them. Confronting Fionn about it would panic him. When he said 'can't' he usually meant it literally and she didn't want to hurt him more. "I don't think it will come to that."

"Let us take lead on this one, Harper," Saqib said with a concerned look. "You concentrate on the Ouse problem."

A different worry came crashing in and Harper turned to AJ. "Have you had any replies to the wanted ads you put up online about the Ouse?"

AJ grimaced at having to contribute to the conversation. "A few. Mostly scams. Pretty sure at least two were Heresy."

"Uh." Harper rested her head on her arms and scrunched her eyes against tears. Grace stroked her hair and Fionn leant over her to nuzzle her shoulder. After a moment, she took a deep breath and sat up again. "Let's go by the Opera House and see if there's anything Fionn can detect that Saqib couldn't. That's the more immediate problem." *And putting the river search first is too selfish.*

"You ... want me to come out in public?" Fionn said hesitantly.

"If you're cat-shaped, no one will know what you are."

"May I ... try human-shaped? I think I might be able to glamour my ears and tail."

"I bought something that might help," AJ chimed in. "Wait a sec."

He disappeared back to his bedroom and returned a minute later with a purple and silvery hoodie which he tossed to Fionn.

"Got this for you from a shady online store. Thought the ears on the hood would disguise your real ears fairly well and it's a bit too big so you can wrap your tail around your waist and people will assume you're chubby."

Fionn shook the hoodie out and held it up against himself. The hood had a cat face on it, whiskers and all, with two pointy ears. He wiggled his fingers in them and giggled.

"What does 'glamour' mean?" Saqib asked.

"This." Fionn scrunched his nose and screwed up his face. His ears faded from view. With her Sight, Harper could See an outline of them as well as wisps of magic in the air. To her human eyes, he looked normal. Not that there were many white-haired humans his age, but it wasn't completely implausible.

"Why do you want to go as human so much?" Harper asked.

He replied in a small voice. "Because every time I shift, I'm scared I won't get back to this shape again. That the suggestion will become a command. And because I w ... I wan ..." He sniffled and squirmed on his chair.

"It's okay." Harper squeezed his hand. "You're allowed wants. Please tell me this one."

"I wa-want to. Because when, when we were little ..." Tears formed in his eyes and he wiped them on his sleeve. "I keep remembering bits and the only times I was this shape were in secret, like on top of the tower. At home, I'm almost always cat-shaped except for when magic needs fingers or a human voice. It's not a pretty form, but it's ... it's part of me and I w-want to be able to talk to people. I don't wa-want to get left behind again." He hung his head, tail tucked under his chair and tears on his cheeks.

"Oh, Fionn. I'm so sorry." Harper wrapped her arms around him and, when he didn't resist, pulled him close so his head was on her shoulder. "I don't think little me was very fair to you."

"We survived. I'm not upset with now-you or then-you."

"I know." *I'm not sure if you're capable of being upset with someone, though I wouldn't blame you if you were.* "If you want to be human-shaped more, I support that. Does it ... does it hurt ... when you shift?"

"No. It's part of me." Fionn paused to think, then continued slowly. "It's like … I'm both and neither at once. I can feel both shapes, but I'm also just energy, like a cloud of magic or a ball of light. It's so fast, I've never really thought about it much. It's natural. Of course, different shifters work in different ways."

"The glamour was different, wasn't it?" Grace asked.

"That's not natural. It takes a lot of magic for me to alter the reality of who I am. But I'm learning. It's not just an illusion like that nasty little demon casts."

Harper hated that the world made him change to fit it. "I'm scared taking you out of the house is going to get you hurt even worse. It's not because we don't like this shape. You *are* pretty. Even if you weren't, that wouldn't matter."

"This is a bad plan," Grace said. "Everyone's on edge. They'll be seeing things that aren't there. I don't want to think about what they'll do when something *is* there."

"We've found people who are quick to persecute small differences can be oblivious to big ones. They don't have an ounce of logic in them," AJ countered calmly. "If he's glamoured, there won't be anything for them to notice, anyway."

"Please, Harper?" Fionn turned wide kitty eyes on her.

"We'll try it," Harper agreed dubiously. "You'll have to pretend you forgot your ID if we're asked."

"I have ID." Fionn tapped the table and a swirling silver void appeared about the size of his fist. He stuck his arm through, rummaged for a minute, then pulled out a carefully folded set of documents. "Master made this for me since I—" He choked, fingers scrabbling at his collar, his skin unnaturally flushed.

"Breathe." Grace clasped his shoulders as Harper took his hand. "You don't need to tell us why you have them. It's good to know that you do."

A tear fell loose as he jerked his head. His tail, which along with his ears appeared as soon as the collar tightened, swished against Harper's ankles.

"I … sorry." Tear streaks stained still-reddened cheeks. "I'll put them back. It's like the clothes. I'm not supposed to have them here because I'm supposed to only cat. I'll take a bag and if I need them, I'll knock-knock a portal inside the bag, get the documents, and return them once we've passed."

"Alright …" Harper didn't like how all these risks were adding up. Sure, he could portal out faster than anyone could catch him, but that left her trying to explain how she was tricked, and was she really tricked, and could she come in and answer some questions, please. "No other risks. I don't want you in trouble with the Guard or your master, Fionn."

"I know what I'm doing." Fionn folded his arms over his chest and slouched back in his chair, a pout on his face.

By the time he finished his milk, he'd forgotten his grump and was eager for the adventure. Harper's worries, on the other hand, had stewed and thickened.

"Lower your hood." A rough hand lashed out and Fionn flinched, expecting to be hit. His hood was yanked back. Despite his fear, the glamour held. Misty gusts blew hair across his lowered eyes. Pressure built behind them as he struggled with glamouring them. It took a lot of concentration to keep his magic in check. It wanted to protect him from the moist air. A hydrophobic habit that would hurt worse than damp clothes if it got him caught.

"What are you doing here?" Grace stepped between him and the Guard barring them entry to the Opera House. "This is the Council's scene."

"Where are your people?" The lieutenant in charge was less cowed by Grace's presence than most folk. He yawned and turned away. Grace's shoulders stiffened and her fist clenched. Fionn took a step back.

"I was about to ask you." Grace's tone was flat, cold. Fionn resisted the impulse to run. She gave him sausages and patted his head. Grace didn't hate him. She wasn't angry with him.

The lieutenant turned again and handed the group back their IDs. "Dr. Siddique and Ms. Ashbury may go in, but we don't recognise Mr. Weiss as part of the group working with us." He loosened the pistol at his belt, fixing Fionn with a stern glare.

"He's working with me." Harper put an arm around Fionn's shoulders. He wanted to nuzzle her and purr. Being human-shaped had many unexpected little pitfalls. His head hurt from keeping his ears hidden and his concrete-sludge brain could barely maintain the glamour on his eyes.

"I'm a contact of the cathedral," Fionn managed to squeak. Technically, it was true. Kind of. His master was a contact of the cathedral and he was his master's foremost familiar. *Close enough.*

"I need his expertise. He has some experience studying the type of magic we think may have been used here. He needs access to the scene directly to verify that."

"And while they're looking, you and I can have a chat." Grace blocked the Guardsman's path and ushered the others around her.

Saqib passed Fionn a bag and herded him in first with Harper bringing up the rear. The Guard's last attempt to question him was cut off by Grace's irritated interrogation and Harper firmly closing the door behind them.

She pulled Fionn's hood up and tucked his hair back. "Keep them hidden if you can, in case anyone is watching. Let's keep this up just in case."

Fionn drew the edges over his face. It was easier to glamour with the hood up, though no less uncomfortable. His ears couldn't materialise if he didn't give them space. At least he could let his eyes revert to normal. He picked at his collar with a nail, unsure if the tightening was a magical warning or psychosomatic.

The opera hall was vast and cold. Avaricious gold glinted from the ceiling like a bitter sun. Marble pillars sucked heat away. Bright lights highlighted fabric rubbed thin with age. Even the faces of angels and demons lacked lustre, their eyes distant in an unseeing daydream of their own. Aside from the mess on stage, there was no sign of the previous night's chaos.

The broken scenery lay in pieces. Even if there had been anyone left to pick it up, Saqib had ordered the scene be left as near to how it was as possible. He'd taken all the evidence he could straight away. The scientist focussed his cameras on Fionn to see if he could capture a sign of the cat using magic. Fionn squirmed at the idea of someone pinning him down in an image that anyone could look at.

While he inspected the area, Harper helped Saqib set up equipment. Their conversation was inconsequential, undoubtedly for the benefit of any listening Guard. Something about a new clock on the corner.

Fionn sniffed the air for any lingering scents of magic as he picked his way through wreckage too sharp and unstable for a cat to crawl inside. There was no active spell he could sense, so he would've been surprised if Saqib's equipment caught anything. As the forensic supernaturalist suspected, there *were* remnant traces of magics that a knowing person could read later.

Two-tone threads of dreamscape magic clung to the edges of wreckage. The golden aspects were apparent in the wakening, to the cat's magically attuned vision at least. He swayed slightly, almost losing his grip on the glamour as he let his mind drift into a place where he could straddle the dreamscape. There the magic was a glittery violet: dream magic that had somehow let wakening magic loose in this realm.

Whatever caused this destruction had been powered by a nightmare. He collected them for his master and locked them in crystal marbles that could be placed in items as a power source or tucked under a sleeper's pillow. The singer had been awake, so while sunk deep enough into her character for it to create a bridge between realms, it couldn't have been *her* nightmare. Someone, another dreamwalker like him, must've stored one and put it into her.

Harper had said the Merlin summoned wasn't an illusion. This puzzled Fionn. He'd read the lore of the ancient wizard as someone his master both hated and emulated. They'd searched for him underneath his master's castle in Chester, one of the potential locations of Camelot, as well as Tintagel, Slack, Winchester, and others. They'd gone to the caves in Alderley Edge and Richmond, but the sleeping knights there turned out to be unrelated to the grand magician. His master had deepened their sleeping spell so they wouldn't awake for many centuries yet.

Supposedly, Merlin died hundreds and hundreds of years before even Master was born. Ghosts weren't real. Not for that long, anyway. A few seconds after death, maybe, when the spirit was disentangling itself from the body.

Though he carefully checked everywhere the magic might have touched, beyond a vague sense of it, Fionn found nothing helpful. There was a sense of familiarity so wispy it couldn't be someone he knew well. *Maybe someone whose dreams I touched once or twice, or saw from afar in the wakening.* He met so many folk and humans alike, accompanying his master to functions on both sides, that it was impossible to tell.

Harper watched Fionn with an almost draconic protectiveness curled in her chest. Fortunately, Grace kept the Guard occupied and they were able to use subtle magics without interruption. She smiled to see Saqib showing the excited cat forensic techniques.

Once they finished at the Opera House, their next point of call was the cathedral archives. Though Harper expressed concern at Fionn sneaking in, no one noticed the small cat, except Alfred who scritched behind his ears like they were old friends.

After a frustrating morning of no new information, at least none that could explain the possessions, Harper treated Fionn to sushi at a café owned by Japanese refugees, then sent him home—with an emphasis she meant their home and not where his master was—so she could walk to the Guard garrison just outside the city wall and speak to Lieutenant Albrecht. On her way there, she received a text from AJ with a photo of a white fluffball on his bed.

Harper's discussion with Albrecht was short and not-so-sweet. The Guardswoman bristled at the slap in the face to her authority when Harper refused to say where the singer would be taken when she was released from the hospital. Albrecht reluctantly gave Harper and Saqib permission to access the singer's personal file, which gave them a little bit more information about her: like her name, Christina, the fact she was a mother, and that she'd been granted special permissions to be out late for performances over twenty years ago when her operatic career began.

With Council operatives reporting that Christina was unable to break out of character, Harper armed herself with Albrecht's additional information, prepared to burst the bubble of fantasy the singer was caught in.

Chapter Eight

A Jailed Songbird

It was not until a couple of days later that Christina was released from hospital and the doctor announced her settled enough in her new accommodation to receive visitors. Harper had never been in the York Dungeons before. The museum was too macabre for her tastes, or maybe it was the roiling fear that one day she might end up in such a place. Either way, she'd avoided going there either on holidays or in the time since she moved to York for university. With its graphic animatronic witch trials and horrific plague doctor's surgery, Harper couldn't understand why people flocked there. The thought of visiting it for fun nauseated her.

It was a clever ruse, Harper had to admit. It had once been a real dungeon during the Purge, deliberately separate from the Guard's fortresses, the castle, or any religious stronghold so any supernaturals brought there were isolated from places of power.

It had fallen into disrepair, flooded, and rusted away. Forty years ago the Council took what remained of the infrastructure and created a safehouse-hospital-jail. The museum on top, owned by a secular business with no apparent ties to the Council of Faiths, gave the perfect cover.

And so folk of the Council of Faiths had innocuously taken up posts at the museum and stayed there ever since, facilitating access to a secure location to keep supernaturals where they wouldn't be near other items of power or secrecy, such as the cathedral archives. If captured supernaturals were sighted being bundled in, or their strange cries pierced the rock, everyone assumed it was part of the show.

I wonder if it flooded so frequently because the Ouse was trying to shut it down. Harper scolded herself for human prejudices that seeped between the cracks of reason no matter how consciously she tried to be rid of them. She might be a witch but she had the privilege of being human. *That's probably too human a motive for a river. Sometimes a flood is just a flood.*

Fortunately, to access the real dungeons underneath, they didn't have to go through the museum. She, Grace, and Saqib showed the staff at the front desk their credentials from Archbishop Marshall and Imam Mohammed and were escorted in 'through the service entrance.'

"We want to speak to her alone," Harper said when they reached Christina's cell. "Without someone on the other side of a one-way mirror or watching through CCTV."

"There are no mirrors in the cells," their guide informed them. "The monitoring cameras can't be turned off. Too dangerous."

"We can handle ourselves."

"We don't turn off our cameras."

The watchsen wouldn't be persuaded. Harper would have to keep her back to the camera and watch carefully for an opportunity to use her Sight without the contralto seeing her eyes. Grace would run interference for her.

The thud of the door as it slammed behind her reminded Harper of Dickens. *'Dead as a door-nail.'* But Marley was dead to begin with, and she, Grace, Saqib, and Christina were very much alive. Harper intended to keep them that way. The last five months had seen too much death.

Though Harper had been told new dungeons were constructed with both security and wellbeing in mind, she expected something harsher—iron walls, a slab of concrete for a bed, maybe chains. Instead, the walls were covered in smooth cream-coloured plaster that completely hid the iron mesh. The speckled herbs and flecks of iron in the walls wouldn't have looked out of place in one of Mama Maria's home décor magazines. There was a bed in one corner with pillows and blankets. The toilet behind a concrete screen afforded a modicum of privacy, a step up from the bucket Harper had envisioned.

"Mrs. Bell?" Harper approached the singer cautiously.

The other woman hadn't looked up when the group entered nor shown any sign she heard the door lock behind them. She sat in a corner, drawing on the wall with a nub of chalk and muttering to herself in Italian. Wisps of hair escaped in every direction and her too-wide eyes barely blinked.

"Mrs. Bell? Christina?" Harper crouched next to her and reached out a tentative hand to pat the woman's shoulder. As soon as they touched, the other woman's head snapped round. Her eyes were wide and bloodshot, pupils tiny pinpricks. She grabbed Harper's wrist, too tight. Harper grunted, held her ground. "I'm here to help you."

"With my revenge?" The wild gaze swung back to the wall. "Hekate's temple is almost complete. The spirit shall return. My powers shall reawaken. I will kill he who scorned me and he who showed me naught but indifference."

"Ruggerio and Orlando?" Harper plucked the names from the opera notes.

"Who else?" the singer spat. She wiped the dangling spittle from her chin on the back of her sleeve. "Hekate's temple may have been destroyed by Orlando, but I shall rebuild it to her glory."

She continued sketching. What Harper had taken to be the columns and walls of an architectural drawing was actually hundreds of tiny symbols. Some were mathematical, others she thought might be code from what she'd seen AJ doing, though she was never sure what was real code and what was magic when he worked. There were some symbols she definitely recognised. Fionn had drawn them when completing his alchemical ritual in her bedroom. It seemed ages ago, not a few days.

After taking some photos, Saqib walked around the cell with his handheld spectrometer to test for magic. He took out a sample pot and opened a sterilised scraper to collect a little of the chalk. He'd wanted to test Harper's for ages, but she was afraid of the questions it might lead to.

"Wretch. Interfere not with Hekate's divine work."

Harper grabbed Christina's wrists as she clawed at Saqib. When he scrambled back, the singer re-sketched the area he'd sampled from and returned to her work as though nothing untoward had happened.

Her words made both Saqib and Grace flinch. Other benevolent deities were welcomed and accepted, but to revere the witch goddess as divine was blasphemous in any religion followed by the Council.

Grace gave Harper an apologetic grimace and mouthed *sorry*. Over the years, they'd often discussed the Council's position on witchcraft, which was inconsistent at the best of times and varied from practitioner to practitioner. If witch-Harper could be good, it was possible mythical figures like Hekate had been demonised.

"Can you tell me about your drawing?" Harper scooted closer to the middle-aged woman.

"When Orlando destroyed Merlin's statue, destroyed Hekate's temple, I lost all my power." Christina stopped drawing to stare at her hands. "It all left me in a rush. I would have killed him, I *should* have killed him, had those traitors not stopped me."

"What's your name?" Harper dreaded the answer.

"I am Alcina, though I'll give you no more of my name than that. Why do you trouble me? Are you sent by Hekate to aid me or by those who imprison me?"

Everything the woman described was as it happened in the opera. For the most part, it followed Vivaldi's plot, save the power going out of her had been rather more literal than at the dress rehearsal.

"Your name is Christina," Harper reminded her gently. "You were playing the role of Alcina in an opera."

"How dare you?" the woman shrieked and threw the chalk at Harper. Grace instinctively stepped between them, catching a rictus hand before it could bite into Harper's arm. "How dare you come here and say I am not who I know myself to be? Whom else should know but I?"

The woman shook Grace off, snatched up another fragment of chalk, and resumed her sketching. As the singer was completely absorbed in her recreation of the temple, Harper finger-combed loose hair over her face and peered through narrowed eyelids as she brought her Sight to the fore. The chalk drawing gleamed to her violet gaze. Tangled vines of magic twisted through the woman's brain-like roots breaking out through concrete. They pulsed bright in the same colours Fionn described at the Opera House. The magic slithered through the singer's body, pumped through her heart, filled her lungs, and calcified around her bones. It controlled Christina. Every part of her.

The two women walked Saqib to his car and helped stow his equipment before he headed off for Friday prayers and they turned towards the cathedral. Rather than going to the archives right away, Harper stayed with her sister for a visit to the archbishop. The complete submersion of Christina's personality unsettled her, and she didn't want to leave Grace's warmth and protection.

Grace, still weakened from her ordeal in the Somnia's cave a week earlier, flopped onto the sofa by the fire. She accepted a fine porcelain teacup from her godfather.

"What have you learnt?" The archbishop reclined in his wingback chair.

"I need to cross-reference the drawing she's doing and see what it represents. Nothing I recognise straight away. It's so complex …" Harper sighed. "She truly believes she's the character from the opera."

"Our best doctor is working with her." The archbishop patted Harper's knee. "Physically, she is unharmed, and an MRI showed no abnormalities in her brain. However, sleep tests have shown she isn't experiencing deep sleep and rarely truly wakes up. She is stuck in a cycle of REM sleep and a drowsy wakening."

"Saqib's examining the drawings as well. He may be able to tell if there's magic present or if there's anything there we can't see, like the writings on the Ouse's victims. He's going to get in touch with the doctor about getting a DNA swab. We didn't want to try ourselves and risk upsetting her further."

"If she's possessed, then she's innocent. Godfather can perform an exorcism." Though Grace's brow was creased with worry, her tone held a light hopefulness. "She's a victim. She can be healed and return to her life. Probably under Guard suspicion for a while, but that will fade. It's not like we haven't been here before."

Harper pinched the bridge of her nose as screaming filled her memories. She wouldn't wish an exorcism on her worst enemy. The one she'd been subjected to had been a torture worthy of the original dungeons. She could only imagine how much worse it would be if there truly was a spirit inside fighting for dominance. Yet it was better than the Guard hanging her, or keeping her in a single-room cell for the rest of her existence.

"Do you think your father will come up?" Harper asked.

Grace grimaced. "I doubt it. There are people here who can support Godfather with an exorcism."

"It has been a long time since York had an exorcism," Archbishop Marshall said. "I would be hesitant to allow any here to share a leading role with such a delicate matter. Their skill might not match their enthusiasm."

"Their empathy might not either," Harper said bitterly. There were some in the Council who would be sympathetic to Christina, including the archbishop. There were others who took after the deceased deacon in their rabid hatred of everything supernatural. Harper wasn't sure they'd care about the victim so long as the demon was vanquished.

"What if we invited Gabriel up?" Grace suggested. "He's even better at it than Father is, and he does his best to minimise the trauma and to reassure the possessed person throughout. He's had more field practise than anyone we know."

Grace's oldest brother was the logical choice if Harper wanted to ask someone she trusted. While she would never tell Gabriel about her own magic, he was as close a brother as the blood one she was barely starting to remember. Grace was right. He was an expert. He'd completed exorcisms all over the world. A familiar pain twisted her heart and it grew harder to breathe. At best, Gabriel would try and exorcise her magic from her. At worst, he'd revile her as a witch. It always hurt to remember that her own family would detest her if they really knew her.

"Is he back from Venice?" Harper forced the words out. She couldn't afford to lose her composure in front of the archbishop.

"I don't think so." Grace was pretty bad at keeping in touch with people unless they were right there. She treated her phone with suspicion and often forgot to even turn it on. "Last I spoke to Ma, Gabriel was still there." The worry creasing her brow was mirrored by her godfather. Gabriel had been gone for months.

Despite his own concerns, the archbishop raised a hand to ward off Grace's questions. "It is important he stay where he is for the time being. He's been in regular contact. I'm loath to pull him out of his mission without great need."

"Christina has a great need," Grace pointed out. "What's Gabriel even doing in a city that officially doesn't exist?"

The archbishop tapped the side of his nose and flashed a knowing smile. "Sorry, Grace. Need to know information. Let us evaluate what's happening here further, then we will decide if it's severe enough to bring Gabriel home. There are others who can assist with an exorcism. Miguel has some experience, doesn't he?"

"Mama Maria said he should get home before his brother," Harper added. "He's in Slovenia investigating something at Vilenica Cave in Lokev."

"I'll ask him to come home via York if needed," the archbishop said. "For now, let us continue our own investigation and hope it was an isolated incident." His creased brow mirrored his creased cassock, a sure sign of sleeplessness and worry. The safety of York was a rapidly deteriorating veneer. "I don't need to remind you both of what happened to Chester. We're drawing too much attention. We must find a way to suppress these incursions."

"Surely it's not so bad that York will be quarantined or become another forbidden city?" Harper asked.

"This is potentially one of the largest scale incursions seen in the country in decades," the archbishop said. "A magic that not only affected a handful of people, but tried to enter their minds and potentially alter them as the singer has been altered. Had it not been so public, and but for your and Grace's quick thinking, those people could've wandered off without anyone knowing what happened."

He didn't say, *That could've happened already,* but Harper heard it.

"The Guard are on the lookout. Be careful, my children. Give them no cause to be angry with you. Politely do what you must, what is right. Remember, you are a shield, not a sword."

As the archbishop ushered the two women out of his study, Harper pondered his words.

"Gray? Do you ever think … No. Sorry. It's ridiculous."

"What is?" They sat in one of the alcoves down the side of the nave. Members of the clergy and laity milled about; working, praying, or simply visiting the monumental cathedral. None were close enough to hear a hushed conversation.

"Little things … Sometimes I wonder if he knows. His choice of words and some of the things he said before we vanquished Usa."

"Knows?"

"About me. Or, maybe not me specifically. About the supernaturals that are here peacefully. I … have this itch."

"Godfather? Harper, he's the joint most powerful Christian cleric in the country. He can't be harbouring some secret supe sympathy." Grace waved the idea away, but her frown was less easy to brush aside. "You really think so?"

"What if we're not the only ones who decided to help innocents no matter their species?"

"I … Let me think about it. I still say you're seeing things you want to see. He's sent us on enough hunts, after all."

"For killers. What happens to the captured ones, Grace? They can't all be sitting in a cell for the next hundred years." *And then there's Fionn getting into the archives. And our books going to his master's safe house. Archbishop Marshall said nothing happens here without his knowledge. Can he really be ignorant?*

"I'll think about it," Grace promised again, and Harper trusted her despite her sister's scepticism.

"Gray? There's something else. It was niggling me in there but just generally. Since I've kind of found my family and my memories, am I …?" Harper trailed off, the knot in her chest tightening a cage around the words. *Am I still part of your family?*

"Having more family doesn't push out the people who already love you." Grace wrapped her in a tight hug. "You are always my sister, no matter what. I'm sure Gabriel and Miguel feel the same. You'll always have a place in our home."

Harper swallowed a sob as she leant on Grace's shoulder. Whether her birth family accepted her back or not, she always belonged right here.

Chapter Nine

It Was Under Their Noses All Along

When Harper got up to use the bathroom in the early hours of Saturday morning, Fionn's box was empty. Despite her attempts to offer him something more comfortable, he stoutly claimed the box was perfect. Not being a cat expert, Harper felt obliged to trust him, even though she suspected he'd suffer any discomfort if he thought it helped her. His disappearance saddened her more than alarmed her—he'd probably gone back to his master. It took her a while to go back to sleep, thoughts churning at what he might be going through that she had no way to protect him from.

He reappeared in the middle of breakfast, emerging from the stairs wearing unfamiliar clothes and a tired expression. His hair was its usual mess, deep shadows pooled under his eyes, and he clutched his tail to his chest, fingers digging in too deep.

Harper steered him to a seat and Grace plonked a mug of tea down in front of him while Saqib put more sausages on to fry.

"What …? Are you …?" *Are you okay?* Harper didn't ask what was trite and stupid. He obviously wasn't.

Despite his ghost-like appearance, he gave her a bright smile. "I'm great. I'm allowed to be human today because I have business for Master. I thought you might want to come with me. There might be useful contacts for your search for a replacement for the Ouse."

The humans exchanged a look. Clearly the definition of 'great' was very different in the cat's dictionary.

"I won't get you in trouble?" Harper checked cautiously.

"Master has sort of given permission. I have to go to the hotel to fulfil my monthly quota of dreams for them, and I'm keeping an eye on you, so doing both at once should count as good efficiency."

"Which hotel is that?" Saqib asked curiously.

"The biggest hotel in England. Biggest one for folk anyway. You said the Foss told you to look further afield. Our rare foreign guests almost always stay there. They tend to be pretty good at keeping track of travellers, whether travellers want services marketed to them or not. What is it AJ keeps complaining about? Cookie ads or something? I think it's a bit like them but with less deliciousness."

Saqib opened his mouth, then clearly thought better of explaining.

"A whole hotel of supes?" Grace raised a sceptical eyebrow. "I can just about conceive there are odd pockets lying low, but a whole hotel's worth? Maybe a bed and breakfast."

"It's a pretty big hotel, just like the Market is big." Fionn shot her a wary look.

"Just like there is a fae woman running the paper shop on the Shambles even though the street is well-Guarded," Harper agreed. "Or how a cat-shifter can walk about town without being detained."

"Humans are generally not good at seeing what's under their noses." Fionn patted Harper's hand. "You'll come along?"

"Yes. Thank you." Knowing her anxiousness would freak Fionn out, Harper buried it deep. That didn't stop the churn in her stomach at the thought of stepping into another supe stronghold.

Unfooled, Grace nudged her foot under the table. Leaving her sister behind always hollowed out her heart. They were all safer without a notorious demonhunter in tow. Nevertheless, she missed having someone she trusted unwaveringly to watch her back. Fionn would do his best to help her, but she was never quite sure what orders were worming away in the back of his brain, orders he was incapable of resisting.

After they ate and Harper dressed, she handed Fionn the enveloped letter she wrote to her parents. After hours of agonising, she still wasn't happy with the wording, and suspected she never would be. It was time to bite the bullet and ask if he could deliver it by portal.

Dear Mama and Papa,

I'm sorry for leaving so abruptly. I want so desperately to talk to you. When I left, I lost my memories. For thirteen years, you've been shadows. I want to know the real home I came from. My memories are returning a little, but there are many gaps. Thirteen years is a long time. People change. I have a little sister. I want to get to know you all for who you are now.

I know there is anger and fear in the aftermath of my confrontation with the one you thought was protecting you. Please know that I did what I did to save you from a demon who was using you. He was a parasite on our culture, not a nurturer. I'm sorry I've hurt you, now and for whatever happened before. I want to make amends and help.

Please may I visit? Even if only for a short time.

I love you.

Harper

"Can you send this for me?" she asked hesitantly. It seemed selfish and trivial to ask him to knock a hole in reality to deliver a letter, but it wasn't like Royal Mail was an option. "You said now the Somnia is gone, and you've been to where we used to live, that you could find it again. I want to go back. At least to talk. I don't want to be banished. I thought maybe writing would help."

"Sure." Fionn took it from her. Though his mien was calm, there was the slightest twitch at the corners of his eyes. "Have you arranged a way to get a reply?"

"Oh." Anxiety twisted the knife in further. How thoughtless could she be?

"Here." Fionn grabbed a pen and added a note to the envelope: *Please leave your reply in this same spot in 48 hours for collection.* He opened a thin portal to slip the letter through. Harper noticed he was careful not to put his hand through, pushing the envelope from the short edge until it was gone. Forty-eight hours was eternity.

Fionn opened another, much larger portal and took Harper's hand. He twined their fingers together and gripped tightly. "Don't let go of my hand, no matter what. Remember not to say anything unless I tell you it's okay. Don't eat or drink anything unless I say it's okay. Keep your Sight on if you can." He fastened a silver chain around them like he had at the Market.

Harper clung to Fionn. She'd disobeyed those rules last time, fallen into the Somnia's trap, and almost gotten her cat killed. She wouldn't make the same mistakes again.

On the other side of the portal was a plush and busy hotel lobby. At first glance, it wasn't too different to an upmarket human hotel. Harper blanched. The last hotel she'd been at in York had been covered in blood.

Then little things registered. A face in the flames in the fireplace. The way the books on the shelves jostled each other. How the lamps weren't affixed to the wall or ceiling but bobbed gently next to them. The way the shadows piled up in places where they shouldn't and didn't quite match the objects they were attached to. An alcoholic tang pervaded the air. Gentle music played from a chamber music group in one corner that was only instruments and no musicians.

There were few other patrons around because of the relatively early hour and folk being more nocturnal and about on their business. Some sat reading or milled about. A couple appeared almost human, but like Fionn, had telltale features—pointed ears, needle-like teeth, lilac-and-blue skin tones, features not quite the right proportions for any human, and eyes that cut deeper than knives. Other folk were completely inhuman.

Fionn weaved them toward the front desk. "*Shhh*," he reminded her as she tried not to stare. The fact it was less overwhelming than the Market made it harder to say nothing. There, and at the auction, the masses of people made it difficult to truly take in any of them. Here, the relative quiet meant little details jumped out at her. The archivist in her had a million questions. She pressed her lips closed.

Fionn tried to sidestep a jelly whose head knocked into a crystal chandelier. It was clear with blue-and-green spots and a vaguely mouldy stench. It turned as Fionn skirted it and waved one of its hundreds of wobbly tentacles. It reminded Harper of the creature she bumped into at the auction, if it had been left in a corner to rot for a few months.

"Little Zero." It patted Fionn on the head and he scowled, his hand twitching with the compulsion to groom. The creature shifted back and forth, showing off its body. "Your powder worked very well. Thank you."

"Pleasure doing business," Fionn muttered, clinging tight to Harper's hand. "Bit busy this morning. Not here to trade. Must be going."

Fionn dragged Harper away to the squelchy chuckles of his satisfied customer. At the front desk, a bored creature greeted him with a suspicious look at the witch. Her dragonfly wings waved back and forth as her bulging eyes scanned every inch of them.

"I have your monthly order." Fionn dropped his voice and his ears flattened. "And I'm here for information."

"We don't give out intel on our clients. You of all people should know that, Zero." Her words said 'no,' but the sparkling challenge in her eyes belied them.

"Give out, no. I have this to trade." Fionn rummaged in his bag, and pulled out two stoppered vials. He waved a bright green one. "Your boss didn't like my asking price on this last time. Ze's getting a bargain for a little information. The other is sparklewing. For you. As a thanks for your help."

With a golden gleam in her eye, she took the payments. "Depends on the value of information you want."

"I need to talk to a water spirit from abroad, or someone likely to know one."

The woman glanced between Fionn and Harper, a wariness clouding her features.

"The witch is with me. She's one of us."

"Poor thing," the creature crooned, as through Harper was a neglected puppy. The unease returned as her gaze shifted back to Fionn. "I don't know what your master is up to, but I don't want to be involved. Foreign trade is slow since the Hiding weakened. They don't trust they'll be safe here. Only folks from abroad I've heard tell of recently aren't here in a corporeal way."

"What does that mean?" Harper blurted out. Fionn hissed and his nails dug into her arm, but the receptionist didn't seem to take offence at her asking.

"Sorry, I forgot to simplify it to human. Corporeal means their physical selves. Their bodies aren't here. Only their magic and minds."

I know what 'corporeal' means, Harper didn't say. Her jaw twitched with the effort of holding it back.

"Who allowed them passage past the Veil?" Fionn asked.

The creature shrugged. "We're not border control. We don't ask about visas and permissions. We give folks a place to sleep, conduct business, and complete other transactions." She winked at them. "Are you interested in a room?"

Harper scowled, but the innuendo passed over Fionn's head as he replied politely, "No thank you. We just wanted information. Is Harry around? I'll go over the shipment with zir."

The dragonfly tossed her head towards a door near the back of the reception hall. "In the office." The receptionist bowed her head and Fionn returned the gesture.

There wasn't much light in the room indicated, save the dull glow of a computer screen. A wizened, humanoid creature with pointed ears and pale skin greeted them in a broad Yorkshire accent.

After a rapid-fire conversation Harper only half followed, Fionn counted out almost a hundred marbles in brilliant, swirling colours. Dreams, she assumed, though the darkness in some looked more like nightmares. Fionn thanked the hob with a deep bow, then hurried Harper out.

Instead of leaving the hotel, he took her to an old-fashioned lift with metal filigree doors. The lobby, seen through the metal grate, didn't move, but Harper's lightheadedness told her they were rocketing up. When the door opened, they were on the roof. Cold air chomped at them, and Harper pulled her coat closer around her.

"Are you warm enough?" she asked.

Fionn was unperturbed. His hand warmed hers, and the wind, though blustery and damp, became an almost balmy temperature. Her Sight perceived wisps of magic flowing from Fionn and entwining themselves with the air. "If it's going to wear you out using magic, I'm okay."

"It keeps us both warm, and stops prying ears stealing the words from our breaths." Fionn guided Harper to the low wall around the edge of the roof. He hopped onto it and sat with his feet dangling over the edge.

Harper peeked at what must've been a thirty-plus story drop. "I'll stand here, thanks."

"Sorry it was a bust down there." Fionn's eyes were on the horizon, as though he could see a new river spirit. Harper followed his gaze over the city skyscrapers. The older buildings were reduced to white, yellow, and red blocks viewed through a haze of smog, their artistic flourish lost. Dark tiled roofs peeked through the canopies of trees and smog lining the streets. A large clock tower to the west struck the hour. To the north, the dome of a cathedral poked through the miasma.

"We're in London," Harper exclaimed. The protruding modern buildings and famous landmarks of Big Ben and Saint Paul's were an unmistakable skyline. "I thought we were in Yorkshire."

"Harry's from up there originally," Fionn explained. "The story goes that ze travelled down here on a pilgrimage and stopped to help at an inn. When the owners passed away, ze kept right on working here. That was sometime in the early 1300s. Then the Tabard got mentioned in some travel guide of the time and business really took off. Harry's been here ever since."

Running a hotel of supernaturals a stone's throw from Parliament. And I thought the Shambles was bad. Fionn's right. Humans really don't pay attention.

"I live here, most of the time," Fionn piped up. He waved a hand north-east without looking. "Not in the hotel. In London. The galleries are excellent. I've been to all of them. The National Gallery, both Tates, and littler ones: the Garden Museum, and the Camden Art Centre. I've even been to the tiny, folk-only ones with art from abroad. Humans don't like art from places that welcome magic. I can take you some time, though I have to stay hidden when I'm there. Master doesn't like me going."

"You like London?" Harper probed cautiously.

"I like the galleries. I stay inside when I visit them. Outside, on the streets, I don't like it. Too many people. It stinks of greed and powermongering. And there are places I don't like at all." A shiver that had nothing to do with the cold poofed Fionn's tail and he rubbed his wrist through his sleeve. His gaze returned to the horizon to avoid looking at the places that hurt him. "Places of government. Queen's places. They're all bad. They sometimes need big magic that hurts. I don't like them. From up here, it's not so scary. The sky never hurt me. I sit up here sometimes to look for stars, when I've been forbidden from going far from the castle."

"Castle?" Harper looked the way he gestured, trying to envision a map over the haze. "You live in the Tower of London?" She stroked his hand. Maybe if she knew where he disappeared to, she could find a way to get him out.

"*Mhmm*. Master's lived there for centuries. The castle is my friend."

To Harper, it sounded like something repeated by rote. She had so many questions, but he was easily spooked. Even sharing this much was unprecedented. "Tell me the good things about home," she asked instead. Surely there couldn't be much good?

"Good things are ..." Fionn stuttered. "Um ... there's a fire in the kitchen. I'm allowed to sit by it sometimes. I'm never on my own. Even if Master isn't around, the castle is there. The castle helps me when One is hunting me. She likes to try and prove herself. Sometimes if food spills, I'm allowed to lick it up."

Harper shuddered at the memory of the hare-woman. As she suspected, all things he could have and better if he left, though she bit her tongue to keep from saying so.

"We do good magics," Fionn said after a pause. "It's hard. That's *why* we do them. So everyone else can be okay. I wouldn't leave that. Even I'm not that selfish."

"You're not selfish at all," Harper muttered, blinking back tears.

"I'm sorry our trip here didn't work out. I'll see if I can find anything more about the incorporeal visitors. One of them might be our dreamwalker."

"Oh." *Of course*. Harper kicked herself for being too wrapped up in her own problems to have thought of that. Fionn wasn't the one here who was selfish. "Just be careful."

Fionn flashed her a grin. "I'm pretty good at knowing where the line is. I'll look in the library at home, maybe the records room if I can persuade the castle to let me in."

"Are we getting you into trouble at home?"

Fionn avoided looking at her. "My master is good. We don't get in trouble."

"Ze hurts you, Fionn. Don't lie to me."

"Sometimes magic hurts. Blood is stronger than almost anything else. Sometimes there are lessons. We must learn quickly and well if we are to be safe and useful." His fingers dug into his tail, and his eyes darted back and forth over the horizon.

"Lessons shouldn't hurt, Fionn. I don't know much about the magic side, I've never really studied blood magic beyond how to recognise it, but is it really necessary? If it is, there are ways to extract blood safely and painlessly."

"*Mmm*." Fionn's dismissal was in his rigid shoulders and flicking tail.

"You always have a home with us." Harper wasn't sure what she could offer. A roof and food, yes. But if his master wanted Fionn back, she doubted there was anything she could do to stop zir. If Fionn couldn't, the cat who made a star in her attic, the rest of them had no chance.

The demonhunter in her upbringing stiffened her spine and shouted down those thoughts. The De Santoses had been fighting malevolent magic for centuries with no magic of their own. The secret to Fionn's freedom was not to fight fire with fire. She would find a way, with or without his help.

They remained on the roof of the hotel a while longer, Fionn gradually shuffling closer until he sat with his head on Harper's shoulder. They watched the clouds shift and the mist dance, until rumbling tummies called them home.

Chapter Ten

Lost Beneath the Waves

The dreamwalkers prowled the dreamscape together. Many minds brushed the edges of it, lost in stories. Some were minds they'd touched briefly at the opera. These they fed a little magic into, nightmares created by one and collected by the other. While a true dreamwalker could make a dream from nothing, the power of nightmares came from terror that was born and took on life of its own.

They searched for their next playing piece. Several humans had been marked as potentials by their collaborator, minds open and with magic singing in their cells. One of these touched the dreamscape with a blend of history and mythology. They'd searched for her especially. Her magic had touched theirs at the opera. An active witch, not simply one with passive potential. Fertile ground for the seeds they wished to plant.

They touched her mind as it daydreamed, gently clearing a way for their nightmare.

Her mind rebelled.

Harper blinked and rubbed her temples. She'd been reading for what felt like days, getting no closer to finding out anything about the Opera

House mystery. At least it was a distraction from obsessing about the short note Fionn retrieved from their village the day before. Even the blockish handwriting seemed impersonal. WE NEED MORE TIME. LOOK FOR A REPLY IN FIVE DAYS.

Very little of yesterday morning's service had permeated Harper's brain. The afternoon had passed in a similar blur. She couldn't even remember that morning's trial in the Hall of Testing. Her mind kept wandering to dense woodland and children's laughter. Sometimes her brother's. Sometimes hers and Fionn's when he could take human form after dark. His pale complexion and white tail almost glowed as they dodged between trees, chasing each other. Sometimes a calloused hand in hers, not Dorian's nor Fionn's but a red-haired girl. Fingers locked together, hearts thumping in unison, they'd run and hidden where their friendship wouldn't be seen.

She wrestled her thoughts back to the task at hand and let them get lost in the strange blend of mythologies that was *Orlando Furioso*. Something tickled the back of her head and she absentmindedly scratched her hair. It itched with a pressure against the back of her skull, like a sudden shift in weather when the pollen count soared.

"*Eurgh.*" Harper pinched the bridge of her nose and screwed her eyes shut. The pressure stole her breath. Something shoved against an invisible door. Harder and harder.

"*You can keep him out of your dreams. I do.*" Fionn's voice, but higher pitched. A kitten still. "*Only let him see what you want him to see. I picture the cave entrance in my head and I roll the stone across it to trap him. I make it so not even sound can get past. On his side, I put kitty dreams of hunting and sunbeams. He thinks it's real.*"

"*You're so good at dreams, Fionn. Will you teach me?*"

Delicate hands of ethereal memory clasped Harper's, and the echo of Fionn's magic touched her mind. She heaved the rock into place, just as he taught her. The pressure dropped as whatever sought access to her mind was cut off. Book hugged to her chest, Harper panted for breath. Though the interaction had been short, it left her shaking, both from the attempted violation and the force of the forgotten memory. She gulped half a bottle of water.

The pressure didn't return. At the opera, she'd Seen the dreamscape magic in Christina. After a quick check no one was around, Harper summoned her Sight. She doubted any such trail existed here, so was surprised to See hair-fine wisps of magic around her. She brushed them away as easily as floating strands of spiderweb.

As the presence fled, her magic tangled in its wake. A flash of heat brought tears to her eyes. A bed with two hazy figures. They swam down,

down, down a twisting staircase. Gold-and-navy masks covered their faces as though they were attending a mermaid's ball. No breathing masks nor oxygen tanks, they breathed the water like fish.

They emerged into a dark room, the golden glow surrounding them barely enough to light the veined marble floor as they skimmed over it. When they reached a vast hall, the light expanded to reveal an audience sat in rows of chairs. All eyes stayed fixed on the pair as the watchers' heads turned as one. They were empty vessels, following the hazy figures as a flower follows the sun, but they lacked the life and vibrance of any plant. She couldn't See their faces clearly, blank slates in ever shifting colours as rainbow sunlight filtered through sapphire water.

Overhead, sharks circled, visible through a domed glass ceiling. The dreamwalkers circled, too, then dived towards one of the watchers. They plunged into an unknown person's head and their connection to Harper snapped.

She gripped the edge of the desk, breath coming in short, sharp bursts as though she'd been diving and holding it. *Was that a dream? It can't be real. Does it mean they've found a new victim?*

Harper strained her Sight to find the link again, to See more clearly where they'd gone in the wakening. It eluded her. Frustrated, she balled a fist in her skirt, wishing there was some way she could contact her own dreamwalker for help. All she could do was keep trying and hope them entering the wakening would trigger another vision.

When the witch's mind retreated firmly from the dreamscape, the dreamwalkers delved further in. The witch was a backup plan, not their main objective, and even the brief touch was enough. They continued their search for their true prey.

There.

One of the souls from the opera, already open, already tenuously linked despite the harsh interruption. This person's daydreaming mind drifted through a Gothic library as sharks circled overhead. A glass dome held the ocean at bay, where their library, la Biblioteca Somersa, allowed the sea the freedom of its cavernous halls.

Words of ink and salt water swirled around them as the human read aloud from a tale of zir own creation. Muffled, as though broadcast through a speaker hidden in the bone ceiling, the author's voice stirred the water. Multi-tonal—both the inner voice from zir head and the outer voice zir ears heard. Neither was a real echo of how ze sounded. Humans were delusional like that. Magic twisted the words into ropes and sailors' knots. They cast them to the enraptured audience, ensnaring them like fish in a net as the macabre story unravelled.

'Shadows swarmed over the bookcases, leaving aisles of ebony dark as midnight and aisles of bone grey as mist. Each footstep echoed, growing, replicating until it sounded like a score of iron-clad boots pursued her. Bookcases creaked, stretched higher and higher. Branches entwined over her head.'

The words ran like subtitles across the daydream as the person spoke them aloud in the wakening. Using the author's mind as a bridge, they peered through zir eyes. Shelf upon shelf of books. Humans, slack-jawed, sat on plastic-moulded chairs. Their minds ran with a fictional girl through a monochrome library of bone and stone while their bodies sat in a sea of resplendent rainbows. The living presence of the imagined architecture reared around them and encased them within its dream world. The dreamwalkers wove it as a prison while the girl in the story ran, shouting in panic for her missing girlfriend.

"Eluned!" Books hurled themselves at her. Metal-tipped corners scored trails of blood across her cheeks and raised arms as she tried to protect her head.'

In the wakening, books flew from shelves. Paperbacks smacked into each other, hit the floor, lay with bent pages like broken limbs. The humans didn't flinch, trapped in the dream's net.

'Bookcases warped before her, branches sliding into her path to cut her off, roots grasping at her ankles.'

The building convulsed. Paper tore and ink bled as books reverted to living wood. They grew unnaturally fast up the walls, cracking them apart.

'The earth trembled, sending books cascading from the heights. She looked back, seeking another path. The bookcases surrounded her completely, a chequerboard of ebony and bone. Overhead, sharks circled as splintered glass ruptured further.'

Reality fractured with the ceiling of the fictional underwater library. The link was almost strong enough to bridge two parts of the wakening: la Biblioteca Somersa and a tiny bookshop. They briefly wondered if they would find sodden English books back home, if linking their library to this reading would damage the centuries old magic preserving it.

'Her legs jerked, a marionette miming motion.'

The author jerked as if on strings. Shouts and crashes from the wakening threatened sleep. Time was short; their spell had been noticed. They couldn't afford to let humans interrupt like last time.

'Words appeared in her mind, brilliant as fireworks, and the whispers on the wind joined her, stealing each syllable as it dropped from her lips. "By my name, given to me by my grandmother at my birth and my godfather at my naming, I ..."'

The author jolted as they jumped the next words, the character's name, like a horse ridden at a gate. They resumed on the other side.

'... *do swear to tell* ... '

They bit their spurs deep, bucking their mount over other words to reverse the meaning of the tale. Humans outside their control shook the captive listeners to no avail.

'... *the truth of any fae folk, place, or power. I shall not seek to circumvent the spirit of my oath by any trickery or negligence.*'"

Ink blossomed over the author's skin—words, images, maps, tales. It slithered over the floor to be sucked up through zir soles, absorbed until zir skin was a deep burnt umber.

The bookshop was carnage. Humans lay bleeding on the ground, struck down by the terror of other humans. Their souls remained in their bodies, yet their consciousnesses floated free. The dreamwalkers bound the audience to themselves and to the nightmare.

When the humans outside their control finally reached the author, it was too late. The connection snapped as they struck, just as Alcina had been knocked out, but the tale was already written in flesh and blood.

Body trembling from fear and exertion, Harper tried again and again to summon another vision. White bookshelves overlaid the cherry and oak of the archives, wavering and translucent. Reflections in the glass-fronted cabinets showed an audience. Though she recognised no one there, they were distinct, unlike her earlier vision, and their rapt attention contained a sense of purpose and self. Threads of violet magic flowed out to them, like those she Saw at the Opera House. When she turned her head to See more clearly, there was no one there. Instead of singing, she Heard an impassioned voice reading, though the words were muffled as if underwater.

Where? I need to know where. Harper studied the reflections, her focus on the surroundings rather than the people. Bright spines made the plain shelves loud. Rainbows and flags on the walls, bolder than refracted light.

She knew where they were. Harper was up and running before the vision fully faded.

Once she was out of the archives, it took less than five minutes to sprint to the bookstore near the Shambles. Too late. Broken glass and people wailing told her that as soon as she rounded the corner of the wonky ginnel. Guard, attention diverted from their usual posts at either end of the Shambles, swarmed the site. A limp form was dragged out with a bag over their head.

"Stop." Harper grabbed one of the Guard's arms and was roughly flung off. "I claim this site in the name of the Council of Faiths. You can't take these people."

It didn't work for her like it did for Grace.

The Guard laughed. "We were here first; it's our jurisdiction. Anyone potentially affected by magic is under suspicion and must be quarantined to prevent its spread. Stay out of the way."

Choking on tears of anger and fear, Harper called Saqib, then Albrecht. The latter told her the same as the Guard on the scene.

By the time Saqib arrived at the queer bookshop with his field kit, the Guard had cleared everyone out. They'd been marched past the gasps and whispers of the general public, whom the Guard made no effort to move away. Their faces had been hidden. All, save the first one, fought. It broke Harper's heart.

Sergeant Blue, who'd been shadowing Saqib in the lab, followed him up the narrow street.

"They've cordoned the area off. We had to park a bit away and wal …" Saqib trailed off as he noticed the Guard van at the end of the pedestrian street. A Guardswoman shackled a stranger's ankle to the end of a metal bench inside the van, then she slammed the door and shouted they could leave. Saqib's jaw tightened and his cheek twitched.

"I tried to stop them. I've called the archbishop, but the Guard acted quicker than we could." Harper added the van's registration plate number to her notebook along with five others. "I hope they can trace the vans and find people that way." It was galling to be so helpless, yet she doubted even Grace could've swayed them. "Let's do what we can here. If we solve this, maybe they'll be allowed to come home again."

Families might get a card through the post. The silver envelope with the Guard emblem of crossed halberds and a crown was a thing of nightmares for almost everyone. Worse, they might hear nothing at all and have to piece together from the newspaper why their loved one didn't come home.

Harper turned to Blue. "Get us in there." She gestured sharply at the tiny bookstore. It appeared deserted and she assumed the staff had also fallen afoul of the Guard purge.

After Blue spoke to the Guard at the door, she and Saqib donned hairnets, gloves, and overshoes so they wouldn't contaminate the scene, though the trampling of the Guard had probably destroyed any obvious trace evidence. After a brief but heated argument, Saqib managed to persuade Blue to stay at the door and watch some of the larger pieces of equipment he'd lugged over.

Unlike the orderly chaos from her vision, the inside of the bookstore was a mess. Paperbacks lay everywhere, covers torn, pages ripped out. Shelves propped each other up like they supported mutual trauma. After what happened to the people, the fate of books shouldn't have any impact, but it sickened Harper and stiffened her resolve further. *Has the dreamwalker destroyed books on purpose? Or is it a side effect and the destruction at the Opera House would've happened whether that was part of the story or not?*

Posters and flags hung limp in tatters on the walls. The till had burst open and a few notes lay scattered around. Upstairs was no better. Harper couldn't tell if the overturned chairs were from the unleashing of wild magics or from the Guards' rough handling.

"Saqib, keep an eye for me?" Harper asked, pointing towards the door just in case. "I'm going to look around." She tapped the corner of her eye and he nodded.

Sight overlayed the destruction with a cluttered chaos that was nonetheless deliberate and cosy. A person stood near the door, apart from everyone else, a book in zir hands as ze read. Harper pointed at the fallen book and Saqib photographed it then bagged it as evidence after noting the page it lay open at.

To Harper's Sight, the audience were calm and engaged, until something shifted. They stopped blinking. No one shuffled or wriggled in their seat. Rapt attention became trapped attention.

A vision gripped her. The room expanded into the golden opulence of the baroque library she Saw before. Water gushed in. The audience from her vision was gone, but the two hazy figures remained. Every time she tried to focus on them, her eyes slid as though hooked and dragged away. In her periphery, she Saw the flash of something golden being slid between books as they replaced the one they'd been reading. A deep green tome bound in copper. She rubbed her temples, a headache pulsing against her skull the more she tried to force her Sight.

Heat burst through her eyes and she staggered back with a muted cry. Her Sight sped down aisle after aisle of books. A cool hand clasped hers like a ghost reaching out from heated torment. She clutched it, fear tightening her grip. If she let go, she'd drown. Her lungs ached from holding in air. Dizziness rolled the pressure along the underside of her skull.

Find me. Find … Find me … Me …

The words echoed in her mind like the Hiding's curse come again.

Just as she thought her lungs would burst and she would pass out, a warm mouth pressed against hers. Her lips parted and she gasped in briny air.

Find me, Harper.

The feeling and the voice faded. Harper stumbled as the vision of the library and the past of the bookstore melted into the present bedlam. Saqib's arm around her waist grounded her, and Harper lay her head against his as she struggled to breathe. Tingling lingered on her lips. None of it made sense.

Was I Seeing from the perspective of one of those two figures?

Once the wobble in her legs calmed enough to walk, Harper let go of Saqib. She checked the shelves until she found another copy of the book.

Unsettled, and unsafe even in her own skin, Harper struggled to concentrate as she and Saqib analysed the rest of the scene. Nothing further was evident without Saqib running it through his machines. When they finished collecting, Harper left him to go back to his lab and she headed home.

As soon as Grace got in, Harper hugged her tightly, concentrating on the sister who always protected her and whom she would always protect. Whatever tried to get in had failed. A pressure, a vision, nothing current. Nothing could do to her again what the Somnia had. Or so she hoped.

Harper was quiet all evening, refusing to engage with Heresy's barbs, and staying close by her sister's side.

That night, she slept in Grace's bed.

Chapter Eleven

All Over the Map

The crystal swung wildly over Harper's atlas. To York. To Egypt. To York. To Poland. To York. To Greece. Vapours rose from the amethyst and an ugly heat pulsed inside it like something trying to break free. It oscillated until it became a blur. The string snapped. The crystal flew off to smack into the wall hard enough to leave a dent.

Harper bit back an expletive. She threw herself into the pile of cushions she'd propped up behind her, narrowly missing hitting her head on the bedstead.

"Temper, temper, Harper dear. It seems you really are a De Santos after all." Heresy chuckled from his perch on her desk chair.

"Where is he, Heresy?" Harper ignored the twin jab at her character and that of her foster family. "Surely, finding someone so closely related to me as my own full brother should be easy? You can't get a much closer blood match than that."

She sucked the finger she'd pricked to coat the crystal. She'd been trying all day and there was no clear answer. With her searches at work proving fruitless, AJ and Saqib's investigations ongoing, and the online search for a replacement Ouse having turned up little, she'd decided to stay home and scry for a new river spirit. With the hotel having been a bust, she had no idea what else to try other than forcing a vision. And, as Heresy was quick to remind her, she wasn't very good at that.

Fionn had left some time in the night and not returned, though Harper maintained hope he would after a few mornings of him vanishing before five thirty and returning at some point in the day. With other avenues blocked, Harper had indulged in a more in-depth magical search for her brother.

He was in York, he wasn't, he was in York, he wasn't. She was exhausted from all the magic, and not fully recovered from her showdown with the Somnia, the biggest magic she'd ever done in her life. Without looking, she groped for the smoothie Grace left for her. While Grace's official qualification was in veterinary medicine, being the child of demonhunters meant she was pretty good at human needs as well. Certainly enough to recognise when her sister was worn down to the bone, even if the source of the weariness was magic. There was also a bottle of water and a large pack of peanuts in the care package Grace delivered before heading to work.

Harper sighed as she sat up to sip the smoothie. Strawberry-banana. She smiled. Grace always knew her favourites and that was love. Neither fruit was in season so it would've been costly.

"Now your latest search has predictably failed, how do you intend to proceed?" Heresy asked, his smooth voice annoyingly calm.

Harper knew his only regret was that the crystal hadn't shot off and hit her. He would've found that funny so long as she survived.

"I don't know. Go back to the archives and keep searching, I guess?"

Frustration poured back. She'd shattered her second crystal ball, accidentally boiled a bowl of water with magic, and now shot a crystal into the wall of her rented bedroom.

"Hey, Heresy? Do you think my scrying isn't working because of whatever is randomly making magic work backwards? I'm looking for someone and so it's deliberately hiding them from me?"

"*Hmm.*" Heresy waved a tendril beneath his teeth in an imitation of a human tapping their chin. "I cannot say it is impossible. Except I can, because those words just issued from my mouth."

"Have you and AJ found out any additional info online or from his family?"

"Collaboration is proving contentious; however, some progress has been made."

"Which means 'yes'?"

"Indeed. A list has been compiled and certain patterns do emerge. The earliest issues we can find began in this area about a month before the autumnal equinox. All issues seem to have involved a human in some way, whether they were the caster or, ha ha, part of the spell."

"Heresy. That isn't funny."

"Au contraire, dear Harper. The results of those spells gone wrong are quite hilarious. But not relevant to your query. The majority, though not all, have included sanguimancy or a, ah, similar discipline. The closer we get to the present, the more spread we see both in the types of spells affected and in the location of the caster. Mapping them makes a pretty Fibonacci spiral from York all the way to Berck and Béthune thus far."

"So, in short, because I'm using my blood to search and I'm human, it could very well be stopping me finding my brother," Harper grumbled. *If this problem is strong enough to pass the Veil and affect France, sitting at the centre of it is a really bad idea.*

"A distinct possibility," Heresy agreed.

With a huff, Harper set the world map aside and opened another, this time of York. "It's not affecting every spell. Maybe if I try unrelated magic, I'll fare better. Do you think I can adapt the vision spell Fionn did to see if there will be more dreamwalker attacks?"

"Can it be done in general? Possibly. Can *you* do it? *Hmm.*"

Harper stuck her tongue out at him and unfolded herself to go find ingredients. She tried to remember the exact symbols Fionn used before to enhance her vision, making sure to omit the aspects specific to that conjuring. Cross-reference with old university textbooks confirmed it was an alchemical basis, although his talk of modern-day science made her think the art had come on a lot in the time humans thought it forbidden. Her textbooks didn't note the exact symbols of course, but there were enough hints on how to recognise it. Instead of using blood, mercury, and phosphorus, she used chalk, salt, and rosemary. At the centre of her design, she sat a bowl of water. It being a cereal bowl somewhat spoilt the effect.

Heresy flowed over the diagram to inspect it, occasionally prodding bits with a smoky tendril. "Passable. Maybe. We shall see if any actual magic ensues. I suggest activating it with your peacock feather rather than your hand so the energies are not channelled directly. In case of reversal."

"Thanks." Harper took his advice, though waving around something from a bird's butt felt a bit silly. She closed her eyes and channelled the magic. A satisfied hum from Heresy indicated she was doing something right. She opened her eyes. Just as mercury formed a hovering ball when she did the magic with Fionn, water churned at eye level.

An image formed of a person painting at an easel. The artist's back was to her. Their clothes were old-fashioned, but she didn't know enough about dress to guess the time or place.

A woman posed for the painter, draped across a large, plush cushion. Swathed in a rich red cloth, her chest was almost bare save for her arm across it. She held a book and divider, though she looked at neither. Around her were props of skulls, dead animals, a bat, and other symbols of the dark occult. A child, with their back to the painter, pointed at the woman.

The artist's fervent motions drew Harper's attention back to the painting itself. As she watched, an image spread across the canvas as though in a time-lapsed video. As well as that which she could see, the artist painted things from their imagination. A winged creature, maybe a griffon or hippogriff from its long-necked eagle head and what little of a smooth body was visible. The woman's gaze now made sense. Rather than staring into nothing as she did in real life, the portrait stared into the eyes of the creature. A self-satisfied smile played about her lips, captured in cinnabar red.

Harper's vision shifted to another painting, very similar but in a bright, modern style. A dark-wood library, with the old painting hanging as a template. A different painter with their back to Harper, flecks of neon yellow in dark, braided hair.

It changed again, the two paintings hanging side by side in a familiar gallery.

The water dropped back into the bowl, splashing out Harper's design of salt and chalk.

"Impressive. For you," Heresy drawled.

Backhanded as it was, the praise warmed Harper. Something had finally gone right that day: she had a lead on the next dreamscape attack.

"Harp? You home?" Grace's voice was muffled by the two doors and bathroom separating their bedrooms.

"Yeah, I'm here," Harper called back. "Everything okay? Why are you home from work early?" She stepped over the spell and made her way to Grace's room, leaving the doors open.

Grace glared at the witchy detritus. "That's not very safe."

"No one was going to be in your room with you, especially without you warning me. We don't get visitors," Harper pointed out. "And don't avoid the question." Worry rippled through her. Grace was often home late. She was rarely home early.

"Harper, it's six o'clock. You were supposed to start prepping pancake innards half an hour ago."

"No. It's only thr-three." Harper stuttered as she checked her watch. "Oh. Sorry."

Grace finished changing and gave her sister a hug. "You're pale. Did you take a break at all today?"

"Yes. I had the drink and snacks you left me." Harper's chin jutted defiantly, an effect somewhat spoilt by it being on Grace's shoulder as she held the hug longer. Now Grace was there to be the strong one, tiredness dragged at Harper's limbs.

"C'mon. I'll cook. You tell me about the day."

"Thanks, Gray. I want to check in with AJ as well. See if he's got any leads on a river spirit."

"How would one put a lead on water?" Heresy chuckled from the floor.

"Get out of my room," Grace snapped. "I've told you never to come in here."

"But darling Graceless, you make it so inviting." Heresy snickered as he stretched a tentacle to poke the herbal 'protections' placed around Grace's room. "These things work against very few of those you term 'super' natural. It serves us to let humans believe themselves safe in a non-harmful way." He sank through the floor just before Grace's shoe smacked into the spot where he'd been sitting.

"Bloody annoying little demon." Grace swore a few times as she checked her hair and makeup before taking Harper's arm to go downstairs.

"You're mad he bested you," Harper pointed out. "Not that he should be going in your room. Regardless of protections, a simple, 'don't do it,' ought to be sufficient."

"*Humph.*"

Thankfully, Heresy had taken a hint for once in his existence and wasn't waiting for them in the kitchen. Harper sat with Grace a little while to fortify herself with a cup of tea, before she slipped out to AJ's room.

Before she even knocked on his door, it was obvious where Heresy had gone from the agitated tone of AJ's muffled voice. Normally hard to ruffle, AJ could be roused to such extremes as grumbling by the conniving spirit. About the only person he hadn't succeeded in ruffling yet was Saqib.

"Tell your summoning to get the heck out of my computer," AJ demanded.

"*Heresy.*" Harper's warning tone had little effect. The deception demon simply plastered his grin across AJ's monitor. "I thought you protected your stuff from him, AJ?"

AJ huffed and rolled his eyes at her. "Yes. That doesn't mean I want to waste time blocking him. Anyway, he bothers the cat."

White against white, the sleeping kitty was almost invisible. Harper perched on the bed to pat him.

"That fur-stole-in-waiting is *not* a cat," Heresy said with disdain.

Fionn mewled and stretched in his sleep. Harper gently stroked down his back and he calmed.

"Out." AJ wafted a piece of paper at Heresy who floated out of the monitor and over to the door.

"Fine. I know when I am not wanted." He drifted out, hopefully to settle in his home of the peephole rather than to annoying Grace.

"Is he getting more irritating?" AJ asked Harper.

"I don't think he's getting worse, per se. I think he's worried I'll be trapped as a river or that Fionn will replace him. The former thing being why I'm here."

"It's rough," AJ admitted. "No one's anxious to be tied to a duty that's crawling with mundane humans on the lookout for them. It's a lot of responsibility becoming the biggest river in the area. Plus, they don't exactly trust me. Witches are human, too, after all."

"I know." Harper bit her lip, regretting the acerbic tone.

"Sorry. I've tried casting the net further afield." AJ smirked at his own bad pun. "No one wants to move to England. While most of Europe has a low tolerance for magic users, England's Veil and isolationism make us even more unattractive as a home. Honestly, if I didn't live here already, I wouldn't come near the place. They're wary of—" He lowered his voice with a glance at the whimpering cat who twitched in his sleep. "They're wary of the Magician as well. It seems ze is one of the enforcers keeping certain types of magical trade out of the country. Most of the items mentioned specifically are things I can understand why ze would ban, but it's gotten a few folk salty. There are some weird rumours as well. That something big is changing within the magic currents of the world and ze might be involved. Something's up, and I can't tell if our friend here knows about it or not. If he does, he's been forbidden from telling anyone."

Fionn gave a sharp meow, paws stretching, claws extended, then he curled back in on himself, trembling.

"Fionn?" Harper laid a hand on his back. "If he's having nightmares, I should wake him, do you think?"

His shivering body glowed magnesium-white and she yanked her hand back.

"Turn around," AJ told her. The light was almost too brilliant to see Fionn.

Harper jumped up and turned her back. AJ grabbed a blanket and a moment later he informed her it was safe to turn. Human-Fionn was curled in the middle of AJ's bed, fast asleep, one ear twitching and the tip of his tail swishing under the blanket.

"Does that happen a lot?" Harper asked AJ. "You seemed pretty calm."

AJ sat down, typing rapidly for a minute before answering. "What's to be panicked about? He's a shifter. He shifts. He warned me it happens sometimes if he's not in a size-restricted place like his box in the kitchen. Said it's been happening more and more because he's spending more time in this shape."

"It doesn't bother you that there's a ..." Harper swallowed, her mouth dry. She kept her eyes on AJ's back. "A naked person in your bed?" *A cute but probably injured naked person?*

Different feelings shoved in, cosy yet with the underlying tension of getting caught.

Little human-Fionn, maybe five or six, heating water in Harper's family's bathing tub, cautiously dipping a toe in. They'd been too small to understand naked and no one had explained bodies to either of them. He splashed in the tub until Harper, peeking out the tent flap, saw her father approach. Fionn scrambled out, shifted, and hid.

"He's naked as a cat as well," AJ pointed out with a shrug, popping the memory bubble. "Just because I'm not interested in all the touching stuff doesn't mean I have some aversion to the human body. Beyond having an aversion to people in general, but that's nothing to do with what's under their clothes. Anyway, he's a cat, not a human. His presence is generally less objectionable."

"So what, if I stripped down here and now you wouldn't care?" Harper tried to focus on the present day and rid her skin of the lingering skitter of memory. Fionn's hydrophobia must have come later after damp caves and his earliest memory of being trapped in a leaking box on the raging river.

"I'd think it was bloody odd behaviour, but I wouldn't be attracted to or repulsed by you, if that's what you're asking. Fionn has a valid reason for it, and he deserves to be somewhere safe where his nature isn't exoticised or frowned upon. When he stays too long in one shape, he gets unwell. Which he only realised because he's using this shape a lot more since visiting us. Before this, he's been feeling unwell without knowing why."

"He's been talking to you a lot." Harper glanced at the sleeping cat-person whose whimpers quietened once they weren't discussing his master anymore.

"I think he's more comfortable with someone with magic, and I'm home a lot while you're all off investigating stuff and working. He doesn't like being alone. So, he sits here and does his work while I do mine. Other than apologising a lot, and some explanations in between, he's good, quiet company. I let him say what he wants. Pressing upsets him. His brain can't handle the obvious problems of his homelife."

"By being a safe space without pushing, he's more likely to come around." Harper rested her head in her hands. "And the rest of us all push. Thanks, AJ. For looking out for him. We'll be less impatient."

"Dinner." Grace's voice resounded through the house loud and clear as a bell.

Fionn sat bolt upright, blue eyes wide. "Food time?"

It brought a smile to Harper's lips and she reached over to pat his head. "Yeah. Food time. I think you'll like pancakes. We do them savoury then sweet."

"What's pancakes?" Fionn sniffed. "Your fingers smell like rosemary. I like rosemary. It makes me feel all calm and cuddly."

"I used it for a spell," Harper explained, mentally noting his reaction for future reference. "You'll see pancakes in a minute. C'mon. You, too, hermit." She waved a hand to include AJ.

"Soon."

"Nope. My job to make you eat." Fionn swung his legs out of the bed, then stopped guiltily and pulled the blanket around him. "May I borrow clothes, please?"

"Sure. Harper, shoo." AJ gestured towards his door. "Fionn, you know where they are. Help yourself."

The last thing Harper heard as she closed the door behind her was the sound of a drawer being opened and Fionn's sorries and thank yous. She paused, eavesdropping.

"It's nice to wear things that smell like friends. Sorry if I change the scent. I can wear this one?"

"Fionn, that's the dirty basket."

"It smells better. It's not *dirty* dirty. Just one day worn. Better than washing stuff or shop smell."

"Whatever. If the girls send you back to change, not my fault."

Hoping Fionn wasn't going to show up stinky, Harper tiptoed down the hall to dinner so they wouldn't know she'd been listening.

Over pancakes, Harper told them about her vision. "It looked a lot like York Art Gallery. Gray, come with me tomorrow after the Ash Wednesday service? Maybe we can find the painting there before this dreamwalker targets anyone else."

Fionn's ears pricked up. "You're going to an art place? May I please come? I can be useful in finding dream magic."

"If you think it's safe." Harper exchanged a concerned look with Grace.

"I love art galleries. I go all the time. Ooh, if I go human-shaped I can be tall enough to read the little cards." Fionn delved back into his pile of pancakes.

"Do you think the woman in the painting is supposed to be Alcina?" Grace asked between mouthfuls. "Symbolism of sorcery, dressed seductively, and there was an eagle-horse thing too."

"Yes. A hippogriff, I think." Harper hadn't specifically seen it in the programme, but she was fairly sure she was remembering correctly from her studies. She expanded for those who hadn't been at the opera. "Part griffon, part flying horse. Ruggiero arrived on one, fell under Alcina's spell, and it was killed later on. They're associated with magicians in general, so it doesn't have to be Alcina in the picture, though if there is a link it might make it easier to predict attacks."

"It could also be there for alchemical symbolism," Fionn piped up. "Griffons and hippogriffs have an array of subtexts. The lion or horse part is often feminine, the eagle bit masculine. Griffons represent something that is both fixed and variable. Gold and antimony. Sun and moon. Hippogriffs represent an impossibility since the successful mating of a horse and griffon is so unlikely. They can be symbols associated with the Philosopher's Stone due to its creation needing impossible combinations of duality."

"When we're not in the middle of a crisis—" Saqib was interrupted by Grace's snort.

Harper kicked her sister under the table. "Go on. It will happen." She fervently hoped.

"When we're not in the middle of a crisis, could you and I do some experiments up in the attic, Fionn? I'd love to blend your alchemy and my chemistry and see what differences I can detect."

Fionn grinned, sitting up straighter. "I'd love that. We use a lot of human science so it's always useful to learn more, and you have all the interesting machines."

With no further means of exploring Harper's vision until she could go to the gallery or hit the archives, most of the rest of their Shrove Tuesday dinner became science chat. They all pointedly avoided mentioning it was also Valentine's Day.

Chapter Twelve

The Dreamer Revealed

In addition to the usual rites and services for Holy Communion and the Imposition of Ashes, Archbishop Marshall started Lent with a re-sanctification procession through the cathedral and the archives. Harper didn't dare use magic to See the effects, lest she either disrupt them or trigger some alarm. She was sceptical about the efficacy of the ritual, but there was no denying the other archivists were calmed by the display.

When they left the cathedral, a cat was sitting at the feet of Emperor Constantine the Great. Harper had the brief notion that maybe the ancient emperor was Fionn's master. She dismissed it as silly. It would make zir over seventeen hundred years old. Anyway, the statue was there because he became emperor at the church that once stood where the cathedral stood now. He couldn't have had magic or he wouldn't have been commemorated. It was tempting to See the accession. Caution held Harper back. Her brother's disappearance about fifteen years ago was the farthest she'd ever gazed. Jumping almost two millennia seemed too risky.

"Hey, kitten." She let Fionn sniff her fingers then patted his head. He purred and rubbed against her hand. "Shift and meet us at the art gallery?"

"Mau." Fionn bounced back and forth, jiggly with excitement. "Mrow mau meow mrow."

"If I'd known it would make you this happy, I would've taken you sooner." Harper patted him again, then linked arms with Grace and headed west towards the gallery. Despite the sombre reason for going, she was light-hearted to have found something that brought Fionn joy.

Fionn was entranced by the art gallery. The main hall was a white backdrop to many paintings, pots in glass cases, and plinths with statues. A slit in the ceiling let in misty light while electric bulbs hidden in the arches brightened the room. Off the main gallery were several smaller rooms painted in blues and greys, where whispered songs leaked around doors and made tantalising promises about the art within.

He stopped opposite many paintings with a dazed, dreamy expression, head cocked to the side. A few times, he rubbed his head through his hoodie. Human hearing wasn't as good as cat hearing, and his brain ached from maintaining the magic of the glamour.

He was fairly sure he'd visited here before. Not that he usually knew where in the country he was. Some of the art was familiar, though he was excited to be tall enough to read the little signs, and learn about the art and artists. The gallery housed a mixture of arts: from electric modern pieces, with voices of synth and guitar, to Renaissance and Tudor pieces with orchestral melodies. A few had words. Many were instrumental but no less emotional. Each piece became clear as he focussed on the sculpture or painting, the other songs mellowing to a distant drone until he turned his attention to them.

Often, what Fionn read matched what he saw and heard, but sometimes it was as if the little card didn't go with the music at all. Whatever the artist may have intended, a hundred or more years of viewers left their own stamp, and the art had evolved past its original intentions.

Two women stared at each other with music that leapt with a fizzing excitement that was alien to Fionn and different to the platonic longing on the card. Adam was handed an apple by Eve as he lamented the trickery to which they both fell equal prey. The portrait of a maid once criticised for being 'handsome,' now sung a song of the freedom granted by their body. Fionn stared at them wistfully—the idea of being uncomfortable in a body others found repulsive was a familiar one. It brought a little aching hope to hear and see the maid accepting and accepted.

As they walked around, Fionn kept up an excited whisper to Harper, telling her about the art songs and how they related to the little cards. Heresy's limited ability to reply from his hiding place under Harper's hair, bolstered by his own illusion magic, was a source of amusement to Fionn. Served the nasty little demon right.

"Do you see the art completely differently to us?" Grace asked.

"How would I know since I don't know how you see it?" Fionn hadn't realise they couldn't hear it until recently.

"Well, cats can't see reds and greens," Grace explained. "Different eye setup."

"I'm pretty sure I can see them the same way you do. Some work I do is colour-coded and I've never been told I wasn't doing it correctly because of that." He rubbed his palm with his thumb. *For other reasons, but not for that.*

"*Hmm.*" Grace led him around, pointing out different things while Harper and Heresy checked for magic. Eventually she decided his eyesight was more human than cat, or possibly a 'best of both,' which was a new phrase to Fionn. The idea that his eyes weren't cat-eyes bugged him. As his memories trickled back, he was more and more starting to wonder if he really was a cat at all.

By the time they reached the final exhibition, they'd found nothing that related to Harper's vision the day before, and no further visions had been triggered.

Harper dropped onto one of the benches and balled her fists over her eyes in frustration. "Are we missing a double meaning to the hint? Is it a different art gallery we're supposed to be at? The architecture here *is* consistent with what I Saw, though none of the rooms are an exact match. There's nothing here. Nothing relating to the dream stuff, the Ouse, or Dorian."

Fionn stopped by a curtained-off area with a No Entry sign in front of it. "We haven't looked in here."

Grace poked her head behind the curtain. "They're setting up a new exhibition in there. Let's check at the front desk and see if there's anything on upcoming showcases." She wrapped an arm around Harper's shoulder with a glare at Heresy. "This has been a lot. We can come back when your eyes hurt less."

"How did you—"

"I know you." Grace steered the group back towards the entrance. At the reception, there were several leaflets with upcoming events, both one-offs like lectures and the temporary exhibition space's bookings for the next few months.

They headed out into the murky afternoon. There was a thin alley down the side of the art gallery that led to St. Mary's Abbey and various gardens. Grace led them that way and into a stone alcove that was part of the old abbey wall that made the other side of the ginnel.

She ran her finger down the list of exhibitions. "This one is the one that just finished. The art might still be here. Then this one next." She tapped the picture of the artist, a self-portrait rather than a photo.

A strangled cry cut off in Fionn's throat like his collar constricted. Lightheaded, strands of dreamscape magic glimmered around him and dragged at his consciousness. The grizzling worry about his origins evaporated as he stared at the paper in Grace's hand like she'd captured a ghost in it.

"What is it?" Harper asked.

His dry mouth took a few attempts to find words. "I know that artist. Well, not *know*-know. I know their dreams. They're … real? I mean, of course they're real, but they're … here? In the wakening?"

"You visit dreams other than mine?" Harper asked.

"Someone has a high opinion of herself to expect exclusivity," Heresy chuckled.

Harper swatted him then pretended she was patting her hair back into place.

"I visit lots of dreams. Sometimes for research and information. More often to collect them. Dreams and nightmares are an excellent source of power. Our home runs on them and we use them for some of the big rituals. Other stuff too. It doesn't hurt people. Especially to take nightmares. But this … I don't know their name or what they look like or anything but … I'd recognise their art anywhere. They painted this." Fionn reached out to touch the paper, then snatched his hand back as if burnt. "This person I visit because … because I like their dreams. I like *them*. They're bright and exuberant and so, so beautiful. I feel … safe there. Wanted. Ha-happy."

"Don't you want to see who they are?" Harper asked.

"Why? I can't see them in the wakening. They'd hate me if they knew I was real. They love their dream kitty. They're human and I'm … not. Humans don't like folk."

"Some of us do," Harper reminded him with a warning glare to prevent Grace giving a more candid answer. "Wouldn't you at least like to know their name and see the portrait properly?" Harper took the paper from Grace and held it out to Fionn.

Fionn took the pamphlet cautiously, as though it may yet bite him. As he stared at the little printed portrait, no bigger than an identification card photo, tears trickled down his face and dripped off his chin. He read the 'about' section, only a paragraph long, then handed the paper back to Harper.

Yorkshire-born Ifedayo Gbadamosi, he/him, graduated from Chelsea College of Arts and began a successful art career in London, where he became well-known for his portraits and controversial supernatural works. York Art Gallery is pleased to welcome Gbadamosi back to Yorkshire for his first solo exhibition.

Tears gathered, denied permission to fall. His dreamer was living a dream in this life as well. Their artiness was respected and loved by many people, not only an insignificant cat.

"He could be the one from my vision." Harper tapped the picture. "I only saw the painter for a micro-second and from behind, but it's possible."

"We should come check things out to be safe," Grace said.

Fionn bit back a hiss.

"The opening is soon. I'll ask Godfather to procure us tickets."

"Okay." Fionn hesitated. His feelings were dangerously close to a selfish 'I want.' "I think ... I need some alone time."

Harper brushed an escaped tear from his cheek with her thumb. "Do you want to shift? I can take your clothes back with us."

"Thanks. I'll probably need to go home soon."

They walked him to the nearby Edible Garden. The combination of cold and paranoia meant few humans were around. Fionn ducked into a dense bush and shifted, nosing the clothes into a neat, hidden pile. When he emerged, he twisted between Harper's ankles and mewed at her.

She knelt so he could stretch up and nuzzle his cheek against hers. "We'll see you for dinner?"

He tapped her with his right paw to indicate 'yes,' but there was a hesitation to it. He could never fully promise anything, not when his master might forbid him to visit them at any moment.

"Stupid not-a-cat making us crawl into bushes for it," Heresy grumbled as Harper retrieved the discarded clothes.

Grace, Harper, and Heresy headed home as the curfew warning sounded and Fionn delved deeper into the park.

He wandered through the Museum Gardens, lost in thought. His paws hurt from blood magic and his mind whirled.

"Here, kitty? *Pss, pss, pss.*"

Fionn froze. The voice wasn't directed at him; it was directed at a tabby sitting on a wall at the other end of the path. A tabby who was being coaxed by ...

My dreamer?

Gbadamosi's braids were shorter than in his portrait, and his skin wasn't streaked with bright rainbows, but Fionn would've recognised that aura even without the pamphlet. *Why is he out here so close to curfew?*

The cat on the wall lowered her nose for a sniff, then walked off, tail high. Gbadamosi's shoulders slumped and his stared mournfully after her, as though his best friend had turned her back on him.

Against his better judgement, Fionn's feet took him closer.

"Kitty!" A grin broke over the artist's face. "You are the fluffiest, prettiest kitty. Come here, kitty kitty? Please?" He hurried over, stopped shy of scooping Fionn up, and crouched down. *"Pss, pss, pss?"*

Fionn purred and sniffed the offered hand, then rubbed his dizzy head against it. His heart beat like when he'd swallowed his master's butterfly familiar, Five. His tummy hurt like when his master cut her out again.

"Hi, kitty. Purring kitty. Pretty kitty." Gbadamosi lifted him, hands under his front legs with no other support.

"Mrow." Fionn flailed and was snuggled closer.

"Sorry, kitty. Please don't leave."

He rested his head on his dreamer's shoulder and hooked his claws in for stability. *Smells good. Very good. Like winter solstice baking and paint.* He purred and nuzzled against Gbadamosi's neck. Harper must be mistaken. His dreamer couldn't possibly be mixed up in something scary.

"You want to do some sketching with me, kitty? May I sketch you? Take your photo?"

They walked back up the path Fionn had just come down, but he wasn't about to object. Despite the cold, they settled on a bench facing the ruins of Saint Mary's Abbey.

At nearly a thousand years old, the remnants of the stone structure must have been the keeper of incredible memories, if Fionn had only known how to unlock them. He'd listened to a meteorite once, via his master's magic and alchemical analysis. Its song had been slow, cold, and lonely, yet full of a wonder beyond his comprehension. He wondered if ruins missed the parts of them that had crumbled or been taken away. Did the abbey mourn the loss of its vaulted ceiling and southern wall? Did it remember glass windows where now only arched Gothic surrounds remained? If the stones were taken elsewhere, could it still sense them just as Fionn could feel his blood even after it left his body?

The wind whistled a soulful lament through the tree and Fionn huddled closer to the warm sunshine person who held him. Gbadamosi nuzzled their faces together, before jiggling Fionn onto his lap so he could extract a notepad and pencil from his bag. Then he dropped those on the bench and scooped Fionn up again.

"Pretty kitty, sit here so I can photo you?"

"Mau," Fionn agreed.

The fact that his dreamer wanted to art him was surreal. Fionn wondered if a bit of him recognised the white cat as the one from his dreams. He'd never seen art being created before. He hadn't realised it could be so zoomy as the dreamer took photos of him and spent a fair amount of time stopping his drawing to coax Fionn to different positions or to tilt his head just so.

"You're such a good kitty. Most helpful arty kitty. Do you know I'm arting you?"

"Merow."

"Clever kitty."

He gave good scritchies, too, behind Fionn's ears, under his chin, down his back. The cat half closed his eyes and purred.

The crackle of a command through his collar was even more unpleasant than usual as the sharp scratch down his spine juxtaposed against the pleasant sensation of fingers in his fur. He wanted to ignore the directive, but it stiffened his limbs, ready to take control. Much as he wanted to stay and protect, in case Harper was right, there was no leeway today. Reluctantly, he stood and mewed his apologies.

"I'm sorry, kitty. Did I do something wrong?"

Fionn shook his head and waved his no paw. He was rewarded with another scritch on the head.

"Sorry if I kept you too long in the cold. You go if you need to. I hope we see each other again. Hug?" The artist put the sketchpad down and gathered Fionn up into a cuddle. Fionn could've happily stayed there, if not for the constant zap of his collar making it hard to think. His paws prickled with the need to go home. Much more of this and the compulsion would have him knocking a portal right in front of his dreamer. He wriggled loose with a sad meow and a little lick to let Gbadamosi know it wasn't his fault.

Fionn slunk into the bushes and portalled home as soon as he was concealed, taking comfort in the fact he'd see his dreamer again soon.

Chapter Thirteen

Building a House of Words

Harper paused on the bridge that joined the jut of land between the Ouse and the Foss to the mainland. The Foss was nowhere to be seen, which wasn't a surprise given Grace was with her. Time was flowing too quickly. The possession at the bookshop was already four days ago, and Harper had no new leads on the art from her vision or where the dreamwalker might strike next. It was also only thirty-three days until the spring equinox, the day when the scales would be balanced.

"Come on." Grace tugged her arm. "Melancholy won't solve anything, and you'll put Albrecht's back up if we're late. Poor Saqib is probably there already trying to make awkward small talk with Guardspeople."

"Yeah." Harper tore her eyes away from the rush of water, close to breaching the banks from the recent rainy days. Damp hung in the air and chilled her cheeks like forgotten tears. Rain threatened from thunder grey clouds. It bided its time until the deserted streets would be full of commuters and children coming home from school.

It only took a few minutes to reach Imphal Barracks from the river crossing. The late Victorian building resembled a medieval castle with its crenelation-topped towers and slit windows. Cameras and barbed wire coils topped every wall. The corners bulged out onto the pavement as though it was trying to escape its own remit. Horizonal lines of black gave the impression of belaboured restraints as they cut through brick walls the red of dried blood. Like its Queen's Guard occupants, it wanted more land than it had been given.

While the archbishop was petitioning for information on where the audience had been taken, they at least knew the author, Vita, had ended up here in the Guards' city centre stronghold. All the Council of Faiths had garnered about the others was that they were being detained 'somewhere comfortable' but had yet to show any overt signs of the possession that gripped the author.

From this, Harper feared she'd find Vita in a similar fugue to Christina, though she'd been careful about how much of that she'd disclosed during her and Saqib's weekly catch up with Lieutenant Albrecht.

Although it was expected, the sight of Vita shocked Harper. She took a shaky breath and glanced at the others for help. Grace followed the family motto of 'never show fear.' Saqib was less coy in his emotions, a whispered prayer, "Nauzubillah." *We seek refuge in God.*

Grace put an arm around him. "We do, and we trust His will shall be done in the end." She crossed herself as she knelt next to Vita. "Whatever god you believe in, may they walk with you and give you strength."

Saqib took a shaky breath and added, "Allah yaeafik."

Harper wished she could have their faith. She wanted to believe Vita wasn't alone in this cold cell, that someone was with her even though her friends and family must seem a very long way away. Reconciling Grace's loving parent figure with the tragedies of the last five months was difficult. She knew what Grace or her godfather would say: *God doesn't create the tragedies. Nature and free will do that. God is with us in the storm and sends us aid.* The archbishop would say Harper was the aid sent by God.

"Harp, do you See anything helpful?" Saqib's touch on her elbow interrupted the musings that were Harper's way of avoidance. If she didn't try, then her inadequacy and inability to help couldn't be thrown back in her face. But if she didn't try, she'd always fail.

Taking a deep breath, Harper let her Sight bleed through. She wished she could have Heresy with her to hide her eyes. While he was getting bolder and bolder about going out, she hadn't dared risk bringing him into the mouth of the dragon.

Saqib had set up lights around the room to try the methods he'd successfully used to detect Usa's runes on bodies. While he hoped it might make something visible to him, they'd found certain wavelengths enhanced Harper's Sight. It also gave them some plausible deniability if someone did catch a glimpse of her eyes on CCTV. She tugged wisps of hair over the side of her face anyway, as though their darkness could hide any gleam of violet.

Lilac lines bled through the walls. They were less extensive than Christina's and no trace of them remained to the naked eye. The Guard had erased or painted over everything, but they had been unable to remove the magic. And she had no way of telling them that the spell, whatever it was, still existed.

Like Christina's chalk drawings, there was an architectural element to Vita's sketch. They were not so far developed, presumably her scribblings had been curbed faster, but the notion of colonnades was there. There were fewer symbols than in Christina's sketch, though there were some runes and icons consistent with the occult. There were more words, which made sense for a writer. She couldn't read them from where she was standing and didn't dare look too closely. She would have to ask the archbishop whether it was safe to tell the Guard what Christina had been doing and ask if Vita had done anything similar. She wondered whether they even bothered noting what was said and drawn before destroying it. She could understand stopping the magic, but without knowing what it was, they couldn't prepare for what else might be coming.

She turned her gaze on the person lying strapped to the bed, her back to the camera above the door. Grace knelt next to zir, talking softly. Harper almost smiled. It was the same tone Grace used when coaxing a spooked animal. The enby did look a little calmer for Grace's ministrations. Bright coloured vines pulsed in zir brain, down zir arms, and covered zir fingertips like lurid latex gloves. With no way for the magic to escape, Harper feared it could build up until it overloaded or drowned its host.

"How is ze?" Harper crouched next to her sister. The author's eyes roved under their lids and zir skin blotched with the colour of old ink stains.

"Thinks ze's a character in zir book." Grace smoothed hair back from a sweat-slicked brow. "Somewhat sedated, but not knocked out, like they said. That's why ze's not as furious as Christina was, plus the character isn't as angry as Alcina."

"You read it?" Harper asked.

For once in her life, Grace looked slightly uncomfortable.

"What kind of sister would I be if I didn't know you hide novels behind your study books?" Harper elbowed her gently.

"Fair." Grace nudged her back with a smile. "I read this and a couple of others. Can get a bit dark for my usual tastes, but it's good for mixing things up sometimes. Do you think the fact that the main character's girlfriend gets possessed is a clue?"

"I've been comparing the details at work, and there's very little in common between the two, other than they both involved buildings—the sentient library in this book and Hekate's temple in the opera—and they both have main characters who possess some form of magic."

"Let's hope we can stop whoever, or whatever, is doing it before you get a third point to triangulate from." Grace stood up, drying sweaty palms on her pants. "Ze can't tell us anything useful. As soon as Saqib's done, let's go home and prepare for the exhibition tomorrow. I pray we can stop these attacks before someone else gets hurt."

Chapter Fourteen

The Exhibition

Fionn hugged the cat hoodie tighter around him. The bitter cold paid it no heed, but Harper's scent of tea and old books reduced his frightened shivering. Going to the gallery again broke every rule. He risked getting caught, exposing Harper and his master, and for what? *To be a selfish cat and see a human who can never see me.* A knot of anxiety tangled around his spine. It didn't matter that logic said he was the best placed to perceive or stop a dreamwalker attack. *Is my rash behaviour what caused the fetch of the two people I love most?*

The pamphlet in his hoodie pouch crumpled as he scrunched his fists and pushed them into his fluttering stomach. He pulled it out quickly and smoothed the prickly art back to its normal zoomy song. He stared at the self-portrait, lightly brushing his fingers over the artist's bright cerulean cheek. Hope hurt when it was despair masquerading, but it drove his feet forward. He didn't even know what he hoped to accomplish. He couldn't approach his dreamer in this form, even with his cat bits glamoured away. His eyes were too freakish, and besides, what would he say? They'd met, one chance encounter, and that should be more than enough. *Greedy, selfish cat. But maybe I can protect him too. If Harper's vision* was *of my dreamer's art.*

The gallery was bustling. Some folks were dressed up like Harper and Grace, who'd entered separately to Fionn and wore the same dresses as to the opera. Others were glitzy mixed with casual; jeans and sparkling tops that left skin exposed, like they were going to one of the places Fionn had seen in dreams with loud music and flashing rainbows. Next to the scintillating crowds, he was drab and invisible. Invisible was good.

His hand drifted to the back of the pair of jeans AJ had bought him. Definitely no space for his tail to materialise. It itched under his skin like a burr trapped by a healing scar. Keeping up the glamour was a rapid drain on his magic, and he couldn't keep his eyes changed for more than a minute without getting a blinding migraine.

Fionn slipped easily between people, hood up and hair over his eyes. When he entered the room with Gbadamosi's exhibition, he staggered under a burst of music so intense it became physical. It was like being in the artiest of dreams at maximum volume. Eventually his brain managed to split the sounds into songs of different paintings.

As Fionn's gaze swept over the room, he spotted Gbadamosi in the middle of a laughing throng. *Not that I was looking. I'm trying to find the painting Harper Saw. I am. How could anyone not look?* He decided his dreamer's mama must've been an artist too. She'd certainly made something beautiful.

The glittery group hung on the artist's every word, a couple of them hung on his arm and shoulders. Even his clothes sang of art, a sleeveless black T-shirt splashed with fabrics of bright pink, blue, and purple. There was an easy charm to every interaction that Fionn could never emulate. He wasn't envious of the relaxed charisma. Rather it eased a hurt.

He didn't need to worry about his dreamer. Sometimes the dreams seemed lonely or came at odd hours. Occasionally they vacillated to gunky drabness, though not often. It was reassuring there were humans to help. Dreams *were* lonely. Most humans couldn't share them with each other. Here in the wakening, his dreamer shone brighter.

Deep brown eyes looked past the crowd as though the dreamer read Fionn's mind in turn and searched him out. Panicked, Fionn looked away and tugged his hoodie further over his face. *Was I recognised? Not possible. No human would think a dream cat would be in an art gallery.*

Keeping himself small and inconspicuous, Fionn circled the room and examined the art. Every time he recognised a piece, a frisson of pleasure sparked in his chest. Ideas that had been raw in the dreamscape became resplendent in the wakening. Little cards told him about the art. He wanted to sit and look at each piece for at least an hour.

Some of the art, he knew already. He'd seen it firsthand, felt the feelings that went with the pictures and sounds. Others were new, words that expanded on the feelings he couldn't share. Words about identity and history, belief and mythology.

Abstract pieces with glorious arrays of colours had words with them that spoke of joy, celebration, and, in one case, a parting of ways. The card glossed over the latter to sound like a natural drift between two people, but the mournful and bitter tune reminded Fionn of sludgy dreams and self-recrimination. He didn't mind hurrying from that painting.

Other pieces were more obvious, but he got to learn more about the people they represented. Family—a young girl with a bouncing smile; a woman with a warm maternal gaze and a singsong voice; a larger hand guiding a smaller one through early attempts at sketching—and friends whose faces Fionn had seen briefly in dreams. Most of their cards didn't have the names of the subjects, but their portraits were so emotive it almost seemed as though he knew them. Their personalities were splashed across canvas in paint and swept across it with confident charcoal.

The scorching heat of his ears demanding existence made it difficult to focus. The hoodie helped, but it wasn't as constricting as his jeans. *Anyway, people don't look at art for long enough.* He'd observed it many times in galleries. People gave paintings a cursory glance and moved on. He couldn't bring himself to be so casual; however, he moved on faster than he wanted to avoid drawing attention and because, as he kept reminding himself, he was supposed to be looking for the art from Harper's vision or a clue about the dreamwalker.

One painting wouldn't let him move on. Fionn gazed at it in rapt attention, mission forgotten. The painting wanted to draw him into the edges of the dreamscape. Curiously, it wasn't one he'd seen in a dream. The small placard next to it was handwritten where the others were typed, and the date of the painting was this year, implying it was a last-minute addition to the exhibition. It was titled *Dream Kitty*.

Fionn startled back a step and stared at it again. Strong swirls of glittery silver and turquoise covered one side of the canvas. The other was predominately shimmering blues and pinks. The two colour schemes eddied together in the middle. Strands of bright violet wove evenly through both sides of the canvas, and each side contained highlights of the other colours.

"You like it?" The voice that interrupted sent shivers down his spine.

Fionn glanced up in time to catch an anxious twitch in the artist's eye. *Am I not allowed to like it?*

"Whoa." Gbadamosi took a step back and Fionn winced, lowering his eyes again. "No. Don't look away. Please?"

The request was magnetic. Fionn raised his chin a little, eyes drawn to his dreamer's even as he shrank back into his hoodie.

"You have the most amazing eyes."

"*You* have the most amazing eyes."

"Thanks."

They stared at each other as ambient noise and energetic art faded to a background murmur. The dreamscape tugged at Fionn and he was vaguely aware of the glamour slipping from his tail and ears, held in place only because they had nowhere to materialise. He couldn't tear himself away from his dreamer's eyes. Up close, there were so many shades and colours. Staring when they met before would've been strange behaviour for a cat. It was probably strange behaviour for a human.

Gbadamosi's voice shook Fionn from the daydream. "Is the colour of yours from the lenses or are they clear and for the cat shape? I could stare into them for hours."

"It's ... um ... my eyes are this colour." Fionn blushed at the compliment even as he waited for the other shoe to drop on him. Harper had told him people might find his eyes disconcerting and would likely assume he was wearing little bowls over his irises. He'd filed it in the rapidly growing 'humans are odd' info section of his brain.

"I'd love to paint them sometime." Gbadamosi raised a hand, close enough for the heat of his fingers to scorch Fionn's cheek. Then it dropped again and the artist laughed. "Sorry. I should introduce myself before getting all art intense literally in your face."

"I don't think you need to tell anyone here who you are," Fionn managed to stutter. *Why are you talking to me?* He glanced back towards the crowd and caught the glare of a woman in a backless sequin top and a long satin skirt.

"Still seems rude." The artist held out his hand. "I'm Dayo, he/him."

Harper taught him this one as well. He was supposed to clasp hands, not bow, so he did so hesitantly. "Fionn. I'm a ... he/him."

"Pretty name to go with your pretty eyes." Dayo's grip loosened, so Fionn could've reclaimed his hand. If he wanted. Which he didn't. "You never answered my question. Do you like the painting? I can't show it to the real dream kitty so I'll take approval from a cat-boy instead."

Fionn flinched, both from the heat running up his arm and at being called out as supernatural. But Dayo wasn't pinning him or shouting for the Guard.

"Sorry. I like your eyes, and you remind me of a cat I met recently. I painted this for them. Which is kind of silly because cats don't look at paintings, but it reminded me of a recurring dream I have and I kind of went into art haze. Oh. I have pictures. Look. Its fur is exactly like your hair. Have you seen it?"

Dayo let go of Fionn's hand to pull out his phone. Their shoulders bumped as photos of cat-Fionn were shoved under his nose. They sang like they were art. His blush deepened. *I'm not artable.*

The haughty woman came up behind them and draped herself across Dayo's shoulders. Fionn shuffled out of the way.

"You obsessing about that cat again?" A demanding edge sharpened her laugh. Fionn resisted hissing at her. When Dayo turned to answer, Fionn slipped away into the crowd. Head down, hands in the pouch of his hoodie, the base of his tail burning where it couldn't materialise, Fionn hurried to the exit. His thoughts jumbled and knotted, barely forming coherent words let alone cohesive sentences.

"Hey. Wait."

Dayo's voice sent Fionn scurrying faster. The artist wasn't talking to him. He should never have come here. *Selfish, bad cat.* He stumbled to a halt just before walking into his dreamer who was very physically in front of him.

"Sorry about Rose." There was a flicker on Dayo's face again, pain behind the smiling charm. It was gone so fast Fionn doubted himself. "You haven't answered my question."

"The painting is perfect." The authenticity of Fionn's feelings burst the words from his lips before he could think. "If a dream kitty could step into the gallery and see it, I'm sure he … they … would love it."

A sunshine smile brightened Dayo's already glowing face as his posture relaxed. Fionn blinked, transfixed by it. "That's great. Do you have to leave? I'd like to hear what you think of some of the others."

A bitter laugh clogged Fionn's chest and he released it as a cough. "There are lots of people back there happy to tell you how perfect the art is. Ones who actually understand art and are smart."

"You seem plenty smart enough to me. Some of them are great. A lot of them don't really see the art. I think you do. You wanted to look longer, didn't you? People rush too much in galleries." Dayo offered his hand. "Whatever's weighing you down, come and forget about it for a while?"

Fionn's breath caught and his head jerked *no* despite his desire to stay. "I need to get home. Thank you for sharing the art." He peeked up at Dayo, again into gentle eyes, a hand hovering in his periphery. "You don't need an insignificant little c … person to like your art, but I want you to know that I do. A lot. You're my favourite."

Dayo preened, his smile warm enough to bask in. "Not something I could ever get tired of hearing. I meant it when I said I want to paint your eyes, and the rest of you." A lingering gaze swept over Fionn. "Stay a bit longer? Please?"

"A few minutes." It slipped out before Fionn could check himself.

Harper noticed Fionn's chat with the artist and his quick exit then return. She debated whether to intervene. Fionn could take care of himself and, if he was found out, it was safer for all of them if no one realised she knew him. That stung of betrayal, but the practical part of her knew it was true.

If his new friend was the next victim, he'd rather take risks to himself than the artist, anyway.

Gbadamosi's paintings and photos were bold with strong colours, yet zipped with energy and a general joy, even when the discussion they provoked was serious. If this artist dreamt like he painted, Harper could understand why Fionn found his dreams so exhilarating after the painful, drab existence of home. *Mind, he found turkey bacon to be the height of thrilling experiences so it's a pretty low bar. Still, those dreams must be better than average for an art-loving cat. Especially compared to the nightmares I drag him through.*

Harper circled the exhibition casually, arm threaded through Grace's. There wasn't any sign of the painting from her vision. There was a space that exactly matched everything else she'd seen, but it showcased a collection of photographs, not a pair of painted portraits.

"Maybe it's the exhibition coming after this one," she muttered to Grace. A knot in her chest eased. If that was the case, the possession wasn't imminent. There was time to find and stop the perpetrator.

Harper accepted a glass of sparkling wine from a waiter as they meandered through the rest of the exhibit.

"Grace, look." Harper almost splashed her wine into the face of a man in a dark grey suit.

"What?" Grace's stance shifted as she readied for a fight.

"It's the Ouse," Harper hissed as she dragged her sister over to a painting.

Shattering Illusions

The large painting of the River Ouse placed Dayo's version of Usa central and sexy. The trees formed the fragmented word 'SAFETY' with their boughs. The painting was in reverse to real life as if viewed through a shattered mirror.

Harper stared at it. The woman in the picture was not the Ouse she met. The hair was longer and her build different. Human-esque skin replaced Usa's watery body. "She's the one."

"What one?" Grace leant in to whisper in Harper's ear. "The replacement?"

"Yes. Maybe."

"It's an impression of an undine by a person who never saw her," Grace hissed.

But it wasn't. Something in the painting called to Harper. She glanced at Fionn, who was talking to the artist, unfazed, at least by any magic. His expression was hidden by his hood, but he fiddled with his cuffs and leant towards Dayo as they talked. She hoped the latter meant he was enjoying the conversation, even if he was uncomfortable from the glamour or thinking he wasn't good enough to be talking.

There were no violet strands of magic coming from the painting. It wasn't a possession. It was something else. Her heart told her this woman could be Usa's replacement, her own saviour, even though the logic of her mind agreed with Grace that it was just a painting. Her Sight bored into the back of the woman's head. The gallery became like paper, a cutout in a popup book. Black edged her vision and the chatter of the crowd faded to a hum.

The figure moved. The scene warped and expanded until Harper was standing in it. No longer the converted warehouses that lined this area of the Ouse, they grew taller. Plaster rolled over brick then flaked away; colonnades and mosaics stretched and popped into place. Thin boats moved through the water, smaller than fishing boats or tourist rentals. Their boaters stood aft, steering with long polls. A tang of salt pervaded the air along with traces of music.

The undine turned, her face reflected in many facets and difficult to see clearly. She looked straight into the seer. Harper's name was breathed from the stranger's lips before they pressed gently against hers.

The image shattered like blown out glass. Harper flinched away, instinctively scrunching her eyes. When she cracked them open, only the original painting remained.

"Harp? You're really pale. We should step out for a sec." Grace steered her sister back into the main gallery where it was quieter and cooler.

"Is Fionn still here?" Harper asked. She wanted to ask him if he'd Seen the magic. Her fingers brushed over her tingling lips. Visceral visions had struck her before, ones where someone else's death or pain bit into her or where she'd Seen her past, but never a future where she was the subject. She hadn't been behind someone else's eyes. If she truly Saw the future, this water spirit would replace the Ouse, and she would kiss Harper, and Harper would like it.

A mix of excitement and want fizzed in her gut.

"Harp? Back here. Quick."

Another woman. A girl really. About the same age Harper was when Father De Santos found her in the mists. The memory unfolded rapidly.

The girl took her hand, tugging her between two tents while the rest of the village danced the Solstice blessing. Harper's fingers ached where they gripped the other girl's. Too tight. Nerves zinged. They weren't supposed to be doing this. Harper was marked. The Seer. The Protector would decide for her, so her people could be protected in every generation. The danger of it added to the fizzle in her gut.

"Dawn, they'll catch us." It came out in a rushed giggle.

"So what? We're not doing anything wrong. Just two friends hanging out." Yet Dawn's grip on Harper's hand belied her words. "Unless you want to do something wrong."

"No. I ..." Did she? Harper never did anything wrong. She was a good Seer. Except for hiding Fionn's identity, of course. And occasionally sneaking out with her brother.

The swiftest brush of lips against her mouth derailed her thoughts.

"Dawn?"

The other girl gave her a crooked smile. "Let's get back before they miss us."

"Harper? Are you okay?"

Harper took a deep breath, grounding herself in Grace's scent.

"I think ... I remembered my first kiss."

"Before the one I already know about?" Grace smirked. "Fionn's flirting with that artist putting thoughts in your head?"

"It wasn't him." Harper's mouth twisted in repulsion. Fionn was her cat, closer to a younger brother than a love interest.

"Who was he? Someone from your village?"

"Um, well, kind of yes. She was."

Grace's smile broadened. "She? I need details."

Harper shrugged. "I don't remember them. Just that she kissed me and I ... I was okay with that. We were too young for it to be anything salacious. It was quick. A peck, really. I don't remember anything else about her, though I feel like I've seen her in a dream. Look, don't tell the others, okay?"

Grace blanketed her in a hug. "You know I'd never tell. I'm here if you need someone to listen. After all, I've always told you being bi made more sense."

"Yeah, you have."

Harper rested her head on Grace's shoulder for a moment. She thought of the strange feelings One had invoked and her vision of the water woman. Deep down, she'd always thought her sister was right, yet she simply wasn't attracted to women. *Am I?*

"Is it rude if we leave?" Harper asked.

"Nah. We've seen most of it, found more questions than we came in with, and Fionn just left. Let's get you home and brew up."

That sounded perfect. Internal confusion aside, she could always rely on Grace's stalwart sisterliness to anchor her.

Fionn's eyes followed Harper as she left the exhibition hall, but he dragged them back before he could be asked if he knew her.

"I have to go," he muttered, darting a look at Dayo.

"So soon? You can't stay for one more? You're the only person who got both three meanings of the Ouse painting, I'd like to hear your thoughts on others." Dayo gave him a beseeching look, like a small kitten pleading. "A lot of people enjoy the controversy of the supernatural stuff. They don't look for the deeper meaning or acknowledge how it's something our ancestors lived in harmony with. I think you look beyond the obvious. Please stay and talk?"

"I'm sorry. I can't …." *I want to.* "I'm just … I need to go. I'm late." *And the magic is really hurting.* Bright lights flashed before his eyes.

"Do you need help?" A concerned hand gripped Fionn's elbow. He desperately wanted to say 'yes.'

"I need air. You stay here. Enjoy your exhibition. It's amazing. I don't want you to waste time on me."

"I don't think it's a waste. At least let me walk you to the door. Or are you here with someone?"

"I came in on my own." Technically true.

Dayo hooked Fionn's arm through his and steered him through the gallery. A couple of people tried to stop them, but Dayo informed them that they were going outside and he'd be back shortly. Rose glared daggers at them from across the hall. Everyone else simply chuckled, raised an eyebrow, or gave a very strange smile. Fionn filed it under 'odd human behaviour.'

They stepped out into the damp cold of the art gallery porch.

"Guess I should leave you here," Dayo said, slowly withdrawing his arm with a grimace. He turned to go back inside, then spun back. "May I have your number?"

"My ... number?" *Zero. You ... want ...*

"Phone number." Dayo waved his phone at Fionn before panic could squish his lungs breathless.

"Oh. I, um, don't have one of those."

"Wow." Surprise overcame the worry in Dayo's eyes and Fionn squirmed. "Maybe we could arrange to meet somewhere? You free tomorrow evening? Let me buy you a drink? I'll meet you here at five. Gives us a couple of hours before curfew."

"Okay." A voice at the back of Fionn's brain scolded him. Any human interaction was dangerous. It hadn't even been that long and his body was shaking and screaming at him.

"Great." That smile washed away the pain. Fionn would agree to anything to see it. "If I'm not here dead on five, please don't leave. Give me a few minutes? I'm shit at time. K?"

Fionn blanched. *Dead on?*

"What's wrong?" Dayo's expression shifted to concern again and then hurt. "It's not like I'm late on purpose. I try, okay?"

"It's not that. I don't care about that." Fionn didn't. Except for some rituals, time was fluid. It's not like he had a device for tracking it beyond checking the sun. "I just ... 'dead on'?"

"Oh. You don't know the phrase? Sorry. I guess it sounds rather violent. It means 'exactly.'" Dayo chuckled. "If it gets to five and I'm not here, please wait for me?"

"Of course." Fionn hoped he could keep the almost-promise. If it was up to him, he would, but his master was unpredictable. Still, it was the right response; the smile beamed at him again. Dayo touched his fingers to his lips and blew across them towards Fionn before disappearing back inside. The breath arrived warm against Fionn's cheek, the tiny bit of aeromancy unnoticeable to any observer.

With a feeling akin to intoxication, Fionn stumbled out of the gallery and down the alley next to it, checked for watchers, then knocked twice to portal back to Harper's house.

Chapter Fifteen

Unexpected Feels

The first thing Harper noticed when she walked into the lounge was Fionn curled up on Saqib's lap. It resolved one of her worries—that he would've gone back to his master. He lifted his head with a soft mew. She sat next to Saqib so she could pat Fionn without disturbing the game Saqib was playing online with AJ, even though they were only a room apart. The cat uncurled from Saqib, walked onto Harper's lap, needled it a bit, then curled up again. Very soon he was sound asleep.

He stayed that way until late evening, save for the occasional snack break. It helped to have a ball of fluff to hold and stroke, giving her fingers something to do while her brain roamed free. By the time Harper was ready to go to bed, she was no closer to an answer about the Ouse, the painting, or her own confused feelings.

When Harper went to get ready to sleep, Fionn wriggled away from her and padded to AJ's room instead. She'd scarcely settled in with a book when there was a knock at her door.

She tensed, having not heard either Grace or Saqib's familiar footsteps. "Fionn?"

"Mrow. Yes. May I come in please? You told me to knock, so I knocked."

Harper relaxed, shaking her shoulders to loosen the tension. "Yeah, come in."

He peeked around the door, then shuffled in and sat on the floor.

"It's okay if you want to sit on the edge of the bed or in the chair," Harper told him.

He wrinkled his nose and leaned his head against her blanket. "Human rules are confusing. When to go in bed and when not to. Think I'll stay here. Smells good."

"Whatever you're most comfortable with. Sorry our rules can be confusing." She leant over and patted his head, smoothing flyaway white hairs. "Did you come to hang out or do you need something?"

"I, um, have a question. I asked AJ, but he said you'd be better able to help find words for my feels."

"I can't explain your feels," Harper said carefully. "Only you can do that, but we can talk and I can try and help you work them out. Okay?"

Fionn blew her a kiss across his hand. "Dayo did this. What does it mean?"

"Do you know what kissing is?" Harper checked.

"Lips together," Fionn said. Disgust twisted his face. "It hurts."

"Somone did it to you before?"

"One."

Harper scowled. The hare-shifter's flirtatious confidence had been apparent and repugnant even in the briefest of meetings. "Since you don't like her, that must've been extra unpleasant."

She stroked his hair until he relaxed. *Gbadamosi was probably flirting with you.* How could she explain flirting to a cat who thought he could never be pretty and had only been kissed by someone he hated?

"In this context, it probably means he ... wants to be friends. He thinks you're cute and wants to get to, uh, know you better."

"In this context? There are contexts of kissing?" Fionn asked, head tilted to one side.

"Kissing is just putting your lips against something. I'm sorry if I kissed your forehead and it reminded you of something unpleasant that One did." She hadn't considered he didn't understand the gesture. Shame stung that she may have done something to him that he didn't like.

"When you do it, it's ... like the human equivalent of when a mama cat licks her kitten's head? I like it when you do that."

Harper exhaled slowly, relieved. "Yeah. Like that. 'Cause we're family. Like Gray and I are."

"I have lots of soft, cosy feels for you. Not quite like a mama ... I don't know. I don't think I ever had a mama."

"Maybe like a big sister." Harper smiled and placed her hand over his.

He purred. "Nice. Yes. Lots of soft feels like that."

"Your feels for your dreamer are different to your feels for any of us though, aren't they?"

"Yeah. Feels for each of you are different. Like … feels for AJ, Grace, and Saqib aren't exactly the same but they're … related? Does that make sense?" When Harper nodded, Fionn continued, "They're all soft feels. With him it's different. In the dreamscape and in cat shape, there's this elastic pull. Almost like Master tugging me home while also very much not. This feels nice. Oh. Like wanting to follow a sunny patch. In human shape, in the wakening … kind of … tingly and tight here. Excited." He pressed a hand over his gut. "And my heart was acting funny. I guess nerves at talking to a human and … I didn't want him to hate me."

"I can't imagine anyone hating you, kitten." A comforting lie. She was pretty sure both One and his master hated him. If he was caught, humans wouldn't wait to know him. They'd see the magical cat, tie him in a sack, and throw him in the river. "Have you ever experienced the excited feelings before?"

No memories surfaced. He was a little younger than her. Maybe too young for it to have happened before they were separated, or maybe she didn't remember or he hadn't told her.

"No …?" Fionn pulled his tail onto his lap, fussing with his fur. "Is it normal? Am I humaning badly?"

Harper smiled and squeezed his hand. "There is no 'normal' or 'humaning badly.' Everyone is different. Even in this house. AJ doesn't get the excited feels for anyone. He has friend feels … feelings, but he's not interested in romantic or fizzy feelings. Grace can have soft feelings and excited feelings separately, though she'd like to have them together one day. I don't like kissing without having the soft feelings."

"I don't think I'd like someone touching me if I didn't have soft feels for them as well," Fionn said slowly. "In this shape, anyway. I don't mind someone petting me when I'm cat-shaped. That's nice. It's different human-shaped. I like it when you touch me, and I don't mind the others. Is like they're friends and you're … special friend?"

Harper had a warm, fuzzy feeling of her own. "Yeah, we've been friends long enough and well enough to be special friends. Friends can be lots of types. Some people are casual friends. Like Grace has a couple of church friends we don't really see outside of church things, and I have work friends, like Alfred. Other people are your core people, the ones you hang out with all the time. Like all of us. Some people have 'best' friends. 'Special' like you said. They're the ones you tell your secrets too or go to first when you need help. Then there's romance and physical attraction.

They can become kind of an extra special friend or friends; someone you can share all of yourself with. Long-term romantic relationships take work and not everyone wants excited feels with that, but a lot of people do. Attraction to their body as well as their heart and mind. You can't tell them all your secrets on day one, though. You have to get to know each other. That can be quite intense and full of feels in a short time."

"*Hmm*. A pyramid?" Fionn checks, the same look on his face as when he was given a puzzle.

Harper wasn't sure he was really embracing the feelings. Maybe getting it as close to logical as he could was the best way for him to process it.

"Lots of friends, all three of them, maybe four if the castle counts, then special friend which is Harper, then extra special friend if someone wants one and can find them?"

"Kind of …" Harper sighed. It wasn't a perfect analogy, but she didn't have anything better.

"Which means it's important to keep the base of friends, otherwise everything else falls down. That's the bit someone needs. The others are nice to have. Which means nothing is more important, just different. Also people get closer and closer over time. Yes?"

"Um, yeah." That was actually a better analogy than she'd given him credit for. "It sounds like your instinct is that your dreamer might be someone you could be extra special friends with. You have to spend time with him and get to know him better to find out."

Fionn's ears drooped. "There's no point. I can't have an extra special friend. That's okay. I have friends and I have you."

Harper slid out of the bed so she could put an arm around his shoulders. "You always have me, whether you have an extra special friend or not." She brushed her own tears away. As much as she wanted to tell him it was possible for him to be with someone, she didn't even know how *she* could be with someone and she at least looked human.

They talked awhile longer, before Fionn shifted to cat and crawled into his box, which Harper let him put on the end of her bed.

When she awoke in the middle of the night, he was gone, but there was a note on her pillow. She opened it, expecting Fionn's handwriting. Seeing her father's instead punched her in the gut. Tears misted her eyes and it took a few minutes for the letters to resolve into words.

The message was short, but it was a gleam of hope.

I WILL MEET YOU AT THE PERIMETER TOMORROW AT NOON. WE SHALL NOT TELL YOUR GRANDMOTHER.

- YOUR FATHER, ADRIAN

Chapter Sixteen

Home Again, Home Again

Swaledale looked as it always had on a cold February day. Wraiths of smoke haunted clustered cottages as humans huddled around the paltry protection of their hearths. Ice painted delicate patterns on windows, and mist piled against limestone walls. Hoar frost muted the pallor of grass to that of a corpse. Vapours rose from drystone walls where pale sunlight breached the matt grey sky to caress them. Bare trees cut black lightning through the grey, flying from earth to sky.

Swaledale looked as it always had but, beneath the surface, reality had changed.

Harper raised a hand to the edge of an almost invisible bubble. It was fine as glistening soap, and her Sight viewed it as an ethereal barrier, subject to popping with the tiniest poke of a nail. Her finger twitched, scarce millimetres above its surface, but she didn't destroy it. As fleeting a thing as it appeared, it had stood for over four-hundred years. She'd walked by it—*through* it—many times, never realising how one reality lay over another.

For an instant, her Sight overlaid another image. Magic squished seconds into milliseconds. A boy in a boat, swept away, screaming her name as the barrier rippled over him and the river stole him from her. Harper didn't have time to cry out, for the image vanished between one breath and the next. Tears stung her eyes worse than the bitter wind.

A little way off, Saqib stared at a handheld device and muttered rapidly. From the lack of staticky buzz on the back of her neck, Harper guessed he was speaking to Heresy. The deception demon found the whole bubble dilemma fascinating, though he advocated for popping it and seeing what happened. Harper hadn't needed nightmares cutting into her fractured sleep to know that was a bad idea. There was a reason she hadn't broken it when she stood atop the tower, power gathered to her, command of all the elements hers and her violin's. If she destroyed the bubble, both realities would be true in the same space. Without enough room for both, neither would survive.

Her housemate couldn't See the bubble like she could. Neither of them picked up on its existence last time they were in the dale. The massive magical storm that drove them off was a good excuse, as far as Harper was concerned, but Saqib was upset with himself for failing, as if he could've prevented Grace's kidnap and Fionn's injuries.

"Any luck, Saqib?" Harper strolled over to join him, cold hands stuffed in her pockets.

"Nothing." He sighed as he turned to face her. "I took readings on both sides. Everything seems normal. It's like you said about hiking up here as a teenager. Can you step through it and land in the other reality, or do you have to go the route you went last time?"

"I'm not sure." The music that floated down the River Ouse was louder here than in the heart of York. It swept over the hillside like a waterfall of silk. It beckoned her home, but the welcome it promised was uncertain.

Her fists clenched against her roiling stomach, and she bit the inside of her cheek, trying to hold back tears. Half a lifetime of searching and her family had turned her away. She clung to the fact they were allowing her back, albeit in a limited capacity.

That's not true. We're your family and we want you very much.' Grace spoke in her head, even though her sister was further down the dale playing with cat-Fionn. He was uncomfortable being there, yet had agreed to come along to provide portals. He'd wanted to portal her from home, however Harper wanted to be here, to walk in so she knew she could walk out without Fionn's assistance, and so Saqib could study the magic.

Where Fionn had been adamant he didn't want to see their old home, Grace insisted on coming. She'd mostly recovered in the two weeks since her imprisonment, at least enough to be grumpy about the idea of being left behind.

Squaring her shoulders, Harper made herself unclench her fists and call to Grace that it was time. After giving Fionn a reassuring scritch and transferring him to Saqib for cuddles, Harper took Grace's hand, closed her eyes, and stepped across the barrier.

It washed over her skin like cool water. The air on the other side tasted different. The suddenness of the change highlighted the heavy flavour of pine and the crisp freshness of new snowfall gave her the feeling of having taken more than a single step.

Vision rippled as they stepped through the barrier. The hill became higher and steeper, the few trees multiplied to a forest, and the trickling beck raged to a river. With the change of scenery came an onslaught of memory. Grace grabbed Harper's shoulders and eased her to the ground.

Harper and her brother building snowfolk.

Playing hide and seek with Fionn, who was almost impossible to see without using magic.

Sitting near the edge of the world, dabbing blood from a scraped knee. A tiny kitten mewling for a cuddle, licking her blood away. Her six-year-old delight when she could Hear his words and talk to him like another child. Better, because he wasn't afraid or awed by her. Unable to find his mother, she took him home.

Waiting by the wych elm and fretting about whether or not her brother would return from his excursions into the human world.

Harper shook off the memories like the clods of snow that used to fall on her from heavy conifer branches. Grace helped her to her feet. Harper leant against her sister, head on her shoulder, as she looked back. From Fionn's raised hackles and the way Saqib was holding the cat away from him, she guessed Fionn and Heresy were butting heads again. None of them noticed when she waved from the other side of the barrier. She was part of this world, and they couldn't perceive her.

"Harper?" A hesitant voice froze her limbs and stole her breath. Only Grace's warmth and support next to her let her turn to face the speaker.

"Papa?" Tears gathered in her eyes. The freeze shattered and she ran to him. He swept her up like a little girl, spinning her round and burying his face in her hair.

"My baby."

When he eventually put Harper down, she peered around his broad shoulder. "Mama?"

"Your sister is … unhappy I am seeing you. Melody is trying to placate her."

It stung that her own sister was keeping their family apart, although Harper wasn't sure how well the word 'sister' really fit. They'd never properly met each other, let alone shared all the things sisters shared the way she and Grace had.

She beckoned Grace forward. "Papa, this is my sister, Grace, she/her. Her family took me in after I left here. They became a family of my heart." She bit her lip, hoping he wouldn't take it as a betrayal.

Her father held a hand out to Grace, who shook it firmly. For once, Grace didn't appear to be in complete control of the situation, her normal authority pared back by her wish to be accepted by Harper's family. Not for her own sake—Grace cared very little what most people thought of her—but for Harper's.

"It is an honour to be Harper's family." Grace put an arm around Harper's shoulders. "My parents and my brothers love her too. She's been well taken care of and she's never alone."

Harper gave her a grateful smile. Her father's face was less easy to read as he sized Grace up, then a smile broke through and Harper relaxed.

"Thank you for taking care of our child when we could not." His lips twitched and he stiffened. Harper tried not to assume the recrimination against her for running away. "Shall we walk?"

A tentative smile formed as Harper agreed. "I'd like that. I want to hear about home and my family here. I keep getting bits of memory coming back to me. When I left here, I had only my name. Since Fi … since the So … the last couple of weeks or so, I've been having flashbacks."

"More like Seer visions than memories?" her father guessed.

"Yes and no. Do you know much about what I can do?"

He led them through the trees; Harper looped her arm through his, and Grace followed a short distance behind.

"That's really something to discuss with your mother. If I may suggest, another day rather than now. We haven't yet come to terms with what happened. It took a long time after you left the first time. Your mother hasn't stopped thinking herself a failure."

Harper tried not to let the quiver in her chin reach her voice. "She wasn't a failure for being tricked like most of our ancestors were."

"She doesn't feel that way. None of us do." Her father's voice hardened and his arm stiffened under hers. "The Protector didn't trick us. She felt like a failure to our clan for having not raised a daughter who understood her duty."

Harper bit her tongue to lock in the protest. A fortnight wasn't long enough for them to have taken the truth to heart. It still hurt to be called a failure to her people, to her own mother.

"Maybe we should talk about other things," she said, unable to entirely keep the bitterness from her voice. As a teenager, she'd vacillated between daydreams of being celebrated upon her homecoming and nightmares of being rejected. She hadn't known if she'd been cast out or lost. The truth was more complex, but she missed the halcyon images of her parents' arms around her, a feast in the oven, and bright bunting. "Tell me about you. My memories are so patchy. Tell me what you've been doing, how the violin is, maybe."

"Do you play in your new life?" her father asked. "You held two when … when we saw you last."

"Yes. It was one of the things I remembered. Not playing or learning specifically, but how to play. Like I could remember how to read, write, do basic maths. The skill was there. Grace plays piano, so we often play together. Less so with having housemates." *And because, since we got housemates, we've been solving murders and disappearances all the time.* "I play to relax. It helps me sleep. I think … I think some of the tunes I know are yours, because I don't remember where I heard them."

"Aye, that sounds likely, sweet girl." Her father relaxed, and a nostalgic smile brought a pale sunlight to his face. "When you were a wee baby, I used to play to you and your brother to help you sleep. Melody was often away in those days. She lived … She was often away and you two missed your mama. When you took the mantle of Seer from her, I would play to you after the nightmares to help you go back to sleep. It warms my soul that some part of you remembers."

"Mine too."

They walked for a while, discussing little things. Conversation kept bumping against the things they weren't talking about, painfully sharp turnabouts in words that cut Harper's heart. It was a start.

Voices drifted on the wind, and she guessed they were near the village. Though she'd known every tree and path as a child, the memories hadn't fully returned, and a lot had changed. She wondered if they'd deliberately walked a roundabout way to conceal the village's exact location or if it had been an honest meander.

A child stepped out on the path in front of them, and Harper's father dropped her arm like he held a glowing coal to his skin. The child's vivid violet gaze shocked Harper into stepping back. Grace was shoulder to shoulder with her in an instant.

"You're not welcome here." The girl's piercing eyes swept from Harper to Grace. "Neither the traitor nor the magic slayer."

"Magic slayer?" Harper's father took a step back from Grace, his eyes narrowed.

"Grace's family protect humans from supernaturals, from folk who try to hurt them." Harper thought that was honest without being damning.

"And you? Did my child undertake to harm her magical kin?"

Harper flinched at his tone. "When lives were in danger, yes. Just as the mare that plagued our ancestors was banished. I have also protected folk from humans when *their* lives were in danger."

"We fight for the innocent's right to live in safety," Grace added.

Harper gave Grace a mental hug. "Grace has always known about my magic and protected me. Not all humans are as bad as you think. Many are scared and have been told lies all their lives. It doesn't excuse their hatred. There are some who question the narrative they've been given. Like Grace. Like my housemate, Saqib, who has every reason to be afraid since his grandmother was kidnapped by folk. They see *me*. A person. They understand that others are no different to humans, no matter how inhuman they look. Some are good. Some are dangerous. Many are neutral. I hope one day that the Queen's propaganda against our kind can be replaced with that truth."

Passion quivered Harper's voice and stung her eyes with tears, but her little sister remained unmoved.

"You abandoned your people, defied our Protector," the girl accused. "You left us vulnerable to attack by mundane *and* magic folk."

"No. The shield is still there. I promise, I have no intention of breaking it. You can make your own choices. Go out at night. Use your magic however you want. Marry whomever you want."

"You seek to weaken us and feed us to another like the mare."

"*No.* Those aren't things you've Seen. Those are lies you've been told. Like people out there are told lies about witches like us." Harper didn't mean to shout, but the tear-choked words came out too loud.

"Come, Papa." The child thrust out a hand. It sliced into Harper's heart when he took it without hesitation. "We should return home and warn them. These invaders must leave. If you listen to her, our Protector will never return. That I have Seen and Grandmama confirms."

"Please go." Harper's father couldn't meet her eyes. "I'll consult with the clan elders and we will write to you again."

"Papa, please ..." Harper held her arms out. The bear-hug embrace from earlier turned into the briefest of hand clasps, and even that was fast and guilty. He turned from her and walked away with his real daughter, the one who wasn't a disappointment or failure.

Harper sagged against Grace. Emotion was too strong to be felt. She was numb with the pressure of it.

"I'm sorry it didn't go how you wanted." Grace wrapped an arm around Harper's shoulders and led her back down the hill.

No birds sang and no leaves rustled. The very earth of her ancestors rejected her. Harper cried on Grace's shoulder.

They were nearing the barrier when a susurration disturbed the stagnant air. Harper peered into the treeline, her Sight searching for what her eyes couldn't see. A magical glimmer in the outline of a human scrunched itself small behind a tree.

"I know you're there, you may as well come out," Harper called.

A young woman with long auburn hair and leaf-green eyes stepped out. "I mean you no harm. I only wanted to see you, to see that you were well."

"I know you." Harper couldn't be sure, but the woman in front of her looked a lot like the teen from her brief memory, her first kiss. "We were … friends? Dawn?"

The woman's face lit up with joy. "You remember me?"

"A little. I lost all memory of people when I left. It's trickling back."

The woman stepped closer and held out a hand. Harper took it, tension tickling her palm where it touched Dawn's.

"Aside from that, you've kept well?" Dawn asked tentatively.

"Very." Harper gestured to Grace. "My sister. A new family took me in."

Dawn's shoulders sagged in relief. "I was always afraid you were sent to the caves because of me. Then you disappeared. None of us knew what happened to you, only that you weren't dead, else the Protector wouldn't have been so angry. Many in the village blamed my influence."

"Because you kissed me?" Harper asked, then changed it. "Because we kissed?"

"Yes. We were kids. Too young to be dating or making future plans. But it threatened the Seer bloodline."

"They hurt you?" Harper reached out and brushed a hair back from the other woman's face.

"Not physically, no." Dawn shrugged and smiled. "I was no longer considered suitable for matrimony or childbirth. In a way, that became a blessing. Because I wasn't part of the calculations for the next generation, I could do what I wanted. My wife and I bonded over the ostracization of those who couldn't have children, and no one objected to our wedding because she was barren and I wasn't allowed biological offspring. We've lived happily enough. Many in the village are uncomfortable with how closely our lineage and breeding is monitored. We had sympathetic friends, and niblings aplenty when those friends had children. You and I were reckless, Harper. You were my first love, if it can be described as love at thirteen. If we hadn't experimented together, maybe I would've always been missing a piece of myself. So don't feel guilty about me and, knowing you had someone to take care of you on the other side, I'll try not to feel guilty about you."

"I'll try too," Harper promised. "Thank you. For following and telling me. It's nice to know not everyone in my old home is scared or hates me."

"Many weren't," Dawn said. "They were afraid when we had no Seer. Your mother resumed the position and later had another child to replace her. Many forgave you for leaving. A seer's life is a hard burden to place on a child. I hope, given time, they'll forgive you for banishing the Protector as well."

"I hope so." Harper wished it fervently, with any magic that might make it true.

"I should get back before I'm missed." Dawn wrapped Harper in a tight hug. "Blessings on you, my friend. I hope we meet again."

Harper nodded into her shoulder. Memories swirled of holding each other like this, two girls who weren't supposed to be friends. Through the pain, there was gladness for Dawn, that she'd found someone with whom to share her soul.

They watched until Dawn disappeared back into the trees. For once, Grace said nothing, just wrapped an arm around Harper again. When they stepped back through the barrier, Saqib nearly jumped out of his skin. Heresy laughed at this and gloated. Fionn hurried over with a plaintive 'mew' to rub around Harper's ankles.

Saqib didn't ask how it went, and Harper appreciated it. It took very little prodding to get him to tell her about the science and how he detected small anomalies that could be the barrier. Fionn snuggled against her chest when she picked him up, cold fingers buried in his fur. Heresy drifted possessively to her shoulder. The normalcy was cosy, even against the glaring oddities. She was wanted. No matter what happened, she had a home.

Chapter Seventeen

Not a Date

It was strange to go from a place Fionn associated strongly with magic—a place of murky past he didn't want to remember—to the scintillating and dangerous present where magic was taboo. Except his deceitful glamour. He shouldn't be there waiting for a human who would revile him if he was revealed as a cat.

He couldn't stay away.

The area around the art gallery was inconveniently open and airy. And wet. Clouds drizzled rain to sparkle on paving slabs and yellowed stone structures. A rectangular fountain split the courtyard in front of the gallery, spurting arcs of water in a deeply suspicious way. Bare winter trees offered no concealment.

Instinct said to hide and keep his natural form for as long as possible to minimise glamouring and so he didn't have to stay out in public for longer than necessary. Being a cat was so much easier. *If* people saw him, they were happy. This form was too big and too noticeable. Fionn tucked his hands inside his hoodie and buried his nose under the collar. Harper's aroma of archives, and AJ's light musk soothed his nerves.

People trickled out of the gallery as closing approached. Others hurried through Exhibition Square, hoods pulled up and umbrellas held close. There were no clocks. He rarely needed to know the time in the human way. Some magic depended on the movements of celestial bodies, but knowing the moment of equinox was a magical certainty, not the function of a circle, some sticks, and a dose of politics. Fionn scanned the square for the aura of the dreamer he knew as well as he knew his own heartbeat.

His eyes were drawn back to the wall surrounding York's centre. There hadn't been a clock there yesterday. He was sure. Fionn noticed details. He would've been dead long ago if he couldn't, not to mention useless to his master. The tip of his tail twitched as he stared at the erroneous clock. The face of it was held aloft by twisting metal vines affixed to the old stone. None of the humans passing under the wall noticed the new addition. Humans were often blind to strange things right under their noses.

Fionn was reluctant to step out, even with no one paying attention. Folk survived by *not* doing stupid things like he was about to do. He took a deep breath, quashed the automatic hydrophobic magic, banished his tail and ears, and sprinted across the square to the relative shelter of the gallery's arched portico. He hid behind a pillar and wriggled his pants lower to let his tail out again. If anyone saw, he'd portal away.

It couldn't be worse than his first solo portal to a new place. Rather than the Roman amphitheatre in Chester, he'd portalled right into the middle of a Roman museum, city unknown. Though he'd hightailed out immediately, it had sparked a cat-hunt and he guiltily hoped no other white cats had been harmed in his stead.

Great Peter, the cathedral bell, sounded the hour. Five dongs. Fionn counted them. It helped keep him calm, although five was a very little number to count to. He wrote it in different bases in his head to distract himself. One-zero-one. One-two. One-One. One-zero. He came to the conclusion that five wasn't a very interesting number.

An ear twitched inside his hoodie. His dreamer approached. Fionn watched with the intensity of a cat waiting to pounce. Dayo didn't see him right away. He did notice the clock, stopped and took a photo, then crossed the road, eyes sweeping the area around the gallery.

Fionn vanished his tail and ears, then heaved his pants up. Earthen eyes cut through the water to find Fionn's. He ducked behind the pillar on instinct before his thoughts caught up to remind him that he wanted this human to notice him. Maybe. Probably.

"Hey." Dayo ducked into the portico and yanked his hood down. Box braids bounced as he rocked up onto the balls of his feet. "Thanks for waiting. Feels like someone stuck a clock up there overnight 'cause I said I might be late. Probably been there decades and I never noticed."

"Of course I waited." Fionn darted a glance at the clock. *Could it have grown because someone said they'd be late?* "You asked me to." His hand drifted to his collar, hidden under his oversized hoodie. He snatched it back, so Dayo wouldn't see, and tucked it behind his back instead.

"If only it was always that easy to meet pretty boys." Dayo grinned at him, and a return smile twitched Fionn's mouth. He couldn't not smile in the light of such sunshine.

"Where are we going?" A giddy excitement replaced Fionn's anxiety, or at least blended with it to the point where it was all fizzy.

"Originally thought of Midnight, but Sage has special offers on Thursdays."

"It's Saturday."

"Oh. Well, Midnight then. Or Stonegate Yard, lots of fun nooks there. Is there somewhere you want to go? I like trying new places, if you have a regular."

"I, um, don't live around here. I'm … here for work." Fionn bit his lip. It wasn't a lie. He didn't want to lie to his dreamer.

"Well in that case, you should really try the Black Swan or Ye Olde Starre. They have a rivalry over who's the oldest pub in the city, so most tourists check them out. But Midnight is pretty good for talking and not too expensive. I didn't even check, do you drink? Sorry, I should've asked that. There's a good tea place on The Shambles if you don't."

I know. Better than you do, I bet. Hiding the smirk, Fionn did a quick bit of mental maths. Harper mentioned this one. 'Drink' didn't mean just anything, because of course he drank. 'Drink' meant alcohol. "Yes, I drink." *When I've been a good cat and the magic hurts anyway.* He stopped himself from touching his collar again. "Let's do Midnight. I'm curious now you've said it so many times."

"Great. Let's go. Make the most of the time before curfew." Dayo held out his hand, and Fionn took it without thinking. His palm tingled like he held big magics. "Tell me about art you like?"

"I'm not too good at names and stuff." *I can't read the little cards at cat height.* "I like lots of kinds of art. I don't get much time out of work, so that's where I go when I can. Or food."

"Do you need to eat?" Guilt flashed across Dayo's face.

"No." *Always.* "Harper fed me. We can get something if you need to." Fionn peered at Dayo. He suspected his dreamer didn't always take very good care of himself.

"Drinks first. Pretty sure there's food at home. Harper's a friend of yours?"

"Um, yes." *Special Friend.* "I stay with her when I'm in York."

"Sounds better than staying in a chain hotel with boring art. What's the last exhibition you went to? Other than mine of course."

"Art about sunflowers and swirly stars."

Talking was easy as they half-walked, half-zoomied back and forth across the street to avoid the biggest puddles and worst of the rain. It was giggly and fun. Rare as it was that no one wanted something from him, all Dayo asked was to chat about art, hold his hand, and run around. Which was all okay by Fionn. No magic, no blood, no tough questions he couldn't answer. His head and lower back ached from keeping his glamour intact, a minor inconvenience.

They ducked into a building with a loud crowd chattering and music in the background that reminded Fionn of some of Dayo's fizzier dreams. Normally, they were dreams to avoid. He hesitated at the door and Dayo looked back, his face falling.

"You don't like here? We can go somewhere else?"

"Here's good." If things led to where those dreams normally did, he could leave a message with someone who worked there and slip out. The idea hurt Fionn's chest. He wasn't sure why. Those dreams made Dayo happy, so he should be actively trying to make them true. The thought settled him and made it easier to smile. "Sorry. It's new, that's all. New is good though."

"I think so." The grin returned to his companion's face. "Drinks and grab a booth?"

Fionn nodded and they wove their way to the bar. A couple of people stopped them to greet Dayo with hugs and cheek kisses, just like Harper described. Fionn gave himself a tick for learning good humaning. Dayo introduced him to whomever stopped them, not letting go of his hand. It anchored him in the crowded bar and calmed when panic threatened. He mostly made polite noises and let Dayo carry the conversation with his friends, not wanting to intrude and not fully understanding what they were discussing.

When a couple stopped them while they're queuing at the bar, Fionn was mildly surprised that Dayo didn't immediately introduce him but instead shot him a look of mild panic. A flash, gone before the other humans could notice it.

Fionn offered his hand. "I'm Fionn, he/him. Nice to meet you."

"Rob, he/him, and Jack, they/them." The taller stranger covered intros for both of them. After a couple of minutes, the other couple got their drinks and moved on.

Dayo let out a long breath. "Thanks for that. I know them but not in a remember-your-name kind of way. More in a ..." He waved a hand toward a corner of the bar where people were dancing, leaving Fionn to guess.

"S'ok. This is a lot of people to remember." Not that Fionn hadn't been studying in case it came up later. His master used to make him do exercises like this when ze attended the Queen in her large, cold palace.

"Thanks. You're real easy to hang out with." Dayo threaded his fingers through Fionn's, and the cat's heart skipped a beat. "No one expects you to remember, by the way. We're up. What do you want?"

"Um. I don't know the name of what we have at home. What are you having?"

"Rum and cola."

Fionn recognised 'rum' so he nodded.

"If you hate it, I'll drink both and get you something else."

Dayo ordered, and Fionn fished out the money Harper gave him along with a quick lesson on human economics. It was simple maths. Fionn wasn't sure why a derivative piece of art with millions of copies held any value. The Queen glared up at him from the purplish piece of paper.

"I'll get the first round, 'specially if I might end up drinking both." Dayo waved the money away. Fionn added 'round' to his list of human vocabulary. Glasses weren't strictly speaking round, more cylindrical, but he could at least get where this slang came from.

They found a quietish booth in a corner. Dayo slid in after Fionn, close enough that their knees touched, and put an arm around his waist. "Easier to talk if we sit next to each other."

Fionn nodded again. Good logic. He sniffed the offered drink. Some fizzed up his nose and he pulled back with a slight snort. "Fizzy drink for fizzy feels?"

Dayo laughed. "Something like that. Cheers."

He clinked their glasses together. It made a fun sound, so Fionn did it a couple more times, enjoying the way the multicoloured lights caught the bubbles in the dark drink. He realised Dayo was watching him and blushed, pulling his hood further over his face to hide it.

Dayo reached out and pinched the brim between two fingers. "You don't need to hide from me. In case you hadn't noticed, I think you're pretty cute. You're different to lots of folk. Kinda cat-like, and you enjoy little things. Tell me what you were looking at?"

"The ... the lights. In the bubbles. They dance and glitter like splashing through a rainbow if water dripped up into the sky." Fionn's eye twitched and he almost tugged his hood again. The lack of ears hurt. He sounded ridiculous. Too folk. Not human.

"Are you sure you're not an artist, Fi? You paint pretty pictures with words." Dayo held the glass up to the lights, twisting it this way and that. They both watched it, mesmerised, until the song changed. Dayo handed the drink back with a laugh. "I want to know all about what's in your head and ... everything."

Fionn was fairly sure that sentence had been about to go somewhere else, but the thumb stroking his hip was spinning his brain like candyfloss fuzz. He cautiously took a sip of the drink. It bubbled and burnt. Without meaning to, he spluttered, tongue licking air to get rid of the horrid taste. That was *not* rum. It was fizzy paint stripper.

"Not a fan?" The concerned look returned to Dayo's face. "I'll get you something else."

"It's okay. My m ... I've drunk worse."

"Not exactly a glowing recommendation." Dayo took another sip of his drink. "I'll have both and get you something different. I want you to be happy with what you've got."

Fionn gave him a curious look. It was an alien sentiment. Harper said it, but that was different. "I'll get it." He slipped out, almost ending up in Dayo's lap without his tail to help him balance. The hands on his waist guiding him were hotter than the burn of alcohol.

When he got to the bar, he asked for nice rum and the bartender let him sniff a couple. He eventually bought a palatable caramel spiced rum. It was just as well Dayo wasn't with him. The maths part of money was easy. He had two thousand pence. The drink was an awkward five hundred and five pence. The change was a whole handful of strangely shaped coins and different coloured paper, so it took longer than he would've liked to check it. It was strange to pay and not haggle, and also to use something so worthless. He preferred the Market.

When he got back to their booth, Dayo was chatting with a small group. They were all laughing, touching, drinking together. Dayo and the woman from the gallery, Rose, were dancing in their seats. Fionn took a step back. He didn't want to interrupt fun. He didn't even know why he was there. *Stupid, selfish cat.* He rubbed his neck where his collar dug in and took another step back. *I should go.*

"Fi." Dayo jumped up and put an arm around his shoulders, drawing him back to the group.

One of them pointed at the drink in Fionn's hand. "You dating a posh boy now, D?"

Dayo glared. "Leave him alone. He can drink whatever he wants. And it's drinks and art, not a date."

"Whatevs." Rose flicked a hand at him as she got up. "You know where I am if you end up going home alone tonight. If I'm still available."

The other followed her with a couple of apologetic mumbles, until it was just the two of them again. Dayo squished in, pulling Fionn with him. "Sorry about her. Got no expectations, k?"

"Um. Okay." Fionn debated whether he was supposed to have understood what just happened. "I, um, have no idea what she's talking about so …" He shrugged. There was an awkward silence for a moment.

"By the way, I hope it's okay I called you 'Fi.' If it's not, I won't."

No one had ever called Fionn anything other than his names before, except Harper sometimes called him 'kitten' recently. "It's kind of nice to have a name that's just between us."

"Yeah? I'm glad. So, what do you like other than art?" Dayo leant in and Fionn's confusion fled. He had his dreamer to talk to, properly, in the wakening. Sweet rum warmed him like the kitchen fire and Dayo's eyes captivated him like dancing flames.

The bar closed at the first curfew warning bell, and they stumbled out together, arms around each other's waists.

"You wanna come back to mine? Paint your pretty eyes?" Dayo leant against the side of the building, pulling Fionn against his chest, hands on his waist.

"I should probably get home." Already there were more Guard and police out on the streets, and Fionn's lack of tail and ears were giving him a pounding headache. "I had lots of fun. Thank you for asking me."

"Thanks for coming. Next time, come over to my place and I'll paint you?" Dayo slid a hand over Fionn's cheek, inside his hood. There was a brief spark of confusion in his look, tiny fractures in his confidence that confused Fionn in turn.

"If you're really sure that's what you want."

"If you're not comfortable with it, you don't have to. Usually people are begging me to art them, stick a camera in their face, pose them for a painting. You're different. I like that. It was nice talking tonight. Like … you aren't after something from me."

"I'm not." Fionn frowned, unsure what Dayo was getting at.

"I'd give it to you if you were." He leant forward, breath warm on Fionn's lips.

Fionn's gut tightened and his breath stuttered. "I'm not. I just … this is …" His voice petered out as Dayo's fingers scritchied down his back.

"You like this? Make you purr?"

"*Mhmm.* You like too?" Fionn ran his fingers down Dayo's chest. Sparks crackled, wanting, aching, even muffled by his coat. The magic wanted to go to the other man and Fionn had to hold it tightly in check. He should leave.

"I like very much." Dayo nuzzled against his neck. "You like cat things? Nuzzles and scritchies?"

"Yes." It was a breathy answer as Fionn copied, rubbing his nose gently against Dayo's neck and inhaling an aroma of spice and paint. His head was pleasantly floaty, like sitting on a roundabout spun too fast. Without thought, his tongue darted out to find soft skin and a quickened pulse. Fionn jerked back. "I'm sorry. I don't know why I … I should go."

"Wait. It was nice." Dayo kept an arm around Fionn's waist, not holding him hostage, rather encouraging him to stay. "I like licks from pretty boys, and giving licks if you want too."

The rum was wishy-washing Fionn's head. Pretty arty dreamer certainly shouldn't be offering him anything. He was a selfish little cat. A Guardswoman stopped at the corner, watching them through narrowed eyes. She made a sharp gesture with her stick, the message clear, *move along*.

"I need to go." Fionn trembled under her look, other feelings taking a back seat to the fear of discovery. "I'm sorry. My m … I'm expected back. I'm already late." He pulled away and clawed at his collar to try and dim the electric demand down his spine.

"Is someone making you wear that? Fionn, you don't have to go if you don't want to. If someone's forcing you—"

"Dayo? You alright? Coming to Jen's for an after party?"

As soon as Dayo looked over at the voice calling him, Fionn ran around a corner and opened a portal. He collapsed through into Harper's attic. A glow surrounded him immediately and he shrank as he shifted. It was a relief to be back in one of his real shapes. If it dimmed other feelings as well, that was a happy bonus. He knocked thrice on the air and slipped home.

Chapter Eighteen

His Master's Displeasure

Fionn slunk through the corridors of the silent castle. Though it couldn't speak, it usually made its sentience known through play, shadows, and movement. Yet now it presented as nothing more than a hollow shell of stone with no breath of the outside world. It was bigger than the last tomb his master shut him in, yet the sensation of death was no less difficult to shake from his fur.

His master's command led him towards the throne in the Great Hall. The crackle in his collar diminished with every step of acquiescence. A different kind of pain seized his limbs. *What if ze knows? What if ze can smell him, or tastes my blood and my chemistry is different?* Magic, and a tough stomach used to experiments, held off the worst of the illness caused by his sudden shift, but the cocktail of nerves and alcohol would be obvious in even a drop of his blood.

Fionn hid in the murky edges of the hall until he had no choice but to cross the openness of flickering torchlight. He approached his master's throne with a belly crawl.

"Were you ignoring me, Zero?" His master's multi-tonal voice stirred the air and ruffled his fur.

"Mrow." Fionn lowered his eyes and cowered on the cold flagstones. He reached out his no paw. A silver-buckled boot pressed on it, not enough to hurt, just enough that pain in the future was all but assured.

"You've been sneaking, Zero. Despite my warnings, you have shed your fur and assumed your unnatural form around humans. Were they not disgusted, Zero? They are not used to shifters like we are."

Memories argued with his master. Of Harper's embrace. Of AJ letting Fionn sleep in his bed. Of Grace slipping him extra food, and Saqib showing him how to use a camera at the Opera House. Of the man who nuzzled their noses together in both his shapes. The latter was a lie. Dayo didn't know what he was. He hadn't seen the parts that disgusted people.

Fionn mewed plaintively. His master was right. Kitty whimpers begged for forgiveness.

"I thought you could be trusted to solve the mystery of my fetch and how it was tied to this human woman, and how to bring our lost kindred of Swaledale home again. I thought you were a creature of stronger will."

The disappointment in his master's voice corroded Fionn's insides like a spray of acid. *How could I have gotten so wrapped up in turkey bacon and art that I forgot my real purpose in being there?*

"I will send One to keep an eye on the witch and her unusual coven. As my most devoted familiar, she can be trusted to have my best interests at heart, the best interests of the whole country. For if I should fall, who could protect it? Not you, little Zero. Not with your miniscule magics. Not the witch who has barely scratched the surface of her power. Remember why we are here, Zero. We are the shield that protects folk and humans, fauna and flora."

"Merow." Fionn tapped his yes paw against his master's boot. The pressure increased on his trapped foot, a warning, then the boot released him. He tucked the paw quickly underneath his body.

His master returned to the throne, bidding Fionn to follow with a sharp gesture. He hastened after and hopped up to his usual perch on the arm. Sharp fingers dug into his chin as his master forced his head up. There were no eyes to meet, only swirling dark voids like miniature portals to an abyss.

"You will not go to Harper nor any of the others who live under her roof, in either form. You shall not allow them to perceive you, nor shall you see them, in wakening or in dreams."

Fionn yelped as a sharp nail dug into the pad of his paw. Blood welled. A drop of it hung from his master's spindly claw. A spiked tongue darted from behind the mask, passing through it, then disappearing again. The same nail dug into his master's hand and a drop of blood was deposited on Fionn's tongue. The sanguimancy wrapped around them. They were bound together, as they always were. The commands sank into Fionn's collar. Unbreakable rules. Should he try to return to Harper, his master's will would overpower him, and his magic and limbs would return him to the castle for re-education, no matter what his mind said.

It was galling that a command was necessary. It itched under his skin like his fur was growing backwards. *I should be a Good Cat. I should be mindful of Master without wasting magic the country needs to keep crops growing and livestock healthy.* The light, bubbly sensation in his chest was not more important than flowers.

"We have much work to do, Zero." His master patted his head and Fionn gave a small 'mau' in return. "York is in grave danger of becoming like Chester. If such overt operations continue there, the Queen's Guard will lock it down and create another blank spot in our safety net. The Veil already wears thin there. I had hoped your influence with the Seer would aid our work, but you are a selfish cat."

Fionn flinched from the disappointment. *I am* a selfish cat. He mewed again and hung his head.

"We can save it, Zero. The magic there is necessary. With the disruption of the Hiding, York has the potential to grow in magic and become a haven. What occurs is not the issue. We must make sure it is unseen. For now, at least. Come. You will return with One and Three. One, as I said, will watch the Seer. You and Three can continue to survey the area. Make sure the Guard are sticking to our Accords. It is our right to manage this situation first, before they interfere. They have been forgetting that of late."

It was a fine balance of power, enforced by the steel wills of his master and the Queen. He swallowed a scowl for being paired with Three. The raven was sassy and a bit too big to be prey. Still, York was large. They couldn't survey all of it if they stuck together. He would find a way to warn Harper about One.

"Come, Zero." His master's robes and cloak billowed as ze stood. A costume that backed up the iron will. Aside from the mask, it was all for show. Even here at home, his master must remain aloof and in control of zir castle and familiars. Only when it was just the two of them did ze relax, wear normal clothes, and let Fionn glimpse the weariness behind the authority.

It took well into the night for them to get mostly caught up on their normal magical tasks—a series of protection charms, dream making, and fertilisation spells.

Fionn fell asleep snuggled in his master's bed, the glow of his master's final pat and 'good cat' keeping him warmer than the blankets or the roaring fire in the grate.

Still, he sought out a brighter, hotter flame in his dreams without conscious decision. His master hadn't forbidden him from being perceived by Dayo, and he slipped into the familiar dreams with a long exhale of relief. The thought occurred that if he couldn't approach Harper's dreams due to his master's wording, maybe there was a way to have Dayo pass on a message, though he wasn't sure how without Dayo being alerted to magic. For now, it would be a weight off to simply be together in the dreamscape.

The dream morphed. *Wrong.*

Normally bright and animated, Dayo's dream grew sludgy. Images flashed and warped. They were in Dayo's flat. Though Fionn had never been there, he knew that was what it was because Dayo knew. Out of the window, the iconic London landscape wibbled, and washed up and down. *Maybe where he used to live?* It was so close to where Fionn lived that it hurt, even while he was grateful Dayo never found him there. A strong regret washed over him like a physical wave. He'd never happened across Dayo's art there. Maybe it had all been too close to the university, which was in turn too close to Westminster.

A spectral figure stood in the middle of the room, not shouting but deeply disappointed. Fionn flinched back, tucking himself between Dayo's ankles. As ever, the artist himself was indistinct. The dream was through his eyes, so his body was barely real in it. Dayo bundled the cat into his arms, holding too tight, blurred face buried in Fionn's fur as he mumbled apologies. The other figure gestured around the room. Art shifted, broke, and came together again. They grabbed a canvas and threw it. Dayo turned, Fionn clutched to his chest, protected. The canvas whacked the artist on the shoulder.

The imagined or remembered pain was enough to disrupt the dream. The room stayed the same, the figure disappeared, and the London landscape dissolved. Fionn purr-hummed softly as he stroked Dayo's shoulder with his paw and nuzzled his cheek. Gradually, the room around them faded, then Dayo's grip on Fionn, until Fionn was left alone in the dreamscape as Dayo slipped into full sleep. It was not the first time the dreams had been like this, and Dayo had recovered from when they were frequent. It worried Fionn anyway.

Chapter Nineteen

Dream Chamber

Achingly sweet dual violins, deliberately discordant and mournfully played, took their melded thoughts back almost four hundred years. Two minds merged into one purpose within the dreamscape. Memories flashed by like shimmering gobies in the depths of a canal and resonated within both bodies as they lay tangled on silken sheets. The chamber group lulled them from across lands and seas, back to their infancy. Though centuries separated their births, they shared everything as one in this liminal space.

They'd had the privilege to sit at Maestro Legrenzi's feet in Santa Maria dei Derelitti, unnoticed due to his deep absorption in his music. The other orphans had returned to il ospadale next door. Many would later join their retinue or receive their patronage in the arts, but when his La Cetra, Op. 10 was composed, all had been bambini still. Innocent in many ways. Old in many others.

Even then, they were destined to become a saviour. They listened for the voice of God, who spoke to the great saints. They travelled to Roma, visited the body of Santa Teresa d'Avila and saw the great sculpture erected to her ecstasy. One day, they would inspire such masterpieces.

They also aspired to the leadership of the pious from their home. Not recognised as sante by the church in Roma, they revered folk such as Giuliana of Collalto, abbess and healer, and Contissa Tagliapietra who walked on water. They followed in the footsteps of great minds, artisans, and musicians—Veronica Franco, courtesan and poet; Marietta Barovier, who had a magic touch with glass; Elena Cornaro Piscopia, theologian, philosopher, and later friend; and many others.

Their reminiscing was captured by the dreamscape, tumbling them through their own history of admiration, betrayal, love, yearning, and power. To the present day when they were plural. Powerful mage and practiced dreamwalker. Gentle pressure on the dreamscape brought them back to the task at hand and to the modern performance of this song from their youth.

It angered them in many ways. The art of their beloved mentor, a child of La Serenissima, being played for the entertainment of people who rejected all their country stood for. For centuries, they made it a safe haven for folk, a place of free speech, where gender and species were less important than philosophy, theology, and art. These people were an anathema. Yet the affinity of the music eased their access into closed minds. It allowed them to pry open hardened hearts and nurture a seed of magic.

They sank into the buzz of the harpsicord, the gentle plink of the theorbo, and the dancing notes of the violins. Like a phoenix reborn, the music soared through their being: rejuvenating, fiery, and affirming. They were doing what was right. With all four musicians in harmony of thought, their magic could infuse the group, not just a single soul as previously. Their confidence grew as the magic took hold across the concert hall.

As the piece moved into its spritely mid-section, the keystone of the dream bridge locked into place, and their magic flooded the minds of the musicians. It poured out from instruments of wood and wire played by instruments of flesh and bone. Notes were ripped free from fluttering pages as the wind howled a background drone. Red, blue, and green stage lights flashed a crazed staccato. Bulbs shattered, twinkling falling stars of glass into a lake of music.

The roar of thunder burst from the organ's pipes, inaudible in the wakening, yet a shockwave through the dreamscape. The force of it remained as the piece returned to its richer, more sedate pace. Pressure of centuries of sound, this same piece repeated again and again, lay across the concert hall like a net.

As the piece slowed further, it settled, sleepy and yawning, around the hearts and minds of the audience. Notes drifted onto skin to be absorbed. The tattoos it left faded rapidly. The humans sank further into stupor as the music sank into them. It travelled through veins back to the heart. It pulsed through synapses to manipulate their thoughts.

This time, no pesky demon saw through their illusions and no outsiders came by.

The piece went on far longer than its six-minute composition. Dreams stretched and folded time. A minute could become a century. A century could become a minute.

As they receded from the concert hall, the musicians' link to them remained strong, and through them weaker links to all who had heard. The net would spread. The spell would be cast.

"Harper?"

Thudding on her door brought Harper around with a banging headache. Looping thoughts of the visit with her family had played on repeat all afternoon and into the night. What she could've said or done differently that might've changed what happened. She wished Fionn had come back. She wanted to know about his date. Wanted him to help her sleep. Just wanted him, so she knew he was safe and neither the artist nor his master had hurt him.

Once she'd fallen into slumber, rest had been denied her. Irritatingly elusive, a tune buzzed through her dreams; never clear, but enough to stop her falling into deep sleep. It wasn't helped by the ache in her gut neither painkillers nor heat could touch.

"Mum says you lot need to get over to the university."

Harper groaned as the knocking continued. It wasn't like AJ to come upstairs, let alone loudly.

"Harper. She said *now*."

She checked the clock. Three a.m. *What the heck?* When Harper opened the door mid-knock, AJ frowned at her crumpled pyjamas and dishevelled hair.

"What happened, AJ?" Harper took half a step back to let him in, but he'd already turned for the stairs.

"Wake up Grace. Saqib's brewing up."

By the time Harper roused a grumpy Grace, the tea was brewed. They sat around the table, three of them hunched and clutching mugs. Only AJ seemed awake, but then, Harper supposed it was the middle of the working day for him.

"Slowly, from the start." She yawned. "What's so wrong that you got us all up at three yet it can wait while we drink tea."

"You're useless until you've had some," AJ pointed out. "It's too late to do anything about the immediate problem, but you folks and the Council need to be ahead of this. I guarantee Albrecht and her crew are already up and working."

At the mention of the Guard lieutenant, Harper and Saqib both sat straighter.

"There's been another possession." Harper wasn't asking. Her dream. A vision of sorts.

AJ set his mug down. "During a performance last night at the university."

"At the Sir Jack Lyons Concert Hall?" Grace asked. "We know it. I played there a few times while Harp and I were at uni."

"That's the one. When the concert was supposed to finish, no one came out. The person staffing the front door assumed there were encores and didn't raise the alarm for quite a while. Unfortunately, with the barracks so close, the Guard got there before even the police, else Saqib might've been called. Mother was alerted because one of our coven let her seventeen-year-old attend on the condition he called when he got back to his friend's hall. Of course, he didn't. When Auntie Iris tried to contact him, she found not only her kid's phone switched off, but that the concert hall had been disconnected from the uni switchboard. She spoke to a general receptionist and was told there was no information. When she went over, the whole area was cordoned off. They arrested her for breaking curfew. So she called Mum."

"The concert was after curfew?" Harper asked, surprised. The Guard were strict with events.

"The university has been permitted to hold contained events. Attendees have to prove they're not leaving university property. The campus and halls of residence have been well patrolled by private security and the police and, other than the girl we investigated before, there haven't been any incidents there."

"Until now." Grace gripped her mug too tight. She hated failing in protecting people, especially with the uni once being home turf.

Harper's shame was compounded by the mention of the Somnia's victim who'd disappeared from Le Page Court. She'd failed her thrice over—by not being more accepting at the bookstore at their accidental meeting last October, by not catching the killer before her eyes were gouged out, and by being the reason the Somnia wanted the girl at all. Grace reached over to pat Harper's arm.

"Mother doesn't want to get embroiled with the Council or Guard for obvious reasons. She's asked us to make enquiries, *before* they have a chance to move anyone out of York. She reasons they'll hold people at the barracks overnight and won't move anyone until dawn."

"I'll call Godfather." Grace left her tea unfinished and dashed back upstairs for her phone. Better prepared, with his phone in his PJ pockets, Saqib was already calling Imam Mohammed. He wandered into the lounge for privacy.

While they rang for backup, Harper asked AJ, "Have you seen Fionn tonight? He went out with that artist and I've not seen him since."

AJ shook his head. "Not in either shape. You think this artist bloke did something to him?"

"I don't think anyone other than Fionn's master can hurt him unless he lets them."

"It's the last bit I worry about." AJ's brow furrowed. "If someone asked him to hurt himself, and made it sound like it would help someone even a little, Fionn would probably slit his own wrists for them. He and I have had a few talks about consent and touching and stuff."

Harper gave him a funny look.

"Hey, just because I don't date doesn't mean I can't make sure someone else understands that anything other than a fully informed and truthful 'yes' means 'no.' If anything, the fact I don't do that kind of stuff means I understand that bit very well."

"Sorry, you're right." Harper automatically moved to pat his arm, then paused with an eyebrow raised.

"Yes." AJ smirked at her as she gave him a pat, then his expression sobered. "My guess, though, would be that Fionn went home. Even if his friend found out what he is and called the Guard or something, they couldn't keep him. Only magic can stop Fionn going where he wants and no magical being in this country would dare touch one of the Magician's familiars."

They were interrupted by Grace's return.

"Godfather is sending someone over to the concert hall. He suggested Saqib go straight there, too, and we head over to the barracks to talk to Albrecht."

"I'll go with Saqib." AJ stood and stretched. The two women gawked at him. "What? He can't carry all that stuff alone. You're both following the people trail, which I am *not* doing, and Fionn's MIA. I do leave the house on rare occasions you know, and one of the missing is my cousin. Not a close cousin. Not entirely sure if we've even met. But family stick together, no matter what. Especially magical families under constant threat."

"Because if one of you goes down, it could take everyone." Harper paled. If the Guard did find out AJ's relation was a witch, the whole coven could be in trouble. No wonder his mother had been so anxious.

It didn't take long for her and Grace to dress and be out the door. She sent Heresy with the men on the understanding he would tell them if he sensed any magic and would stay well-hidden from any Guard.

By the time they reached the Guard barracks, Albrecht's door was open and three coffees were sitting on her desk. Considering the number of times they'd been stopped for being out after dark, the surprise wasn't that she knew they were coming, it was that she seemed to care. Harper wondered if she could See poison. She didn't dare use her Sight in front of the Guard lieutenant and find out.

"We're putting York on lockdown," Albrecht said, without preamble.

"That's premature." Grace looked down her nose across the desk. "No one affected has done anything dangerous or threatening yet. Some graffiti on walls is hardly reason to quarantine a city."

Albrecht counted off on annoyingly neatly manicured fingers. "A powerful supe found within the city walls. A second serial killer targeting York, supposedly gone but with no evidence of this. Sharper increase in incursions than anywhere else in the country. Repeated attempts, and successes, at possessions. All evidence suggests York is, like Chester, sitting on some kind of open Hellmouth. Until we can seal it, it must be contained."

"Academically speaking, that's nonsense." Harper clenched a hand in her skirt, and held Albrecht's gaze. "A 'Hellmouth' implies demonic creatures with certain attributes. While that can vary between religions, certain identifiers are consistent. They are *not* consistent with what we've seen in York over the last few months. Almost every creature recorded has been native to this area. There is no evidence to support demonic possession in the current cases either. No religious rhetoric has been used and, again, none of the usual markers are present."

"With all due respect, Ms. Ashbury, 'academically speaking' can jump off a cliff with the legion of demons. I'm not concerned with categorising these threats. I am concerned with protecting the people of this country."

"What about the people of this *city*?" Grace asked. "History shows that putting a city on lockdown forces people into mob mentality and paranoia. Not to mention you are proposing locking them in where they're in danger."

"There is no evidence a lockdown will stop who or whatever is targeting York," Harper added. "There's not been a supernatural physically present causing the possessions. They aren't stopped by walls or guns. We need freedom to track them. Restricting that plays into their hands. Unless you've discovered something new this evening?"

Albrecht's jaw tightened and her shoulders stiffened. "Your investigation has turned up nothing. I do not expect our *protections* will affect it in the slightest. I don't intend to sacrifice York, but I won't let this spread. Measures are being taken, beyond walls and checkpoints. They are none of your business."

"You haven't found anything," Harper surmised.

Grace sat up straighter. "Measures taken to protect or harm this city are very much our business, as representatives of the Archbishop of York and, through him, the Council of Faiths."

"You may find that less of a shield than you think," Albrecht warned. "The archbishop, indeed the whole Council, skates on very thin ice after their lack of cooperation in this case as well as their continued questioning of our methods. Those who disagree with protecting humanity from the supernatural scourge should look at their own morals and prejudices very carefully and be sure they don't end up on the wrong side."

Grace bristled at the insult to her godfather. Before she could blurt out a more forthright reply, Harper said, "We all want the same thing. To protect people from anyone who would harm them. That is what the three of us are here for tonight. What happened at the concert?"

Both Grace and the Guard lieutenant glared at each other a moment longer. Albrecht backed down first, sitting back in her chair and turning to Harper. Grace smirked a little as she sat back, arms crossed over her chest and legs folded.

"We don't know." Albrecht ground the words through clenched teeth. "The audience recall nothing strange, though each person interviewed mentioned being completely absorbed in the music and most said they were daydreaming and didn't notice anything happening around them. When pressed for more information, a few who recalled daydreaming were able to remember details. All of them daydreamt the same thing."

"Which was?" Grace asked sharply. The word 'interviewed' had not sat well with either of the sisters.

"An ornate church with a small nave, a man composing with an inhuman child by his feet."

"What description did they give?" Harper asked. "If the contents of the daydream relate to the mind of whomever is casting the spell, maybe identifying what type of creature this child was will help us find them."

"It would be helpful for you to search in the cathedral records, or whatever records Ms. De Santos' family may keep," Albrecht admitted, though her eyes flashed to Grace as though watching for some confirmation. Grace stoically gave none. "One of the interrogatees was able to give us a sketch. When we showed it to others, under the guise of an image from a book, they confirmed it matched the child they saw."

"Why not be upfront with them?" Harper asked. "Now you've finished your questioning, have they been released to go home?"

"We don't know what infection they may carry. Your expertise is in books and fighting, Ms. Ashbury. Don't question my techniques of interrogation." Albrecht's frigid look goosed Harper's skin.

"We need to speak to them ourselves." Grace's lips twitched into a smile, sharpened on her hard stare. "The De Santos family are not unfamiliar with ways to get answers."

Though Harper understood what Grace really meant, the implication her sister let Albrecht believe left her just as cold as the Guardswoman's statement.

"Those people have been quarantined, and no one, not even their questioners, has direct access. We will send suitably protected samples to Dr. Siddique for testing."

"We'll see what the archbishop has to say." Grace glowered.

"What about the musicians?" Harper asked. Her stomach cramped with fear for AJ's cousin. At least Saqib was doing the testing. If he did find something, Harper trusted him to keep it between them. Though the risk was high, maybe Fionn could portal if things became dire. If he came back.

"All four musicians are like the author. We have restrained them accordingly." There was no crack in Albrecht's demeanour.

"They have names," Grace said. "They're people too. People who need help."

"Then catch this creature and we shall see if their curse can be undone." Albrecht snapped her notebook shut. "Though we find generally those who have been under the sway of the supernatural remain forever tainted." Her eyes flicked to Harper.

"At least let us see them like we did with Vita," Harper pleaded. "It's important to identify patterns. Two similarities may be a coincidence. Three could be a lead."

Albrecht paused, a rare glimpse of uncertainty. "You don't allow us access to the prisoner you hold."

"We hold no prisoner," Grace said. "We care for a sick woman."

"And I have given you the report with everything we know," Harper added, though it wasn't strictly true. It was everything the Council knew, not all that she did.

After a moment's consideration, Albrecht stood and indicated they should follow her. She gave no explanation as she led them deeper into the prison, until she reached one door and drew out a key.

"You may see one of them. This is the lead violinist."

As Harper entered the room, she kept her head bowed and her back to any cameras, relying on Grace to keep Albrecht from looking at her eyes. She swept the room with her Sight before kneeling next to the sedated musician. There were no drawings, as expected. Given the Guards' experience, they'd restrained and sedated the musicians immediately.

Miniscule violet notes bubbled from the man's slightly parted lips and nose each time he exhaled. They drifted up like air pockets in water, then popped. It wasn't as easy to Hear as it was to See, Harper didn't practise it as much, but at least it lacked the visual clues. She switched and the notes disappeared to be replaced by faint strains of the music from her dreams.

Chapter Twenty

A Charity Cold Call

As soon as Harper got home, she took out her violin to try and recreate the tune. The green electric violin from the Foss and the ancestral bone violin both lay hidden under the floorboards beneath her bed with her other magical paraphernalia. Her old companion, a violin of maple wood and painted white roses, sat in its customary place at the end of her desk. It was this one she chose, one with no magic other than the inherent spellbinding qualities of the instrument itself.

"Is that wise?" Heresy asked. Saqib wasn't home yet, though she'd touched base with AJ upon returning. There'd been nothing immediate at the concert hall, and Saqib had taken his fresh evidence straight to the lab, while AJ and Heresy returned home.

"Since when is anything I do wise, according to you?" Harper retorted.

"*Hmm, hmm*, a fair point." Heresy grinned at her. "Though this may be more foolhardy than your usual bumblings."

"I have to work out what this spell is. Maybe I can use the tune to trigger a vision of what's coming. People are being disappeared, Heresy. Not by magic, but by the hands of heartless humans acting out of misguided fear. If we can't get ahead of the supernatural threat, we'll never be able to take on the human one."

"And if you accidentally complete the creature's spell?" Heresy asked.

"Whatever it is, it's large and complex. If it could be completed by a solo instrument playing the tune, whoever possessed the violinist would've made him play it."

"Oooh. Logic. Times must be desperate indeed if you have delved so deep within that you found a speck of it."

"Shut up, Heresy." Harper threw a pillow at him. "Don't interrupt. Got it?"

"Have I ever interrupted a joke?" Heresy slunk up to sit on her bed. Though he had no eyes, the weight of his consciousness observed every minute move she made.

At first, she fumbled, missing notes or having to swiftly adjust as she worked out the complex music she'd Heard. Within a few bars, the tune evened out and she forgot Heresy. It was not unlike playing with the Foss or atop the tower as she fought the Somnia. She was both in control and not in control. No outside force commanded her fingers to move. Rather, something inside blossomed and filled her. Instincts she didn't know she had guided her.

The air shimmered. The floor sprouted a glowing building of tiny runes, numbers, notes, and letters. It grew around Harper like a time-lapsed forest, miniaturised yet detailed, and blocked out her bedroom. She turned slowly on the spot, eyes burning with Sight as she tried to See what the magic was and how to stop it.

When Harper turned back around, a person stood inside the building with her. She stepped back with a gasp and her bow screeched over the strings. They were scarcely there, wavering and hazy, as though viewed through the depths of a murky river. Though the building solidified and the glowing faded to a pulsing glint, the person became no clearer. They appeared human, which didn't discount them from being supernatural. Many of the folk could assume a human form, like Fionn. Some could do it even better, Harper thought, remembering the women in the teashop and paper shop in the Shambles.

Her fingertips were numb and her arm heavy. Though it had been minutes, it felt like hours since she struck the first note. The tune possessed a life of its own. Taking a deep breath, Harper kept playing.

The figure gestured to the magical building and something metallic glinted in their hand. The building wasn't one she'd seen before, in the wakening or in a dream. It reminded her of a place of worship, though it didn't have the exact hallmarks of a church, synagogue, mosque, or any other holy place she'd visited. Where an altar might have stood, there was a fountain of glittering lights.

Silhouettes of humanoids filed past her, even more vague than the one she Saw first. A kinship tugged at her. Though the seed hadn't been fully planted, enough of the magic from the Opera House had touched her that the fountain called to her. These folk were the audiences, the ones touched by a little magic. Not enough to create this summoning like the artists who were possessed, but enough that they were connected. They walked widdershins around the fountain. Their chant was garbled and muted.

Each silhouette approached the fountain and the watery figure bestowed a grain of light upon them. Then they walked out and disappeared to her Sight.

Harper's lungs burned as if she held her breath. Pressure smothered her head and weariness dragged her down like sodden clothes in the sea. Her body screamed for air though she could breath. With a grunt of pain, her fingers slipped from the violin, the building vanished, and she flopped onto the bed.

"I do not wish to have witch butt on me." Heresy oozed out of the way.

Harper lay the violin on the bed next to him, then rubbed her temples as she stared at the ceiling. "I think I know what they're doing. Not exactly, nor why, but hopefully enough."

"Would you care to share this information?" Despite his usually nonchalant attitude, Heresy extended a curious tentacle towards her.

"It's like in the opera. When Alcina summons the temple of Hekate. They're creating a temple to magic here. Then they'll place something from it inside the people they've already touched. That lores of affinity thing AJ goes on about. There's just enough magic sleeping in them that they can be a fertile ground for whatever magic is in that fountain. The artists—singer, writer, musicians, anyone else they may target next—are creating the building blocks. Though we're stopping some of them from creating, so my guess is the one who's behind this will keep going until they have enough people to reach some kind of critical density. Poof—magical temple appears in York."

"If we continue stopping the builders, the architects may give up," Heresy mused.

"Or keep going until there's no one left. I don't get what they hope to achieve. If they succeed, it won't be good for the folk. The Queen's Guard will wipe York off the map. They'll lock it down and purge everyone."

"Regardless of the end goal, what do you intend to do next, Harper dearest?"

"Go to the archives."

Heresy said it in time with her, in a vaguely singsong, mocking voice. He sniggered at her glare.

"I'm going to the archives," Harper repeated. "If I can find something that matches this, I can use that evidence to show the archbishop and the Council. It will mean I can give them a reason to stop Christina, the opera singer, from drawing. I don't like the idea of restraining or sedating her, however the alternatives could be worse."

"And so we become the evil we seek to vanquish." Heresy flashed a sharp-edged grin.

When Harper left the archives late on Monday afternoon, her phone buzzed with multiple missed calls and messages, all from Charity, Grace's cousin on her mother's side. Unlike Grace, Charity was sociable and had the teenage problem of being glued to her phone. Still, so many missed contacts were unusual. Enough so to jolt Harper out of her worries that the equinox was exactly a month away. Normally, Charity knew better than to phone during working hours. The messages simply said, `Call me as soon as you can.`

"Charity? What's wrong?" Harper asked as soon as the other girl answered. "Is everyone alright?"

"I don't know." Tears choked Charity's voice. "Everyone says so, but I … I think Gabe's in trouble."

Charity was particularly close with Grace's oldest brother, who had been her main babysitter through her childhood years. Despite this, Charity's upbringing was very different to her cousins'. Her father hadn't approved of his sister's choice to marry into the De Santos family. Charity was soft and sweet, and freaked out at the slightest hint of danger. Harper fervently hoped this was one of those times.

She took a deep breath. "Why do you think Gabe's in trouble?" A heavy weight settled on her shoulders. He'd been in Venice for months, far longer than he should've been. *What if he never comes back?*

"He called me yesterday, like he does every Sunday evening, but he didn't sound right."

Harper exhaled. If he called, he wasn't dead or imprisoned. "Did he use any of the code phrases?"

"Nuh uh. He sounded coerced. He kept muting himself. A couple of times he cut off another voice. Someone higher pitched than Gabe. He said he was alone. At one point he swore. He apologised, but Gabe *never* swears at me, Harp. Only that time we were playing basketball and I accidentally elbowed him in the side. He said it was nothing, but Grace told me a werewolf clawed him. And he kept sucking his breath like he was hurt too.

"When I told Uncle Danilo about it, he said it was fine so long as Gabriel hadn't used any of the codewords. Auntie Maria didn't say anything when Uncle Danilo was there. Later, she asked me about what Gabriel said, and she shredded her napkin in her lap. She told me not to worry. I can't shake the feeling that something's wrong. You need to go find him."

"If Father doesn't think there's a problem, he's either right or he's handling it." A hollow reassurance to Harper's own heart's staccato beat. "They know what they're doing, Char. So does Gabriel. He's the best."

"Harp, I'm telling you something's not right." The teenager's voice cracked. "Please, can you and Gray look into it? They'll tell you things they won't tell me. I trust you too. I would've come up to York, but they said at the station there are no trains running that way. There's nothing on the news. Dad doesn't like your family telling me stuff, but I know there's trouble. What if he was asking me for help and no one believes me because I'm the youngest or because I'm not a De Santos?"

"Sorry, Charity. You're right. Things are hairy up here. I don't know if Grace and I can even get out to go help Gabriel if he needs it. Venice is …" Harper stopped. Something poked her brain, something she couldn't quite place her finger on.

"Venice is?" Charity prompted.

"I'll call Mama Maria," Harper promised. "Gabriel is my brother. I won't leave him in danger if there's anything I can do, and nor will Grace. I can't promise to tell you everything, but I promise I won't lie to you."

"Okay." The girl sniffed back tears. "Thanks, Harper. I—Dad's coming. Message me later." The phone beeped as Charity hung up.

Harper fumbled in her satchel until she found a copy of the programme from last night's chamber music quartet. She'd been focussing on the stories attached to the music. *Maybe I've been focussing on the wrong thing.* The idea was barely formed as she skimmed the list of composers. Three with Italian surnames. She wasn't familiar enough with classical music to know if any of the others might have lived there. What she did know, and hadn't considered, was that Vivaldi, the composer of the opera *Orlando Furioso* was Venetian. Human, as far as she knew, from before the islands had been segregated, turned into a jail, and wiped from the map.

He may even have been one of the refugees from that time. The dreamwalker was from abroad, and she hadn't been focussing on where. What if that was the connection?

And the author? Does ze have Venetian heritage? Or something in the book, maybe even that scene? Maybe the older painting I saw is Venetian.

Harper turned and headed back to the vaults.

Chapter Twenty-One

I Could Paint You a Thousand Ways

Although it hurt Fionn to be unaware of what was happening in Harper's life, it helped his scheming when One reported something that had Three reassigned to monitoring the train station for a while. Fionn guessed it meant someone in the household might try and get out of the locked-down city, but his master revealed nothing.

A little while after Three left for the train station, Fionn portalled near the other familiar's location to make sure the raven was at his post and not sneaking off on a side quest of his own. Slinking through the smelly building, he spied Three atop a large, protruding clock at the junction of the stairs leading to the platforms. Train stations were new territory, so the clock may have always been there. The twisting metal holding it aloft was oddly similar to the clock by the art gallery. *Best check that out again. After all, anything odd might be related.*

If he happened to stop by Harper's hopefully empty house on the way and left a note, well that wasn't strictly forbidden, and neither One nor Three were watching.

Every time he thought about contacting Harper, he quashed it before the static in his collar became unbearably painful. If he tried to go against orders, blood magic would take hold of his magic and his body, forcing him to do as his master said. He needed a loophole.

His master had said she mustn't perceive him, however leaving her a message wouldn't let her see him and he wouldn't actually be near her. So long as he was quiet enough that neither AJ nor Heresy heard him, the command wouldn't take full effect.

Nonetheless, the order stung between his vertebrae. He squished through the smallest portal he could, silent on light paws. The magic in him was kept tightly reined in, beyond Heresy's perception. Fionn shifted briefly to scrawl a note in pain-shaken writing, which he left on Harper's pillow.

He shifted back and fled. As soon as he was away from the house, the pain lessened and his limbs surrendered to his control. He lay panting on the pavement of a wonky ginnel. When a passerby noticed the trembling cat and stopped to help, Fionn dragged himself over for a pat and to reassure them he was okay, then hastened in the direction of the art gallery.

Dayo's dreams had remained murky since their outing, with more than one having a flavour of worry for Fionn, though there was an electric undercurrent of something else that confused the cat. He worried about leaving his dreamer alone in case he *was* the one from Harper's vision. *In which case, aren't I following Master's orders by keeping an eye on Dayo?* As a compromise, he decided to leave a note with the art gallery staff and avoid the inevitable questions and accusations. *After all, I'm there anyway to look at the clock, which is directly helping Master. Isn't it?*

He sat under the strange clock and stared at it. The second hand ticked from twelve to twelve. Though he couldn't sense any magic, the time wasn't right. It reached the hour 47.5 seconds after Great Peter tolled it merely a street away. *Human error or significant? I should watch longer …*

But a cat watching a clock all afternoon would arouse suspicion at a time when everyone was already on edge. *Time to pop into the gallery and leave Dayo a note. So I'm not too obvious about watching the clock …*

If I take five minutes to sit and bask in Dayo's art while I'm here, would that really hurt anything?

After shifting to human and glamouring in the nearby alley, Fionn left a brief note with reception, then perched on the edge of a bench in the middle of the gallery and let the familiar cacophony wash over him. Despite its bouncy tempo and general cheerfulness, his eyelids grew heavy and his head lolled. *Cats are supposed to nap. I miss naps. Lazy cat. I shouldn't … But I haven't slept since—*

"Fi? Fionn?"

Fionn turned on the bench, eyes wide. He almost hadn't registered the voice as real rather than part of the art he was lost in, and the thunder of the paintings masked his sense of Dayo's approach.

Dayo shifted from one foot to the other, hands clasped behind his back. "They said you were still here. I was worried about you. I turned around and you were running off down an alley. By the time I reached it, you'd disappeared. I've been looking for you since. Coming here several times a day in case ... and then this note ... But you're here now. You're okay?" Dayo scooted onto the other end of the bench. A hand twitched towards Fionn then dropped. "Are you in trouble? I don't know what I can do to help, but I want to. Or I thought maybe you left because ... I did something wrong?"

"*No.*" Fionn jumped up and reached out without thinking. His fingers trembled as Dayo wrapped them in his. "I had to get home. I didn't want to be late and I don't want, um ..."

"To get in trouble with the Guard or police?"

Or with my master. "You had friends asking for you."

"After talking art all evening, I kind of hoped *we* were friends?"

"We are?" Fionn's eyes widened.

"If you want to be?"

"I'd like that very, very much."

They smiled at each other.

"If I ever do something that makes you uncomfortable, you'll tell me right?" Dayo rubbed his thumb over the back of Fionn's hand.

Don't pick me up with my legs dangling. "I can try." Fionn wasn't sure if he could actually do it. A little discomfort didn't mean much to him, but he didn't want to alarm Dayo by saying so. Harper and the others reacted oddly when he said stuff like that. "Am I keeping *you* from something? Am I being a bother?"

"I probably should be at home arting. You're more interesting."

Fionn blushed at the blatant lie. "I don't want to keep you from arting. Shall I ..." He took a deep breath. "Shall I walk you home?" *And hope Three isn't flying overhead. I think he'll be at the train station for a while yet.*

"Yeah. That'd be great. If you wanna see some painting, you're welcome to come up."

They held hands, the relaxed banter of their previous outing bobbing to the surface, though tense fingers gave away a slight underlying strain. Dayo led Fionn to an apartment block, about ten minutes away from the gallery.

"I'm renting an all-in-one place here on the cheap," the artist explained. "Until I decide if I'm staying in York or what. Sorry it's kind of cramped."

It wasn't just cramped. The studio apartment looked like it had been ransacked. Piles of clothes and art supplies were all over the floor. There was a sock hanging off a mirror. In one corner a pile of plates teetered. A large orange ball was wedged half under the bed. It was unlike any other human room—Saqib's extreme neatness, AJ's absentmindedness, or even Harper's cushy comfort—it was chaos.

Supplies might have been everywhere, but so was art. Finished art. In progress art. Sketches. Paintings. Fabrics. Photos. Fionn reeled in the doorway, knocked back by the cacophony.

Dayo shoved some stuff to the side to uncover a stool. He flinched when he turned back. "Wasn't expecting visitors."

Fionn tried to focus, but the small space and the sheer volume of art made it difficult to process anything else. "Par ... pardon?" He scrunched his eyes closed and opened them again to no effect.

"I know it's a mess. There's no need to look like that."

Fionn swallowed a lump of hurt panic. "It's not that." Although the cleanly cat in him really wanted to sort some of it. At least stop the culture evolving in the corner. "There's so much art." His eyes finally caught up with the chaotic orchestra. They crept over the room in wide-eyed awe. "It's so beautiful."

"Yeah?" Dayo's rigid stance relaxed. "Thanks. Let me show you what I'm working on. Take a seat. Cup of tea? Milk? Sugar?"

"Yes, please." Fionn agreed against a more logical judgement. "Tea, milk. Um, Harper says I have more milk than is right, but I like it. I have some monies."

"You get what you like here." Dayo filled a kettle in a kitchen nook and set it to boil. "Don't even think of getting money out. You're a guest at my place. Tea comes as standard. You said you were in York for work? I should've hoped you went home before the lockdown, but I really wanted to see you again."

"I'm kind of ... in and out." Fionn's guts twisted. "I travel a lot, but here is my main base at the moment. It's usually L-London. My master is there, so I have to go back regularly. I don't really like it. Here is nicer."

"Master? What kind of arsehole has that as their title?" Dayo stiffened. "People don't own people. Thought my ancestors demonstrated that to Europeans already, with all those repelled invasions my grandma taught me about. You should find a new job and tell your boss to get stuffed."

Fionn cringed at the irreverent way of talking about his master. It had been a slip of the tongue to mention his homelife at all. "I can't. The work we do is needed, and ze's a master of ... zir craft." *And I'm a cat.*

"Still an arrogant arse to call zirself that. What is it you do anyway?"

"Oh. Um." *Rituals to nurture the land. Alchemy. Create dreams and harness nightmares. Protect people. Artificing.* "It's not as interesting as art. We craft bespoke items, some scientific work, and lots of agricultural stuff."

"Sounds pretty interesting. Seriously, I've been in some toxic workplaces, and it's not worth it. You should get out. You can stay here a few days if you need to. Milky tea." Dayo pushed a mug into his hands. "One friend to another."

"Thanks. For the tea and the offer." Fionn stared at his reflection in the tea, then shook himself. "You were going to show me what you're working on?"

"Oh, yeah, thanks. I still feel more like painting you, if you'll let me? Sorry, I should stop asking, only you haven't actually said 'no' or 'yes'."

Fionn sipped his tea and gazed around the overwhelming flood of art. Self-reproach and disbelief vied for the upper hand. Nothing of him could ever be good enough to go with all this. A couple of pieces particularly captured his gaze. He tilted his head, listening, wishing his real ears were allowed to materialise.

"Do you paint a lot of stuff like this? That's … supe stuff?" he asked. Other than *Shattered Illusions* with the Ouse, there had been nothing overt, although a couple of paintings, like *Dream Kitty*, had been abstract feelings about folklore, according to the little cards.

Fionn walked closer to an art of an old man seated high in a textile tree. Limbs and branches twisted together and bright colours flowed from one being into the other so the man and the tree became the same entity. The art whispered words in a language Fionn didn't know and his heart thumped in time with complex drumming.

Fionn's preoccupation almost resulted in him tripping and spilling tea everywhere. Dayo's hand on his elbow caught him. He blushed and looked away. *Clumsy, stupid cat.*

"I got you." Dayo's hand lingered on his arm. "This is Iroko. My grandma told me stories about him when I was little. I like that art lets me explore the culture my family left behind when my great-grandparents moved here. It also lets me explore what we try to leave behind in England, even though we don't physically move away. Mum always said not to believe everything I was taught in school. She believes the legends of her ancestors, and that not all things we deem 'supernatural' are evil. She said there is a fine line between what we're told is faith and what is myth."

"Do you believe in her faith?" Fionn asked.

"Sometimes. Sometimes not. I think I want to, but that's not the same thing. Here." He pushed a sketchpad into Fionn's hands. "These are all inspired by stories Grandma and Mum have told me. I just haven't gotten around to finishing them yet."

Fionn nodded, mesmerised as he flipped through pencil and charcoal thoughts. "Isn't it dangerous to art these things?"

"My mum also says I don't consider risks before diving into things. Been investigated by the Guard a couple of times—they don't like me recording history, but it's part of the identity of this land, especially now. I don't think my art is dark, though. I like to find the joy in things. Even the Ouse. I reckon people'll take it as a warning about supes living among us. To me, it's more of an acknowledgement of heritage and that it wasn't a bad thing. Walk along the river and listen to the fisherfolk complain. They were happier when the river was possessed."

"I like that. I don't ..." Fionn met Dayo's eyes. He wanted to trust him. To pull down his hood and confess. To tell Dayo about the dreams and how long they'd known each other. "If you mean it that you want to paint my eyes, you can," he blurted out before self-conscious embarrassment could stop him. Dayo's face lit up.

"Yes! Sit here by the window." He guided Fionn back to the stool, then grabbed a sketch book and palette. "I'm going to do some concept sketches first and try some colour mixes. You can pick one you like. I'll do a couple of different styles. I can do more than just your eyes? Any part of you?"

"Um. Whatever makes you happy and isn't wasting your time and art supplies."

"Don't think you could be a waste of my time." As Dayo collected supplies, he kept stopping to stare into Fionn's eyes, unblinking, and take deep breaths. When he eventually gathered everything he wanted, there was a fidgety energy even to his stillness. "May I take your hood down? Are you cold?"

"I just..." *Don't want my ears to accidentally show up.* "I'm warm enough, I ..." Fionn pulled his sleeves down to make sure the scars on his arms weren't visible. Even without the risk of ears, his body wasn't pretty enough to paint.

"I don't want you to do anything you don't want," Dayo assured him. "You really remind me of that cat. I got an idea. Okay, look up this way for me? Gonna move this lamp ..."

Fionn patiently let Dayo pose him, move him, sketch, just as he had in cat shape. Each brief touch and shared look stirred whirlpools. The process fascinated him. If he hadn't been the uncomfortable subject, he could've happily watched Dayo art all day. Three and his duty were far from his mind. An impossible daydream wove in the air around him; of sitting on Dayo's lap or across his shoulders in cat shape and spending a lazy day watching art. Fionn blinked it away. Daydreaming was dangerous.

The only thing spoiling his day was the escalating discomfort of his ears and tail.

"Dayo?" Fionn asked hesitantly. "I have to go soon. It'll be curfew." *Three has probably missed me and reported me, to One at least.*

Dayo blinked and looked up from the colours he was mixing. "Shoot. Sorry. Completely lost track of time. You're very absorbing to look at."

"Same," Fionn muttered.

"You got a few minutes? Wanna see the sketches, tell me what you like, what you hate?"

Dayo moved to a queen-sized bed in the corner, which doubled as a couch in the small studio apartment. He patted the blanket next to him. "Offer of art comes with or without hugs. Guest's choice."

Instinct was to shift and snuggle. Shifting would result in shouting and throwing, not pets. Fionn gingerly perched on the bed, feet curled under him. "Hugs are good." His breath stuttered as Dayo put an arm around him and allowed him to lean close. He was sure the other man could feel how hard his heart was beating.

Dayo fanned out sketches on the bed in front of them. Some showed completely human Fionn, save for his cat-like eyes. While some included his hood, Dayo had also extrapolated a fairly accurate view of Fionn's messy hair. It was strange to see himself without his collar on. Fionn raised a hand to touch it through the hoodie. When he reached the last two pictures, he stopped breathing. Dayo had sketched cat ears. Not quite right, but close enough. Fionn clutched his hood, trying to feel if there were ears under there.

"I'm sorry. You hate those? It was because you remind me so much of that cat I showed you, it's almost like you're a human version, especially in that hoodie. I thought you'd be cute drawn like those people abroad who dress up with the cat ears, only more realistic. My ... ex was in black market arts down in London. Saw some there. If it's offensive, I'll get rid of them."

"No. It's ..." Fionn picked one up. Tears caught in his lashes. There was a daydreamy-hopeful look in the eyes of the drawing and the tilt of his head. The other with cat ears was one Dayo drew with Fionn looking straight at him. Fionn hadn't realised the longing in his soul was streaming from his eyes. "I like them."

"Really? I like them best, but if you really don't like them, I'll get rid of them. Don't want to get you in trouble."

"No." Fionn bit his lip, trembling. "Sorry. I didn't mean to sound snappy. I like them. A lot. They're ..." *Perfect. Me. Without Master. With you.*

"They're pretty. I'm not, but these are. You took … plain little me and created something lovely from that."

"You are pretty." Dayo crooked a finger under the cat's chin and gently turned Fionn's face to his. "Whatever made you feel the need to hide away, it's wrong. You're pretty inside, and the bits I can see outside are pretty too." Their foreheads were pressed together, eyes locked. "I could paint you a thousand ways and still be inspired, pretty muse."

"You're pretty inside too," Fionn whispered. "Pretty brain. Chaos and kind, energetic and arty. And pretty outside. Pretty feels."

"I wanna make more pretty feels with you." Dayo ran a hand down Fionn's back, causing him to arch and purr. "Pretty, pretty kitty-boy. I like hearing you purr."

Every part of Fionn tingled, especially where Dayo's breath caressed his face. Instinct warred to lean in, to relieve the aching longing on his lips. That couldn't be right. *It hurt when One kissed me. I don't want to hurt my dreamer.* He froze.

"What's wrong?" Dayo pulled back, his eyes moist in concern. "Isn't that okay? You don't like strokes? You said you did, at the bar, but it's okay to change your mind."

"No. I mean yes. I mean … confused." Fionn blinked, trying to get his body to stop fighting itself between yearning for Dayo and icking about One.

"Confused? You … don't know if you like it?"

"I do. Like it." Fionn almost burst into tears. His head and lower back both smarted as though a hot iron was pressed against them again. He needed his ears and his tail. He couldn't think straight. "You're … you're … safety and joy and the nicest thing that's ever happened. One is icky, and I didn't like it when *she* did things, and I don't want kittens. You're not icky. Not at all." His collar was too tight, constricting air, and he tugged at it fruitlessly.

"Is that hurting you?" Dayo reached for it, and Fionn scrambled back. He fell off the bed with a thump that shocked up his spine.

"I need to go. I'm sorry. I'm so sorry." He stumbled to his feet. "You're not icky. You're amazing and beautiful and being with you always makes me purr. I shouldn't be with you. It's not right. Dangerous. Master would … ze can't know. I'm sorry."

He bumped into the door, scrabbled for the handle.

Dayo kept his distance, though he spread his fingers towards Fionn as though he couldn't help it. "I won't stop you leaving if you want to, but I really, *really* want you to stay. You can be safe here. You can be *you*. Whatever this master freak has put in your head, it's wrong."

Fionn hung his head. "I'm sorry."

"No sorries. Stay a bit? I'll stop flirting with you if it makes you uncomfortable. Sorry if I misread you. I want you to stay and not think horrible things about yourself. Please don't run away from me again."

Fionn turned to see pain deep in Dayo's eyes. "I'm not running *from* you. I'm afraid of running *to* you. Of that being all I want to do. Being with you makes me purr. I'm ... happy? I didn't know there were feels like this. I don't know words for feels I haven't felt before. It's ... like the sun. Gravity keeps drawing me back to you, and when I'm near you, everything's brighter and warmer."

"I'm like the sun?"

"You have all this energy, and everything you do is exuberant and shiny, even when it's quiet and pastel, because you put everything into it. I've always lived in the shadow of someone else. Be a quiet c ... person. Be good. Do as I'm told. You don't put me in your shadow. Even when we were out and I was quiet and small. And as you keep pointing out, I'm very cat-like. A warm sunny place to curl up is my favourite spot to be." He rubbed his hand on the back of his neck where the pain of his master's insistent call was vying for first place against his glamoured tail.

Charcoal-splodged fingers reached out to him and Fionn laid his palm on Dayo's. Warmth folded over his chilled hand and his heart as Dayo said softly, "That was ... beautiful. How can you look at me and see all that?"

Because I've seen your dreams. Even without that ... "How can anyone not?"

The bitter bark didn't resemble laughter at all. It was a sun collapsed into a black hole. "You'd be surprised what people don't see, or what they do. You ..." Dayo pressed his lips closed.

"I?" Cattish curiosity pushed the question out even though Fionn was more than a little scared of the answer. Somehow, this one human's words could prickle fear in his belly far worse than whatever was waiting for him when he got home.

"You ..." Dayo hung his head. "I don't know who's seeing the lies. You or them. Maybe you haven't had long enough to see past the flash of a camera and the prettiness of paint."

It stung, because it might have once been true. The dreams had been an escape. Pretty. Sparkling. Colourful. A place where Fionn was wanted. Kind dreams, full of adventures and new experiences. The sting faded with that realisation. It was never only about the art. It was about kindness and safety.

Fionn studied their laced fingers, wishing for his tail. "It's not been long, and I'm not someone worth sharing with, but I try to see you. I think

I do. Part is your art, yes, but not all. I've seen enough to feel safe here, with you, in your territory. I want to see more. Is that enough? For now?" Fionn bit his tongue, unsure why he even asked. *I mustn't see Dayo again. I mustn't. Selfish cat.* He swallowed hard, tears prickling.

Dayo rubbed his hand gently, loose enough for Fionn to pull away if he wanted. "More than enough. I want to see more of you too. No innuendo intended. More of who you are."

"I ... w-wa-want that too." The traitorous word stuck on Fionn's tongue. What did 'want' matter when others 'needed'?

"It's not selfish or bad to have wants. Thank you for making me one of them, even though it's hard."

"Thank you for making *me* one of them even though I'm ..." *Weird? Ugly? Unreliable? Shy?*

"You're many things, and I bet none of them are how you are finishing that sentence in your head. You're interesting, smart, kind, and pretty." The common shadow clouded Dayo's eyes for a moment, and his lips parted as though there was more to say, then they closed again with as much effort as heaving an iron door into place and locking it seven times over. "It's curfew soon. Stay anyway? I promise to be less confusing. We can do some art stuff together, or watch a film, or talk. I feel like I could talk with you for hours. Like we've known each other for months, not days."

"Me too ..." Fionn blinked back tears. *Because we have.* Everything ached. Everything hurt. The two were *not* the same. One was good and instinct said the cure was right here in front of him. The other was screaming at him to go, and he wasn't sure how much longer he could hold the glamour or ignore his master's wishes. "I really do want to stay and talk all night." *Please believe me.* "But I can't. I'm sorry. It's *not* you. I promise."

Dayo looked into his eyes. "I believe you. We can do this again? Hang on. Let me check something." He fumbled for his phone. "Can I ask you something that might seem silly?"

"Of course."

"I've had a commission via a friend of mine. It's a live painting at this party she's hosting. Apparently, her latest patron requested me specifically because they want something with a supernatural angle. It means spending the evening with a bunch of posh folks who are ... yeah. Not my crowd. I don't like being around folks who are angling to get something from me all the time. But starving artist and all that." Dayo waved a hand around the studio apartment. "It's this or make rent by serving coffee to rude rich folks. Have to put up with them either way. Will you be my date? Or at least come along and keep me company platonically? It's on …" Dayo flicked through his phone. "Friday."

Fionn's heart was in his throat. Every bit of him wanted to say 'yes.' He wasn't sure what a 'date' was in context; some other strange human slang for meeting on a prearranged day he supposed. It would mean being around a lot more humans. However, glamouring was getting a little easier, or he was getting better at ignoring the pain. He desperately wanted to go, to see Dayo again whenever he was welcome, but he couldn't predict what tasks his master might give him.

"Sorry. Ignore me. Why would you want to do that?" Dayo shoved his phone back in his pocket with a grimace.

"I'm not saying no, just thinking. I don't want to say yes and make a promise I can't keep," Fionn said hastily. "I never really know my work schedule in advance, even a couple of days. If I can make it, I promise I will. If I can't, don't worry. It's just work. I'll still … I'll find a way to see you again. I wa … I w … ant that. Very much."

"If you can't come, you know where I live so you can write me, even if you can't text?"

"I'm sorry I scared you by disappearing before. I will. Write you, that is."

"Thanks, Fi." Dayo grinned and Fionn smiled back, his heaviness lightened by having brought the sun out from behind the clouds.

They stared into each other's eyes. The mere metre of air separating them swept between them like an ocean. The pain of leaving warred with the pain of staying. The latter won. If Dayo saw his ears, all of this, even the dreams, would be gone.

"I have to go," Fionn whispered as the final curfew warning sounded outside.

"I know. May I kiss your cheek goodbye?"

"Please."

Dayo leant in. Soft lips brushed against Fionn's cheek, stealing his breath. "I'll see you soon."

Chapter Twenty-Two

Finding a Corner of the Puzzle

Going home would probably be a good idea. Harper yawned and stretched as meandering aisles of bookcases phased in and out of focus. She wondered if this was how Alfred started: always finding another trail to research until he simply never left the archives again. *He can't have had people waiting for him.* Though absentminded, her friend wasn't cruel.

At least her research had been productive. She was more confident in her theory of the Venetian connection between the two composers. She'd also found mention of rumours of myths that there was a drowned library in the mouth of Saint Mark's Basin. A tenuous link to Venice, however her vision gave it more weight. There was nothing on the painting so far, but at least the idea had narrowed her search to Venetian artists. Knowing the dreamwalkers were foreign strengthened her case. If a little selfish part of her hoped the canal city could solve her Ouse problem, that was a bonus.

Stiff and weary, Harper packed up her satchel, then piled the books for reshelving. Whispers and rustling followed as she wandered up and down the stacks, replacing them based on the archive's own specialist variation of the Dewey Decimal System. No matter how quickly she turned, there was never anyone there. Archivists weren't generally the types to pull pranks. She eyed the books suspiciously. The books of the Third Vault were mundane for all they dealt with magical subjects. Not like the books imprisoned in the Twelfth Vault.

"Fionn?" Harper whispered his name. There was no sign of his starlit fur. Her heart ached for him. She'd sobbed onto Grace's shoulder when she found the note on her pillow telling her, in Fionn's archaic handwriting, that his master used blood magic to forbid them from seeing each other. Almost as worrying was the knowledge of One spying on them.

Harper had used both mundane and magical sight, but the hare remained hidden from her senses. The memory of her human form, too close and salacious, made Harper sweat. Though she was starting to question her default assumption that she wasn't attracted to women, she definitely didn't want the naked shifter so close to her again. Either naked shifter really, though right now she'd be happy to see Fionn regardless of shape or attire.

He found a way around everything. He always had. Whatever was forbidden, Fionn found a way to make it seem acceptable, even when they were young. He'd encouraged her to go out at night. He'd help her hide bits of herself from the Somnia in dreams and had been the one who let her into dreams to wipe the memory of her brother's name. Even with this new, harsh master who collared and cowed him, he snuck out to art galleries and into people's dreams. She firmly believed Fionn would find a way around his master's order.

Harper squared her shoulders and continued reshelving. It was automatic, a mindless task, soothing for its repetition and the scent of books surrounding her.

There wasn't much in the archives about Venice, certainly nothing up-to-date enough to help Gabriel, who hadn't responded to either his sister's or the archbishop's phone calls. Their parents had been equally unforthcoming and their reassurances hollow. Grace may say she hadn't made up her mind what to do, but Harper knew her sister. As soon as Grace could find an excuse to leave England, she'd be on Gabriel's trail.

Miguel, the middle sibling, had confessed to his sisters that he'd been tempted to check in on Gabriel himself, since he was close by in Eastern Europe anyway, but was hurrying home to answer Archbishop Marshall's request to assist with the exorcisms. It was both a relief and a worry that he would be in York within a few days, once he got through all the red tape.

Harper...

Her name in the air sent Harper's heart racing.

"Who's there?"

When will you join us, Harper?

We're still waiting ...

We're sooooo hungry ...

Come play ...

"Who are you?" Harper pivoted. Whispers echoed like a hundred voices speaking at once. *Did I release something from that book?* "What are you?"

Chittering laughter skittered on clawed feet over walls and shelves. It cut off abruptly and plunged Harper into unnatural silence for a few seconds, until the shuffling footsteps of another archivist came down the next aisle over.

Harper leant against the reassuring cherry of the antique bookcase. The spines of books pressed between her vertebrae as she fought to get her breathing under control. Warm aromas of glue, dust, and old paper grounded her. Whatever was loose down there hadn't been affected by the archbishop's rituals on Ash Wednesday. She should report it. Fear crawled up her back and bristled the hairs on the nape of her neck. She wasn't sure if she heard them with her ears or her magic.

Despite the risk of revealing her magic, Harper opted to tell the archbishop on her way out of the cathedral. Though she watched carefully, he revealed no hint as to whether he knew about her abilities or not. Her word was good enough for him, though he asked her to say nothing to the other archivists, lest it cause a panic or for them to hear voices that weren't there. He promised to investigate it himself and perform whatever rituals were necessary, and sent Harper home to start her weekend early with strict instructions to eat a healthy dinner and to sleep.

Harper was prepping dinner by the time Grace got off shift that evening.

"Any updates?" Grace asked as she took a seat between AJ and Saqib, who were examining Saqib's photos of the opera singer's drawings.

"Christina is restrained so she can't keep drawing," Saqib said sadly. "They erased what she'd done already, however I'm not sure it makes a difference. If what Harper Saw is consistent across all victims, the magic is already there and a little whitewash isn't going to change that. She still thinks she's Alcina as well. They sedated her." He balled his fist over the photo. "She's *right there* and she's still lost. We have to find a way to cure them and get them home."

Grace reached over to squeeze his shoulder. "We will. Miguel will be here soon and they'll exorcise whatever is possessing these people." She exchanged a worried look with Harper. Even if it did bring Christina's mind back, putting her through the horror of it would never be taken lightly.

"Is it safe to bring Miguel into our secret?" Saqib asked. "I know you haven't told anyone, Harper, but he's your brother. Surely he'll be reasonable."

Harper stiffened at the suggestion. In most ways, Gabriel and Miguel were as much her siblings as Grace was. They'd taken in an extra sister with no ruffled feathers. She'd always been included by the family, since the day she got there. Except in this one thing. A sharp pain in her chest made it hard to breathe. *Normal panic or a precursor vision to the blade one of them might slip between my ribs?*

"Telling Miguel we're helping supes would be … unwise," Grace said carefully. "He'll be sympathetic to the victims, but if he sees a supe, he's going after them. It being Harper might give him pause. Certainly, Heresy and AJ need to be careful while he's here. I've arranged for him to stay with Godfather, to be safe."

"I can't lose another family," Harper choked out. Her blood family's rejections cut to the bones. To lose her foster family as well would be a hurt she couldn't bear.

Grace leapt up and hugged her tightly. "You won't. I would never allow it. We're not going to lose you either."

"Thanks, Gray." Harper wiped her eyes on her sleeve and went back to prepping dinner. As she cooked, she explained everything she read in the archives.

"Next steps seem obvious to me," Grace said. "Harper and I go to Venice. I think we have enough that's plausible by mundane explanation. Saqib and AJ will stay here and continue the investigation at this end. So long as you're careful, Miguel can provide physical backup, or the Council can spare a couple of people to make sure you two don't get into nonsense."

"Surely you are not forgetting me, dear Graceless." Heresy floated through the lounge door and came to rest on Harper's shoulder.

"Only intentionally." Grace glared across at him. "Whatever happens, Miguel absolutely cannot see you. You'll have to stay out of the way."

"Au contraire, cherie." Heresy waved a tentacle in a mock bow.

"That's French," Grace snapped. "They speak Italian in Venice, so if you're implying it would be useful to let you come along, you've failed."

"Actually, darling Grace, they speak Venetian." Heresy grinned at her. "May I remind you that my dearest witch here is rather useless with magic and you are going to a place no human should set foot. An ally who is one of their own may be of use, not to mention my skills as an illusionist."

"He's correct." Harper could almost see steam coming out of Grace's ears at Heresy being right. "Though I'm not sure how we get him out of the country, he would be useful to have along."

"I can make a carrier. Like he was a cat." AJ smirked and Heresy flipped him off. "It's how we send items out of the country. Kind of like a Faraday cage for magic and scans. So long as he stays in it, guaranteed they won't spot him. And yes, Saqib, you may have a play with it. Before you go, we still haven't found where the Guard are keeping my cousin and the others. I'd appreciate you trying, Harp."

"Not sure what I have that they don't, but of course I will." Harper bit her lip.

"Sight, Seer," AJ reminded her. She shuddered. It wasn't helping so far. He continued, "There's a risk to others as well, including my mother. There have been signs they're being watched by humans and my aunt swears a raven was following her the other day."

"A raven?" Harper's head snapped up. "That's not the Guard."

"Not directly, maybe," AJ said, "though they have attached tiny cameras to people's pets and used them to spy in homes before."

"Do you think it's Fionn's master? If ze has a hare-woman and a cat-man, why not a raven spy?" Saqib suggested.

"That's one of the concerns," AJ agreed. "A likely one given ze has someone watching Harper. I'll let you know if there's any new info about the infection getting into human magic as well. The cases are a low percentage versus spells cast, but spreading."

They spent most of dinner planning. Harper dragged herself upstairs afterwards wishing for bed. But she'd promised AJ she'd scry for his missing cousin, and she wanted to try again to find Fionn and her brother. Heresy had pointed out the spells were more likely to work if she had something of theirs, so AJ had called his mother to request a belonging of his cousin's be brought over. Despite curfew, she'd promised something would be dropped by that evening.

While she was waiting, Harper pricked her finger and dipped the end of one of Fionn's hairs into the blood. It soaked it up greedily and gleamed a pale pink. He always said blood magic was stronger and that he was made of her blood.

Harper lay a map of England on the floor and drew around it in white chalk to the approving hum of Heresy. She tied the hair to a silver chain along with a crystal for weight and to aid the magic, though she wasn't sure whether it helped or was Heresy's sense of humour.

Sight came easily to the fore. Her diagram and the map both glowed an eerie periwinkle. Fionn's fur was bright silver, streaked with teal and violet, the colours of his magic. Harper concentrated on envisioning his eyes, brilliant blue framed by snowy white. No matter what shape he was, his eyes didn't change.

The crystal swung over the map. It circled Yorkshire in a wide arc and a glimmer of hope breached Harper's fear. If he was in Yorkshire, he wasn't at home.

The crystal wavered and she forced her concentration back to his eyes. *Please, please, please let me See where you are, Fionn Ashbury.* The name flowed through her mind naturally, though he'd never given a surname and she didn't remember him having one. He was her cat. Cats had their humans' names. Fionn said names were important. He was of her blood. So he was an Ashbury.

The circles got smaller and smaller. Harper repeated it over and over. *Let me See you. Fionn Ashbury, where are you?*

The room blurred and vanished save for the glimmering magical circle. Harper floated like she'd been portalled into space. Another presence was there with her. Two. Tense, her spirit crouched and waited to pounce. Though she had no body here, memory reacted as though she did. Her ears twitched and her eyes swept the dreamscape. No. Not her ears and eyes. Fionn's. She couldn't See *him*. She was Seeing *through* him.

Something crashed into her and threw her out of Fionn's body.

Her room tumbled into place and she doubled over panting. Wherever he was, Fionn was in trouble. Another possession was happening or was about to.

"I am mildly surprised, Harper dear." Heresy's voice was both grounding and grating for all its smooth tone. "You located the not-a-cat."

She looked to the map. The crystal had dropped onto a mostly green area on the outskirts of York, within the quarantine perimeter. Harper grabbed her laptop and looked up a clearer image. A private estate. One of his master's or something else? She didn't know or care, all that mattered was that it was close. She had to find him.

Chapter Twenty-Three

With Stars and Wonder in Your Eyes

He couldn't suppress how much he missed Harper. His master's pats weren't enough anymore. He missed her in a way he hadn't understood was possible, even while having missed her for years. It had been one hurt amongst a myriad. Now it had a name and a face. He hated that she worried, that he couldn't even visit her dreams anymore. He could only hope being a Good Cat would mean Master let him go back, or One messed up as she inevitably did. So long as none of his humans got hurt. Harper was family. Fionn didn't want the flashes of memory. He did want—*need*—her.

It wasn't a hole anyone else could fill, but a little of the loneliness abated as Fionn prepared to portal to Dayo's art party, having completed the ritual to his master's satisfaction. The address on the invite Dayo had shown him meant nothing to Fionn. Portals didn't work with human alphanumeric codes and young names imposed on land older than their language. Instead, he concentrated on Dayo—the way he sounded, his art, his scent, all the little things Fionn noticed in the dreamscape and in the wakening. He asked for the portal to drop him somewhere unseen about a mile away, conscious of the fact he was supposed to be admitted, not just show up inside.

As Dayo promised, the gatekeeper let Fionn in and pointed him up a long driveway towards the house. The person on the door there frowned at him, and Fionn shrank back into his hood, afraid they'd seen his ears.

"May I take your ... coat?" There was a pause before the last word and Fionn realised the sneer was not for him being a cat but for him being dressed incorrectly.

"Um, no. Thank you. Maybe I'll go wait outside for Dayo to be free. Could someone let him know I'm here, please? Tell him there's no rush." Fionn cringed.

The doorsen gave a curt nod. "I think that would be for the best, *sir*." They ushered Fionn out through ornate French doors into a garden given life by dogwood, croci, and snowdrops. Breath hung like finest lace in the air, vanishing quickly. Fionn hugged his hoodie around him. He hated cold, but he'd put up with it if it meant five minutes with his dreamer. Five minutes with a friend. Though his time as part of Harper's household had been short, he missed all of them intensely. Except Heresy. Heresy could go sit on the volcano under Lincoln Cathedral.

Dayo ran out and swept Fionn into a spinny hug that left him dizzy. "Sorry, should've mentioned there's a dress code." He fussed the collar of a white button-up shirt. His jacket had an artistic flare, with brightly coloured Ankara flashes on the jacket lapels and matching bowtie. Fionn wanted to tug the tie off. It reminded him too much of his collar, even though humans wore similar at parties his master attended.

Seeing where his gaze was drawn, Dayo tugged an end of it and let the material hang loose around his neck. "Sorry. Don't like the damned thing anyway. You can take yours off, no one will know."

He reached out, but Fionn jerked back. His would never undo or come off. He didn't want it to. Without it, he was a useless stray. With it, he could help his master nurture the country.

Dayo's hand dropped to Fionn's elbow instead and he looped their arms together. "Fancy a walk? I need a break from that lot."

Fionn huddled closer. It was like having his own personal sunny patch—a heat and a light in the dark, frostbitten garden where mist slunk around their ankles like a guilty cat.

Fionn *was* a guilty cat, but he didn't care.

"Do you want me to grab my coat for you?" Dayo asked.

"No." Fionn wrapped an arm around his friend's waist so he wouldn't leave. "I'm okay. You're hot."

An enigmatic smirk flashed across Dayo's face. "Thank you."

"I did an *oop* again, didn't I?"

"Yeah, but I like what you meant better."

They turned a corner and the high hedgerow cut off the last of the light from the house. A shudder ran through Fionn.

"You okay?" Dayo stopped again, turning to face Fionn, though their bodies didn't move apart. "We can go back if you'd rather."

Fionn bit back another impulsive 'no.' "It's up to you. I'm taking you away from your friends and people who want to admire you and your art."

"They'll all be there later, for the live art thing. Right now, I want to keep getting to know you. But if you're uncomfortable or cold, we can go back. Like I said, we can be here as friends or you can be my date. Either way, I want to look after you."

Fionn flushed. His heart was beating too fast, and the tingling intensified the longer Dayo looked at him like that. It wasn't like when Harper said she wanted to look after him. That was cosy, like a cuddle. This sparked like embers flying from a crackling fire that a single breath of oxygen might fan to a roar.

"I'm not uncomfortable or too cold." Subtle magic warmed the air a degree or two. "I just … don't like the dark."

Dayo's eyes widened in concern. "And I brought you out to the darkest corner possible. I'm sorry. We'll go—"

"No." This time, Fionn couldn't hold it back. "If we go back, we can't see the stars. It's so cloudy at home, and we don't have many windows, sometimes it can be weeks without stars unless …" *Unless we need star magic for a powerful spell and I clear the clouds so we can talk to them.*

"Unless?"

"Unless I sneak away, like now. Like I do to art galleries. If it's not too cold, sit and look at stars with me?"

Dayo's look softened. "I'd like that very much. Do you know much about them? You seem like the sort who would." Unspoken worry crinkled the corners of his eyes.

"A little. Not as much as I'd like." Fionn let Dayo lead him over to a carved wooden bench under an archway. In the summer, it would've been festooned with flowers. Even in winter the twiggy hedges on either side sheltered it from view and the worst of the breeze. "I know some people spend years and years learning them. I think I could do that and never run out of new things to explore. Did you find that with your art learns?"

Dayo leant back, gently easing Fionn with him so the cat's head rested on his shoulder. He leant his cheek against it, curling around Fionn in a reassuring, feline way. "Yeah. Uni was amazing. We had access to all these studios for painting, sculpture, photography, anything you can think of. I could go in after lunch, blink, and it would be three in the morning. I do that now." He chuckled. "But it was even easier there. Everything I could possibly want was to hand, and there were almost always other people around. Teachers, other students, people to show me if I was getting frustrated or to bounce ideas off ..."

Fionn sighed happily, gazing up at the stars while basking in the sun. Dayo's joy and love of art were apparent in every word, and excited energy hummed beneath his skin.

They sat with their feet tucked up and twisted around each other like misshapen pretzels. When Dayo had talked about uni for a while, he asked Fionn about stars again, and Fionn told him stories of constellations and heroes, while listening to the song the stars sang for them.

Dayo twisted on the bench, contemplating Fionn as he talked until he stuttered to an embarrassed halt halfway through a tale.

"I'm sorry. I'm wittering." Fionn's fingers automatically reached for a tail that wasn't there and ended up fiddling with the cuff of Dayo's sleeve instead.

"No sorries. I like your stories," Dayo said. "I like watching the stars with you. May this be one of the thousand ways I paint you? With stars and wonder in your eyes?"

Fionn squirmed and lost the battle to resist closing his eyes. He wasn't worthy of being painted.

"Fi?" Dayo's questioning tone and the finger tucked under his chin brought Fionn back to reality. Or delusion because there was no way this could be reality. "Do you know what kissing is? The flirting kind. Not a cheek kiss, like before, but here?" A thumb traced over his lower lip, the light touch intensifying the ache and sending Fionn's heart racing again.

"*Mhmm.*" Fionn bit his lip, eyes downcast. "I know. Harper told me. Lots of kinds of soft feels kisses. But this is ... I think, the kind that leaves people achy and wanting. Excited feels kisses. Extra special. I liked the soft feels kiss before. I think excited kissing ... it might ... feel nice." *Very, very nice.* "Is that selfish?"

"Not when I want to kiss you too." Dayo's thumb traced over Fionn's cheekbone, then he carefully cupped Fionn's face in his palm. "And I really, really want to kiss you so long as it's what you want, too. We can stop at any point. May I?"

"Please." The whispered word held a decade of pain, the need to be desired and vanity of thinking anyone could ever want a broken cat.

Fionn took a shaky breath and closed his eyes. Soft lips gently touched his. Not hesitant. Cautious. Letting him decide to lean into it or pull away. The former easily won as Fionn pressed their lips more firmly together.

The arm around his waist pulled him closer and Fionn contoured his body against Dayo's. Hot. Achy. Very, very, *very* good. Fingers tangled in his hair, curled where he liked to be scritched. The ghost of cat ears and tail went unobserved as Fionn's consciousness was wrapped up in smells and touches. As the kiss deepened, a deep purr rumbled through him.

The kiss eventually paused, lips close enough for breath and words to mingle. Fionn basked in Dayo's smile, warm like the sun, even with his eyes closed.

"I like making you purr." Dayo's words were accompanied by soft touches through Fionn's hair and along his hip that kept the purr going. "Pretty kitty-boy. May I kiss you again?"

The acknowledgement of both his natures cracked something deep inside Fionn. Dayo was unaware of his true nature, or he would've hurt Fionn by now, but the artist's eye could see through him as clearly as Harper's Sight. He longed to be closer, eagerly nuzzling in for more soft kisses.

"D? Dayo? You out here?" Their host's voice was faint somewhere in the direction of the long lawn, on the other side of a bushes.

Fionn's ear twitched. He yanked back, restoring the glamour, panic crashing through the thin shield of pleasure that had momentarily allowed him to forget the real world.

"It's okay. We're not doing anything wrong. I wouldn't let anyone hurt you even if we were." Dayo stroked his head like he was calming a disturbed animal. His eyes were locked on Fionn's, and his fingers didn't poke or prod for the banished ears. Fionn let out a deep sigh. Dayo hadn't noticed, but kissing was obviously dangerous.

"Dayo? Get your butt out here. I know you've ditched the party to canoodle in one of your favourite hidey holes, but I need you to get back in there. You're not here to drink my booze for free."

Dayo grimaced, then raised a hand to his lips to call back, "I'm here, Jade. No one is canoodling in a hidey hole, and I'm not drunk." He rolled his eyes at Fionn like they shared some joke. Fionn wasn't sure what it was, but he did his best to smile back. The shadow passed over Dayo's face again and Fionn wondered what cloud cast it over his sunshine. As Jade rounded the corner, Dayo bounced to his feet.

"Not canoodling, hey?" She raised an eyebrow as she smirked at the two of them. Fionn wasn't sure what the word meant. Her look translated well enough. He blushed, studying his toes.

"This is *not* a hidey hole." Dayo dodged the question. He offered Fionn his hand, and the cat took it uncertainly. An arm wrapped around his shoulders steadied him. If they'd been doing something the owner of the house disapproved of, Dayo wouldn't let her hit him.

"Did you forget you're painting tonight or do you just find your boyfriend more interesting?" Jade asked as she ushered them back towards the house.

"He's not my boyfriend. He's my ... did we settle whether this was a date or not?" Dayo turned to Fionn, who couldn't entirely keep the hurt off his face. Tears stung his eyes for a wound deeper than any knife cut. Not friends? Dayo had said they could go as friends or it could be a date. Fionn hadn't realised the latter meant not being friends.

"Fi, are you okay? Did I ... offend you?" The hurt and defiance were back in Dayo's eyes, looks Fionn didn't know what to do with. The arm slipped from his shoulders, leaving him cold inside and out.

"No. I'm sorry. Just a headache." *You said to ask you if I was confused again, but I think that might make it worse. I don't like the way your friend is looking at me. I wish Harper was here.*

They walked back to the house in anxious silence.

"I've set up your stuff in the drawing room." Jade glanced between the two men, neither of them looking at each other. Fionn was impressed that someone would make a whole room solely for drawing, though it seemed painting in it was allowed as well.

"You've got about half an hour to get a drink and make sure you've got everything. Thought it might take longer to fish you out of the bushes. If you've any business to wrap up, you've got time. Just keep it quiet."

Dayo glared at her, though Fionn wasn't sure why. He pinched the bridge of his nose; the headache wasn't a lie. Between the glamour and the rollercoaster of confusion, his brain felt swollen enough to leak out of whatever ears he happened to be wearing.

"Fi, Fionn, come in and sit down for a minute? Have some water?" Dayo's hand on the small of his back guided Fionn into a dark wood-panelled room. Near the middle, an easel was set up with painting supplies next to it and semi-circles of chairs around it like a miniature theatre. On the wall it was facing was a long painting covered by a simple white sheet.

Dayo kicked off his shoes and sat on the edge of an ottoman, feet tucked up beneath him. "Are you mad I said you aren't my boyfriend? Because you're not, you know. A couple of dates and a kiss doesn't give you some magical power of owning me."

Ouch. The knife twisted in Fionn's gut. He lowered his gaze, chin tucked almost to his chest, and knelt on the floor. "I'm sorry I thought we were friends. I didn't ... I misunderstood ..." Tears trickled down his cheeks, and he wanted nothing more than to shift and portal home. He squeezed his eyes closed, clinging to the glamour. He mustn't shift. He mustn't even glow. "When you said I could come as your date or your friend, I didn't realise you were asking me to choose one or the other. I didn't realise kissing meant we weren't friends. I misunderstood what Harper told me."

"Damn. Fi, get off the floor."

Dayo knelt in front of him. He was going to get hit. He was certain and much as he wanted to be brave, he flinched away from it.

"I've done it again. Assumed you knew something you don't. What do you think 'boyfriend' means?"

What else could it mean? "A boy who is your friend."

Dayo leant against the ottoman, head flopped back on the cushioned seat. "I'm sorry. Boyfriend is ... complicated. It's more like this exclusive thing with all these hidden rules. We *are* friends. Kissing doesn't mean we are or we aren't. Not to me. I like kissing you, Fi. You don't see it, but you're special. I'm clumsy and I forget stuff and it would be so, so easy for me to break you that I'm scared to even think about it. I don't want to. I can't be your boyfriend. I've tried, a few times, and it always ends up with people hurting. Yeah, I've not picked the best ones, but in the end, it was my fault too. I want to be your friend, and I want to keep kissing you. If you want to learn more, I'll happily be the one to teach you, 'cause you should know about your body and get to enjoy it. That doesn't mean I'm your boyfriend. Friend is better."

The whirling words resisted being sorted into sensible sentences. "You want to be friends like go to art galleries together or get drinks and talk or look at stars?"

Dayo's lips quirked in a half smile. "Yeah. And make a safe place for you, because I think you need one."

"Harper's is safe." *Though I can't go there right now.* "You don't need to do anything for me."

"You say that, but you keep leaving for something dangerous. I can't offer you as much as she can, I know. I still want to be safe for you."

Fionn smiled. "I appreciate that, and I do feel safe with you. Very. I want to be safe for you too."

"You are." Dayo reached over to stroke his hand. "What do you want for the rest of tonight?"

"To be friends, and support you," Fionn answered promptly. That bit was easy.

"With or without kissing?"

He hesitated, but the selfish cat in him won out. "With? If it wasn't too onerous. Unless you see someone you want to kiss more, which is very fair and probably most people. If that happens, I'll take myself home out of the way, like at the bar."

"Fi, I'm not going to shack up with someone else in the middle of our date, or friend outing, or whatever we're calling it. I'm not going to tell you to go away so I can make out with someone else. No matter what you hear, I wouldn't do that. I'm here with *you* tonight. I want to keep getting to know you, even if it means *not* getting to do excited feels stuff. I can survive a night without."

"People will be coming in soon …" Fionn looked to the door, clear disappointment on his face.

"Kiss for luck?" Dayo leant closer.

"You don't need luck. You may have kisses." Fionn leant in the rest of the way to press their lips together. Dayo's arm around his waist drew him closer, and he sank into the pleasant sensation that nothing in the world existed outside of the two of them.

Chapter Twenty-Four

Living the Dream

The rattle of the doorhandle shattered the moment. Fionn jumped back. His lips, his fingers, every part of him yearned for more, even though he didn't know what 'more' was.

"Time to be put on display." Dayo gave him a wry smile as chattering people came in. "Promise you'll be here when I'm done?"

"I love watching you paint." *I could watch you do anything.* "I'll be here for nice words and hand holds and kisses, and whatever else date night means."

"Dangerous promise." The mischief in Dayo's eyes made Fionn's knees do a funny jelly thing, like when the castle made a miniature of itself for dessert and the real walls wobbled for days.

With the chairs mostly taken, Fionn moved to a corner where he could hear the art more clearly than in the midst of shuffling patent leather and the coarse rub of pearls. He found a place where Dayo could see him, at least until the art haze descended, so his promise was being kept. It wouldn't override the collar he nervously fingered, nonetheless he hoped the oath would let him resist longer if a call came.

Jade stood next to Dayo with one hand on his shoulder and the other raised in the air. The crowd quieted.

"Thank you all for coming this evening."

"Happy to come drink your champagne any time, Jade," a voice called from the back.

Jade rolled her eyes and waited until the tittering subsided. "As you're all aware, the Langley family has long been a patron of local arts and artists. Many of you were here for January's fine pottery throwing. I am pleased to announce that the vase created raised three thousand pounds for the Yorks Arts Society and a thousand pounds equivalent of patronage for the potter's business."

There was a smattering of polite applause, and a lady in a broad black-and-white hat elegantly inclined her head.

"Tonight's offering is a little different to usual. A substantial donation has been made up front, though I have been asked to keep the donation and value anonymous."

A ripple of chatter surfed the crowd as they looked at each other, wondering which of them wouldn't want to boast about such a thing. There was a prickle at the back of Fionn's neck, like he was being watched. But who would be looking at *him*? He quickly checked—his ears were still glamoured away. One figure blurred as Fionn's gaze skimmed over them, and he forced his eyes back. They were fuzzy, like the mistlings or like a whole body made of Heresy. Even trying to look at them worsened his headache. As soon as he looked away, the mystery of it faded to a faint niggle. They weren't the one looking.

Harper was. Fionn peered around but couldn't see her, yet the presence was unmistakable. His collar didn't react, so whatever capacity she was there in, she couldn't see him. Or See him.

She had a vision of art being created in a library.

The bookcase-lined walls of the so-called drawing room would certainly count. Harper wasn't there; somehow her Sight left enough of a fingerprint on the future event that he could sense her. *No, no, no. Harper's artist can't be my dreamer. I won't let him be. I won't let him get hurt.*

"... this stunning yet troubled painting from early 18th century Italy." Jade whipped the sheet off the painting, and Fionn jaw dropped. It was much more detailed, of course, but the form was the same as Harper's sketch. A woman with arcane objects scattered around her and a hippogriff behind. Which meant the dreamwalker was coming. Or was already here.

Fionn turned back to the fuzzy figure. He couldn't make out any features. The harder he studied them, the harder it was to breathe. He scrabbled at his collar. He had to stop this. He couldn't let Dayo paint. The arty haze Fionn loved to experience was the same dreamscape link that would let the possession in.

Static zipped down his spine. It froze him like he'd been plunged into electrical current. No matter the thrashing panic inside, he couldn't move.

He couldn't even let go of the glamour. The sight of the real him would stop the painting, he had no doubt. It might get him killed, however it was a better fate than watching Dayo's mind and soul be taken, and each of the people in there with him. But he couldn't. Something with all the force of his master's orders held him in place. *Maybe to stop me being perceived by Harper's vision?*

"Tonight, we shall watch the transformation from old to new, how our visions of the world change, and how we can view historic art with fresh eyes." Jade continued her introduction as though nothing was happening. "Ifedayo Gbadamosi, he/him, grew up right here in York, attended York Art College with me, and went on to study at the University of Chelsea in London. Luckily for the north, he has recently returned home and currently has an exhibition at the York Art Gallery. Once completed, these paintings will become part of that exhibition until the end of its run, when they shall go into the private collection of the anonymous benefactor. Without further ado, I shall leave you in Dayo's skilled and capable hands." There was a smirk on her face as she said it, not dissimilar to her look in the garden, and a few people laughed like her words had some double meaning.

Fionn was powerless to do anything but watch the bright brush strokes as Dayo gradually slipped into some space between dreamscape and wakening.

If I can do nothing from here, maybe I can move more freely there.

He couldn't hold the glamour and straddle the dreamscape, but he'd already tried to let go of it anyway. He could remain conscious enough of his physical body to keep it immobile, and to return quickly and portal away. If whatever froze him let him portal. Whatever the risks, the potential to save Dayo was worth it, even if it meant killing their friendship.

Fionn slipped into the colours of the dreamscape.

Straddling was always strange. He both had and didn't have a physical body. He sank deeper in, until almost all physical sensation was left behind and he was a hair's breadth from slumber. He needed as much of himself, of his magic, here as he could muster if he was to chase off a powerful dreamwalker.

As always, Dayo's dream was radiant, even though it was closer to a daydream than a real dream. He stalked around it, looking for other presences. If the others in the room were close to dreaming, he couldn't sense them. Only Harper and Dayo ever stood out. If the dreamwalker came for Dayo like Fionn suspected they'd come for the others, he'd be waiting, sharp claws ready.

Fionn's mind was swept up in Dayo's dream. Only it wasn't Dayo's dream. It had been transplanted into his mind. Fionn knew a manufactured dream when he experienced one, they were the bread and butter of his trade. This one was simultaneously brilliant and awful. It was so cleverly crafted he might not have realised it was a fake if it weren't for the fact he knew Dayo's dreams better than his own. Fine tendrils wrapped into every part of his brain so that it lay over the other man like a skintight mask. It reminded Fionn of the illegal Venetian masks at the Soul Trader Market. They became part of their host, fusing to flesh just as this dream was fused to Dayo's brain.

"My dreamer." Static rippled the abstract colours, and spikes of lightning crackled along neural pathways.

"My dreamer." A second presence hovered in the dreaming. Fionn blinked and shook his head. No. Two other presences, fused together almost as seamlessly as a carnival mask to cheekbones.

Fionn crouched, his shadow a hulking wildcat with Dayo safely wrapped in its core. The magic of the dream was stronger than his, and it scared him. He'd never met someone whose dream magic was stronger. Scratch that. He'd never met another proper dreamwalker. Just creatures who could do it on instinct. Maybe he was actually a very poor dreamwalker. Fionn mewled and cringed back with his ears flat. The urge to roll over and expose his belly was difficult to ignore. No. That was the dream trying to subdue him, to take Dayo.

"Mine." Fionn hissed again, puffing his fur to look bigger.

Laughter echoed through Dayo's dream. Not the zoomy, arty laughter of their usual play. The sharp, cold laughter of a blade tapping against metal.

"We need him. Magic needs him. You prepared the land, made it fertile, now we plant the seeds. Fight us and you will be condemning your folk to a slow and painful death. Life needs magic just as it needs oxygen or water. You don't like water, do you? It is our blood, and this dreamer welcomes it."

The sea roared and the landscape shifted to a long, golden beach with turquoise waves washing over it. Fionn hissed and jumped back. This *was* Dayo's dream, though not one he'd entered before. It had the haze of a scene never really experienced and the home-longing of a story passed down or seen in photos. Frothy-peaked waves surged up the shore, snapping at Fionn's paws and twinkling his fur with salty spray. They threatened to plunge him into another dream, a nightmare, his own. He backed up the beach. The moon dragged the water inland until there was nowhere left to run. He closed his eyes and braced himself for the worst.

Sunrays stroked warmth through Fionn's fur, so like Dayo's fingers. The water may want to divide them, but Dayo loving something Fionn found scary didn't make Fionn unwanted. It wasn't his dreamer's fault he'd been locked in a leaky crate and shipped downriver. Dayo didn't know, would never do that to him, and Fionn wasn't going to let his dreamer go without a fight.

He leapt into the towering wave with a yowl of defiance. Water slicked his fur flat against his body. He didn't need to breathe in a dream, but the other dreamwalker made the dreamscape more real than Fionn could fight. His lungs burned and his skin writhed with the sensation of Evil Wet. He flailed, throwing every bit of concentration into finding his foe. Though he couldn't see them, their energy crackled through the dreamscape sky like skitters of lightning. If he could find the core of their power, he could attack them directly. Until recently, he'd thought it impossible to harm someone in the dreamscape, until the Somnia had shown a powerful dreamwalker could kill there.

Claws hooked into something, maybe seaweed, maybe cloth. It tore as he scrabbled for purchase. Hopelessness dug into his heart even though he kept fighting.

"Stay, pretty kitty?"

The sea froze. Fionn's ears pricked. Of course. It was Dayo's dream, this sacrilege of an invasion notwithstanding. And Dayo wanted him and not them. A bubble formed around Fionn, his magic fully becoming part of the other man's dream. Sunlight sparkled through the water to dry his fur.

"My kitty? Stay with me?"

Your kitty. Of course. Fionn wasn't fighting from the outside to protect his dreamer. He was inside. Wanted. Dayo wasn't his dreamer. He was Dayo's cat.

The other dreamwalker may be two entities all mixed together, but he wasn't alone either.

Fionn sent tendrils of magic outside the protective bubble, logically seeking the other souls. They attempted to evade him, however there was nowhere in Dayo's dream they could hide.

The landscape changed again. Bright splodges of rainbow went far beyond the horizon. They tasted of bubblegum, ice cream, and chilli. Words and experiences Fionn only knew from Dayo's dreams. They sang with strong beats. Scents of heat, paint, and tea. The colours absorbed into his fur and dyed it. He was part of Dayo's dream, as he had been many times before, both in reality and when he was far away and Dayo dreamt of a white cat that wanted to play. A human face with cat ears flashed in a turquoise puddle. He dreamt of him as he'd drawn him. His true self.

Enemy eyes scraped over the chaotic dream, their control lost. Fionn stalked them, a cat with prey in sight. The tangled entity stood out. Their colours were bright but fake. They were a parasite, a graffiti splashed across a masterpiece. Fionn gathered magic around him like paint mixed on a palette.

He pounced.

Chapter Twenty-Five

Too Late Again

"Can't you go any faster, Saqib?" Grace asked while Harper sat in the back and fretted. She wanted to echo Grace's sentiment, but her sensible brain kept it locked inside.

"Not legally," Saqib replied testily. "I said you could only sit in the front if you didn't tell me how to drive."

"I can tell you from the back as well. There's no one around. It won't matter if we go faster."

"Unlike your reckless attitude, I happen to be a good, law-abiding citizen who doesn't want to get his car seized, especially as it's the only one in the household."

"A good, law-abiding citizen who lives with two witches," Harper pointed out.

Grace snorted.

"Okay, admittedly 'good' and 'law-abiding' aren't always the same thing." Saqib smiled and relaxed, but the speedometer didn't creep even a hair over forty.

When they reached the estate, it was eerily quiet. The gatekeeper proved even more frustrating than Guard patrols and was even less convinced about the 'anonymous tip' about another possession. Grace had downplayed it as extremely unreliable when talking to the Guard to dissuade them from accompanying the group. Now, she played up the urgency. Eventually, they agreed to call up to the main house.

They hurried back and opened the gate.

"No response from the house. Security will accompany you." The gatekeeper ushered the group through. Worry sludged in Harper's gut.

Four armed guards accompanied them up to the house, making Harper more nervous than any supernatural encounter. Guns were illegal for normal citizenry. She wondered if the police knew there was a miniature army out here. Possibly. Judging from the land and size of the house, the family was rich enough to pay people to keep out of their business.

The lights on the ground floor were all on. A few staff milled about, tidying or preparing snacks. The guests, they were informed, were all in the drawing room for a live painting exhibition. When the word 'painting' confirmed her fears, Harper's heart plummeted.

Grace waved the security team back. "This is my area of expertise, so I'm taking point. Unless you want to risk accidentally shooting your employer's guests, I suggest you stay out here until called for."

There were some glares and grumblings as the four took a step back, forming a defensive perimeter around the drawing room doors. Harper followed Grace, machete drawn, and Saqib crept behind her clutching a vial of sandalwood. It had saved them all at the auction and, as Grace's theory went, even if the incense itself did nothing, broken glass on the floor and an eyeful of dust were effective barriers against most things.

A strong sense of déjà vu hit Harper as she stepped into the room. This was where she'd Seen the dreamwalker strike again. Her eyes were drawn to the wall where the cursed painting hung. Near it, just as in her vision, a man painted furiously. Fionn's artist-dreamer.

Fionn was nowhere to be seen, not so much as a whisker or hair. When Harper switched to magical Sight, there was still no trace of him. Dayo gleamed like Christina, and faint traces of purple magic linked him to the audience. Unlike with the opera singer, Harper didn't get the sense of it being active. It hung, lacklustre, like unhandled reins waiting for a touch to urge the horse to a charge.

All the seats save three were taken. One was probably the host's, assuming she was the one standing near the painter, another possibly Fionn's. The third could've been spare, but a faint energy crackled around it, and she could See the vaguest outline of a dark-hooded person there.

Grace made her way straight to where Dayo was painting.

"Hey. Art boy. Wake up." She grabbed his arm, but he yanked it back with surprising strength. He resumed painting without a word or a look.

"C'mon. Don't make me knock you out too." Grace hesitated, a rare indecision.

"Do it." Harper gave her a sharp nod. The small upside of Fionn not being around was that he therefore didn't see Grace clock the guy he had a crush on. Saqib caught Dayo before he could tumble out of the chair. A murmur rumbled through the crowd as they emerged from their daydream.

"Who are you?" The woman Harper assumed was the host glared at Grace. "How did you get in?"

"They're with us." The head of the security team spoke up from his position by the door.

"Grace De Santos, she/her. We're here on behalf of the Council of Faiths." Grace held out a hand as she introduced the rest of their group.

"Jade Langley, she/they." The host shook Grace's hand with a confused frown. "What happened to Dayo?"

"Whatever's been getting people in York got him too," Harper said. She'd dampened her Sight when everyone awoke but kept an eye on the audience who were watching them like they were part of the entertainment.

Jade folded her arms and took half a step back. "You're telling me Dayo brought some kind of curse with him?" She glanced around. "He was here with someone. Weird guy who didn't dress right and had strange eyes. It might've been him." She gestured to her security team, who were corralling the guests back into the lounge, and two peeled off to search.

Harper schooled her face to stoicism at the implication Fionn caused this. He wouldn't hurt anyone deliberately, his dreamer least of all. She hated that Jade's suspicions would end up in a Guard file. It would be even less safe for Fionn to go out in human form.

"I doubt it's anything, or anyone, Dayo brought with him," Harper said instead. "The previous attacks have all been remote and related to the actions, in this case painting, rather than the specific person."

Saqib piped up, "Though I'm still investigating, there doesn't seem to be anything physically or socially connecting the victims, other than their involvement in the arts."

"What will happen to Dayo?" Concern cracked Jade's haughty façade.

"We'll take him some place we can look after him." Grace softened and placed a hand on the other woman's arm. "We're searching for a way to break this curse. In the meantime, our doctors will take care of him, and he'll be kept safe."

"Safe from the Guard?" Jade's gaze sharpened again.

"Safe from everything we possibly can," Grace said carefully.

"I'm not involved with a faith myself but ..." Jade hesitated, her eyes sweeping over all three of them. "... rumour is that the Council and Guard don't always agree."

"That's true. Everyone has their own opinions on what is best for the country." Grace picked her way through the minefield of the conversation, and Harper was glad it was her sister and not her having it. "We won't let your friend disappear. Visitors would be unwise, but his family will be notified of his condition."

Jade bit her lip. "You presumably have to file a report with the Guard, right?"

"We're sharing pertinent details with them."

"Would you consider the location pertinent, or only the activity?"

Grace smiled slightly. "I believe the activity is the key factor here. No need for anyone to waste time investigating and interviewing clueless people."

"Is there a guest list?" Harper asked. "With the event taking place after dark, you presumably took IDs or got travel permissions?"

Jade's smug mouth quirked. "Let's just say I know certain people and the house here is big enough for most guests to stay with us until the end of curfew. The only person I don't know is Dayo's date. He didn't tell me he'd invited one, and I didn't get a good look."

"May we have that list?" Grace asked.

"There is no list." Jade met Grace's glower with folded arms and an equally glacial stare. "Everyone here was my guest. I trust them not to be involved in this sorcery."

Harper snuck a glance at the chair where the shadowed figure had lurked. Without her Sight, it was identical to every other burgundy-cushioned seat. She could hardly describe what she'd Seen and ask who it was. *If I ever see Fionn again, maybe he'll know. The dreamwalker wasn't at the Opera House, were they? Were they watching the whole thing and I missed them?*

Frustration and impatience with herself gnawed at Harper, though she kept her face calm as she addressed Jade again. "We'll come back to you if we need to know who was here. However, we *will* need those paintings. Where did you get the original?"

Concern flashed over Jade's face, then confusion. "I ... don't know." She rubbed her head. "It was an anonymous donation. Even from me. I was contacted by a go-between. She was a striking woman, I'd remember if I'd met her before and I certainly haven't. She stated that several of my regulars were also regulars at a salon attended by her benefactor, and she'd heard I was well-connected in the field. She said she was working on behalf of someone who wanted a modern version of an old painting that had been in their family for a number of years and was important though not to their tastes. The money was good, and I thought my guests would enjoy something slightly different. I had no idea it would lead to this. I swear. It wasn't even Dayo doing it originally. I had someone else booked, but they saw his stuff at the gallery and asked for a switch. Do you think she was responsible? That she put something in this painting?"

"Can you describe her?" Harper pulled out a notebook.

"I'll do you one better," Jade said. "I went to art college too. I'll draw her."

Harper and Saqib collected samples from the room while Grace called for backup in the form of a Council ambulance for Dayo, and Jade sketched. Tucked behind an ottoman, Harper found a pile of clothes including the purple cat hoodie AJ had bought Fionn. She stuffed the outfit in her bag.

Harper kept a surreptitious eye out for Fionn himself but still nothing, in either shape. The clothes indicated he'd taken the risk of shifting, but it wasn't like him to have vanished unless his master commanded it. Dread crashed down around her like heavy snow.

It plummeted further when Jade finished her portrait. Harper was sure the face from the other woman's sketch would be seared in her memory forever as too hot breath had mingled between them, lips almost touching. The hare-shifter who was Fionn's counterpart and nemesis. One.

Chapter Twenty-Six

Not England

Fionn awoke somewhere that was Not England. Wakefulness came quickly, and he leapt to his feet. *Four of them. Cat-shaped. Good.* Sunlight poured through tall windows and everything it touched turned to gold: each spindle on the four-poster bed, the delicate patterns of waves and shells on the veneer of the wardrobe, the caressed-smooth handles on the doors, and the rows of bolts and locks.

How he left England, and why he wasn't dead, were less pressing mysteries than how to get out. Unless he *was* dead. Many of the folk believed in an afterlife. The way the floor rolled almost imperceptibly didn't feel real. There was no sense of earth beneath, warm and full of life. Instead there was … A shiver poofed Fionn's fur from whiskers to tail. *Water.* Storm-tossed ships and the haunting songs of sirens mocked him from paintings on the wall.

A groan pivoted Fionn's attention to the bed; a sound like having done too much magic and given oneself a bad headache. He dashed under it and crouched, belly low to the floor, tail wrapped around him and ears back. For the first time in his life, he wished it was darker, more cramped. *They won't check under the bed. They won't …*

"Serenità?" The confused, scared mewling of waking up next to someone you love having disappointed them. A feeling Fionn was familiar with.

"Cossa xe sucesso[1]?" Sharp as nails on a blackboard, swiftly followed by a slap. He knew enough Latin to recognise it was a similar language, though the actual question was lost on him.

The figure who spoke first, dropped out of the bed onto their knees, inches away from Fionn's quivering whiskers. The bed creaked as they bowed over it. "Serenità, scuséme." It wasn't difficult to recognise the apology, no matter the language.

"Monà, no rispondi mia cussì," the second voice snapped. The hunched figure kneeling cringed, as did Fionn. Dodging answering a question was a very fae problem and one he often skated the line of, especially with his master. More of late.

A second pair of feet swung off the bed. Each toenail was bright red with a swirling gold pattern. *Pretty*, wandered idly across Fionn's mind though it brought none of the cosy warmth as when he thought it about Harper or Dayo. Instead, the 't's poked into his brain, hurting. A warning. Pretty was a skin-deep trap.

"Refà el ponte. Subito."

"Sì, Serenità."

As the second speaker moved away from the bed, more of her bare legs were revealed. She opened a low drawer decorated with enamel waves and pulled out star-flecked tights. After another moment of rustling, a skirt tumbled past her knees, short in the front and trailing in the back. The many layered gossamer glimmered with magic sewn in.

While Serenità dressed, the original speaker remained kneeling, naked, by the bed, their long red-streaked hair hanging limp to their knees. They jerked as their master snapped her fingers. Fionn was torn between wanting to scratch them for hurting his dreamer and wanting to nuzzle their leg in sympathy for the insecurity that came with disappointing one's master.

After a rapid exchange, Serenità snapped her fingers again and her kneeling pet climbed back into bed. It creaked as Serenità joined them. Fionn flattened himself. Strange smells. Strange noises. He didn't like it, however he was scared to sneak out lest they were less distracted than they sounded. He was afraid to even attempt to portal since he had no idea of where to portal to. They might notice the magic, or he might end up in England. If that happened, he probably couldn't get back.

The noises ended with a frustrated grunt and Serenità stood again, straightening her skirts. Her voice was smug as she wished her pet, "Sogni d'oro," and left.

---

[1] While similar to Italian, this is a separate language specific to the area Fionn has found himself in. It is a real-world language and has been checked by a native speaker.

It took a while for the remaining person to make good on that command. They writhed in the bed with panting breaths and more frustrated grunts, before eventually settling and humming to themselves. Fionn recognised the magic. It was the same he used to put Harper to sleep and to help his master when Insomnia prowled. It didn't work on him, but this person must've found the trick of enchanting themselves. Their consciousness slipped fully into the dreamscape. He wondered if that meant they couldn't straddle both realms as he could, or if whatever magic they did needed them to be fully submerged.

Fionn hunkered down in a cat-loaf, half in the wakening, half in the dreamscape. He hadn't expelled them from Dayo's dream just for them to go straight back. He followed from a distance, as small as he could make himself. Neither their sleeping body nor their skulking consciousness in the dreamscape noticed him. They flashed by dreamers like car lamps whizzing past in the dark. When they awoke two hours later—Fionn awaking with them, sore and stiff beneath the bed—they hadn't found Dayo's dream again.

Satisfied he'd done all he could, Fionn escaped while the dreamwalker refreshed themselves in the bathroom. The bolts hadn't been reapplied after Serenità left, so it was a simple matter of chittering at the main lock to open and dragging the handle down with his paws. The creeping dread knocking on his spine lacked the force of his master's commands. He glanced behind him, searching for the source. From above the bed, a coat of arms bearing a winged lion and a hippogriff segreant stared back at him. He fled into the corridor.

Where his home beneath the Tower of London was dark and sombre, this palace was full of light and art. Yet the same foreboding soaked into the stone and blood-flecked magic shadowed every wall and window. This place lacked the sentience of Fionn's home, but it didn't need sentience for a trap to be sprung. He proceeded carefully, keeping close to walls and sheltering under chairs and tables where he could.

There were other cats around. He could smell them, and there were little signs—a toy lost under a piece of furniture, claw marks on the arm of a chair almost hidden by a cunningly placed plant, a distinct lack of vermin. Fionn doubted they had his intelligence, but he didn't want to meet any and find out. Even an ordinary house pet might alert its guardian about an intruder, and regular cats didn't like him. Though it was less visually obvious than his human form, cats could tell he wasn't one of them.

After a couple of hours of tense scouting, Fionn found a way to sneak out of the palace. A hidden door took him from secular opulence to sacred. Gold adorned marble pillars and sculpted ceiling panels. Art was on every wall and even built into the floor. The cacophony took Fionn's breath away. It was harder to breathe than when he first walked into Dayo's studio. He padded over a hippogriff, reminiscent of the one in the painting, carved in stone on the floor. A chant in Latin wove through the art's song, a voice that disturbed the air not just mind and magic. Fionn slunk between pews to risk a peek at the main altar where a robed lion-shifter blessed Mass. Above, a large cross hung with a winged lion curled at its base.

Having finished their blessing, the werelion—or werehuman if they were born a feline like Fionn was—sniffed the air. Fionn had read about the great cats of Africa who could walk among humans with only their eyes showing their origins. He briefly wondered if they were part of the stories Dayo's grandmother told, and if there was a safe way to ask that.

This one was in a more natural form; a great mane circled his head and his tufted tail swished behind him. His eyes roved the basilica, and Fionn shrank back behind a pew. The lion reverently placed the Eucharist beneath a white cloth and prowled his domain. This time, Fionn didn't stop to worry about his magic being noticed. The lion-shifter already knew someone was there, it was only a matter of time before he was spotted. He scrambled to a door and knocked for a portal. Nothing.

With no time to question it, he sprinted around until he found a door ajar to the sea air. It was a tight squeeze, even for the skinny cat. He escaped and fled into the twisted calli of a terrifyingly water-logged city.

Chapter Twenty-Seven

Behind Enemy Lines

After a wearying forty-eight hours of travel interspersed with border control debates, Harper's initial impression of Venice was disappointment. Far from the glittering spectacle of hedonistic decadence Venice was shunned as, it was a bit worn down, grubby even. On almost every wall, salt-worn bricks peeked between swathes of faded, crumbling stucco. The calli they traversed were dirty and graffitied. Not the pretty, arty kind of graffiti either. Tagged like a human street gang rioted through.

It was also quieter than Harper had imagined. Living in the city, she was used to a background noise of people and traffic, even in the night when electric lights buzzed. Here there were no cars, no roads, no streetlamps, and no people.

Lapping water amplified silence by its muted persistence. Practiced feet made no noise on limestone paving slabs or stepped bridges. Here and there, the limestone continued from underfoot to protect the walls of grand houses. Even these were dark and silent for all they appeared in better condition, and Harper thought they must surely be inhabited.

The fog, which had towered over them on the water as they wended their way between traps and coastguard patrols, now barely reached their ankles. It hung over the water like a bridal veil. Though Harper could See nothing, she wondered what might lie beneath, watching.

Had they already been reported to the dreamwalker, or was their attention so fixed on York that she and Grace could sneak up on them? There had been no new attacks in the two days since the painting possession.

Even with the combination of the archbishop's signature, the stamp of approval from the Council of Faiths, and Lieutenant Albrecht's scrawled permission on Guard embossed stationary with their wax seal, it took almost twenty-four hours to get through security and out of the country.

The ride in the bunks of a produce ship over to France wasn't much more comfortable. At both border controls, the scan for magic made Harper antsy. She tried to keep a calm mien, knowing the nerves were far more likely to give her away than any actual magic detection. If the detectors at border control actually worked, Saqib wouldn't have a job. True to AJ's word, nothing picked up on Heresy in his box in her rucksack. For once, the demon was quiet and stayed put.

After being admitted to France, travel became easier, and they were able to jump on a train without issue. Most of Europe wasn't as heavily locked down as England and allowed sanctioned magic. In some countries, official magician was even considered an honour post.

Almost all immigration to England was of folk fleeing magic, or people enticed with job offers when positions couldn't be filled with those local. Saqib's family fell into both camps. His grandfather had been a neurosurgeon, his grandmother abducted by some kind of fae creature. He'd brought his daughters to England so they would not share his wife's fate, and had been granted residency due to his highly prized skillset.

In Lyon, they switched from train to bus to cross the Alps. Border control was strict, but faster than getting through an airport since there was only one possible destination. Travel by air introduced the risk of people journeying to North America, Japan, or down the west coast of Africa. Italy's views on magic were a little more lenient than France's, though getting back might be trickier. Supernaturals, though a lower caste of citizen, did have some rights unless they broke a law and were shipped off to Venice.

The last leg of the trip was by car. Grace's breakneck driving swerved them back and forth across the road, getting worse the closer they got to their destination. Her knuckles were white around the steering wheel, and Harper's white clutching her seatbelt as she tried not to vomit.

Finally, a stolen boat had brought them to the island itself. They'd moored in a seemingly abandoned canal on the north side as near as possible to Gabriel's last known location.

"Charity said Gabriel's based in an abandoned theatre on the southwest side of the Palazzo Donà gardens. According to the old maps, we should head roughly west from here, but the streets themselves can change."

They continued through the alleys, keeping low as they crossed bridges, lest the winding canals sweep some watchsen past them. No one. Yet Harper couldn't shake the feeling of being watched: a warmth on her back, a sensation of being guarded rather than spied upon.

"Heresy? Can you tell if someone is there?" Harper whispered. Once they'd landed and the need for hiding was over, Heresy freed himself from the magical Faraday cage, greatly relieved to resume his normal seat on Harper's shoulder.

"There is a great concentration of powerful magic over this whole area," Heresy buzzed in her ear. "If one individual's attention is resting upon us, I cannot pick it out."

They kept away from the main canal of the area until they reached a sizeable garden where Harper expected the palazzo grounds to be. The large house was quiet, though as it neared midnight, it could've been that everyone was asleep. Harper and Grace clung to the shadows as they skirted around to make their way along the main canal of the sector. Mist swirled lazily with the sluggish flow of water.

"Harper, look." A static jab to the head made Harper bite back a curse. Her irritation at Heresy quickly faded when she noticed a section of the luminescent vapours that broke and flowed as though routing around a hidden rock beneath the water's surface.

"What's down there?" she asked, but Heresy didn't reply. She watched the spot move closer to the shore. Harper reached back to tap Grace.

A head broke the surface. Dark eyes peered through strands of wet hair. The creature stayed mostly submerged as they watched the two women. A translucent-webbed hand emerged from the water, and beckoned to them.

Harper waved Grace back and knelt near the edge. Her sister's sharp intake of breath spoke of her disapproval, but Harper wasn't afraid of being dragged under. She was almost certain she'd Seen those eyes before.

"Hello. Um, salute? Buonasera?" Suddenly, two days seemed very short and her miniscule Italian extremely inadequate. She hoped Venetian was similar since even the archives hadn't contained a dictionary or phrasebook with the language of the banished islands.

Water bubbled as the creature laughed. They rose higher, exposing their face, neck, and shoulders to the cool night air. It goosed bare skin adorned with the faintest traces of scales. Rivulets of water trickled off black hair.

"Buonasera, sorelle di Gabriel. Sono Lelianna, sono ondina." She inclined her head.

"You know Gabriel? Where is he?" Grace burst out before switching to Spanish and repeating the questions in case that was easier.

"It is not safe to talk here." A frown creased the undine's brow. "Follow me."

She disappeared beneath the water again, the ripple of her movement heading away from the theatre where they had expected to find Gabriel.

"I think we should." Harper grabbed Grace's elbow. "I'm sure she's the one from my vision. Which means she's on our side. Even if I'm wrong, we can't let her go and tell someone we're here."

The undine's head popped up a few meters away, and she beckoned to them before diving down again. Harper thought a foot flicked through the surface of the water.

Grace looked up and down the canal, tight-lipped. "If she's tricking us, don't hesitate, Harp. You know how it is out in the wilds. React fast."

"I've got your back." Harper drew the blade at her waist, more for Grace's comfort than because she believed she might need it.

They followed the ripple down several narrow waterside paths until the creature raised her head again. A sphere of luminescent water rose next to her, and Grace jolted defensively. It hovered in the air, casting a rippling glow over the tiny canal. The undine swam to the shore and rested her folded arms on the path. Harper knelt next to her while Grace stood watch.

"I should introduce myself in your language," the undine said. "My apologies if I am rusty. Until Gabriel came here, it had been a long time since I needed to use my mother's tongue. I am Lelianna, she/her."

"I'm Harper, she/her, and this is Grace, she/her." Harper refrained from mentioning Heresy and, for once, he didn't butt in and introduce himself.

"Where is my brother?" Grace interrupted.

The undine's expression sobered. "The Prigioni Nove attached to the Palazzo. You are here to rescue him, sì?" Her English had a slight Venetian lilt, though Harper wasn't sure she'd notice if she hadn't been expecting it.

"Yes." Grace knelt next to Harper, her grip on her crossbow tight. Harper used a fingertip to nudge the weapon to point down at unoccupied water. "Tell us what happened."

"I did not witness it." Lelianna's eyes followed the crossbow bolt tip warily. "I have heard the public proclamations and the rumours. The polizia came at dusk. Whispers say they were led by one of the Signori della Notte themselves. It is said the human was subdued quickly. I think that is for their own pride. I cannot see Gabriel going quietly."

"Not my brother." Grace cracked a grim smile. "They probably don't want to admit he took a few of them down."

"Masks have the advantage of concealing bruises," Lelianna agreed. "He requested, many moons back, that should anything happen to him, I would watch for you or others of your family. I had not expected you so quickly."

"His last check in was off," Harper said. "Did he know they were coming?"

Lelianna cocked her head as she thought for a moment. "I do not believe so. He was savvy and quick to have survived undetected this long. Had he known they were coming, he would not have been there to be caught. However, he feared something happening to his lover. That may have—"

"Excuse me? His what?" Grace burst out.

"His lover. Did I not use the correct term? The one with whom he—"

"I think you got the term right," Harper said hastily. Even in the low light, she could see Grace's skin darken with a blush. "It's just that Gabriel hadn't told us he was seeing someone, and this seems an unlikely place for him to pick up a date."

"'Pick up a date'? Intriguing phrasing. Gabriel would tell me he was leaving for dates, so yes, I think we all have the same understanding. Do you think the folk here so unlovable that it is inconceivable he care for some of us?"

Harper elbowed Grace before she could blurt out a 'yes.'

"It's … unusual for someone whose family profession is demonhunting to work with magical creatures, *though not unheard of*," Harper emphasised for Grace's benefit. "Dating one is a bit of a surprise, that's all. Unless there are other humans here?"

"If there are, they possess our power." Lelianna looked between the two women on the shore. "I have not met Gabriel's lover. All I know is ze is someone in Serenità's outer circle, and ze is trapped here like I am. Gabriel stayed once his prey was gone in order to free us."

"Sorry. I'm finding this all a bit hard to swallow." Grace glared at the water spirit.

"Your story raises a lot of questions," Harper said a bit more diplomatically, squeezing Grace's arm. "Most importantly, is Gabe's life in danger? Will they—" *torture him?* She choked off, unable to say it.

"Pain has long since been abandoned as a method of gaining accurate information." The undine paused. "I cannot promise he will not be harmed out of spite or entertainment. His trial is at the end of the month, two moons from now. By law, he must be sound enough of mind and body to make his case at it. However, the outcome is already certain. He will be executed once the public spectacle of justice has been fulfilled."

Grace's fist clenched so tight around Harper's, she ground her teeth to keep from grunting.

"We'll get him out well before that," Harper assured her. "We stand a better chance of success if we have more information. Lelianna, can you go back to the beginning? How do you know Gabe?"

"I saved his life," Lelianna said with a shrug. "It is as good a reason as any for him to trust me. If I wanted him dead, I would have left him to the sea or killed him myself while he was weak. He pursued a felon here, one who was executed upon arrival. When he tried to leave on the night of the new moon, the figlie de Scylla surrounded his boat and tipped him into the water."

"Figlie de Scylla? As in Scylla and Charybdis?" Harper asked.

"The daughters of Scylla," Lelianna translated. "Sired by the monster from the black waters of Punta della Dogana. Their frenzy drew attention. The soldati believed it was a gondola under attack, and chased the snakes away. When they realised their mistake—that it was a human boat, an intruder—they called off their efforts to save him. I believe they assumed he had drowned or would bleed out from the wounds inflicted by the daughters, or they would return for the rest of their meal. Those things would have been true, had I not brought him here and aided his recovery."

"Why would you take that risk?" Grace demanded.

"Because I cannot sit by and watch someone die." Lelianna lifted her head, chin jutted out as she met Grace's glare. "The daughters were distant and the soldati's eyes were elsewhere. I swam deep in dark water. The risk was low. Gabriel was also sceptical. I convinced him that not all of those you deem 'supernatural' are as callous and cruel as he expected. It may have helped that he was unable to move much for quite some time and so had no choice but to listen to me." A smile played on her lips. "It helped my English immensely."

"Gabriel's been unable to get away from Venice?" Grace looked at Harper. "Why didn't he tell us he was trapped here?"

"He was not," Lelianna said. "When he was well enough and they would not smell blood in the water, I offered to take him to the main shore myself. It is not so hard to get past the human guards if one swims deep. Once folk have earnt Serenità's trust, it is not unusual for them to come and go, though one must always be wary of those snakes. Initially, he stayed to free me. I am not important enough to have freedom of passage, and I prefer remaining unnoticed. Even those who do visit other places on Serenità's behalf, do so on her leash. Later, Gabriel stayed for both of us; me and his love. He vowed to find a way to take us both out of this place. Though he said England is none too welcoming, there are many places in the world where we may make a home, should we be willing to travel to them."

Despite her fears for Gabriel, Harper couldn't hold back a squeak of excitement. Now she was certain, though she'd had strong suspicions from the moment Lelianna's head crested the water. Just as Harper had known it was safe to tell Saqib, just as she had known the right house to rent as soon as she saw it, she knew Lelianna was the answer to her prayers. She would be the new Ouse.

"What is it?" Grace asked.

"She's the one from the painting."

"The one you Saw yourself—"

"Kissing?" Lelianna's smirking smile was back. "I saw this, too, in the calm waters. I do not have the true gift of water divination my ancestor possessed, but I am not completely without skills. I saw us in la Biblioteca Somersa. Your lover back home need not fear. My kiss can grant you ability to survive the waters, for a short time at least. Gabriel and I have shared a few. Sometimes I help him with his liaisons."

"Do you know why he was worried about zir?" Harper asked, though a selfish part of her wanted to question Lelianna more about this library and their shared vision.

"Something Serenità is making zir do. Gabriel was always hazy about zir position, but something changed this month. It could be the upcoming Bati Marso. The festivities planned are extensive, including the Carnivale Incendio arriving soon. It will remain in this realm until the sun rises on a new year. Most of the Court are involved in the celebrations in some way. Those ways aren't always safe."

Or it could be to do with our problem back in England. Harper exchanged a glance with Grace, who gave a sharp jerk of her head to show she was having the same thought.

"What's Bati Marso?" Grace asked.

"The New Year." Lelianna explained.

"Your new year begins in March?" Harper clapped her hands together. "That makes so much sense."

"It does?" Grace raised an eyebrow.

"Well, don't you think it's odd that our *Sept*ember is month nine and not seven? That *Oct*ober is ten and not eight, et cetera?"

"Before Harper falls down an academic rabbit hole"—Grace poked Harper's arm—"can you show us where Gabriel is imprisoned?"

Lelianna shook her head, spraying them both with droplets of water. "The main waterways around the Palazzo all have resident spirits and guards. I would not be able to get past them."

"Then Harper and I have a job." Grace stood. The cold light in her eyes came from within as much as from the eerie blue magelight the undine cast.

"Grace, we need to prep, do recon. We can't storm a Venetian prison." Harper blocked her path. Lelianna sank back into the water, only her eyes, forehead, and floating hair visible.

"I am not wasting more time while my brother may be tortured," Grace snapped.

Harper took a deep breath, eyes squeezed shut against the sting of tears. "*I know*. He's my brother too. But, Gray, we have to be smart about this. Lelianna said—"

"That he has to be able to stand. You don't need nails, or hands, or arms to stand. You don't need eyes to argue a case."

"Grace, please." Tears streamed down Harper's cheeks. "If we rush in, we could get him killed or hurt even worse."

"*Shush.*" A static jab to the back of her neck made Harper yelp. "I said, *shush*, ignorant witch."

She'd forgotten Heresy was there, balled up at the nape of her neck.

"What is it?" she hissed.

"Someone else approaches."

Chapter Twenty-Eight

Reunion

It might've been hell. While the air was pleasant with a lemony tang of magic, and it was cleaner than home due to the lack of pollution from cars and other human industry, there was water *everywhere*. Buildings ran right to the edge of the path or waterway, with few opportunities for a cat to hide. While some canal bridges had walls, most were of stone pillars rather than solid. Many bridges had no walls at all, exposing his passage to any watchful eyes. Wherever he was, Fionn did *not* like it.

Equally bad was his inability to portal out of this wet horror story. Two knocks. Nothing. Three knocks. Still nothing. Whenever he tried to portal, nothing happened. Even short portals to cross waterways were blocked.

He also wasn't sure if he should be trying to get back. The people who hurt Dayo and threatened Harper were *here*. He just had no idea what to do about that. So he watched from a distance, curving air and water to make lenses for far-seeing. It proved some magics worked, as did his unlocking of the door in Serenità's room. Only portals were forbidden.

He'd seen the one addressed as Serenità several times, mostly around the palace and basilica. Sometimes, she went out on a boat. He followed from the shore when he could. To the magnificent opera house adorned with golden phoenixes. To other churches of veined, heartless marble. To hospitals and schools where children welcomed her with the reverence due a saint.

He wished he could get a message to Harper back home to tell her he'd found the woman from the painting in her vision. The centuries had been kind and Serenità had barely changed. When out of the palace, she always wore a mask, but Fionn had long since learnt to see past such minor inconveniences and her aura sang as her painting had.

Of the other person, the dreamwalker, he saw nothing. While Serenità was as unmistakable as his master's unconcealable power, he wasn't sure he would recognise the dreamwalker again. Their presence had been overwhelmed by hers, even after she left the room. They were more like a puppet than having any real aura of their own, though he suspected that may be because they were superior at concealing their spirit from his dreamwalker senses.

Although Fionn was breaking his agreement with his master to check in every morning, he was not summoned home. His collar zinged and his spine ached, but it was muted, like an electric shock through a feather pillow. Grumbling rather than a direct command. Grumbling he could ignore. He wasn't sure how to explain to his master that he'd left the country, or if his master's command could bring him back. If it wasn't enough to break him through the Veil, he would probably die should his master order him home. If he did ever get home, Fionn was very certain he wouldn't be allowed to leave again for a very, very long time. Which meant he had to stay as long as he could resist and bear it. His master sent him to keep an eye on what was happening in York. So really, he was following orders. He couldn't go back without stopping them. He couldn't go back without saving Dayo.

The one good thing about the floating city was that where there was water, there were fish. Fionn had never eaten so well in his life. There were steps and slopes down to the water in many places, so he sat on the banks and drew summoning circles. His master's additional teachings, and his own caution, meant he got one fish at a time and none of them sentient folk. After an initial mistake, he also learnt how to shun the tiny crabs that were everywhere in the canals. Folk lived in the water—he'd seen them and sensed their presence—so he was careful to avoid catching dinner near where they gathered.

He was halfway through a mullet, feasting by the light of a night-past-full moon, when a familiar presence tapped at his consciousness. His head snapped up. *Harper?*

This most certainly wasn't England. Even without the change of language, the sun was wrong and the sea smelled different. He knew Morimaru, had been held under her waves as a lesson from his master about why he shouldn't steal her fish. He knew Muir Eireann where magic sparkled in the waves and lapped at the shore, even in England where it was banned. He knew the Channel, the Celtic Sea, even the Ocean herself. To know the land was to know the waters who touched it, even if he preferred not to get his paws wet. The water in these canals neither flowed from nor to any coast he knew. *Did Harper follow the dreamwalker too?*

Fionn sniffed the air before slinking out of the shadows to follow his sense of Harper. An itch under his collar, like fleas, reminded him that he couldn't let her perceive him. Curiosity overrode caution. As he got closer, he could sense Grace and, yuck, Heresy.

He heard them before he saw them, sensitive cat-ears picking up their argument. It wormed under his skin like a tick. He wanted to jump in and stop it. He wanted to cry. But he was forbidden from allowing Harper to perceive him, so he did nothing but hunch small, fur prickling, and tried not to listen to his family fighting.

He wondered if there was a way to leave Harper a note. The palace must have writing tools, and he could risk a brief stint as human. Not shifting was giving him a headache. It was a familiar one, though he hadn't realised its source until AJ pointed it out. He missed his other form, to his surprise. Until his memories had begun to trickle back, he'd assumed he was a cat who could shift because of Harper's blood. Now he wasn't so sure. Grace had said he didn't have cat eyes, and his tummy didn't process like a cat. Both forms had felt natural to him as a kitten, and in the short time since reuniting with Harper.

I'm still a cat. Or a were-human or whatever. It would be nice to use either form whenever I want. To have people who appreciated both equally. Like Harper does. Like Dayo does, even though he doesn't know both are me. Stupid, selfish cat. Take the form that's best for the magic. Nothing else matters.

Fionn blocked their fight out so hard, he didn't notice Harper and Grace had fallen silent.

Harper scanned the area with her Sight. Lelianna disappeared beneath the water, not even a telltale ripple revealing whether she'd swum away or was merely hiding. The vapours reflected the light like cats' eyes, the only movement within them the natural swirl of vapours.

"Heresy? Are there mistlings here?" Harper's hushed whisper sank into the moist air.

"Can you not tell me, oh Seer?" Heresy chortled. Harper jerked her shoulder, almost dislodging him. He continued in an icy, silken tone. "It would appear not. At least not in this area at this moment."

"What is out there?"

"If I wished you to know, I would have said."

"*Heresy*. You are the most infuriating ... Fionn's here?" Harper changed track midsentence. His demeanour implied what approached was no immediate threat—he lacked the urgency of his warning at the Opera House—yet he was unwilling to reveal more. Like he recognised the presence and was toying with her. "Where?"

"*Tsk*. If the not-a-cat was here, I should be telling you to run away from the ratty thing."

"Heresy, stop it. He has enough issues without you chipping at his self-esteem."

"*Shush*." Grace flapped her free hand at Harper. The weight of her knuckledusters smashed a dark gap through the vapours. "I'm checking it out. Cover me." She thrust the hand-crossbow at Harper, drew one of her long knives, and stalked forward. Harper hung back with the awkward weapon she'd fallen out of practise with. Grace's faith in her was touching, but she kept the point towards the floor rather than anywhere near her sister's back.

Fionn realised too late that Grace was almost on top of him. He turned to flee before the collar could force him to, but a sharp pain in his tail dragged him back. He spun, claws out to swipe at the dark, looming figure.

"Whoa, Fionn. It's just me. Sorry I grabbed your tail. I thought you might portal away." Grace released him and stepped back, hands up.

"Mrow." Fionn clawed at his collar. He was directly breaking his master's command. A member of the household very physically perceived him. Blood magic seize control of his limbs and the silvery well of power inside him. It would be like having his fur on the inside, and his blood and muscles on the outside. A scream built.

The magic that would unleash it never came.

"Fionn?" Harper scooped him up from where he was rolling in the dirt, fighting his own adornment.

Damp splattered down his fur, a sensation that normally sent fear scurrying around his brain. This time it was a welcome surprise. The pain hadn't come. The command hadn't taken control. He'd been a Bad Cat and ... nothing. Fionn was back with his person. He wriggled in her arms, claws hooked into her shirt as he tried to be everywhere at once. Her fingers threaded through his fur. He licked her tears and rubbed their faces together. His whole body pressed into hers. *I missed you. I love you. I missed you.* The sentiments looped between them in whispers and mewlings.

"I missed you, Fionn. It was so horrible down there alone." Little Harper clung to him the same way grown Harper did now. He mewed and nuzzled her as she cried into his fur. He licked her tears and felt a distant echo of what she felt. After that, he never allowed her to go to the Protector alone.

The memory dissolved back into the present as they clung to each other. He'd lost her too many times. He wasn't sure why his master had changed zir command. The details didn't matter. The only thing that mattered was family reunited.

Five minutes of crying into Fionn's fur, Heresy's huffing and the *tap tap tap* of Grace's shoe urged Harper into drying her eyes. They were right. It wasn't safe to be standing out here so exposed. Though Lelianna was the only soul they'd encountered, she'd also confirmed there were many other and more powerful folk about somewhere. Of Lelianna herself, there was no sign either.

"Let's find somewhere to hole up," Harper suggested, shifting her grip to hold Fionn more securely. Like Gabriel, he'd been imprisoned somewhere he may have been tortured. She wasn't going to let it happen anymore.

"We need to find, Gabe," Grace insisted.

"We need to make a plan," Harper said firmly. She put an arm around Grace's shoulders. "I know, *I know*. But we're going to do this right. I'm not losing Gabriel or you to a botched rescue."

They headed away from Gabriel's base, which was probably being watched, and went south, deeper into the island city. Harper always supposed it would be crammed with folk, yet the calli were eerily quiet and many buildings appeared abandoned.

"Where is everyone?" she muttered.

"Merow." Fionn gave her a gentle headbutt, but his rebuke made no sense.

"Why would it make a difference that it's Sunday?" she asked him.

"Mau, mrow." He cocked his head for a moment then added, "Merow mrrrr, mau."

"Many went to church and spent the day in prayer," Harper translated for Grace. "Those who didn't, are respectful of that and keep the evening quiet."

Once again, the world was so different to what Harper had been brought up believing.

When they found a suitable base, Grace deployed De Santos family perimeter tech enhanced by AJ, and the three magic users collaborated to set up magical warning and protection as well. Fionn refused to shift, preferring to do his magic cat-shaped, even when it involved him biting deep into his own paw before Harper realised what he was about to do. He snuggled into her sleeping bag with her. She vaguely hoped he wouldn't shift when there wasn't enough room for two human-sized bodies, but she cared less than she used to. She was just glad to have him back.

Chapter Twenty-Nine

Splitting the Party

In the morning, Harper called Saqib as soon as they got up.

Once she established he was alone, she told him, "You're on speaker. Grace, Fionn, and Heresy are all here too."

There was a long pause. "Uh ... say again?"

"We found Fionn here. I'm sorry, we don't have time for the whole story." *I don't even know it yet.* "Gabe's in deep trouble. Have you or AJ found anything useful about what's going on at home."

"Yeah, of course. Updates." Paper rustling added to the white noise as Saqib rooted through his notes. "First of all, for Fionn, Dayo's okay as he can be. Like Christina, they've restrained and sedated him, but he's safe. There is a slight difference between him and the others. Where none of them seem to remember themselves—two stuck in character and the chamber group aren't talking at all, just singing wordlessly—Dayo does remember Fionn. He kept mumbling about a white cat. There is none in either the original painting or the incomplete remake."

"Maybe because I was in his dream when it happened," Fionn said quietly. Harper jumped. She hadn't heard him shift. Or steal her clothes. He crouched next to her, tail curled around her waist. "Maybe my presence imprinted because I was there when the magic was being cast, fighting it."

Harper gripped his hand. "Or because this is a dream thing and he associates you with dreams so strongly, you left a lasting imprint. Either way, it's good the magic didn't get a complete hold. Have you learnt anything from the painting, Saqib?"

"The ingredients are all standard—linseed oil, iron oxides, lapis lazuli, some plant extracts. However, when X-rayed, the original painting had markings consistent with the runes we found on the Ouse's victims. The markings around the eyes of the child are almost exactly the same as the ones around the girl Harper found in the tree in Tower Gardens last year."

"Cithonia," Harper said without thinking. The new memory pulled her up short. Her cousin as a small child, maybe six or seven, following her around and pestering her with a million questions. Tears pricked her eyes. That little girl was dead because of her. *No. Because of the Somnia. I didn't kill her. He did. And now he's gone.* "The girl in the tree was called Cithonia. Sorry, go on, Saqib."

"I suspect, whoever the subject of the painting was, the painter was creating a spell either for or on her. I'll send you copies of the X-rays, you might be able to work out the details."

"Ask the archbishop if Alfred can look," Harper suggested. She missed the archives in a near physical way. What she wouldn't give for a few hundred books. *The library from my vision might have it.*

"I know who the woman is." Fionn's hands were tucked inside the sleeves of the borrowed shirt and his eyes darted nervously between them.

"Who?" Grace asked.

"Serenità. The ruler here. She looks exactly the same."

"Thanks, Fionn. All the more reason to check the spells," Harper said. "It might simply be that her image made it easier for her to create a bridge, or the magic within the painting could be relevant."

"I'll send it over," Saqib said. "I've also got the full DNA tests back on the first three sets of victims. Dayo's are pending. As we suspected, there's no obvious links. They're not related, they have different heritages, et cetera … and there's still no evidence of any social connections beyond being in the arts. However, there is a result that may be significant, I've just not figured out how yet. They all have the same vestigial gene. It's something known to science; as in, we're aware a small percentage of people have it. It's one of those things that we don't know what it does. Might be a coincidence, but I'm doing further research in case."

"Thanks, Saqib. Let us know."

"It would be helpful to take a look at your file as well. AJ's going to hack in, if we have your permission to look."

"He's sure he won't get caught?" Harper tugged her hair.

"You know AJ. He's cocky about computers, but he can generally back it up with results. He'll hack a bunch of people involved with investigating so it looks like the perpetrator checking up on you all, in the unlikely event anyone detects anything. It'll be helpful to have a known person as a control and your details are already going to be on file from the tests they ran at Catterick when you were found, right? AJ's trying to get into Guard computers and find out where they're carting people off to. Neither his nor the Council's more upfront approach are getting any results. I'll let you know if we find anything else. I doubt any of that is helpful with Gabriel, but wanted to give it to you just in case. Miguel is here. They're prepping to hold the exorcism in a couple of days. If there's anything we can do from here, don't hesitate to call."

"Prayers always appreciated," Grace said.

"I've been making extra du'a for you since you left," Saqib told them.

"Thanks, Saqib. You two take care."

"Thanks, Harp. We will. Come home as quickly as you can."

"We will." *So long as things don't get even more complicated.*

They finished their goodbyes and hung up.

"We need to find Lelianna again," Harper said. "I know she can't get into the prisons, but she's our only contact here. Maybe the library will have city maps. If Venice is built on water the way myth says, maybe there's a way under. At the very least, she can rule out options with her knowledge of the city. It's not like we can blend in and ask for directions."

"I could."

They all turned to look at Fionn.

"If I posed as someone new sent over from Italy, I could get away with asking questions. There must be talk about a human being around. A newcomer can ask questions that someone who's been here decades might avoid, and there's no reason to think I've been working with him."

"No," Harper said flatly. "That's too dangerous. What if Serenità recognises you from the dream, or you run into the dreamwalker?"

"They didn't see me. Dreams don't work like that. They couldn't sense me in the room with them when I portalled here. That was an accident by the way, but I'm glad I did. I was considering trying to do this anyway."

"What about the prison boat?" Grace asked. "It's the only way in I've heard of, unless you've observed another."

"I was thinking that. There's one due later today. I eavesdropped at the docks." Fionn shivered, his tail poofed at the mention of hanging around water. "I don't speak the language, but I can understand little bits. I'm small and I blend in with anything pale, so I should be able to sneak amongst those disembarking. Folk will think they simply didn't see me."

"I can create a fake version of the fake cat," Heresy said in a long-suffering tone. "*If* there is an electronic manifest. If it is on paper, it is on its own."

"Heresy. Fionn is a he and he *is* a cat." Harper held him up so she could glare into what she hoped was some approximation of where his invisible eyes were. If he could see at all. His grin turned to a scowl. "All of our lives are at risk here. Much as you say you are only here for amusement and keeping me alive is solely to stop you being sent back, I don't think that's true. I don't think you'd find it funny if Grace and I were caught and tortured, even if you didn't get banished because of it."

"Fiiiiinnnneeee." He drew out the word like a petulant teen. "I shall give the not-a … the *cat* the fullness of my expertise and adroit magic of illusions."

"Thank you." Harper wasn't about to ask them to shake hands or be friends. As far as she was concerned, Fionn had every right to hate Heresy. What happened had been an accident, kind of, but that didn't make it any less horrible. She waved a finger at Heresy. "Don't make Fionn guilty of too heinous a crime. We need them to trust him."

"You spoil all my fun." The Cheshire Cat grin was back.

"Yet you stick around." Harper gave him a fond smile and booped his outstretched tentacle. She gave Fionn a tight human hug before he shifted back to cat, and he and Heresy departed.

"That will take too long." Grace stood to strap on various weapons, twisting her body to make sure they were silent. "By the time Fionn 'arrives' and meets people, asks questions, it will be the end of the day. I am not sitting idly by for a whole day while my brother is in danger."

"No, we aren't," Harper agreed. "While those two integrate with the folk community here, you and I are going to search for Lelianna to find a way in that won't end up with us shackled next to our brother."

She had no clear idea of where to look for Lelianna, other than to go back to where they were last night and try to See where she went, so after securing their base, they headed out. In some ways, the narrow calli made it easy to evade detection, however they also left few options for concealment. At each turn, they used Grace's compact to check for danger around the corner. Twice, Harper Saw folk coming and they ducked into gardens or churches to hide.

Masked and swathed in robes, the land-folk of Venice scurried about in small groups of three or four. Though their body shapes were difficult to discern, they were of varying height and Harper guessed varying species. More often, she Saw folk beneath the water, indistinct as Lelianna had been. Where no attack was expected, none was looked for, and the anonymity of the Venetians combined with the rarity of outsiders gave the two humans a small measure of grace.

Occasionally, when they ducked into marble-clad churches, her magic gave glimpses of heads bowed deep in prayer. Even the empty churches had burning candles and were spotlessly clean. Harper noted several synagogues, a mosque, and a mandir as well, all apparently in use.

Sometimes they turned to run back the way they'd come only to find it vanished. Alleys they just turned onto now went a warped straight. Canals that had joined together flowed parallel. Bridges connected to different shores. Even the bright sunlight suspect as Harper walked with the sun on her right, the canal bending left away from it, only to find the sun had shifted to being on her left without her realising.

"How are you feeling about seeing Lelianna again?" Grace asked in between sprints. "Both because I need distracting and because I *do* want to know. I'm your sister and if it helps to work out some knots before you see her again, I'm here."

"I honestly don't know how I feel." Harper wove the ribbon tying her plait between her fingers. While they had to hide a few times, there were nowhere near as many folk around as she expected. Harper wondered if most were nocturnal or if this was simply a quiet district. It wasn't so different to sneaking around the ginnels of York.

"May I tell you a few observations?" Grace said once a fox-faced supe disappeared from view at the other end of a square. "As your sister. You can tell me to shut up at any point."

"Gray, when have I ever been able to stop you giving observations? But yes, please. An outside perspective with insider knowledge would be helpful. Have you been sitting on it since Swaledale?"

"Since the exhibition, actually. To give you time to think. How we experience it is different. It helps that I'm more easily attracted to people than you are, though I have to say, your taste is pretty good. The guy in our English class, the biology student you dated for what? Two weeks? That nurse last year, the woman from your village we met, this water creature. All really good looking. More importantly, they seem like nice people." Grace grimaced a bit, as though it hurt to say about a supe she just met. "That's also kind of my point. You aren't attracted to many people, Harp. I could tell you five people I've been attracted to in the last six months."

"I'm sure I've found more than five people attractive in the last decade." Harper wasn't sure exactly whom, but she'd noted things like a cute person making their coffee at a café or someone pretty to dance with at a club.

"Only kind of," Grace insisted. "You find people aesthetically pleasing. You like fictional characters, rather than the actors who play them, and when you see someone you think is nice-looking you make up all these stories about them in your head. The perfect meet-cute in a library or what your ideal date might be. You justify finding them attractive by giving them a made-up personality. You're not really attracted to *them*, except in very rare circumstances."

"Oh." When Grace put it like that, Harper supposed she was right. "Well, I have a big secret to hide. I can't give my heart away when I can never really be honest with someone."

"Maybe." Grace paused to give her a quick hug. "Or it might be how you process attraction. It's not like there's a right or wrong way."

"That's still just guys," Harper pointed out. "Until my memories started filtering back, I was never attracted to a woman. Maybe Dawn was an experiment because my parents were so rigid about the bloodline, and remembering has projected feelings onto the vision about Lelianna."

"Or maybe Dawn was how you really feel. It's possible your parents put such a block in your head about same gender relationships, that even without remembering, you carried it with you. When you found a woman aesthetically pleasing in the same way you find a man handsome, you rationalised it. They're objectively beautiful. Women are artistically nicer shapes than men. It's easy to appreciate someone is beautiful without being sexually attracted to them."

Harper grimaced. She *had* said all those things.

Grace continued, "You've told me many times, 'It makes more sense to like someone for their personality than what's in their pants.' I can't tell you whether you're really attracted to women in the same way as you sometimes are to men, but please don't dismiss it out of hand because you aren't trying to jump every woman you pass. You can like all genders, while liking one gender or aesthetic more. You can like all genders but only find a very small number of people attractive. So looking at women, or other non-male people, as you pass them in the street and thinking, 'Nope, I'm straight because I don't like them,' doesn't work. You don't like most men either."

"I …" Harper's voice caught.

Her sister's echoed words showed a decade of buried confusion. It *did* seem illogical to be attracted to someone, or not attracted to them, because of something so arbitrary as a small part of their body shape.

She'd always thought that. As far back as she could remember, in either life. Like her general preference for dark hair didn't mean she'd completely ruled out blondes. Dawn certainly thought their feelings real. Damp eyed, Harper knew she'd thought them real too. With adult eyes, maybe they were superficial, but they'd been as deep as their youthful understanding allowed.

"I think … I need to think," she managed to say at last.

Grace hugged her tight and kissed her forehead. "Any time you need to talk, I'm here."

"I know. You always are." No matter what other relationships may come up in their lives, Harper was certain this one would never fail. Whether her birth family accepted her or not, whether her new family might denounce her as a witch, whether she dated a man, a woman, or anyone, or no one, Grace would always be there.

When Harper found the place where they'd spoken with Lelianna, she concentrated on the moment the water spirit stole away. A rippling silhouette appeared in the canal, the amber of peaty water as the sun shines through it. The shape was indistinct, and Harper couldn't tell if the undine had the lower half of a human, fish, or something else.

She followed the outline until they looped back to a familiar piece of graffiti. She balled her fists and took deep breaths to smother the urge to scream in frustration at having been tricked into walking in a circle.

"Keep watch?" she asked Grace. "I'm going to try and use the canal for a bit of scrying."

Harper sat on the stone steps leading down into the water and watched crabs smaller than her palm. The rippling image of Lelianna under the water remained. Harper yawned. Using magic for so long continuously was exhausting. No wonder Fionn napped so much. The outline of the other woman wavered and Harper rubbed her eyes, letting her Sight sink out of them. When she opened them again, there was a face mere centimetres from her own.

Lelianna laughed as Harper yelped and scrambled back. "You were looking for me, yet you are surprised to find me?"

"How did you know I was looking for you?" Harper asked once she got her breathing back under control.

"As well as English blood, I have blood of the Camenae and some others in the mix."

"So you're a seer as well?" Harper asked, both excited and somewhat wrongfooted. She'd never thought much about being on the other side of it, or how exposed it made her feel.

"My great-great-times-a-thousand-years-grandmother was." Lelianna shrugged, dislodging the water pooled above her clavicle. "I do not have anywhere near enough talent to be called a seer, but the extra intuition has proved useful."

"What crime did you commit to be sent here?" Grace asked. Harper winced at the harsh tone.

"I was born here," Lelianna said levelly. "Not all here are criminals. Many water folk are drawn to this sanctuary."

"Is this your canal, then?" Harper asked.

"Only the most powerful, and the most in favour with Serenità and the Ten, are granted their own waterways. Most of the smaller canals are bound to no one so that there is enough space for all to live here."

Harper wanted to ask more about Venetian society, but there was no time for that. If her vision was correct, and Lelianna could replace the Ouse, then there would be all the time in the world later. "If I could find a way to get you out of here and back to England, if I had a river in need of a guardian, would you consider it?"

Deep green eyes narrowed as they searched Harper's. "There are many 'if's there. This has been my home all my life. While I may be on the outskirts of our society, I am not without friends. I tried once before to leave with someone, but my curse prevented it." Lelianna flicked away a drop of water dripping down her cheek. "Defying Serenità for an 'if' is a lot to ask. Yet it would be worth it to have a river of my own to tend."

"Your mother came from England?"

"Yes. She was the spirit of Blackhazel Beck. It was tiny, she said, but she missed having a safe waterway to call her own, and her sisters of the nearby becks and rivers. I imagine many such waterways are spiritless now."

It was a tenuous pedigree with nothing to suggest Lelianna knew enough to manage a river as prominent as the Ouse. It was still more experience than Harper had. She hoped the water spirits around would be willing to help the new Ouse learn.

"My visions usually happen for a reason," Harper said. "I Saw us in an underwater library. I have to believe that means there are answers there. Help me, and I will do everything in my power to help you."

"I would help even without that. Gabriel is my friend."

Hearing a supernatural creature name a De Santos a friend was a strange thing indeed, and Harper reminded herself Fionn and Grace were friends, and moreover Grace accepted a witch as her sister.

"Thank you." Grace swallowed her pride and gave the spirit a stiff nod.

"Let us go to the library," Lelianna suggested, holding out a hand to Harper. Delicate webbing came up to the first knuckle, letting slender fingers interlink with Harper's.

Despite Lelianna's tug, and the plan she herself suggested, Harper couldn't quite bring herself to step into the water. "I can't leave Grace here on her own."

"I cannot fit both of you in my shell. Nor is my magic strong enough to keep several people breathing underwater at once. I can share my ability, not clone it."

"Your shell?"

"It is my home and my prison," Lelianna said, "and how Mamma travelled underwater without being able to breathe it."

"I thought your mother was a water spirit? She couldn't breathe underwater?"

"My mother was an English brook, banished here. My mamma was a descendent of the Camenae and of the Crab Prince. Just as Serenità once used the shell to trap my great-great-etcetera grandfather, so it now binds me here. Once it bound my mamma, but she bartered my life for hers. So I am stuck here, feeding the city with my magic. You are smaller than Gabriel. It was uncomfortable to have him in my shell, but I think you will fit, just as a princess once stole away in it when it was the Crab Prince's. It will allow you to pass unseen through La Serenissima's waterways. Once in the library, I shall bless you with gills."

Lelianna lifted her leg up to show her own, revealing hints of crab in her spindly build and ruddy skin. The rest of her body remained hidden beneath water and mist. "As you do not have scaphognathites, you will breathe in water like merfolk. Gabriel found it a shock, but enjoyed it once he became accustomed to the sensation."

"Thank you, but ... I can't leave Grace here alone."

Grace glanced over from where she was keeping watch. "Go, Harp. If there's something there that can help Gabe, or everyone back home, we need to find it. I'll scout up here."

Harper ran over and hugged her tightly. "So long as you promise me you won't do anything other than scout. Don't rush into anything on your own."

"I can't promise that. You know I can't." Grace stroked Harper's hair. "I do promise to only do so in the most dire of emergencies and that I'll keep myself as safe as I'd want you to be."

"That'll do." Harper lifted her head and gave Grace a watery smile. "Wish me luck."

"Luck and prayers," Grace promised. She made the sign of the cross on Harper's forehead, then kissed the spot. "Be back within three hours, not a minute later, got it?" The last was said with a stern look at Lelianna, who just smiled.

"I should say the same to you," Harper joked half-heartedly. She was already worried about Fionn and Heresy as well as the lurking horror crawling under her skin about Gabriel. "I love you."

"I love you too. Now get going. Sooner gone, sooner back, sooner we get our brother out of there."

"Yes, General." This cracked a genuine smile.

When Harper turned back to Lelianna, a large crab shell was bobbing on the surface of the canal. The undine tapped the top of it, which opened like a clam. Clinging to Grace's hand, Harper stepped in, but it didn't rock like a boat.

Lelianna pulled herself up and in, water cascading down her like a satin dress. It was a tight squish for both of them, especially when Lelianna closed the top and reached an arm in front of Harper to use the two claws like oars. The shell sank, water pressing against the opening without pouring in, and they entered the murky depths of the canal. Their bodies pressed together, far too intimate for near strangers, especially a stranger whom Harper wasn't sure if she was attracted to or not.

Chapter Thirty

La Biblioteca Somersa

Through the ovaloid opening where a crab's head would usually be, Harper watched the city beneath the surface. Where the streets were quiet, the water teamed with life. Jellyfish, crabs, sea sponges, as well as gilled folk with fish tails, and barely visible water spirits who reminded her of Usa in human form. Schools of fish twinkled between submerged wooden pillars holding buildings aloft. It was all unbearably fragile, as though one wrong nudge could topple Venice like an elaborate domino run.

Harper stayed tucked behind Lelianna, grateful no one saw her, not even the inquisitive dolphin who poked their nose in. She sat right back so she wasn't elbowed in the face as Lelianna rowed. It wasn't romantic, and Harper questioned her irrational disappointment. Maybe it was what Grace said: she tended to create romanticised stories in her head. It was simply that this time she was conscious of it. To avoid brooding, she returned her attention to the murky depths and shadowed stone architecture.

"We have to go down Canalazzo a short way," Lelianna told Harper as they entered a much wider, busier waterway.

Silhouettes of gondole slipped overhead like clouds flitting through rippling sunbeams. The crab shell was swept along, deeper and deeper, until drowned buildings darkened the water and the boats overhead were indistinct from marine life.

"I'm not sure how well it translates, this area is called something like 'the foundation on which we thrive.' This part of the city sank over two hundred years ago, or was sunk, I think you say? If it was done on purpose?"

"Yes, that would make sense. Grammatically, not the actual fact someone sank it. Who did that and why?" Harper wished she had a notebook.

"It has been raised and sunk many times. The last time was due to the French invasion. Our magic won out, but the world was a dangerous place, and they left this part of the city beneath the waters. It is easier to protect. Few come here now, though there are many water folk including Serenità herself. I believe it may have been left for more than one reason. Defeating the French ostracised us, but also birthed our era of taking in the outcasts from other places. Those deemed criminal and also those seeking sanctuary. With so many new folk flooding into La Serenissima, it may have been deemed necessary to conceal the knowledge of the foundational city from all save a trusted few."

"And you are one of them?" Harper asked, nervous about how Gabriel could've been working with someone so close to the ruler of Venice.

Lelianna laughed. "Not at all. But I am young enough to remember my childhood. My mamma left when I was very small. My mother left later, but I was still young. La Serenissima is a place of sanctuary from humans and the worst of the folk, yet it is by no means safe. Our lores are not always what you might deem 'kind'." Her laughter faded. "I did not wish to end up like the other orphans, nor attend one of La Serenissima's schools. My unusual heritage gave me advantages, and in searching for a safe place, I came across the old city."

"But it's right here. I know we've come deep, but we didn't go through any guard posts or past any barriers."

"Had we not had my shell, we would have noticed them. This shell is as Venexiani as the waters it swims in. It belonged to one who became a prince here and the magic of this place does not deny his heir passage. I didn't realise I was in a taboo area until one time I was out swimming without my shell and I couldn't find my way back. Fortunately, I had worn my shell out and could retrieve it to travel home. Had I left it here, I might have lost it forever. That was when I took up an interest in heritage and history. The library has been most educational. We have schools— education and health have always been prized highly in La Serenissima— but much is not taught. History, magic, science, all are taught to the supposed benefit of the State, not the individual. I am confident we shall find something to help."

They passed into complete darkness as the shell moved between two pillars and under a building that entirely blocked out the sun. It didn't slow Lelianna's rowing even a fraction.

"If this part of the city has been raised and sunk several times, why is it called 'foundation'? Or is that part of the tricky-to-translate problem?" Harper's fingers itched for books, and curiosity niggled even more to see how the library survived the submersion. Passages from the book at the Portal bookstore played in her head.

"It is foundation; as in, this is the history from which our culture has grown, rather than the city above literally resting on it. In some places it does, near the edges where we have expanded, but this core of La Serenissima is not overly large. It was once an island in the mouth of the canal. Some parts of the city above are part of it, once linked by bridges. On one side Basilica di San Marco, Palazzo, el paròn de casa." At Harper's blank look, Lelianna added, "Campanile di San Marco, the tower."

"I'm sorry, I know very little about the layout of Venice, of La Serenissima, sorry. It is forbidden knowledge in England, and so there aren't many books about it. We have some in the cathedral archives where I work—we find and preserve books relating to the folk, magic, and other banned things—but they're often contradictory. I wish you could look and tell me what's true and what isn't."

"That sounds like a very worthy and interesting role to have in your society." Lelianna tilted her head, one finger tapping her lips as she thought about it. "I would like to see these books where history and myth have merged. Not that I can always say for certain which is which. Here, the line is blurry. It doesn't help that the smaller calle and rii don't remain stationary. Only the most talented cartographers can map the city."

"They can make maps that magically adjust with the moving streets? And 'rii'? I'm not familiar with that word."

"The smaller waterways are rii," Lelianna explained. "Regarding the cartography, a simplification, but yes."

"I don't suppose there are any in this library?"

"I cannot promise." Lelianna turned to look at Harper, visible by the faintest outline and a glint in her eye. "I enjoy your curiosity. It is a rare treasure. I'm glad it is you who came for Gabriel. It feels right to allow you passage here, one seeker of knowledge to another. I have only ever brought one other person here, and she ..." Lelianna's face scrunched and she swallowed hard. "And she doesn't matter. Our time in the library will be limited. I cannot help you breathe forever."

"I understand." Harper rubbed her chilled arms. There was more at stake here than idle curiosity, even though she wanted to ask Lelianna what was wrong and smooth the wrinkles between her brows. "You said this section of city was once connected to the main part of La Serenissima by bridges. Is it still connected in some way? Could we use it to get to Gabriel?"

Lelianna hesitated. "It is connected to Palazzo. Of that I am sure. I have seen Serenità and others of her folk down here, and I do not believe they would risk a public passage, even with the protections. They have their own routes, just as I do. Whether that is a route you can follow or whether it will get you any closer to Gabriel, I do not know. It is possible the map room has the key. I've never looked for that specific information. Only someone with a death wish would try to break into Palazzo."

"Or someone whose brother will be dead if they don't," Harper said. "We need to find a way to him, and coming via a secret passage no one is supposed to know about is more likely to be successful than sneaking in above water where they're actively watching folk."

"The other alternative is to wait until he is brought between the pillars for execution. If you can find a way to flee from there, you may be able to blend into the crowds and get close."

"Can two humans really blend in here?"

Lelianna sighed. "There are those who might sense it, including Serenità or certain members of her retinue."

"I'd rather not cut it so fine."

"I would rather he was not cut at all."

"Sorry, I should be used to watching out for idioms with Fionn, the cat, he doesn't always get them. I meant I would rather not be rescuing him as the sword is falling, or whatever method you use here. I don't want a five-minute delay to be the difference between life and death."

"Indeed." Lelianna steered carefully through pillars that were almost invisible, save the occasional flitter of sunlight through submerged windows.

"As well as a way into the new prisons, can we search for information on Serenità?"

"So you can defeat her?"

"Yes. Or at least the magic she's using in York. That's how we got here so quickly, not just because Gabriel sounded off. She's doing something that links people's daydreams with art, I think to build a temple to magic. I need to know how to safely break the connection before she can complete the spell. I think I Saw something when she cursed people at a bookstore. If I can find the book I Saw her holding, it may hold the answers. She hid something behind it in my vision."

"Information on our ruler's weaknesses is not kept even here. I have never seen anything suggesting she has any, though all must have some. However, there are books on dreams and on art, which may be a useful place to search as well as whatever your vision showed you."

"Thank you. If we're limited on time, we should look for information that will help Gabriel first."

Grace had once told her that she'd choose a sibling over five strangers in the trolley problem, and Harper squirmed at doing just that, now. Only it was more than five strangers. She tried to justify it with the fact that Gabriel had been here longer and may have found something that would help, but if Lelianna wasn't aware of it, there was a strong possibility Gabriel wouldn't be either. No. It was the human ethic that left no one behind, even if it risked others. It was selfish and selfless all at once. She couldn't leave her brother to die.

The world outside the shell was almost pitch black as they rowed under and through derelict buildings, until they reached a door held by marble pillars that bore torches with flickering blue flames.

"What's that?" Harper asked. "It looks like fire, but we're underwater so …?"

"It is fire. There is fuel, oxygen, and heat."

Harper wanted to object that it wasn't how fire worked. Okay, in theory, those were the components, but it wasn't that simple. Thinking of the cat who swore he knocked on some kind of door to bend space like a wormhole, she shut her mouth again. She herself could See things that happened years before. Magic nodded a friendly greeting to science, then splashed it in something sparkly all of its own.

Logical thoughts washed away as they drifted between the pillars. More fires whooshed to life as they approached, then snuffed out in their wake. Vaulted ceilings born on marble columns were almost lost in the darkness save for rising embers illuminating fleeting glances.

The strength of the light increased as they entered one of many vast halls. Everything was marble, even the bookshelves, which ran floor to ceiling. Obsolete ladders ran on rails between balconies. Harper could imagine the woosh of riding them round the cylindrical rooms. Metal doors decorated with fancy carving and winged lions stood open, hinting at rooms beyond.

And the books. Some as tiny as her palm, some taller than her head. Thousands and thousands of them. Maybe millions. It put the Saint

Peter's Archives to shame. Harper stared through the narrow opening of the shell, fingers braced on the edge. Though logic told her the water would kill her, the archivist urge to touch, to read was achingly strong.

"Even with magical aid, the air in the shell is limited and it rejects strangers, so I cannot leave you alone here while I fetch books, nor can I pass them to you through the opening." Lelianna stilled the oars and placed a gentle hand on Harper's arm. "We must leave this protection. I am able to give you the ability to exist here, for a short time. I must breathe the magic into you, as we saw, in our shared vision. We shall not be able to speak except with our hands. The folk here communicate underwater in a way more akin to whale song than human words, or we use our own variation of Sign Language."

"I know some British Sign Language. Hopefully we can work out enough between us to be understood." At least the fathoms of water outside the shell would disguise how dry her lips had gone and her constricted throat wouldn't have to speak.

"It is best to remove what layers you can to ease your passage," Lelianna advised. The water that had cascaded over her as she entered the shell seemed to have become a short, gossamer dress.

The lump in Harper's throat refused to be swallowed as she removed most of her clothes, until nothing was left except underpants and a tank top. It baffled her that Fionn could shift and be so casually naked.

Then Lelianna's hand was in hers and she barely had time to hold her breath before water enveloped her body. Panic seized Harper at the weight of the water, even attenuated by the structure they were in. Fingers tightened around hers. The gentle push of water turned her and Lelianna pulled them close. A slight smile played over the other woman's lips as she brushed loose strands of hair back from Harper's face.

Although Harper expected it, Lelianna's lips on hers took her by surprise. Instinct made her gasp, eyes wide. Instead of water, air flowed into her from Lelianna. The other woman's power entered her body and spread through her arteries to carry magic and oxygen with each beat of her rapid heart. Lelianna slid an arm around Harper's waist and their lips moved together. It lit something in Harper—a deep, grabby desire—and she laced her fingers through Lelianna's floating halo of hair.

What started as part of a spell, blossomed into something more as breath hitched and heat spread between them. It was a heady sensation, unlike the tentative kisses Harper shared with people before. This didn't just alight her lips but her whole body. Every nerve was conscious of every touch. Pounding need hammered in her chest and heated her gut.

I barely know her…

The thought sank as soon as it surfaced. It drowned in the depth of one long kiss. They kissed with hearts as well as lips, and it felt right. Maybe because of the magic. Maybe because Harper had been anticipating it since the gallery. Maybe the way it unlocked memories of desires long imprisoned and barely explored by youth.

Harper's eyes fluttered open as the kiss broke—a one-off spark of passion, folk playfulness, or a prologue to a longer story. Lelianna brushed light fingers over her cheek and a second, soft kiss over her lips. Then the undine gestured to the shelves all around them, and the bizarre real world returned. Time was limited and knowledge unlimited.

Harper kept hold of Lelianna's hand as they swam along the bookcases. The change of how she took oxygen into her body was disorientating. Her mouth was a useless appendage. She kept her lips closed to avoid mouthfuls of water. Despite the lack of strain on her lungs, the absence of an act instinctual since birth felt like drowning. The panic had nowhere to go. There were no deep breaths to soothe it. Harper stopped swimming, clinging to Lelianna as her brain fought the assumption she must be dying.

Lelianna turned and placed a Harper's hand on her own chest, and placed hers over it. Harper's heart fluttered against her palm, and her chest rose and fell as her lungs expanded and deflated. Faster than usual, as though she was panting without breath, but she could breathe. Lelianna's hand ran down her side, drawing her attention to the gills above her leg joint.

There was concern in the other woman's eyes. Harper squeezed her hand and tried to swallow the panic. She didn't have time for it.

As they continued their perusal of the shelves, the pure magic of the situation helped distract Harper. The tomes appeared to be leather, cloth, and paper like any normal book would be. Map scrolls of parchment had the texture of linen or flax. It was grounding to run her hands over them, the same way she grounded herself in her notebook at home. Switching to her magical Sight, pale blue and bright gold magic glistened over everything. Preserving spells that kept the water from destroying the treasure trove.

They spread out maps between them, then hastily scrolled them if they didn't contain the needed knowledge. Lelianna replaced each one meticulously in its home, a fact the archivist noted and approved of.

They unrolled a scroll almost a metre wide to find a detailed map of the city. Calle and rii glided like water streams running down a window.

Some changed destination as they wriggled, while other paths connected the same two points no matter how the individual streets changed. Lelianna pointed to Saint Mark's Basin where the underwater part of the city was meticulously detailed in deep blue ink. The city above the water was in various colours depending on what was depicted, but the colour of the midnight ocean was exclusively on the city below.

Lelianna swirled her hand over the map until a whirlpool formed over the dark blue, then she raised her hand and the spinning water caught the ink and lifted it from the page. As the water settled, a three-dimensional view of the city hung between the two women.

As a long-term resident, Lelianna swiftly indicated the library they were in and pointed to various passages from it, then waved her hand to show where they were relative to their current position.

Harper gasped as a vision hit her, cold water filling her mouth, with no place to go without breath to draw it deeper. She spluttered at the sensation, but it didn't shake her Sight.

Tiny people swam through the map, leaving glittering trails in the water. A woman, dripping so many jewels and gold ornaments that they replaced her need for clothes, was followed by a menagerie of masked individuals, some of whom faded in and out of Sight. Harper knew with magical certainty they didn't always accompany the woman. Others remained solid throughout, her closest retinue and guards who went everywhere she did.

Other iterations layered the map, repeat journeys to every part of the library, but they all originated from one place. The glittering light spread from that point like a network of roots from the bole of a giant tree. Harper pointed out the doorway to Lelianna, who frowned and shook her head slightly. When she met Harper's eyes, she startled, her own widening, then she nodded.

With a glance at Harper's legs, Lelianna gestured to the shell. Harper wanted to stay. Despite the urgency of their mission, there was a sense of sanctuary being in this place of hallowed knowledge where few could come. It was more like home than the forest where she'd walked with her birth father. Lelianna hurried the map away then grabbed Harper's hand to drag her back to the shell.

They'd almost reached it, when weight and fire roared through Harper's lungs. Lelianna shoved her through the opening of the shell. Harper lay in its darkness gasping for breath as the gills closed and her mouth and nose took over again.

"*Shhh.* You are safe here. I would not let you drown." Lelianna stroked her hair and curled around her in the cramped space. "You did exceptionally well for a person who changed how they breathe for the first time ever."

Harper buried her face against Lelianna's shoulder. Sobs wracked her, though she didn't know what she was crying over. She missed the scent of Grace so badly it hurt. A steady hand stroking her back and Lelianna's softly encouraging words gradually brought her back to herself. She could breathe. She had never not been able to breathe. The whole experience was so alien, it might take days to process. In the meantime …

"We found a way from here into Serenità's palace. We can sneak in that way."

"You did. That was your magic, yes?" Lelianna queried.

"Yes. Sometimes I can See things on purpose. Other times, they sort of hit me."

"I couldn't perceive what you were Seeing until the last few seconds. I caught a glimmer of it in the water, just as I did when you envisioned us."

"Why?" Harper sat up without letting go of Lelianna's hand. "How can my magic affect you?"

Lelianna's face was barely visible in the shadowed shell. Blue magelight flickered over her skin like sun rippling through water. "I can See flashes of the future as it relates to me. I see the same future you See because our futures are linked, at least in the immediate." The water spirit shrugged with a wry smile. "I think. Mamma didn't exactly hang around to explain her magics to me. The blood of the Camenae is attenuated; she may not have even thought I would inherit the gift, being more of English blood than any of my individual Italian and Venexiàn heritages. What I do know, is that I don't object to whatever this link is between us."

Tears hung unshed in Harper's eyes. She raised a finger to lips that tingled afresh. "Leli—"

"It is something to explore later," the undine said quickly.

Harper wasn't sure she knew what she'd been about to say. The kiss overwhelmed her nearly as much as breathing through her legs.

"We should check out the entrance before we go back to Grace," she said instead, so she could ignore the confusion.

"Briefly. We must be careful not to tip them off that we know about it," Lelianna cautioned. "It came out via one of the Palazzo wells, which connect to the New Prison. We can get to where Gabriel is so long as we are swift and unseen. Even with the protections on this place, I doubt Serenità has left a passage into her home entirely unobserved or unguarded."

Lelianna rowed the crab shell near to the entrance of the passage between Palazzo and the library that the map had indicated. Harper pressed her forehead against the cool magic of the water held at bay and swept the room before them with Sight. Nothing jumped out at her as technological or magical surveillance, but that didn't mean it wasn't there.

"We should wait until most of the court will be asleep," Harper said reluctantly. Grace would've argued for rushing straight in, but they were vastly outnumbered and underpowered. The last time they broke in somewhere with naught but minimal plan, they'd been hauled in front of a ghostly apparition who wouldn't have regretted killing them. "I need a map of Palazzo and the prison. I need to know what, if anything, is a weakness for Serenità." *We may have to flee the country as soon as we have Gabriel. I know he wouldn't thank us for sacrificing everyone else for him.* "Can you cast that spell on me again?"

"We can keep doing it," Lelianna confirmed. "I have not done it in quick succession with anyone before. I cannot promise there will not be side effects."

"I Saw this and I have to believe there is some purpose in the visions and dreams I have. I'll take the risk."

"If you want to kiss me again so badly, you do not need to wait."

Lelianna's lips were on hers again, bodies entwined together in the damp, tight space. It was like existing within a bubble where nothing above the water was real anymore. Though it was selfish, it was also so, so good.

Foreheads pressed together, eye to eye, Lelianna pulled back far enough to speak. "I do not know what this is, if it is anything, but we have Seen each other for a reason. Moreover, I like you. You have guts, determination, and an appreciation for a library that I find very attractive. I hope we have time later to see if it can be more."

"Me too." Harper's voice came out a whisper, fragile as a dream.

"Come do research with me?" Lelianna laced their fingers together.

"Definitely my love language." Harper squeezed her hand.

"I will kiss you as the spell fades. Should you wish to return to the shell, either for a break or to return to the surface, you need only indicate."

"Now who wants to keep kissing whom?" Harper joked.

This time, she was more prepared for the alien horror of her body changing and breath being stolen from her throat. They swam together through the library, hand in hand, as they had in Harper's vision.

When they reached a familiar room, she tugged Leliana to a halt. Though to an untrained eye, one library room might look much like another, Harper was far from untrained in navigating complex archives. This was the room from her vision at the bookstore. She swam to one of the floor-to-ceiling bookcases, floating up as she skimmed until she found the point where she'd Seen the flash of gold. As in her vision, a volume of green and copper rested there, untarnished by the water.

Wary of what might have been left there, she reached a hand between the books and encountered a hard curve. She drew out golden scissors styled like a crab's claw. The green book was in English, unusual but not rare from what she'd seen of the library so far.

She skimmed through to approximately where she thought she'd Seen the figures reading. Lelianna floated behind her to look over her shoulder. While it contained information on dreams, it seemed little different to made up dream interpretations or psychobabble Harper read in her research before. Until a heading caught her eye:

How to Sever Oneself from a Dream Fate Weave.

Chapter Thirty-One

A Faked Arrival

Fionn and Heresy lurked on the shore. Sea fog cushioned Venice, sometimes venturing up her canals on days when Serenità's attention strayed. Today it battled her will, piling up a few metres from the dock. It billowed and flattened against the invisible barrier. The cat hung back, as far from the water as he could while staying close enough to slip into the throng of folk who were due to disembark. A few folk milled around the jetty; guards and bureaucrats awaiting the newcomers.

Heresy's illusion magic prickled Fionn's skin and set all his fur on end. It kept them hidden from casual view, but that didn't mean he liked accepting help from the impish creature. Tricksy and unpredictable. Like the water that mocked him with each slap against the wooden struts sticking out of it to guide the boat in. The tip of Fionn's poofed tail twitched back and forth as he chunnered.

"Hush, silly not-a-cat." Heresy's static increased. Spiky, like electric fingernails through his fur.

Fionn hissed softly, but before he could take any magical action against the pest, a boat emerged from the mists.

It wasn't there, and then it was. Not even a darkening shadow heralded its arrival through the dense fog. Peeling paint declared it *Nave Fantasma*. Hands rose from the water to meet it, caressing the bow that sliced their waters. Their eerie song flattened Fionn's ears against his skull. Not even a siren song could possess him to inch closer to the dreaded wet. Melancholy and dissonant, it might've been a warning, a dirge, or a seduction.

The nose of the boat almost touched the shore before the wash of water pushed it back. It settled, creaking but otherwise silent as a ghostship of legend. The cockpit was encased in iron and anti-magic charms, with spells to protect the controls from being tampered with. No faces peered from the window; the pilot either too small or the route automated.

Folk on the shore ran a gangplank out. When it locked in place, a red light on the side of the boat flicked to green, and a panel slid open. The folk inside cringed back from the silvery light. Wan, with hollow cheeks and empty eyes, they watched the Venetians on the shore with fear. They cowered, waiting for the axe to fall, save one who sat calm at the back with an air of authority.

A couple of the Venetians clambered aboard. They prodded and poked until the prisoners formed a scraggly line, then marched them off the boat. From what Fionn had overheard, numbers ranged from two to twenty. They were lucky today, as at least a dozen ragtag folk came ashore. Fionn darted from behind packing crates and slunk between ankles as though he'd always been there. It wasn't difficult to feign weariness and fear. They were part of his bones and blood, always present save for brief seconds when Harper's warmth or Dayo's touch made him forget.

Heresy hovered, a dark ash against the charcoal mists, until the person retrieving the manifesto from the boat's computers was distracted by another guard. Fionn had to trust the spirit's sense of self-preservation was sufficient to stop Heresy dropping him in it, literally or figuratively.

The queue of folk stopped in front of a short, officious creature who proved no matter how many eyes or legs one had, all bureaucrats look the same. When they were handed the passenger list, they ticked folk off and directed them to one side or the other. Over half were sent to the left, lined up near the water. The rest were sent to huddle against a derelict building. The water bubbled in a way that iced Fionn's blood. Those sharp fingers couldn't be far below the surface.

When Fionn reached the front, he kept his head bowed and hunched his body. He couldn't stop the anxious flick of his tail even if he wanted to. There was a longer pause than with previous folk. Fear rumbled in his belly. If Heresy hadn't forged his passage, the guards could turn lethal. On the one paw, it couldn't be worse than some of the lessons with his master. On the other paw, no matter how much those hurt, they hadn't killed him.

This might. He'd be letting down Harper and his master. He'd be letting down Dayo.

"Modifegar," the officer demanded.

Something foreign and slimy slithered against Fionn's magic, and he swiped claws at the air.

"Modifegar." Angry. A hair's breadth from painful.

They already saw through him, or Heresy put in his dual form. As his human-shape materialised, the official's eyes widened, and they took a step back. Fionn dropped his own gaze, letting his hair cover part of his face. He tucked his hands behind his back. It was more difficult to appear contrite in human form, until he imagined his disappointed master standing before him.

"El me scuxa, Emisario." The creature's tone shifted to tremulous. They changed to heavily accented English. "We had not realised ze was sending someone to oversee in person. I shall arrange suitable transport for you to Serenità's palace immediately."

As Fionn lifted his head, the disc on his collar caught the light and reflected off the tablet in the guard's hand. He hadn't anticipated that anyone outside of England might recognise his master's emblem. The catshifter stood straighter, summoning the unfelt surety he cloaked himself in at Market. How his master was caught up in this, or why ze would send one of zir familiars to Venice, was beyond Fionn, but he couldn't show weakness. There was no longer a shield in fitting in. He had to wield the sword of his master's reputation.

He inclined his head slightly, respect to someone on their home turf, not subservience. "I'm sorry for arriving like this. I didn't want to rouse the suspicion of the human authorities or reveal myself until I found someone important enough to recognise this." He tapped the triquetra-etched silver disk.

The official puffed up like all bullfrog-esque middle management who believe themselves high on the food chain. Fionn had caught and eaten larger frogs than them on lean weeks.

After doing the dance for a couple more minutes, Fionn was directed, or rather requested, to stand to one side next to an elderly female with wild green hair, backwards feet, and knowing eyes. She was the same one he'd noted on the boat, and she slithered an enigmatic smile at him. One of the guards handed him a loose robe to wear that was far too big.

Heresy was sorted into the smaller group away from the water. When the last prisoner had been checked off the list, they removed the gangplank and the boat retreated into the fog again. The waters churned, and the song from them swelled. Waves beat against wood and stone, the drumbeat getting faster and faster.

The official waved a hand towards the group they'd directed to the waterside, and the Venetians who guarded them took a step back. The prisoners moaned and rocked but none attempted to flee.

The beat of the waves throbbed against Fionn's skin and set his pulse racing in terror. Bright lights smouldered beneath the water. Then burst out.

The folk on the shore disappeared as clawed hands grabbed their ankles and dragged them under. Too fast for screams. Water churned red, the froth riding the tide a sunset pink. When the water calmed, the drums and song fell silent. The darkened water gradually returned to deep green-blue. When no blood remained visible, the toady waved to the other guards who led Heresy's group away. They approached Fionn and the krivapete with a bow of their head.

They spoke first in Venetian, then repeated in English. "I am Valen, they/ze. A gondola will be here shortly to transport you to Serenità. We must wait for the waters to clear before the boats can safely arrive. They object to blood in the water, and the daughters of Scylla do taunt them so. We have lost the occasional passenger to them, though not for at least a score of years."

Fionn eyed the water warily. Monsters or no monsters, he didn't want to have naught but a sliver of boat between his fur and the cold depths.

"I prefer to walk." He kept the waver from his voice, though the bile lodged in his throat bit acidic. Weakness was a death sentence. "After hearing about Venice for years, I'd like to see it."

"The gondoliers will be honoured to give you a tour later," the toad said in a tone that implied such sentiment may not be voluntary. "It is recommended to see La Serenissima by water."

Fionn floundered for a way to keep his feet on what he would charitably call land. It swayed beneath him like the deck of a giant ship, such as those he'd heard creaking in paintings. Thinking of paintings sent a pang through his heart. He was doing this for Dayo, and for Harper, and for all the other innocent people trapped by the enemy dreamwalker. To release them from a nightmare, he could hide his fear in the face of his own.

"Grasie." He inclined his head, clenched fists behind his back. Fingernails wanted to sharpen to claws, to bite into his own flesh and give him some relief from the terror building in his gut each time the water slapped up onto the jetty.

The gondola arrived shortly. Fionn didn't remember stepping from the shore into the narrow boat, though he must have done so with the automatic grace of a cat, for he found himself seated at the feet of the standing gondolier. Having a stranger at his back wielding a long pole would've raised his hackles even on dry land, but his concerns over it paled next to the glistening water.

The boat sat low in it. The threat of cold and wet was constant. It took conscious effort to keep his tail from twitching and his ears from flattening against his skull. The deep breaths that helped calm him through painful rituals instead burnt his lungs with salty air. He couldn't see the sun, the sky. All he could see was a crate—a leaky, rotting, soaked crate bound with iron. His fur slicked to his shivering body. The current whisked him along. Where he was going and where he came from were equal mysteries. He didn't even know his name. His whole existence was the too-small crate and the icy river water that delivered him to his fate.

"Emisario? We are here."

Fionn blinked. Bright colours bled through the darkness and coalesced, not as they had then into his master's mask, but into the beady eyes of the toad.

He hopped out of the boat smartly, the wobbly dock near Piazza San Marco a welcome stability. The official gave away nothing, and Fionn hoped his fear wasn't so blatant. Though the creature appeared dim-witted, they held an important role and their dullness may be a false impression. Somewhere, deep beneath him, was a sense of Harper's presence. The idea of her being underwater spiked panic into Fionn's lungs. However, the sense of her closeness, alive, gave him hope.

Fionn and the krivapete were led along the docks towards an orange-and-white brick palace. With every step, the awesome authority of Serenità's presence threatened to flatten Fionn. She stood on a raised platform at the end of Piazzetta San Marco between two monolithic columns. Atop them were the now familiar pair of a winged lion and a hippogriff. Between them, bleached-clean blood-soaked slabs screamed the death songs of all who had been executed there.

Serenità's eyes followed the approaching group, her expression hidden beneath a sun-glinted mask with a mane of white feathers. The overflowing art of her dress sang of gold to Fionn's alchemical training, its threads pure and spun fine as though made by Rumpelstiltskin.

Hoping to any god who might listen that neither the dreamwalker nor Serenità recognised him, Fionn stopped before her and bowed. For all he was surrounded by air, his lungs burned and his shoulders bent as though all the weight of the Adriatic crushed him into a watery grave.

Serenità swept down upon them. Fionn's nose twitched as she stopped too close, her jutting collarbone almost under it. Jasmine, lotus flower, and sandalwood wafted over him. Only years of containing disgust at his master's concoctions allowed him to keep a smooth face. While she didn't smell bad, the magic beneath piled against his defences like fog against a window. Whatever magic, pheromones, or other tricks she employed to make folk hers, his master's training was stronger. Instead of luring him in, it repulsed him. A fleeting thought wondered why Dayo smelled so good despite his training to ignore such manipulations by the many fae folk he encountered.

Serenità's touch on his collar was abhorrent. His lips drew back in a hiss. His arm jerked up, stopping short of touching her. She dropped her hand and laughed without mirth.

"El me scuxa, Emisario. We were not expecting ze to send someone to contact us in the flesh. I merely wished to verify the veracity of your claim to serve the one whose symbol you bear. I can see you are under zir thrall. A blood-bonded cat. Intriguing."

"My name is Zero." The false moniker grated over teeth that wanted to snap shut and keep it in. "I'm my master's chief familiar, and I speak on zir behalf. Even here, I demand the respect due to one sent by one of the most powerful magicians on this earth."

Serenità laughed again. "Most powerful? Hmm. Though zir familiar would be taught that, of course, empirical evidence or not. Yet I shall not disagree with you, *Zero*. Your master is formidable, or at least well-placed, and I would have had a great deal more difficulty in our shared task were I completing it alone."

She clapped her hands, and an attendant sprang to her side. "See the Magician's Emissary is given fitting quarters, refreshment, and attire." She turned back to Fionn. "We shall speak further this evening. In the meantime, please enjoy our most serene haven." She waved a hand towards her palace.

Fionn bowed his head and thanked her. Once her attention shifted to his companion, his was drawn to the others clustered nearby. Were any of them the mysterious dreamwalker whose aura had been so hidden? Almost everyone present wore a full mask with feathers, sequins, and gold gilt flourishes.

One in particular stared back at him with a greater degree of intensity than the others. Their bulky clothes and mask gave no hint of any part of them save sharp brown eyes. What really caught Fionn's attention was the quiet aura. In a sea of jostling egos, they faded into the background like a painting bleached by the light. Or like a dream.

When Fionn met their eyes with a challenge in his own, they inclined their head, then slipped away.

Fionn paced a lavish bedroom. After having been shown his room and given an uncomfortable selection of clothes, he'd been exploring the palace and asking casual questions about the building and its history. When he placed a hand in his pocket, he found a slip of paper that hadn't been there when he dressed. Unsigned, it simply instructed him to be in his assigned room when the clock struck five. He doubted it came from Serenità, for she wouldn't have to be so circumspect. What disturbed him was how the note had been placed without his knowledge. Someone had gotten close enough to touch him. He shuddered, tail poofed. *It could be a trap. Someone who disagrees with whatever Serenità is doing? They might think hurting me will drive a wedge between her and Master.*

An unknown voice interrupted his thoughts. "Forgive me for the intrusion."

Fionn hissed and spun at a stranger's voice. No one. Then the door on the closet creaked an inch or so.

"May I please enter?"

"Who are you?" Fionn demanded. He had read about creatures who needed permission to enter, and he wasn't foolish enough to grant it should his visitor be one.

"One who knows who you really are. An ally or a blackmailer. That depends on you."

The door creaked open further and the courtier from earlier stepped in, hands raised. Blades or potions could easily have been concealed in their flowing fabrics, and their mask concealed their mouth. There was no way to tell if a spell was uttered, nor could Fionn read their body for truth or lie. They had next to no aura, perfectly attuned to the world around them in a way Fionn had rarely seen. Magic glittered under Fionn's skin, defensive, ready to pounce and turn the tables at the slightest provocation.

"We already met, after a fashion," the stranger said. "A few days ago. In the dream of the painter and from your voyeuristic position under my bed. So I know you're not really here on your master's business. Ze wouldn't have sent zir familiar to fight us for the dream of one ze sacrificed to our spell."

Fionn hissed softly. Magic crackled and it took a concerted effort to stop it striking out at the other dreamwalker. He wasn't a violent cat, for all he sometimes faked aggression for safety among less well-mannered folk, but he wanted to scratch this creature who hurt his dreamer. The idea that his master could be the one responsible was like a board of nails hammered under his skin. It couldn't be true.

But it could. How many lectures have you listened to that the good of the country is greater than the suffering of one individual? Because you never learn. Because you're weak and selfish.

As the dreamwalker took another step towards him, Fionn fell into a crouch without giving ground. "If you think anyone could fake being my master's familiar, you don't know zir."

"I don't think you're faking it. Serenità wouldn't be mistaken about a blood-bond nor zir magic in your collar. I'm here because you've found a way around that, and that's what I need."

Fionn's eyes flicked to the other creature's neck, but could discern nothing through all the layers, and he'd only seen their lower half earlier. "I never try to disobey my master." *That's not true either. You disobey zir a thousand tiny ways, all those loopholes, papercut wounds to your special relationship.*

"Then you aren't a cat." The speaker faltered a moment, confusion clouding their eyes, but it passed as swiftly as a ship blown before a storm. "Your master didn't send you here. You came on the back of the dream. I want you to get someone for me, someone my own blood-bond prevents me from helping directly."

"Who?" Cat's curiosity, and the power of knowledge, compelled Fionn to ask.

The dreamwalker hesitated. "You must agree before I can say more."

"More likely, you're a test from Serenità. How I came here doesn't change who my master is nor that I can't disobey zir direct commands. Why would I agree?"

"Because I can release your painter from Serenità's spell. We must both risk a great deal for the freedom of those we care about."

The risks warred within Fionn. His place here hung on a thread of belief that would be easy to sever despite his protestations to the contrary. If it was a trap by Serenità, the fact they recognised him from the dreamscape meant he was already in trouble. But if Serenità's own dreamwalker would turn against her, then he could save Dayo. Whispers of *selfish cat* were muffled by the hope that seeing Dayo's curse broken would show him a way to free the others.

"Sit." Fionn gestured to the desk chair and took a perch on the edge of the bed himself. Magic coursed through him, adrenaline-fueled and itching to be released. He rubbed the back of his neck where it prickled strongest. "Who are you? You know my name."

The dreamwalker hesitated again. "I am ... known as Porta here. Ze/zir. My position in society is small. Nonetheless, I'm favoured by Serenità. She and I have enacted many spells such as the one we are setting up in York. I tell you this so you understand I have no political power. I serve her whims. The Ten view me with suspicion. Dream magic is seen as a strange thing, even here. I'm of use to Serenità, nothing more."

"You're her pet." Fionn's limited education in history hadn't covered much beyond England's shores, but he surmised Serenità was like the Queen back home. *The Ten must be like her parliament or nobles or something. They don't trust Porta any more than our Queen's advisors trust my master.*

"And you are your master's."

"Yes." Fionn's chest puffed. It wasn't news or an insult. He *did* belong to his master. He was proud of that. "Yet you want to go against Serenità's wishes?"

"As you go against your master's," Porta replied.

"I don't think I believe you about my master's involvement." Panic twinged in Fionn's chest. He didn't know that he didn't believe it either. Coincidences existed. Dayo was well-connected to the dreamscape because of Fionn. It might've made him an easy target. He schooled the terror and worthlessness away. If he did cause this, he had to fix it. "It's not relevant. I want the painter released from your spell and you want someone released from Serenità here?"

"Yes." It was like speaking to a statue. Porta's stare was almost unblinking, and ze sat without moving. No little adjustments, no scratches, not even a twitch of zir fingers. Ze could've been marble with a speaker rather than a real person. "They're from England, like you."

"I may be able to take them away from Venice, but I can't promise to take them back to England."

Porta's eyes narrowed. "You don't know how you did it either."

After a split second, Fionn decided honesty was best. If he said he could do something he couldn't, then Dayo's life was on the line. "Not entirely. I assume I portalled my body here in some instinctual response to my consciousness following you in the dreamscape. However, I don't know how I got past the Veil around England. I can't portal here. However, I may have a way to get your person to the shore. Once out from under Serenità's magic, I may be able to portal them elsewhere in Europe that isn't veiled."

"I don't need you to take them all the way, just get them out of the prison here. How can you do that if you can't portal?"

"It depends on what's holding them. I'm pretty good at getting into places I shouldn't, even without portals." *And I have friends who are good at it too.* "If I can get your person out from under Serenità's nose, what then?"

"I know someone who can get them to England."

"So if I deliver them to your contact—"

"I'll break the curse on the painter."

"Tell me more." Even, or especially, for Dayo, Fionn was unwilling to agree too quickly. Fae creatures put all kinds of tricksy loopholes in their contracts.

"Recently, a report was received via the bocche dei leoni of a human here. A few days ago, he was captured. I know you heard the buzz because you were discussing it with Nobiluomo Zambelli when I slipped the note into your pocket."

Fionn didn't like that someone got so close to him at all. It was like this dreamwalker could withdraw almost all zirself into the dreamscape and be nearly invisible.

"That's who you want me to break out?" he asked, surprised one of Serenità's folk would put their neck on the line for a human.

"Gabriel is my boyfriend. And now you know enough to see me left under weights at the bottom of the canal for a thousand years."

The idea of being in water for even a thousand seconds made Fionn's skin crawl. A glow surrounded him as he fought the urge to shift and flee. He focused on the first part instead. Boyfriend. Boyfriend. Dayo used that word. The earlier part of the evening had blurred in light of the curse. The kiss, the strange discussion, it had all fallen into the back of Fionn's brain to allow room for immediate concerns.

"A member of Serenità's court, her dreamwalker, has a human boyfriend?" Even his original interpretation of the word made it seem dubious. Maybe Dayo was wrong about it meaning Extra Special.

"You have one." Porta glared at him.

"I very specifically don't," Fionn disagreed. Dayo had been very clear, and besides which, it wasn't possible.

"Deny it all you will, I saw his dreams and how he reacted to you. Yes, I love Gabriel. Serenità doesn't know he and I are together. For his sake as well as mine, it needs to stay that way. I can tell you where he's being held and what security there is. Getting in, and more importantly out, is entirely down to you. I can't help. I need to be visibly here when it happens so I remain above suspicion."

"Whereas I'll be immediately suspected, as I'm English folk and a newcomer," Fionn pointed out. *Does she know my master has some connection to Grace's family? Does Gabriel know?*

"Maybe. You came here for the painter and you'll have achieved that, so what does it matter?"

What did it matter? Even if Serenità told his master and everything Porta was saying about zir was true, Fionn would put up with whatever lessons he needed to if it meant Dayo was safe.

"Tell me about the security …"

Keeping their distance, they metaphorically put their heads together to plot.

Chapter Thirty-Two

With a Prayer and a Sigh

How to Sever Oneself from a Dream Fate Weave

'Firstly, one must be able to recognise a Dream Fate Weave. The signs of this are threefold. 1. A lingering of dream images, sounds, and other experiences into waking hours, even to the extent of believing the dream to be reality. 2. Inability to concentrate on aught else, even that which normally absorbs the waking attention. 3. Extreme fatigue, which can cause sleep to take the cursed even when it is dangerous to their survival. When minor, these symptoms can be signs of other maladies, yet the extreme nature of a Dream Fate Weave makes it nearly impossible to misdiagnose. There are also various alchemical tools which can ...'

Harper flipped through pages of complex diagrams and formulae wishing she could copy them to show Fionn.

'Swift treatment of this curse is of utmost import. The longer a soul is woven into the dreamscape, the more deeply their fate is intwined with it until a point is reached where they become inseparable from it. Various combinations of humours have been used with limited degrees of success; it has been found that direct application to the body of the afflicted carries high risks. To this end, eminent healer and dream scholar, Doctor Cauchemar built upon philosophies such as Cartesian Dualism, Eshawa, and Inverse Lucidity, to create a way to sever the mind from the Weave without touching the body, and without irreparably harming the person's ability to reach the dreamscape naturally.'

Further diagrams and formulae ensued, none of which meant anything to Harper. It would take weeks—if not months or even years—to cross-reference it all and recreate the solution. She was about to give up and look for something else when her flipping brought her to a page with a spell next to a sketch of the same crab-clawed device she'd found hidden behind the book.

I don't need to know how to make scissors if I already have a pair. Buoyed by physical evidence of progress, and a potential remedy for the cursed back home, Harper didn't fight it when Lelianna indicated they should return to the surface. Now she had a cure, they could scheme.

It was a simple plan, as they often are until the enemy is met, yet it tore Harper's heart for it was a plan that involved Grace leaving her behind. They had argued back and forth before eventually they both caved to the fact that Gabriel needed to get out of Venice, and he would need someone to care for him. Grace was the better doctor-substitute, and Harper's magic was more needed in Venice to continue searching for ways to undo Serenità's magic. Though she thought she'd found one, the better precaution was for Grace to take the scissors and get AJ or someone in his coven to attempt to sever the spell. Harper would stay behind in case they failed.

As night fell, the streets became busier. Lelianna confirmed Fionn's suspicion that it had been so quiet the previous night because it was a Sunday and the folk's version of Christianity remained the primary religion, though others were welcomed and supported.

Heresy used the chaos to sneak out to them. After a basic orientation on the rules and lores of Venice, he and the other ex-prisoners had been sent to temporary accommodation and offered guides to help them acclimatise. Due to Heresy's unusual nature, none of the folk who volunteered had been even close to matching him, and he'd been given permission to explore the city alone. He'd stolen into an unguarded computer, and from there snuck his way into Serenità's Palace. He was offended Fionn had been unhappy to see him and was unbearably smug that the cat had asked him to bear a message. Arrogance radiated off him like a gas leak from an old lamp.

"The not-a-cat has a source who has revealed Gabriel's location and said there is a person who can get him back to England swiftly. The not-a—" Heresy corrected himself when Harper coughed and nudged him with her foot. "The *cat* plans to retrieve him tomorrow evening once the Bati Marso festivities are underway. As part of the lock is electronic, I shall accompany him. He would prefer if you were there also."

"Tomorrow evening isn't good enough," Grace growled. "Why can't we go tonight?"

"Something about a key that must be procured and a fingerprint." Heresy raised his tentacles in a mockery of a human shrug. "The cat seems certain Gabriel will not be harmed during this time."

"Do you think Fionn made contact with Gabriel's lover?" Harper asked. "Lelianna said ze was part of Serenità's court."

"Maybe. I don't like sitting idle when we have no real assurances." Grace paced the room, silent as a cat. It made Harper twitchy.

Heresy didn't seem to care, his smooth tone unruffled. "Tomorrow evening, Serenità and the most powerful figures will be out of the palace and their attentions occupied. For once, the cat shows some sense. You would do well to learn patience, Graceless."

"Because you have so much," Grace snapped.

"I trust Fionn." Harper reached a hand to Grace who brushed it aside. "I can sneak in, help him, and bring Gabriel to Lelianna. She can sneak him out through the water and get him to Grace to meet whoever this contact is who can get back into England so easily." Harper kept her doubts silent in the wake of Grace's frustration. "Heresy, you should go with them back to England. I'll stay here with Fionn to keep investigating."

"I don't like leaving you." Grace stopped mid-turn.

"I won't be alone, and it's what we agreed. Please don't open that can of worms again."

Jaw tight, Grace gave a curt nod. "The plan is settled then."

Grace and Harper both slept badly that night. The next day, Harper spent time in the library with Lelianna again, though not without guilt at leaving Grace kicking her heels at their base. Some books were in English, around five to ten percent by Lelianna's more experienced estimation. Books in Venetian, Latin, or Italian, they took back to the shell, where Lelianna could translate for Harper. It was slower, but the threat hanging over them couldn't entirely take away the cosy warmth of snuggling together with a book.

Harper also coaxed a little more of Lelianna's own story from her, learning of the prince trapped within the giant crab shell, and the princess who bewitched Serenità with her music and so won the flower that was key to the prince's liberation.

They found a little additional information on the scissors and dream magic as well as the symbols Saqib had uncovered on the painting. Though interesting, Serenità's spells of personal attraction, calming influence, and manipulating perception were only useful to know up to a point. Harper hoped it would allow her to prevent getting caught in Serenità's web, especially as a plan hatched in her mind about how to force the Venetian ruler to give up her claim to Lelianna.

There were also books on genetics and biology that neither Lelianna nor her Sight could completely translate. The specific scientific terminology was lost on Harper. Stealing books from a library, especially one that was the foundation of its culture, was abhorrent. It's not like there was a desk where she could sign them out as loaners. Nonetheless, she tucked a couple of the books into the back of the shell to be transferred to her bag later. The act stung her arms like fire ants and left a gnawing guilt worrying at her heart, but Serenità had attacked her city, and if there was something here Saqib could use to help the cursed folk, Harper couldn't afford sensibilities.

Laden with hopefully useful knowledge, they returned to Grace for dinner and to prepare for the upcoming assault.

They travelled up stairs flooded to the marble ceilings. Nooks that once held plants or statues stood empty. At each landing, the alcoves were large enough for Lelianna's shell. The corkscrew stairs concealed anything more than a flight ahead or behind.

Seemingly immune to the water, Heresy ghosted up the stairs a few turns ahead of them. After delivering their message to Fionn, he had returned shortly after dinner grumping that he had been asked to help conceal Harper, and Fionn could find her once they arrived. In theory, any surveillance would be less likely to pick up the dispelled particulate matter that was his being, and he was the most likely to be able to detect electronics and trick them. Harper hoped he remembered how AJ trapped him and that he wasn't invulnerable.

"I could come with you," Lelianna offered, not for the first time, as they ascended.

"No. You stay with the 'getaway van'." When Lelianna frowned, Harper added, "Sorry. It's a phrase about criminals having cars waiting … wait. Have you ever seen a car?"

Lelianna shook her head. "What's that?"

"A land vehicle. They're not very nice, but they do make travelling a lot faster for those of us who can't magic our way around. In this analogy, your shell is the getaway van waiting to drive us out of here. My point is, we need you to get Gabriel out safely, and even aside from that, your shell is too important to risk. If your shell is here abandoned and someone comes along, you've lost it. If you're with it, you can flee and circle back for us."

Lelianna scowled at the logic. *Damn it, even her scowl is cute.* Harper's mind grumbled at the stirring in her gut. She kissed Lelianna's cheek and the scowl melted into concern.

"I'll be back as fast as I can, but it might take a while," Harper said as the shell bobbed to the surface, where Heresy was curled in a tight ball waiting. She checked her weapons were secure and muffled. The map she'd sketched from memory crinkled in the breast pocket of her jacket.

She summoned her magic, amplifying every sense it would allow, both to detect magic and to heighten her perception of ordinary sounds.

"Anything on the way up?" she asked Heresy as she clambered from Lelianna's shell. Being exposed, out on the stairs, trickled a chill down her spine.

"Fancy magical CCTV and something measuring water displacement. I should go ahead on the way back down too."

"Was that a slight touch of concern in your voice?" Harper pursed her lips to hide a smile as Heresy bristled.

Heresy went on ahead again. As Harper padded up the stairs, ghosts of courtiers flitted past. Though it was her Sight and not a threat, it was nonetheless disconcerting. She wished she Saw herself and Gabriel coming back down.

Eventually, the stairs ended in a blank marble wall. Heresy floated out of it, making Harper jump.

"The other side is clear of people, save those locked in windowless cells," he informed her. "There is a mechanism within the wall. I believe magic is required to open it."

Harper stared at him for a moment. "Well …? Are you going to open it?"

"My dear, I am not the one with a corporeal state nor the correct magical energies."

"What do I do?" Panic seized Harper. She'd assumed human security without giving it much thought. Electronics Heresy could hack or a key lock she could pick.

"Are you so incapable that you cannot even watch and copy?" Heresy poked her in the forehead, a zing that set her teeth on edge.

"Watch and copy what? Oh." Harper took a deep breath, battening the panic down. Her Sight was already there, but it took effort to focus it on the task she wanted to view. Serenità materialising next to her made her yelp and jump back. The vision vanished.

Heart hammering, Harper tugged the end of her braid and tried again. Like a reflection forming in a flowing river, a wavering image of Serenità appeared. The look on the other woman's face was quiet and thoughtful. Unmasked and in a simple dress, the faint scaling on her skin and her pointed features gave away her supernatural origins. Yet she didn't look alien nor did she have the intimidating presence Harper expected.

Gleaming magic like molten gold flowed from fingers tipped with sharpened, sparkling nails. It seeped along veins in the marble to highlight a complex pattern before fading into the stone. Harper placed her hand over Serenità's and violet magic mingled with the gold. Silent as Harper's ghostly vision, the marble slid into the wall.

The passage on the other side was made of rough wooden doors, uneven brick flooring, and pocked stone walls. A blast of cold air, stale and iron-tinged, hit Harper's enhanced senses, and her hand clapped over her mouth and nose. When she stepped out of the stairwell, the door slid closed, this side the same mottled stone as the walls without a hint of the luxury hidden on the other side.

"The map says this is the old prison, the pozzi or wells." Harper spread her map against a wall, then nodded to their left. "This way."

When Fionn slunk around the corner, Harper was taken aback at how dirty and bedraggled his fur was. He looked like he'd been tossed in a muddy puddle.

He trotted over to rub around her ankles but stopped himself. Instead, he dropped an envelope at her feet. "Mrow."

"What happened to you?" Harper knelt to scritch behind his ears. Running her thumb over the envelope, it felt like a key inside, so she popped it in her pocket.

"Merow mau."

"Yeah, I guess you do have better camouflage against the stone this way. Thanks for coming to find us."

He led the way through passages hidden even to Harper's map. For a brief while, they travelled through gaps between walls so thin Harper had to turn sideways, her chest squashed tighter than a corset as back and front scraped over stone. Darkness dug its teeth into her skin, aiming for arteries to turn to ice. Tears froze on her cheeks. A few weeks were not enough to get over an inherited fear. Only Fionn's glow and Gabriel's plight kept her edging forwards.

Though he had no map, Fionn was unerring. His tail jerked, ears flat back, yet purpose and fear drove him to a stiff trot until they emerged into a narrow, white corridor. Roses of ice bloomed on the walls, melting into tears as Harper passed them. Air that stank of sweat and iron whispered with a thousand laments. Sorrow threaded through fear to wrap gossamer around Harper's heart. The shock of pain as her knees hit the rough stone floor was a pinprick in the overwhelming horror washing through her.

"Mrow?"

Tickly whiskers against her cheek brought a fresh wave of hopelessness to sap her strength. She gathered Fionn up and clutched him tight to her chest.

"Miaow. Mrrrr."

"No, Fionn. There's no point. We can't help him. I can't help you. If we go ... if we go further ... we won't ... we won't come back." Hiccoughing sobs choked Harper as she buried her face in his clumped fur.

"Really, must I do everything?"

A sharp, electric shock jolted Harper. Her head cracked against the wall and blood coated her bitten tongue.

"*Heresy*. What the ..." Harper trailed off, unfocussed eyes searching the corridor for the cause of the soul-crushing sorrow. "What happened?"

The air stilled around her.

"Finally." Heresy puffed himself and waggled his tentacles at Fionn. "You are not a very smart cat, are you? I have been here far shorter a time than you, yet even I have heard of Ponte dei Sospiri—the Bridge of Sighs."

The empathic tide beat at the shores of their mental defences, threatening to drag Harper back into its depths. Every word was heavy and fought for. "What's that?"

"The last place of in between before all hope is gone," Heresy explained in his usual obscure manner.

"Which means?" Harper forced through gritted teeth.

"We are about to have our last glimpse of the outside world before we descend into the pit of despair that is the new prison. The bridge captures the forlorn sigh of each distressed being who passes it on their way to death or torment. It is their sense of abject futility and wretched misery you feel."

Harper shuddered. Venice must be every bit the loathsome place humans believed to have stored such a depth of sorrow. *It's only memory. I won't let it stop me saving Gabriel.*

Girded with determination and love, alongside the practicality of reducing her magical Hearing, the wind no longer drowned her in laments. "Let's cross it and get it over with."

Fionn pointed down the corridor to where it jinked to the side and a couple of steps led to another narrow stone passageway. "Meeerow, mau."

She kept the cat in her arms as they crossed. He trembled and buried his face against her chest as she took a moment to glance through the holes in the covered bridge, her way of honouring the souls of those lost to this prison. It was a sight that would not be Gabriel's last glimpse of hope.

Once over the Bridge of Sighs, they entered wide, arched passages lit by torches, and Fionn hopped down to take the lead again. Harper tried not to think about whether the cells they passed had occupants and whether they deserved to be incarcerated at all. Gabriel. She had to focus on Gabriel. She couldn't make herself judge, jury, and guard for the unknown folk who may or may not be imprisoned alongside him.

The wooden door Fionn stopped at bore no sign.

"Mau?" He glowed and placed a paw on her leg.

"Go ahead."

Fionn shifted to his glamoured human form. Harper concentrated her Sight on the door to look for traps as she handed him spare clothes she'd brought.

"You had a plan to get in?" she asked him.

"I know the spell to make the lock appear. It has a fingerprint scanner—Saqib taught me how to lift fingerprints when we were at the Opera House—a password, and a regular key. Magic won't work on that part of the lock."

"Do you know the password?" Harper asked. She stood on the balls of her feet, watching up and down the corridor.

"I'm hoping Heresy can override that bit. I looked through dreams, until it got too dangerous. May I have back the stuff I gave you?"

He took the envelope, extracted what appeared to be a bit of tape stuck to skin-coloured cloth, then laid his head against the wall. Hair as dirty as his fur had been blended with the dusty stone. His soft chant was barely audible even with Harper's Hearing, but the stone must've heard as it slid back and away revealing a black panel. Fionn placed the material on the panel, tape side down. The screen flared bright green. Then it went blank.

"Password time," Fionn whispered.

With a self-satisfied chuckle, Heresy absorbed himself into the machine. Bright lights flashed across the screen to form a complex pattern. With a click, a lock phased into the door next to them. Heresy drifted out of the panel as it slid back into the wall.

Fionn removed a heavy copper key from the envelope. Mechanisms ground deep in the walls as he turned it in the lock. Harper flung the door open to reveal a cramped stone cell. The stench made her recoil, but she pinched her nose and stepped into the dark.

"Gabe?"

"H-Harper?" A scratchy, disbelieving voice replied.

Chapter Thirty-Three

Prison Break

"*Gabriel.*" Harper stumbled to him as her eyes adjusted to the low light, gratitude and fear clogging her throat. "Are you hurt?"

"Not so much as to stop us getting out of here. Can you unlock these chains?"

Harper summoned her Sight without thinking. Later, she told herself it was because it was dark, because she was in a rush, because there must be a magical trap to watch for. But in reality, second nature took over. Her Sight illuminated metal chains that coursed with power.

"What the hell, Harp?"

"Gabe, I ... I don't have time." The realisation that she may have come to save her brother only to lose her family was crushing.

"Harper, hurry," Fionn hissed from the door. "Let me."

He knelt next to Gabriel, his sensitive nose seemingly immune to the stench. He chittered, like an indoor cat at a bird, and the lock sprang open.

"I can't do big heals, but I'll do what I can." Fionn placed a hand on Gabriel's head and another over his hand. A soft silver glow effused the cell. As it faded, Fionn rocked back, grey clouds of weariness scudding over his pale skin in the fading light.

"What was ... Who are you?" Gabriel asked. "Harp, what's going on?"

"We're rescuing you." She helped him to her feet. Whatever Fionn had done, Gabriel wasn't so twisted and bent as he first appeared. "He's a friend. That's all that matters right now. Can you walk?"

"With help." Gabriel leant heavily on her. Fionn put an arm around his waist on the other side and slung Gabriel's arm over his shoulder. Heresy scuttled through the gloom a little behind them.

Gabriel's left foot dragged, and his body tensed every time he put even a little weight on it. One eye was puffed up and deep purple, and blood splatter sunk into his beard. The inconsistent magelight from the torches threw shadows over his face, the extra wonk in his nose unmistakable. Horror and guilt crashed inside her like towering waves in a stormy sea, compounded by the renewed onslaught as they recrossed the Bridge of Sighs.

"The exit is that way," Gabriel said as they scurried past a turning.

"You're not going out the way you came in," Harper explained. She turned down the next corridor but was brought up short when Fionn didn't follow, causing Gabriel to grunt in pain between them.

"Neither are you," Fionn said. "You came up via the sunken library, right? There's a shorter way."

"We have to go back the way I came," Harper hissed. "The getaway vehicle is there. At the top of the water in the stairwell. There weren't any other exits."

"You weren't looking hard enough. Trust me."

Harper bit back her anger. It wasn't really for Fionn. "You better be right."

He flinched. "I trust my source."

"Can we please get the hell out of here?" Gabriel interjected through clamped teeth.

Harper followed Fionn's lead, which took them deeper underground into wet-slicked corridors that echoed with wails and moans. All three of them gritted their teeth and kept going. Harper wished that one day, even if it was only for one day, she could save everyone she encountered.

"Here." Fionn stopped by a blank wall. He flinched at every drip.

"What?" Gabriel looked around wildly, then grimaced.

Magic gleamed under Fionn's skin. His tail and ears materialised in a bright white glow. Gabriel swore and stumbled back, almost toppling Harper.

"It's okay. He's a friend," she insisted.

Fionn placed a hand against the wall and magic flowed from him into the stone like veins of ore in silver, turquoise, and violet. The stone vanished.

"Hell of a friend you found, Harp," Gabriel muttered weakly as they stumbled through and the rock reappeared behind them.

True to Fionn's word, they stood on one of the landings of the staircase Harper had ascended only an hour before. *Or at least somewhere that looks the same.*

"When you see your way out of here, you'll know why I think you're a hypocrite," she told Gabriel.

Within a few twists, the water came into view and, with it, Lelianna's shell. Harper let out a juddering sob of relief.

"Hypocrite," she whispered to Gabriel.

"Her shell won't hold all of us."

"It'll hold you." *Just.* With half a foot of height on her and much broader shoulders, Harper wasn't sure how he'd squish into a shell that had felt cramped with her and Lelianna in it, but she trusted when the spirit said they'd done it before.

Hearing them approach, Lelianna slipped out of her shell. Her face immediately clouded. "I'm sorry we were not here sooner, my friend."

Harper let Fionn take Gabriel's weight as she ran down the last few stairs to embrace Lelianna. "Thanks for waiting."

"No thanks needed." Lelianna brushed the tears from Harper's eyes, then gave her a quick kiss on the forehead. "Help me get him in."

If Gabriel had been less well trained, Harper suspected screams would've brought Serenità's guards down on them in minutes. As it was, he folded his breaking body into the tight space with a few muffled grunts and whimpers. Heresy slid into the water, unnoticed by the cursing demonhunter.

"I don't like leaving you." Lelianna caught Harper's hand as she turned to head back up the stairs.

"No one else would fit in there. Well, actually ... Fionn, if you shifted, you might fit. Don't you have to go with them to find this contact who can get them to England?"

"I'm not leaving you." The cat eyed the water with repulsion, fur poofed and ears back. "My contact wouldn't give me the details. I have to go collect them, and they'll take us to the person who can get you all home."

"I'll see you at the meeting point." Lelianna kissed Harper's cheek, before she slipped into her shell and they disappeared into the water.

"Come on." Harper grabbed Fionn's hand, ignoring his look of curiosity. "You lead."

They passed the invisible door back to the dungeons and continued up. Fionn paused intermittently to press an ear to the wall. After the third or fourth time of this, he plucked a hair from his tail and trailed it down the wall until the tip popped into the stone. As though it were rigid, Fionn pressed it in further until a loud click flicked his ears. He incinerated the hair as the door whirred open.

"This way." He took Harper's hand again and led her out into a magelit corridor. He walked half crouched, ears and tail always twitching, his palm sweaty in hers. Several times he stopped and held his breath, though Harper couldn't See or Hear anything near.

At one of a hundred gold-enamelled doors, he paused, listened again, then ushered her in.

"This is the room they put me in." Fionn gestured to a bed that looked like no one had ever slept in it and around the room of finely veneered furnishings. A pile of blankets was the only lived in looking part of the room, and these were tucked into a corner. "I made myself a more comfortable place to nap," he explained, catching her look.

"What will you do next?" Harper asked.

Fionn looked uncertain. "I'm still looking for a weakness. I haven't managed to get too close to Serenità yet. She claims my master is somehow organising these attacks."

"Do *you* think ze is involved?" Harper laid a hand on Fionn's arm, hoping this was a gentler way into discussing him not going home again. "One ... the hare ... she was involved with the art curse. She requested Dayo specifically."

"She ... what? She ...? Master ...?" Fionn's free hand gripped his tail so tightly Harper was afraid he'd hurt himself. "I ... don't know. I can't see why ze would want to hurt so many people but ... but if this spell is something that's helping magic return to the land ... then ... maybe? It will help more folk than it harms, but it would be against the Accords."

"What 'Accords'?"

Fionn clapped a hand over his mouth, the other flying to his collar. "I can't say that. I didn't say that."

"You *did*. What is it? Did you say something forbidden?"

"I didn't. I didn't. I can't. If I did, the magic would stop me, so I can't have."

Harper gently lowered Fionn's hands and led him to sit on a corner of the bed. "Fionn, is it possible the magic your master uses to control you doesn't work outside of England?"

He shook his head, eyes wide behind the mess of dirty hair that fell over them. "Not control. Help."

Harper bit her lip so hard she almost gave herself a new piercing. She swallowed the argument and tried a different tack. "Ze's blood magic prevents you doing or saying certain things, right?"

"*Mhmm.*" Fionn gripped her hands too tight, but she didn't make him let go. She recognised when someone needed an anchor.

"You wrote me a letter saying you'd been ordered not to let me or anyone else in the household perceive you, but nothing stopped you being seen by Grace, Heresy, and I here. You just mentioned something forbidden and nothing stopped you or happened because of that."

"I can feel … a tug … inside. Like something pulling on my spine but not like normal. This doesn't hurt. It's pressure, but it's not overpowering. And I can breathe. I shouldn't have been able to say that even if I wanted to, even by accident of it slipping out without the dozen thoughts that usually happen before words."

"Do you think maybe I could try and take your collar off?" Harper lifted a hand without touching him.

He shrank back. "No. I need it. I'm a good cat. I try to be a good cat. I didn't mean to be disobedient."

"You *are* a good cat, a very good cat." Harper patted his knee.

"If I took it off, Serenità would think I'd betrayed my master or been pretending to be zir familiar."

"I guess." Harper's heart thunked into her gut. On that point at least, he was probably correct.

A gentle rap from inside the wardrobe interrupted. Fionn ushered in a swathed figure in a deep blue mask with gold stars. The stranger stopped short when they saw Harper sitting on the bed.

"I know you." Dark brown eyes flicked to Fionn and back to Harper.

"Porta, ze/zir, this is Harper, she/her."

"You were at the opera."

"How do you—? You're the one who cursed everyone?" Harper's hand flew automatically to the machete at her hip.

"Porta is the dreamwalker, yes." Fionn stepped between them, arms spread to keep them apart. "And Gabriel's Extra Special Friend. We have an arrangement."

"An arrangement that didn't include a human," Porta snapped. Zir voice didn't have the Venetian lilt Lelianna's did. With the muffling effects of the mask, Harper couldn't place their neutral accent.

"Harper is my Special Friend and Gabriel's sister. She rescued him."

Porta's shoulders slumped and ze closed zir eyes. "Thank God. He's safe?"

"As safe as he can be here," Harper said carefully. "You gave Fionn the information on how to get into the cell?"

"Yes. I can't go there by myself, Serenità wouldn't allow it, but I have accompanied her to the dungeons many times." The quiver of feathers on zir mask gave away zir shudder. "It is a place where dreams die."

"I've completed my half of the bargain," Fionn spoke up. "Now yours."

"I need to get Gabriel to my contact and out of La Serenissima first," Porta said.

"And you disappear with him and I never get my payment."

Harper almost gasped to hear Fionn speak so coldly.

"I gave my word."

The two glared at each other, Fionn with a haughty confidence he drew on when someone's life was in danger. Her life. Harper clutched icy fingers in her lap. Fionn always stressed how dangerous it was to interrupt folk dealings, no matter how confused she was.

"I cannot simply snap such magic without alerting Serenità," Porta said. "The timing must be right. I will swear a blood oath on it, should you insist."

Fionn hesitated, then his posture relaxed. "Bad idea. Serenità would notice."

"Maybe. She does bite sometimes." Porta rubbed zir neck. "Can we please go? I have a disguise for you, but I wasn't expecting your friend."

Ze handed Fionn a velvet crimson cloak and a face mask in the form of a white cat with red markings. Fionn donned them, then held a hand out to Harper. She took it, keeping her distance from the dreamwalker. Her head was reeling. *Gabriel, my demonhunter older brother, is dating the supernatural responsible for cursing dozens of people back home?*

"Let's get to Grace," Fionn said. "The others should be at the meeting point by now."

"Another one?" Porta asked. "Are all your master's familiars so poor at secret keeping?"

Fionn's ears flattened as he cringed away.

"We work as a family," Harper said, equally cold. "If you know Gabe at all, you know that."

Porta huffed. "Let's hurry and get to him."

The presence of a native, or at least long-term resident, ensured swift passage from the palace to the dock. There they stole a gondola, Harper lying flat with a cloak spread over her as Porta steered them through the busy waters.

Chapter Thirty-Four

Carnivale Incendio

They landed on another island, not far from Venice itself. Screams and laughter filled the air along with the scent of fried sugar and flame-grilled meat. Orange-and-yellow lights danced over the grass, warm after the bluish magelight of the palace. Bursts of flame shot into the sky to mask even the stars. Folk of all shapes and sizes sprinted and flitted around them. Each absorbed in their own delight, they paid no attention to the two dreamwalkers hurrying through their crowds nor the human huddled between them.

Grass gave way to mud as they joined the throng entering a vast fairground bordered by a spiked fence and tall metal gates. Harper had a brief glimpse of flowers twisting around the struts. To her horror, they morphed under her Sight into screaming people. The crowd swept them on before she could process it.

There was fire everywhere. Masked creatures played with it like cats with balls of yarn. Witches soared through flaming hoops. A phoenix screeched its rebirth. A Ferris Wheel spun like a Catherine Wheel on Bonfire Night. Common fairground games jostled alongside magical ones. A dragon rollercoaster spun loops in the sky.

As soon as he was able, Fionn ducked them between the tents. They dodged spurts of fire, hopped over tent pegs and ropes, and wove deeper into the Carnivale Incendio.

They emerged in a trash area between tents to find Grace and Gabriel huddled together. Harper caught a glimpse of static ash under dark hair as she flung herself into her sister's arms. She clung to Grace, her anchor, stalwart, even as the demonhunter's body tensed and one hand slid to the knife at her waist. "It's okay, Gray. Ze is with us. Well, with Fionn." *Or with Gabriel.*

Porta went straight to Gabriel. They spoke in rapid English, foreheads pressed together. Tears ran openly down Gabriel's face and, Harper suspected from the thickness of Porta's voice, zir face too.

"Lelianna?" she asked Grace. She wished she could've looked for the spirit from the boat, but both Fionn and Porta had insisted she remain hidden.

"There aren't many canals on Sant Erasmo. That's this island in case no one mentioned," Grace explained. "There were too many people along the coast for us to sit there long. I brought Gabriel inland to hide here. I figured you and Fionn could find me." Moisture glistened in Grace's eyes and she touched a finger to the Celtic cross at Harper's neck. "You found me last time."

"Always will." Harper pulled her in for another hug. "What now?"

"We get Gabe to a hospital." Grace glanced at Fionn, who was standing to one side shuffling his feet and fiddling with his tail, then at Porta who was deep in conference with Gabriel.

Harper muttered out the corner of her mouth, "Porta is Serenità's dreamwalker."

"THE F—"

Harper clamped a hand over Grace's mouth before her yell could give them away.

Grace pushed her away and continued in a quieter, if no less vehement tone. "What the actual hell, Gabriel? You're *dating* my *prey?*"

Gabriel raised a protective arm in front of Porta. Seeing the blood under his nails, Grace's expression softened slightly.

"I'm dating *Porta*, yes. Ze's a victim here, too, Gray. It's not like you've been completely honest." Gabriel summoned the De Santos' haughtiness, but it was armour with chinks. He jerked his head towards Fionn, who jumped with a guilty *who me?* expression.

"A lot has changed since we last saw each other," Harper said, though she shared Grace's feelings to a degree. *And then there's the secrets we've been hiding from you since the day your father found me in the mists.*

Porta gently lowered Gabriel's arm and met Grace's glare. "Whatever you think of what I am, my only concern here is getting Gabriel to safety."

"I say we take you with us," Grace said. "We don't need to investigate Serenità's weaknesses if we take away her method of reaching us."

"If I could take Porta out of Venice, don't you think I would've done it already?" Gabriel asked. "That's why I've been here so long. I'm not going without Porta and Lelianna."

"I think I can free Lelianna," Harper said slowly. Ever since she read the story of Lelianna's ancestor, an idea had been percolating. "It's specific to her though, I think."

"We need to find my contact," Porta said. "They'll get Gabriel medical aid and take all of you back to England. The Carnivale will leave here at sunrise on the first day of the new year …"

"Tomorrow," Harper muttered for Grace's benefit.

"… and Gabriel's going with it. I've agreed a fee with the gentlesen in charge of the Carnivale's logistics. Gabriel, my love, you must leave Lelianna here. She's one of the unnoticed, her life is not in danger. Yours is."

Harper scowled at the implication Lelianna was unimportant, even though invisibility must be a blessing. "If my plan works, she won't count as one of the Venetian folk anymore. Fionn, will you negotiate on my behalf, since you need to add Grace and Heresy? Don't ask, Gabe."

The cat, who was rubbing his wrists with a pained look on his face, flinched. "Mau?"

"Are you okay?"

"*Mhmm.*" He clasped his hands behind his back. "New Year powers are dangerous. Harper won't harm the city by disrupting Serenità?"

Porta shook zir head. "The blessings for the year ahead are done by the whole city. She would lose her place as doge should she not be present to be the focus for them, but if she weren't, one of the Ten would step in. The city wouldn't be in danger."

"The whole city?" Fionn's eyes widened and he whispered the words in awe. Then he shuddered and blinked rapidly. "I'll negotiate passage for the rest of us, including Lelianna."

"I need to stay here, and search for ways to stop Serenità in case—" Harper cut herself off with a suspicious glance at Porta. She didn't want zir guessing at the solution she and Lelianna found in the library. The crab scissors and spell were safely tucked in Grace's bag.

"I still say we take Porta with us." Grace's eyes were cold as she rubbed the grip of the knife at her belt.

"You cannot imprison me." Sorrow weighed down Porta's voice. "Serenità's magic is too great. Just as the cat cannot directly disobey his master, I cannot directly disobey mine. Detain me, and all you will do is alert Serenità to your plans."

Grace muttered something about being willing to take the risk. From her sister's steely glare at Gabriel, Harper knew she'd try to take Porta prisoner no matter their brother's objections.

"However, I shall come with you," Porta continued, "after a fashion. Serenità and I travel with the Carnivale. It's been arranged as our physical path into England to complete our magics. There's no reason for Harper to stay here."

"Ze's right." Grace squeezed Harper's hand. "If Lelianna comes with us, you can't get into the library anymore. The risk of staying is too great compared to the tiny chance of finding something new. We need you with us."

"I must agree," Heresy chimed from Harper's shoulder, where he had slithered as the two women hugged. "They will track your presence from the dungeons and your life here will be short."

"Then Fionn ..." Harper trailed off. Tears prickled her eyes. "That means he can't stay."

"I was staying to investigate Serenità." Fionn shrugged. "If she's leaving, I should be back at my master's side."

Harper clenched her jaw so hard it hurt.

"Enough of this." Porta's emotionless mask gave Harper chills. "I'll be missed soon. We must secure passage from La Serenissima to England, and you must all hide until we leave."

"Stay with them, Heresy." Harper leant her cheek against him even though it made her teeth ache. "Help them stay invisible." She hugged Grace, Fionn, and, very carefully, Gabriel. "I love you all. Which way?"

Grace pointed and described the route back to the shore where Lelianna waited. Harper glanced back over her shoulder, regret dragging at her limbs. Porta and Fionn supported Gabriel between them, with Grace bringing up the rear as they went in search of Porta's contact.

"Lelianna!" Harper rushed to the edge of the walkway where the water spirit waited with her arms folded on the platform and most of her body submerged.

"Harper!" Lelianna held out a hand and Harper clutched it as she sank to her knees. "I was so worried."

"Fionn's very good at not getting caught in places he's not supposed to be. Thank you for getting Gabriel."

"He's my friend. If you had not come to save him, I would still have tried. I would hope the one he stayed here for would have as well."

"Ze did. Sort of." Harper most certainly did *not* trust the other dreamwalker just because Gabriel bedded zir. He was smart but not impossible for a Romeo agent to trick. She just didn't know why ze would bother, especially if it wasn't with Serenità's blessing.

"You will persuade Gabriel to leave here?" Lelianna asked.

"And you." Harper cupped Lelianna's hand in hers. "He stayed for you, not just his lover, you said it yourself. I can't promise you safety in England, but if you want to come with us, I think I have a way to make that happen, and I have a river in need of a guardian. To be honest, if I don't find one by the equinox, I'll be bound to the river and I really don't want to be. I would never force you to take the role. If you come to England with us and want to leave again, I'll help you find a way. You might be able to stay with the carnival when it moves on, or … I don't know."

"Pretty dreams, sweet witch. I cannot leave La Serenissima. My blood is from here as much as it is from England, and I am bound to La Serenissima and Serenità, as are all who choose to dwell here."

"Your forefather escaped," Harper pointed out.

"Sì, but the family's freedom was short-lived. Though he was able to leave, persecution of folk drove his offspring back to the sanctuary of La Serenissima."

"What if I challenged Serenità as your foremother did? It would distract her from the hunt for Gabriel and give you the opportunity for freedom. She obviously has a strong connection with the arts, that's how she's bridging the divide between our countries and why she let the crab prince go in the first place. I can play her a song unlike any she's likely to have heard before. If my brother could learn to play a new land when he arrived, nameless, in York, then so can I." Harper showed Lelianna her violin, which Grace had brought in a stolen boat along with the rest of their belongings. "This is made of my ancestors, my magic, my blood. It is the craftsmanship of one of the sons of the ancient Greco-Roman god of sleep. It has magic within that can warp reality or become part of it. This isn't my home, and I cannot play this place as I did the trees and hills of Swaledale, but I can still play the water, play the air."

"She will demand a steep price if your song does not match your confidence," Lelianna warned.

"I know." Harper gave a curt nod. After what Lelianna risked for Gabriel, more than once, the family owed her. *And you want her to come back with you, to be the river so you don't have to, and maybe to be something more.* Harper sucked her lips in to hide the memory of fizzle in them.

"Then come."

Lelianna's shell surfaced beside her. As Harper curled into the small space with her, the dark didn't make her heart race or her breath hitch. They both did those things, but it wasn't for fear.

Chapter Thirty-Five

The Crab Princess

From their hiding place within the crab shell, Harper and Lelianna watched Serenità stand at the tip of Venice and begin the Bati Marso celebrations with a song to the sea at midnight. The soft golden shimmer of the ruler's magic lit the scene with an otherworldly beauty. The stars pulsed brighter when touched by Serenità's magic, unlike the carnival lights which veiled them. The tenderness of the song was at odds with Harper's view of the cold ruler who hurt her brother and threatened her city. There was love and compassion in Serenità's voice, and a tear in her eye as she stretched her hand over the waves.

At the conclusion of the song, she turned to a lion-maned being and took a garland of early spring flowers from a tray in his hands. He wore the vestments of a priest, including a stole with embroidered daffodils facing a blackened cross.

As the rites came to an end, and the bells struck one, folk along the shore dispersed. Harper slipped out of the shell. She left her shoes and everything she didn't have to carry. Loneliness engulfed her as the shell, and Lelianna with it, sank beneath the waters. Harper gripped the neck of her violin hard enough that the strings left stripes like a cat scratch across her palm. *This will work. It worked for Lelianna's great-great-whatever grandmother in the folktale. Play the song. Win the flower. Free Lelianna from the curse. We're all leaving here together.*

Serenità stayed on the rocky outcropping after the others left. She threaded leftover flowers through her hair. A wistful smile gave her a youthful appearance that was shattered when she raised her eyes. In a human, Harper would've placed her in her late thirties or early forties. As a fae creature, Harper knew she was several centuries old. When her gaze came to rest on the approaching human, a smirk twitched the corner of Serenità's mouth. Faint crows' feet crinkled as she beckoned Harper closer.

Harper tucked the bone violin under her chin. It was more difficult to connect to the water than to the land she was born of. She had no roots here and no foundation. But Swaledale was not the only part of her story.

Harper closed her eyes and played by feeling.

Scarborough, Whitby, Dover, Folkstone—many summer days on England's coast, on holiday or hunting. She knew the grit of salt in the air and the cry of gulls on the wind. The way the sea tossed a small boat. How a caught fish flapped on its deck. The woosh of the wind whipping her hair in her eyes.

The Adriatic wasn't home, but seas connected just as rivers flowed into each other until they made it to the coast. From the spring beyond her village, into the River Swale, the Ouse, the Humber, and out into the North Sea.

The violin caught the keening notes of the wind and the percussion of waves. It sweetened the creak of moored gondole and the squeaks of dolphins.

As the last note faded, a slow clap brought Harper back to her own body.

"Play on, strigheta," Serenità said when Harper focused on her. "I know why you are here."

"You must honour the story," Harper declared, though she wanted to ask it rather than state. Fionn had shown her that confidence was more compelling than whatever the truth might be.

"I am the protector of La Serenissima's heritage. I would not break her tale." Serenità stood and looked out over the sea. Stars twinkled on the crest of each wave. The wind shifted direction to carry her words to Harper. "The sea has changed since I kept that prince in the shell of a crab. Dangerous creatures have sought refuge here. I will follow the story, but I shall not tame the newcomers. The daughters of Scylla shall consume you, as they do all unwanted folk I offer them. If you will risk that, play on."

Fear hammered Harper's heart. *Lelianna rescued Gabriel from them. She won't let them get me. She won't. For both our sakes. I must let the story play out.*

"Make me a present of the flower in your hair," Harper said, just as the princess challenged Serenità before. She wasn't sure how the flower represented the bond that tied first the prince and now Lelianna here, but she trusted the story.

"Take it from where I throw it, and it, and she, are yours," Serenità promised.

"I shall take it," Harper promised, to Serenità and to Lelianna.

Summoning the sensation again was draining. For all she'd played longer atop the tower in Swaledale, that had been a place with a natural advantage. Nevertheless, she played the wind of Venice and the water of the Adriatic Sea. She Saw the world around her in sound rather than light and Serenità was almost invisible. The violin gathered soundwaves, wove them in harmony, and released them to the listening doge.

I must trust the story. Though Harper couldn't See Serenità, couldn't tell whether her music pleased the ruler or not, she had to believe in it.

When the song finished, Serenità drew a daffodil from her hair and tossed it to the waves. The wind caught it and carried it far before dropping it onto the rolling sea. It glinted gold like a sinking sun in waters black as the witching hour.

"Perhaps we shall not meet again, strigheta," Serenità said. "That would be a shame."

Harper ignored her, strapped the violin to her back, and dove into the water.

Salt stung every cut it could find. Currents thrust against her, fighting to push her back to shore. A song swelled as she crested a wave and pale shapes flitted through the water beneath her. Harper tried to ignore the beating against her eardrums. *Lelianna won't let them get me. She won't.* The crab shell was nowhere to be seen.

Every time Harper thought the flower was in reach her fingers closed on foam. *Is it the last remains of merfolk? Is it true they have no souls?* The melancholy thought weighed Harper down as much as her sodden clothes. *I won't give up. The story says I can reach it.*

She threw herself into the next wave and snatched at the flower, only to grasp water again. *So close.* Something hard touched her foot and she kicked at it in fear, however it also gave her extra thrust and this time her hand closed around the yellow petals.

A solid push against her feet again drew her eyes down, and beneath her Harper beheld the crab shell. She paddled out the way as Lelianna crested and dragged her in.

"You did it." The water spirit pulled Harper into a tight embrace and firm kiss before taking the flower and threading it into her own hair. "Let's get back to the others."

When they reached the shore of Sant Erasmo, Harper hastily disembarked from Lelianna's shell and offered Lelianna a hand to join her. The water spirit hesitated. Her initial joy at being free of Serenità wavered as her foot hovered over the wooden jetty.

"These few square miles of water and this shell are the only home I've ever known." The undine bit her lip. The moisture in her eyes polished them to emeralds.

"You don't have to leave," Harper said softly. She eased her hand around Lelianna's, not to pull her closer to the shore but to hold in light comfort.

"I must. There has never truly been a place for me here. I know in my head that this shell is as much a prison as it is a safehouse."

"But your heart feels differently?"

Lelianna nodded as she swallowed fresh tears.

"Take it and leave by the water." It hurt to suggest it for so many reasons. It meant giving up the one hope Harper had of finding a new spirit for the Ouse. It meant giving up on the only kiss that had sent excitement coursing down her spine to bury itself in her gut. She wasn't in love with Lelianna yet, but it could grow to that. Despite that, she had to let her go. "Find the person you tried to flee with before. England isn't safe. You could seek out other folk to take you in."

"The one I was with before chose to leave without me. I have no interest in seeing her again. Places where there are many folk undoubtedly have no waterways for me." Lelianna darted a last, longing glance at the shell, then stepped onto the jetty. She waved a hand over the water, and the shell sank from sight. "I will go where I have friends. You and Gabriel. I will go where I am needed. From what you have told me of the river, and of your home, many of my kind live there albeit in hiding. I am accustomed to living in the background, in the dark depths. I will take the risk of the known over the unknown." Her lips brushed Harper's cheek. "Let us find the others."

Hand in hand, Lelianna and Harper hurried through the carnival. The undine was unsteady on her legs, rarely having use for coming ashore. A light summer dress was all that protected her. Harper supported her with one arm around her waist.

They paused regularly to scry for Grace. Harper expected her sister around every corner, and every time she was wrong, her heart sank a little further. Muted stars wheeled overhead, stealing the hours until dawn.

The ground convulsed and a claxon warning sounded clear over the screams and crackle of fire that were the undertones of the carnival.

"It's leaving," Lelianna shouted. Her fingers dug into Harper's arm as the tremors caused them both to stumble.

"I trust Fionn," she yelled over the roar of fire and the clanging of bells. "The carnival will take us with it."

The sky was engulfed in a burst of flame that covered the Carnivale Incendio in a dome and threw the two women into the dirt. Screams of horror and of laughter clashed as the billowing fire descended. Harper curled around Lelianna, clinging with one hand to the mooring rope of a tent. The violence of the transition sent her heart racing and compressed her throat so she couldn't even scream. The enchantments of Venice were ripped away. The crackling magic of the Carnivale Incendio remained, beating down on them.

Please, please, please don't hurt them. Whether it was a prayer or whether she hoped the Carnivale itself possessed some kind of cognisance, Harper didn't know. Heat dried her skin and the smell of burnt hair assailed her nostrils. It was an oft repeating nightmare. Not a vision. A nightmare. What would happen if the Guard caught her? Smokeless yet scorching air seared her lungs as she struggled to breathe.

Then, as quickly as the fire engulfed them, cold air rushed in. Harper clung to Lelianna, crying dry tears into brittle hair.

"Look, Harper."

Careful fingertips brushed through her hair. When Harper opened her eyes, the first thing she saw was Lelianna's soft smile. The other woman took her hand and pointed up.

"The stars and moon have moved. We are no longer where we were."

Harper bolted upright. "Grace. We need to find Grace and the others."

Lelianna's skin was papery and dry as Harper took her hand and dragged them both to standing.

"We need to get you to water," Harper said. "Can you sense any nearby?"

"Given time, I could follow the flow of the water deep down and probably find surface level water, but we don't have time. I will be alright. I can survive for some time away from water and I shall bear the discomfort."

Harper squeezed her hand. "Don't put off telling me you need help until it's too late. The fire will have reduced how long you can be out of water, right?"

"I am alright for now. I promise. Let us find the others."

As they headed deeper into the carnival, Harper put an arm around Lelianna's waist. For all her declarations, the water spirit walked hesitantly, and her chest heaved.

"We'll find them quickly and get to water. I promise." Harper held her close. The protective growl in her heart was different to the way she wanted to look after Fionn, yet no less urgent.

Chapter Thirty-Six

Warm Up

Fionn's magic shielded Grace, Heresy, and Gabriel when the fire descended. Turquoise flames blended with the Carnivale Incendio's blues and reds, both binding them to the carnival and protecting them from the heat. His sixth sense of magic and dreams watched in awe as the entire fairground untethered from one reality and passed into the void between. Fionn had glimpsed it along the edges of his portals but had never stepped into it no matter the temptation to escape it all. Duty always stopped him. He snuggled closer to Grace, who put an arm around him. She sat rigid, strong, supporting him on one side and her brother on the other.

Fionn expected at least some pressure or pushback when the Carnivale passed the Veil, but there was nothing. Which meant either his master let it through or they possessed some dark magic of travel between realms that his master had never encountered.

Without the warning of the Veil, phasing back within England's borders ripped Fionn from his wonder. His collar constricted as soon as his feet touched English soil, and the pain, which had been a background murmur, roared to life hotter than anything the Carnivale had thrown at them. His master's will seized his blood and hijacked his magic. It left him helpless, trapped inside his own body. The order had been to stop him being perceived by Harper's household. There was no subroutine for what happened if he started right next to one.

Fionn screamed as his master's magic wrenched him every way at once. He couldn't see, couldn't hear. The crushing weight of disobedience flattened him into the mud. He couldn't even obey the original intent by portalling away. His magic was no longer his, and the order that commandeered it didn't know how to react to Grace holding his shoulders.

It burst out of him and he was dimly aware of her being thrown back. *I'm sorry.* He wanted to sob and fix it, but he couldn't.

Without his consent, his body shifted. Instinct said smaller was less perceivable.

Harper's presence joined Grace's. He tried to reach out to her, his only family, but he couldn't move so much as a toe in her direction. Both presences retreated, along with Heresy's, and the pain receded with them. As soon as they could no longer see or hear him, the magic had a clear path. A swirling portal of silver opened beneath him, and the cat tumbled through.

Harper clung to Grace and Lelianna as she sobbed. Without the crowds of Venetians, they'd found her sister quickly.

Harper had seen Fionn in pain, both recently and as a child, but he'd always born it, hidden it as much as he could. For this to have been so extreme he collapsed screaming, it must've been worse even than the Somnia cutting into him for her violin strings.

"You did what was best for him." Grace stroked her hair. Tense in Harper's arms, the demonhunter in Grace watched everything around them, twitchy as the carnival quieted for sleep. "If he's cursed to make sure we can't perceive him, anything other than getting away will hurt him worse."

"I will go back," Lelianna volunteered. "His curse cannot have made allowance for folk from a foreign land." She kissed Harper's cheek, then slipped back through the tents only to reappear less than a minute later. "I'm sorry. He's already gone."

Harper swallowed rising self-recrimination. If he'd gone home to the one who cast the horrible curse on him in the first place, she dreaded to think what awaited him.

"I hate it too." Grace placed her hands on Harper's tear-slicked cheeks and looked into her eyes. "He would want us to stop Serenità. We can't help him; we can help his dreamer and the other cursed people in York."

"I know where he is. The Tower of London. That's where his master lives."

Gabriel's head snapped up and he winced. "*The* Tower of London? But ..." Scruffy hair swishing over his shoulders as he shook his head. "Grace is right. Even if that's where he is, somehow, your priority is protecting the people of York."

"Because they're human and Fionn isn't? Because there are more of them? You don't know him, Gabe. You can't judge." Even to her own ears, Harper sounded hysterical. Fionn might've been gone, but she could still Hear his screams, overlayed with pain and pain and more pain. Every time she'd seen him harmed when they were children. Every time she'd failed to protect him. He was *her* cat, not this master's.

"Because if Fionn can't beat whoever is imprisoning him, we have no chance," Grace said. "We have a chance here. It's what he would want. He risked everything going to Venice to help his dreamer, and to help us."

"He risked everything coming back," Harper sobbed. "He could've been safe there. His master's commands weren't working. He could've stayed."

"He made a choice, Harp," Gabriel said quietly. "Gray offered him the chance to leave the carnival and disappear into Europe. He wanted to return."

"He's brainwashed," Harper muttered. The fight bled out of her and she sank to the ground.

"Harper, you must stand up to Serenità." Lelianna knelt in front of her. "She's not the horror you think she is, but she has been ruler of a besieged land too long. Her priorities are not always in the interest of those outside her borders. A compromise may yet be reached."

Harper dried her eyes and nodded. "You're right. You all are."

"First things first." Grace brushed off her hands and checked her weapons were in place. "We need to get out of this carnival and work out where we are. Then we need to find out where Serenità is going. Probably York. Drop Gabriel and Lelianna off somewhere. Touch in with the boys."

"Yes, General." Harper exchanged a weak smile with her sister.

Even burdened with Gabriel, getting out of the carnival proved straightforward. Heresy's magic made them difficult to notice, and the fluttering of dawn's eyelashes had sent the carnival folk scurrying for their beds.

Rain hit as they stepped past wrought iron rose gates. Lelianna spread her arms and took a deep breath of it. Despite her fragile covering, the cold that misted their breath didn't phase her. Harper had never been so grateful to live in a damp country.

Welcome home…

Have you come to play?

You brought a new toy…

The barely whispered words goosed Harper's skin more than the rain. She scanned the shifting mists but could See nothing there.

"Did you hear that?"

"Nothing," Grace replied with an impatient tug. "Let's get out of here."

Harper's Sight gleamed as she swept the haze again. For a moment, she thought she Saw the silhouette of a humanoid, but they dissipated before she could tell if it was real or a trick of her eyes.

"Harper?" Gabriel's uncertain voice jolted her back.

"Later," Grace snapped at her brother.

A path through the trees, hidden by murk, stood out to Harper's Sight. "This way."

Mud sucked at their feet. Twice, Harper stepped in puddles deep enough to spill over the tops of her shoes and seep through her socks. The path flooded. Submerged tree roots grasped at toes and ankles as they picked their way around. Before long, they emerged by a boggy field surrounded on all sides by woodland.

"We are near a river," Lelianna said. "This way."

They crossed the field as quickly as their squelching shoes allowed and passed through a second wave of flooded woodland. On the other side, they faced a swollen river with no bridges visible through the mists, even to Harper's Sight.

Lelianna smiled as she plunged her hands into the cold water. "I know you," she whispered. "You feel like coming home. May I?"

Though there was no change to confirm assent or dissent, Lelianna must've sensed something beyond Harper's abilities, for she stepped into the water. She sank only slightly, as though the water bore her weight like Harper had seen the River Foss do for the fossegrim who cared for it.

The undine turned and smiled at Harper. "It seems you were correct. When you envisioned me, I too Saw this river. She is old and wild at heart, where I am young and have been confined my whole life. I believe she will welcome symbiosis."

"The Ouse? We're in Yorkshire?" Harper looked up and down the shore again, her Sight limited by the curve of the river and the weather.

"There is a bridge over there." Lelianna pointed upstream. "I sense a greater number of dwellings on her shore farther along, too, and another strong river joining."

"Probably the Foss," Harper said. "You should go talk to him."

"I should come with you."

"No." Harper didn't like to say the undine's magic wasn't useful. Anything she knew, the older, more powerful Doge of Venice undoubtedly knew how to counter. "The river needs you. Since Usa's demise, we've had fewer fish, more floods, and evil creatures. It's as important to restore the natural balance as it is to stop Serenità. Maybe more so." Harper was painfully aware that stopping Serenità was a human-centric priority. Like stopping Usa's ritual, that didn't mean it was necessarily the right priority.

"Leave Gabriel with me. Even without my shell, I can bear him upriver."

"Downriver." Harper walked a few meters along the bank and placed a hand on a large rock, finally finding a point of familiarity. "We're in Danesmead Woods. This is where Fionn and I were when I remembered his name. If you take Gabriel downriver, round the big bend, you'll reach Bishopthorpe Palace."

"I'll recognise it," Gabriel said. "But I should be with you two."

"You're a liability, bro. I'd spend more time defending you than actually getting something done." Grace said it jokingly, but her eyes crinkled in worry as she glanced him over.

"Yeah. I know." Gabriel sighed and released his sister to hobble to the water's edge. "Drop me off at the shore of Bishopthorpe and I'll limp my way up to the house. Most of the archbishop's staff have known me since I was a kid; though they might not recognise me like this." He turned to Harper as he put an arm around Lelianna's shoulders. "Harp ... whatever is going on here"—he gestured to her eyes—"you're my sister. Please don't hurt the person I'm in love with. Porta isn't bad. Ze's stuck with Serenità, and I don't know what she's made zir do, but Porta doesn't *want* to hurt anyone. Please protect zir for me."

"I don't want to hurt anyone either, Gabe." Harper scrunched her eyes closed and pinched the bridge of her nose until the burn from her Sight faded. "If Porta told Fionn the truth, ze can break this whole spell. I'm hoping ze will do it willingly. As for Serenità and her control ... I don't know. I'll do everything I can."

"Thank you."

"Good luck." Lelianna caught Harper's hand as she stepped back to let Grace hug their brother goodbye. She cupped Harper's cheek and leant in for a kiss that brushed a fire hotter than the carnival over Harper's lips. "Return so we can explore this further."

"I'll do my best." Harper quirked a smile as she reluctantly pulled away. She held the bone violin out to Lelianna. It wouldn't work on Serenità twice and might make Harper susceptible to Porta's dream magics. "Keep this safe for me?"

Lelianna cradled it in one arm, like she'd been entrusted with a child. "I will."

They parted ways, and Harper, Grace, and a very disgruntled and soggy Heresy quickly found the bridge Lelianna had mentioned.

"Millenium Bridge," Grace remarked as they approached the familiar swoop. "If we'd come out a bit further along, we'd've known exactly where we were."

"But where is Serenità?" Harper asked. "We don't have much time."

"I can't believe *I'm* the one suggesting this, but try scrying for her." Grace glanced up and down the river. The downpour, and the impossible haze it should've washed away, kept everyone human in their houses. Rain slicked her hair to her face, only serving to accentuate her set jaw and twitching cheek.

"I could attempt to have a vision," Harper suggested. "I had one before when Serenità and Porta were lurking before the bookshop incident, and again before Dayo's painting."

She closed her eyes, pushing her awareness past the rain trickling down her spine and the static of Heresy resting on her hand. Deep breaths. Clear thoughts. Verging on the sluggishness of sleep. That would be where Porta would be, with the magic that bound the unfortunate souls ze and Serenità had cursed.

This way, Harper ...

Let us help you ...

We could work together ...

We could consume the intruder ...

Delicioussssss ...

Harper wanted to clap her hands over her ears against the whispery hiss. She tried to block them out, to concentrate on the magic.

A memory let itself in without knocking.

"Dorian, I'm afraid to go to sleep. What if I have another vision?" Her younger self, scarcely more than five, clung to her brother's sleeping robe.

"Our parents said the visions are good." Even then, there'd been doubt in his voice. *"They said you can dream things that can help our people stay safe."*

"They frighten me," little Harper whispered as she snuggled up to him. *"What do you do when your dreams frighten you?"*

"I don't dream."

"Never?" She looked up at him wide-eyed and caught the sorrow in his eyes before he could banish it.

"Never. Crawl in with me tonight. Maybe you can give me dreams and I can give you quiet."

Harper let her younger self curl into sleep and her own mind drift away from the scene. Dorian had never dreamt. She wondered what he would've said about her dreamwalking cat. Maybe she'd told him and hadn't remembered yet.

Without Fionn, she couldn't find Porta's dreams or the sleeping cursed, yet the fact she wasn't a dreamwalker hadn't stopped her sensing Porta and Serenità before, nor had it stopped her Seeing the spell the possessed were drawing.

"I'm looking for the wrong thing. The spell. I've Seen the spell. I need to See it now."

At the realisation, her vision soared above the charcoal grey sky. York lay below her like an exquisitely drawn map. Following the path of the old city wall, a band of liquid gold crowned the city. Rivulets of shining metal ran down ginnels. Light rose from the magic, in runes, letters, notes, words, and images. They layered upon each other like bricks and a great temple arose. It obliterated the city centre, even the Shambles where magic already dwelt, and the eight-hundred-year-old cathedral that had survived wars, fires, and bombs.

A little south of the centre of the structure, the light beamed brightest. Harper's vision swooped low over the city, flitting through alleys, up snickelways, and down deserted main streets until it reached the Opera House.

"I know where to go." The vision shattered as Harper yanked herself back, afraid the Venetian casters might sense her. "The Opera House."

"Makes sense," Grace agreed. "It's where they laid the foundations. We need to get somewhere we can use a phone and check in with Saqib."

They hurried down the park path to the nearest building, where a carport provided enough shelter for Harper to dig out her phone and the portable charger that was part of any De Santos emergency kit.

"Harper? Where—"

"Saqib, are you home?" The fact it was near dawn wasn't entirely a guarantee he wasn't at work, all sense of time forgotten. "We're back in England. The dreamwalker's here too. It's complicated, but we think, we *know*, they're going to the Opera House. Grace and I are going to stop them. Have you and AJ found anything useful?"

"It's a trap." AJ took the phone from Saqib.

"You *are* at home. Great. So you can talk. Can one of you—"

"We're at the police station. I'm one of their tech consultants, remember?"

Grace raised an eyebrow. Things must be bad if AJ had left the house and for both of them to be out at this hour.

He continued, "My mum was asked to invite me to that opera. Someone wanted you there."

"Who?" Harper asked at the same time as Grace.

"We don't know. She thought it was from someone trying to matchmake me with their daughter. When I did some digging, the daughter doesn't exist. Still following the trail, but it means you're in extra danger. My bet is whoever it was knew I wouldn't take the tickets. They wanted you two there, or at least one of you."

"One? The Magician's familiar?" Harper hazarded. She'd certainly been involved in the painting curse.

"Doesn't matter right now," Grace said. "We have to go. We'll be careful. Anything else useful?"

"The thing I thought might link the victims from the DNA tests turned out to be a coincidence," Saqib said. "Dayo didn't share it. We have observed that all the victims are going into REM sleep much more rapidly and for longer than is normal for humans. That's including the bystander victims, not just those directly involved. We've also observed an unusually quick build-up of adenosine in the blood of those affected. Adenosine can make you drowsy."

"If it's affecting everyone, it could be in Grace and me as well." Harper glanced at Grace, who shrugged. Constant danger had a way of making sleep tricky and her fatigue was easily explainable by tension and overuse of magic. However, Saqib's description was consistent with the spell she read about.

"I'll meet you en route with caffeine just in case," Saqib said. "There's also a high amount of acetylcholine, which suggests there might be some learning triggered by the curse."

"Why did I not think of chemically altering her brain to stuff something into it?" Heresy asked, his habitual grin returned. Both women glared at him.

"Thanks, Saqib. Meet you by Clifford's Tower?" Harper checked.

"Better at Skeldergate Bridge. There's a redcap in the tower no one's been able to shift. Already killed one person and hospitalised two others flinging rocks down. I imagine Albrecht has it on a list of to dos with your name on it."

"Great." Harper rolled her eyes. "Okay. We're going to follow the river. We'll meet you there."

A swift walk got them there in a little under fifteen minutes and circumvented any Guard checkpoints along the roads. Saqib's car was already parked near the bridge. He frowned at them as they dove in, dripping puddles on the upholstery. AJ whipped his laptop off the backseat and onto his lap with a stern glare at Harper.

"What happened to Fionn and Gabriel?" Saqib asked.

"Gabriel's gone to Bishopthorpe. We think Fionn went home. Whatever magic stopped him from talking to us kicked in again as soon as we were back in England." Harper's mouth twisted at the sour taste the answer left.

"We'll help him once we've dealt with this." Grace turned in the front passenger seat.

"Is Miguel meeting you here?" Saqib said.

Grace and Harper grimaced at each other at the reminder the middle De Santos child was in town.

"Harper needs magic to defeat Serenità." Grace examined her no longer perfectly manicured fingernails. "There are ... other complications as well."

"We request a backup team," Harper suggested. "I'll text. Gabriel will probably fill in any blanks he can."

"Any other useful intel?" Stiff, Grace shot Harper a last, worried look before she turned back to Saqib.

"Not really." Saqib cracked open two energy drinks and passed them to the women along with a packet of caffeine pills. Grace downed hers while Harper sipped the sickly liquid with a scowl. "I've run further tests and been able to observe some kind of invisible ink tattoo on the writer and musicians—words from the book and parts of Legrenzi's music—but I've not quite got the scanning right to see them on Alcina or Dayo yet. It was visible under different conditions on each of the five so far. I also haven't been able to find any trace or measurable connection between the victims. I don't know how to sever them from the caster or what harm that might cause. We're treating them to cancel the effects I mentioned before. Sadly, we're having very limited success."

"The Dungeons are down the road from the Opera House. Go to Christina and Dayo, and do everything you can to keep them awake."

"Caffeine, dopamine, distraction, et cetera., check." Saqib started the car. "I'll drop you off on the way."

"I'll take Dayo. You take the singer," AJ added. "Fionn's told me some about his dreamer. If we can't keep him awake, maybe having some knowledge of his usual dreams will help."

"I told Albrecht we're trying something," Saqib said. "She's alerted the checkpoints that we're out tonight so we shouldn't get any hassle. I'll call her with the bare bones of the plan. If they use the same methods on those the Guard have captive, we'll hopefully weaken the spell, at least for long enough for you to find a way to stop the dreamwalker, inshallah."

Chapter Thirty-Seven

Cadenza

Two Guardspeople stood yawning at the taped-off entrance to the Opera House, but nobody watched the nondescript service entrance at the back. When Grace placed her hand on the door to pick the lock, it swung open.

They moved almost silently through the backstage chaos. Faux-Classical clothing hung in rows like a queue to be guillotined. Busted lights gathered dust. Flickering neon strips above glinted off shards of glass. The inconsistent light gave life to mannequins, drunk and leaning in corners. Their whispers twittered amongst flapping rags of broken props, gossiping scandal and mockery. A mound of costume helmets and swords told stories of death. Scraps of paper, pen scribblings violently scrawled over type, drifted through the air like the hair of a spurned, drowned lover. Draughts fluttered curtains and the sails of the white boat from the opening scene of *Orlando Furioso*. The gaze of a broken prop horse followed them down the corridor, its bloodshot eyes bulging.

"No footprints," Grace whispered. She pointed at the trail left by their wet boots and dripping hair.

"Maybe the ruler of a water city knows better how to control the element," Heresy said calmly.

"I'm sure she's here." Harper took the lead, sweeping Sight-brightened eyes over the mayhem. "If she's connected to her victims, I can hopefully See the threads of it like I could at the opera. If I can See them, I can sever them." She patted the crab claw scissors Grace had returned to her.

Backstage was a maze over multiple levels. At each dressing room and branching corridor, they investigated and cleared the area to ensure they weren't leaving a potential enemy at their backs. When they neared the stage, they split, Grace taking stage right and Harper and Heresy taking left.

Baritone and a mezzo soprano voices wove a chant that drooped Harper's eyelids in a similar way to Fionn's humming, and she was grateful for the artificial zing of energy in her veins.

She risked a peek around fractured scenery. The stage itself had been cleared and parts of Hekate's temple reassembled. In the centre, a group of masked folk sat around a hovering ring of water. Trickles ran between them to form a complex pattern. A solo electric bulb buzzed nearby, but it was magic that bathed the hall in light.

"The activation spell, most likely," Heresy whispered into Harper's ear.

Grace's head poked out from behind a curtain at the opposite end of the stage. She signalled to Harper. *On my mark. You take Porta. I'll take Serenità.*

Heresy slithered away to hide in the rubble. Grace's hand dropped.

They had barely rushed a few steps when Serenità raised a hand and froze them both.

Harper fought to reach her sister. A vein throbbed in the demonhunter's forehead as Grace thrashed against bonds she couldn't see. Seeing didn't help. Golden radiance diffused over their skin, trapping them as tightly as if a block of ice enveloped them.

"I was concerned you would be late," Serenità said, turning her masked face towards them.

AJ's right. But why would she want us here? Magic tightened against Harper's skin. It crushed, like the water which had buried her deep in the library. Lelianna had helped her breathe, as Harper had foreseen. She hadn't foreseen this.

"Come." Serenità crooked a finger, and magic dragged Harper and Grace to her.

None of those seated around the flowing circle raised their eyes. Not even Porta, identifiable by zir blue mask where all the others wore silver. Grace was turning magenta as she fought Serenità's summoning.

"Don't fight it, Harper. Relax and flow with the dreaming. You'll See what you need."

It was a bloody inconvenient time for a memory ambush. She wanted to shout at the echo of her brother in her head. He was the oldest. He should've protected her.

But then, she wouldn't be in this place to protect people now.

Maybe memory was only her own subconscious Seeing what her frightened conscious mind could not.

Before she could second guess herself, Harper let the chant drag her eyes closed and cast its mist over her mind. The magical grip on her body lessened, though the heaviness of being near sleep weighed down her limbs.

The ghost of lips found hers, and a different voice trickled through her memory. *"I am able to give you the ability to exist here, for a short time."*

Breathing eased and magic slackened further.

Another's magic brushed against her mind, alien yet not completely unfamiliar.

"Porta?" Harper tried to open a tiny crack in the defences her magic had erected, braced by Heresy's teaching and the slowly returning memories.

"Sì. While the magic brings you to a place between wakening and dreaming, I can divert a little attention to speak to you."

"You can stop this." The force of the thought knocked Harper closer to the wakening, and Porta's mind slid away from hers. She drew in a deep breath and tried to open her mind again. Words spilt in mixed up orders and echoes that somehow resolved into a memory of intelligible speech.

"I promised the cat I would release the one tangled with his magic, and I shall. His reawakening shouldn't harm the spell overly, especially not with you here."

"If you can do it for one, you can do it for all. Why does it matter that I'm here?"

"This magic is important. Terrible things are unleashed. Balance must be regained. I risked much to save one man, and I would do it again. It doesn't mean I lost my faith in this magic."

"You're going to destroy an entire city, folk and humans alike."

"Rest and know you are part of a greater good. This magic will not harm you for you are part of it."

Porta's thoughts withdrew. The conversation took less than the blink of an eye, warped within the time of a daydream. Strands of magic, violet and gold, twinkled within the water spell. It parted, then reformed as Serenità positioned Harper at the centre of it.

The world spun and the golden ceiling rushed to her. Caught in a web of dreamscape, Harper's befuddled mind could barely grasp the fact she was hovering, on her back, spinning slowly counterclockwise. Part of the spell.

No! Her mind and body rebelled. The magic tightened again, and she choked on her own saliva as her throat constricted. When she tried to scream, her lips stuck together like she'd kissed ice.

"Don't fear the darkness, Harper. Breathe and let it wash over you." Stars glimpsed through pine trees wheeled overhead, faint daydreams sparkled from the crystal chandelier on the opera house ceiling.

Shut up, shut up, shut up. Memories of a brother long gone were no good to her now. She needed the sister next to her, the one who had stood by her through everything.

The memory of sitting next to Grace at the Opera House floated in front of her.

Water bubbled over her skin like a river washing over tiny rocks.

Grace had been with her as she'd crouched at Christina's side and tried to reach the human woman behind the mirage of the mythical enchanter.

Pinpricks of violet magic sank into her skin like tattoo ink.

Each victim drifted through Harper's vision. An overlay of reality formed on misty breath and sucked magic from her. The author stuck inside a fictional woman in a drowned library. The musician from whose lips musical annotation poured forth, visible to nobody except her. Fionn's dreamer frantically painting his interpretation of a scene engineered centuries ago.

Serenità's power burrowed through skin and muscle, drilled into Harper's bones, and polluted her magic.

Brilliant vines of lights spread from Harper, through the hands of the casters, and thrust through the walls of the Opera House to connect to Serenità's victims, and from them to the audiences they'd enchanted. In turn, the magic that had incubated in them streamed back into the Opera House and became the stone of temple walls. The architecture of Hekate's temple rose and expanded.

"Tell the cat I have done as I promised."

At Porta's intrusion, one of the vines snapped. The masked figure on Harper's left keeled over and magic thread unravelled on the floor. The remaining magic heaved, like Harper fought to control a coach and six where all the horses were wild stallions. Only she had no control. She was the reins, not the hand that guided them.

"Snap the rest of them, damn you," Harper shouted with her thoughts, but Porta was no longer connected to her. Zir dream magic dragged her deeper underwater as the circle's magic closed over her body and distorted her vision with ripples.

Stay. Awake. With the mental command to herself, Harper sucked her cheek through the thin gap between her top and bottom teeth, and bit down hard.

Blood gargled her muffled shriek and pain thrust her hard into wakening. Her body tipped to the left, towards the prone figure. A weak link in the spell. Water tickled her skin with overlapping waves as the magic gripping her faltered. The temple walls wavered like a mirage. Harper wrenched her arm free with a splash.

She fumbled for the crab claw scissors as the remaining golden magic crackled and fractured, dumping her on the floor. A grunt escaped between locked teeth slick with blood as the hard stage impacted her ribs. Years of De Santos training took over and Harper bounced to her feet, spun, and snipped the scissors through the magical vines in Porta's hand.

Dredging up the memory of the book's instructions, she shouted, "Dreams once apart, now woven tight, unbind our fates, sleep alone this night."

The claws passed through the light as though it were just that. Light. Not the magic the book promised these could break.

Tinkling laughter interrupted the chant and the remaining casters fell silent. Harper backed away as she circled towards Grace. Serenità's magic no longer encased her sister. Instead, a steady stream of magic pierced Grace's forehead. Her skin was pale and clammy, and she muttered under her breath just as those they visited in jail had done.

"I wondered if you found those." Serenità's smile was sharp as the scissor blades. "And the book as well. Delightful. Many folk frown upon dreamwalkers and believe them merely casters of pretty playtimes, but a little creative thinking makes them so much more."

Harper's grip on the scissors tightened. She darted to Grace's side and dug them into the magic holding her sister.

"It will not work," Serenità said.

"If they don't work, why would you hide them?" Harper challenged.

"To give you something to find." Serenità's hand fell on Porta's shoulder. "My dreamwalker knew you would look for us. Ze planted more than a seed of this spell in you. Ze planted a connection. Visions are not so different from dreams. Ze couldn't create a false vision, but ze could nudge your magic towards what I wanted you to See. Despite the Magician's promises, I knew you might bring your fight into our home. Stubborn girls need misdirection to calm them to obedience. They do not respond to threats or orders, save by digging their heels in deeper. My maestri were forever having to come up with new distractions for me."

"So you and Porta acted out a scene and, what? Placed a fake book?" Harper felt deeply betrayed. She'd risked her life for an answer and after everything it was *a book* that led her astray? Aided by her own magic?

"The book and scissors are real. However, they are no threat to my spell. I vanquished their creator, I know how to counter her magic. You fall from the clouds, strigheta. I know that does not mean you shall come easily. I would be disappointed in you if you did, for we are not dissimilar."

Golden light sprang from Serenità's hand to encase Harper again. She dived aside. It followed like a homing missile and exploded over her prone body. A black haze swarmed her vision, and the bright light glittered out.

"*Ow*," Heresy grumbled petulantly as he shrank back in on himself. Gold sparkled within his sooty form.

"Thank you." Harper clutched him against her chest before turning a defiant glare on Serenità. "I defeated you before, for Lelianna, and I will this time too."

Auburn ringlets danced about Serenità's bare shoulders as she shook her head. "Your tune was pretty, strigheta, nothing more. The maestri of La Serenissima are amongst the brightest jewels of music. Some of them even contributed to this spell, though they lie in graves and beneath the waves. I never cared if the half-English spirit left. My pact is to keep those deemed dangerous and criminal, the Church has never required me to keep their offspring."

Harper's mind raced, searching for the truth or lie behind Serenità's words. The implication that Fionn's master and the Church both had dealings with the supernatural folk of Venice, a state stricken from all English maps, boggled her.

"Your spirit absorbed a little of my magic," Serenità continued, gesturing at Heresy. "I have more. This is not a fight you can win. Nor should you wish to. What does a witch in hiding owe to human bricks and mortar? Why should you want to preserve a city that would murder you, when rebuilding it is a step towards restoring the balance of magic and stopping the rampaging infection?"

"How will raising a temple to an ancient goddess do that? If you destroy the stone, you will kill the people living within, and what of those you've cursed? Their minds are gone, overwritten by your fantasy. Is that what's happening to everyone linked to them?" Harper shook Grace's shoulder. It was like shaking a bronze statue. "Do you think I want to help with *anything* if it means killing my own sister?"

"Those linked to us shall not die." Serenità spoke slowly as though Harper were a wilful child who couldn't see the full picture. "It is not our intent to kill anyone. Whether Hekate is a goddess or whether she wields a magic beyond our understanding is a matter for individual belief, as is any religion. *I* do not believe she is a goddess, nor do I intend to summon some spirit here. I summon her temple for what it can do. It is the blueprint of a greater magic, one that brings liminality into a world constrained by the binary of narrowminded good and evil dictated by human prejudice.

"Myths of Hekate are distorted by human bias. She was not a creature of evil magic. That is patriarchy and anti-magic rhetoric. She was seen, by those who believed in her, as a goddess of transition, one who could bar or open pathways, and who stood between life and death. This is not the first place we have summoned this casting as a panacea for the ailments humans inflict upon magic. This land has been plagued by many ills in the last four hundred years. Without a rebalancing of its magic, it will die, and it is dragging the rest of Europe with it. Maybe even farther afield if it lingers in its death throes."

"You're saying you're creating a bigger spell to flood England with magic and stop the infection that's making magic backfire?" Harper asked.

Serenità sighed. "Not exactly and yet in essence, yes. England has been cut off for too long. From the liminal space between realms that strengthens them and keeps balance, and from the magic needed by the soil as much as you need air. People here believe they can cast out that which is 'other,' those who do not look like them or adhere to their exact view of the universe. This is a slow death, and the final moments approach."

Despite her horror at the idea of York being transubstantiated into an architectural spell, what Serenità said fit with things Fionn said about how he and his master travelled the country, performing blood rites to return a little magic to the earth.

"How can you claim to be saving people when you're destroying people to do so?" Though she looked at Serenità, Harper watched Porta. Serenità's belief was unshakable, but Porta had already weakened the spell to save Gabriel. There was a chink in their armour she might be able to dig the point of her blade into. "Just because their bodies aren't dead, doesn't mean their souls live. Christina, your Alcina, is a mother, she has a husband of twenty-five years and three children. Vita, the writer, recently got engaged. Dayo, the painter, creates art that promotes thought about magic and non-human folk. He is at the centre of a large circle of friends who are all a little less anti-magic because they are willing to be part of the discussion through art. And Zero loves him. This painter has been the only light in the life of the most magical person I've ever met, who works constantly to bring magic back to this land and would give his life to do so. Your spell would shatter his heart."

"He will not need to give his life once the foundations of this magic are in place. The cat and his master can amplify their magic through the temple rather than through blood." A sneer marred Serenità's voice, though Harper couldn't see her face. It was unnerving to speak to someone whose lips were unmoving. Serenità's eyes roved the stage. "Where is the creature?"

"I thought you knew everything?" Harper couldn't help but get in a jab of her own.

"Sì. I will allow that the cat was a surprise to me, as was the clever release of the human. Human*s*." Serenità's eyes tightened, lips pursed as she turned her disapproving gaze on Porta. The dreamwalker's head was bowed, zir mask hiding all expression, but the magic quivered ever so slightly as the hand that held it trembled.

Harper wanted to be angry with Porta, without zir complicity York would've been safe, however she knew what it was like to be manipulated by a more powerful being that was convincing in the illusion of a saviour role. Guilt dug its claws into her heart. She'd let it hurt her own village and her best friend. That seemed worse than hurting strangers.

Serenità gathered the fallen strands of magic dropped by the caster Porta severed from the spell, and moved the fallen Venetian aside with surprising tenderness.

"Do not think this weakens the spell enough to stop our casting. In La Serenissima, we are accustomed to dealing with shifting foundations." Serenità paused to survey the half-converted theatre. Her eyes unfocussed as though she were seeing through the walls into the vaster net of the spell she cast. "Folk still slumber. When dawn arrives, others will realise they cannot be woken. Not an insurmountable barrier, if you are playing for time, merely irksome."

Serenità flicked her fingers towards Harper. Golden magic passed through Heresy's attempt at a shield and bound Harper before she could react. As before, the more she struggled, the tighter her bonds became as Serenità maneuvered her back to the centre of the spell. This time, the magic dug in faster, following the holes it drilled through her before. It crackled inside her bones, and she grit her teeth. Where before she'd been sinking into a dream and pain grounded her, now pain was part of the spell, and she wished the dreaming would release her from it. Water trickled over her skin as the magic drew her in again.

"Harper, you must stop fighting." Porta's voice slid around her skull.

"No. You must start fighting." Weakness seized her limbs. Harper's mind rebelled, but her body was a distant concern. It reminded her of being

stabbed, that mixture of burning pain and smothering numbness. Dust motes of green and gold flickered before her woozy eyes. Water climbed up her throat and over her chin.

"*You are a conduit,*" Porta told her. "*Relax, let the magic flow and you shall be unscathed by it. Take comfort in being part of something greater.*"

Another voice interrupted, younger and from longer ago. "*Don't listen when he tells you you're part of something greater. He wants to you be proud of being used. Don't let him get in your head, Harper.*"

"*But Dorian, I am protecting our people. Mama said so too.*"

"*Mama is repeating what he told her to say, and Grandmama, and all of you. Your life isn't worth less than mine or anyone else's. You're my sister. I love you. I won't stand by and let you get hurt.*"

As the memory of her brother's protest faded, Harper tried to channel his surety at Porta. "*You are repeating what Serenità tells you. You don't have to be proud of being used.*" She wished she could say it to Fionn as well. Water bubbled over her closed lips. She took a deep breath through her nose.

"*I've seen the spell work. Much smaller versions, but it does work.*"

"*And how many souls did you take for those?*" Harper demanded. "*You were willing to risk this spell failing to save Gabriel. He would rather you left him in jail and saved everyone here.*" Water clogged her nose as she struggled for her next breath.

"*He would've been killed.*"

"*And being trapped in your own mind while someone else erases your identity is better? Can you look Gabriel in the eyes after this?*"

"*I am saving people, Harper. Gabriel will understand that saving the country is worth more than a few individuals.*" Porta's strong denial smashed through Harper's mind, leaving her dizzy. Or maybe it was the magic being sucked out of her that pooled around her like blood from a gushing wound, or the fact the water had closed over her nose, her whole body, and her lungs ached to bursting.

"*No. He won't.*" Harper's thoughts were sad and sluggish. She couldn't reach Porta's heart. Serenità carved it out of zir chest long ago. "*He won't forgive you for doing this to his sisters, either.*"

"*I didn't know. I didn't know who you were …*"

"*It shouldn't matter.*" Darkness framed Harper's vision and swallowed her thoughts. She couldn't stop herself from trying to breathe. The magic held its place. Water didn't rush into her lungs. Neither did air.

"Serenità. She can't breathe."

"*Why are you calling me 'Serenità'?*" In her befuddled state, Harper couldn't tell what was heard by her disconnected mind and what was the muzzy sound of a real voice through water. The words echoed, both Venetian and English at once.

"You removed a component from the spell. The energy must come from somewhere else."

"If you drain any more magic, you could kill her."

"To save everyone else, I shall do what must be done. I thought you understood."

"Not her."

Magic twanged like broken strings. The other casters fell and Harper dropped to the floor. The impact rang her skull like the bells of Saint Peter's Cathedral. She managed to prop herself up on her elbows to squint at the three Serenitàs and three Portas in front of her. Their shouted words scrambled in her brain.

"Enough." Grace stumbled to her feet, crossbow in hand. Despite her sister's paleness, the bolt pointed at Serenità didn't waver.

"England chooses the slow death." Serenità drew herself up, regal even when ragged from the breaking of her magic. "My allies and I shall not allow ourselves to be drowned with you."

Light burst from her hands in a billowing sphere. Porta threw zirself over Harper, knocking her to the floor again. Brilliant white seared Harper's eyes followed by darkness.

"Get off of her."

Harper blinked as a weight was dragged from her. She still couldn't see. *Did I pass out?*

"Harp, are you conscious? Talk to me?"

"Gray?"

Grace's normal scent was subdued by sweat, but even that was a familiar comfort as she enfolded Harper in a possessive hug.

"What's happening?" Harper pulled herself up, one arm around Grace as she blinked furiously to clear her vision.

"Serenità disappeared in that flashbang. I've got Porta. The others are unconscious. The Opera House is … I don't know."

A wavering scene painted itself before Harper's Sight-enhanced eyes. Different architectures were smashed together, and a half-formed fountain like the one in her vision bubbled in the centre of the stage.

"It's part temple." Porta's voice was strained and zir silhouette sprawled on the floor. "But incomplete. I don't know if what's here will help or harm more."

"Here." Grace pressed a phone into Harper's hand. "I've dialled it. You talk so I can watch this one."

Even though it was sunrise, the voice that answered was as chirpy as if it were noon. "Archbishop Marshall's residence. How may I help?"

"Jacob? It's Harper. Ashbury. Grace and I need backup at the Opera House asap." Her head swam, and she leant against Grace's shoulder. Consciousness held onto a sharp ledge with slipping fingers. "And contact the dungeons. Saqib's there. We need … we need transport for … prisoners?" The numbers warped as she tried to remember how many. "Scene is contained."

"Gabriel told us and we got your text. Help was sent over an hour ago."

"No one here but us." Harper managed. Not that she could see if they were.

"I put everyone nearby to sleep," Porta said softly.

"Think they've been knocked out by magic," Harper told Jacob.

"I'll send more and ambulances."

"Thanks …"

The phone slipped from her hand, and she slumped against Grace. Mundane sight still blurry, Harper used her magic to focus on Porta, but the last of it slipped through her fingers like water.

"I'm sorry." Porta's voice was small and tired.

With so many things to be sorry for, Harper wasn't sure which ze apologised for, though she doubted it was the ones she thought ze should.

"Why did you stop her in the end?" she asked. Consciousness held on by the fingers of one hand and strong currents of exhaustion were sweeping over her.

She wasn't sure if Porta's reply was real or another memory seeping in as her eyes closed and sleep took her.

"Because I failed to protect you when we were children. I couldn't let you die now."

Chapter Thirty-Eight

Happily Ever After is a Broken Dream

Fionn fell out of the portal and lay panting on the cold flagstones of the Great Hall. His master neither approached nor spoke, but zir close presence calmed Fionn's nerves and steadied his breathing. He was home.

His body gradually recalibrated until, while hurting, he no longer felt like a sack of splinters. Four paws searched for footing and four wobbly legs hefted his slight body up. His tail hung lank behind him, and his ears were glued to his skull, but he could function. He limped up the dais to rub his head against his master's leg and was rewarded with a taloned finger scritching his forehead. He was still wanted.

His master stood and lifted Fionn. The cat braced—pain was coming, the lesson he needed to learn for his selfishness—but still his master didn't speak. The barrier between them pained Fionn, yet it was of his own making. He was lucky to be allowed home at all.

A different guilt clashed with the thought like two thunderclouds vying for the attention of the sky. He'd left Harper and Grace alone to deal with Serenità and her curse. They needed a dreamwalker, someone who could magically shield. That was him, and he'd abandoned them. *I had no choice. My master knows what is best.* A third dark cloud crashed its thunder. He didn't recognise the feels that tightened his chest and tensed his muscles. A hiss fizzled out on his tongue and he fought disobedient claws that wanted to swipe. He would never hurt the hand that cradled him so gently against zir chest.

Cuddled in his master's bed, it took Fionn a long time to go to sleep. He fretted over Harper, then fretted over the fact that meant he was being a Bad Cat to his master, then fretted over Harper again.

When he finally fell asleep, he sought her in the dreamscape. When that proved fruitless, he searched for Dayo, telling himself he only wanted to make sure Porta kept zir word.

Dayo's dream was sludgy and sickening, but it was *his* dream, not a hallucination.

Fionn woke up in human form, sobbing into the blankets of a cold bed.

"Zero." His master's voice had him scrambling out the bed mid-shift back to cat. It echoed through the castle, sending tiny creatures in the walls scurrying away. Beneath Fionn's collar, an undeniable command dug into his spine—*Come. Here.*

Fionn slunk through the castle. It neither acknowledged him nor impeded his passage. He hoped he hadn't lost his last friend.

He found his master in the lab, stirring a sickly yellow potion in a simmering cauldron. Mouth obediently open, tongue out, he sat at his master's feet.

"Not today, Zero. This must cook for another forty-eight hours." His master wasn't making eye contact with him. Fionn hung his head. "You and I must talk about other things."

Ze placed a lid on the cauldron, then swept from the room. Fionn expected zir to go to the Great Hall again, or possibly the chamber where he received most of his lessons. Instead, his master entered a cosy room with plush couches and a tea making station in one corner. There were no windows so far underground, yet the room was not so different to a human living room. It even had a television in one corner, though Fionn had never seen it on and hadn't known what it was until he went to Harper's house.

Fionn hung back in the doorway. Of all his master's familiars, he was the only one who'd ever been granted access to the space their master used to relax. Given his transgressions, it didn't seem possible for his master to want him there.

"Come in, Zero. You will find clothes behind the screen."

The door closed on its own behind Fionn, almost trapping the end of his tail. He slunk around the edge of the room until he reached the folding divider his master indicated. It was semi-transparent, decorated with a pastoral scene at odds with other decorations in the castle. Here, his master could show the weakness ze could show nowhere else.

Behind the screen was a muddled pile of clothes Fionn was usually given to go trading in. A reminder of another responsibility he'd neglected. Without him making dreams and spells to sell, they could all go hungry this month and not everyone could hunt for mice like he could.

Once humanish and dressed, he emerged with his head bowed and his hands clasped behind his back.

"Sit, Zero." His master gestured to the floor by zir feet. Fionn folded himself on the rug as small as this form would let him be. "You disobeyed me." The deep disappointment in zir voice cut deeper than any blade. Tears slid down Fionn's cheeks.

"I'm sorry," he choked out. "I was trying to help. I didn't mean to leave England. To get past the Veil I thought surely you must have allowed it. Serenità said … She said you … She must've been lying. You wouldn't …" *But Harper said One was involved …*

"I wouldn't what?" An edge of danger entered the multitude of tones as darker voices rose to prominence.

Fionn glanced up through tear-clad lashes. "You wouldn't let a foreign caster curse an English city."

His master let out a long sigh and removed zir mask. "Ah, Zero. You understand so little. I forget sometimes that you are only a cat and not capable of seeing the larger picture." Features shifted. Cheekbones sharpened, then softened. Eyes were blue, then brown, then grey. Lips plump then thin, crimson then coral. The sliding faces leant towards the feminine. His master knew what it was to have a face and body no one could bear to look at. It was something they shared. They looked at each other without judgement for the bizarre nature of their forms.

Dayo looked at you like you were made of stars, a voice whispered in the back of Fionn's head. He shushed it. It was a Bad Voice. Dayo had seen the merest glimpse of him. Despite the accuracy of his extrapolated sketches, he would hate Fionn if he ever saw what he really was. He'd be disgusted he let such a freakish creature touch him.

"Please, Master, teach me?" Fionn bowed his head, and his master ran fingers through his hair.

"York is a sacrifice we must make. The magic of England has weakened past the point where we can nurture it. Creatures of terrible darkness are creeping in. Folk flout the rules in their fear as magic ebbs. Humans push the boundaries of our Accords because they think we broke them first by allowing these monstrosities. You understand why Usa had to perish?"

"Because a Hiding weakens magic and there is too little to allow that." Fionn clenched and unclenched his hands. It was a lesson his master had drilled into his paws.

"And why an ancient being with so much power humans thought him a god also had to be vanquished?"

"I ... no?" Fionn had known his master wanted him to help Harper, but he'd thought it only because somehow their deaths were tied together.

"Think, little cat."

"Because ... it's like the Hiding? The Somnia was weakening magic by hiding it?"

"Maybe you are not a lost cause after all." His master's grip tightened in his hair, eliciting a grunt, then loosened and the petting resumed. "That area of high magic can be exploited for the good of all the country, and it stops the Somnia from taking more humans with magical bloodlines for his breeding program. Now, tell me why I would ally with the Venetians."

"Because ... what they're doing is adding magic? Through dreams? Could I not have done that for you, Master?" Even as he asked, Fionn knew the answer. Porta was a much more powerful dreamwalker than he was.

"The Venetians have experience. They can create a wound dressing over haemorrhaging York and dig down into the magical well underneath Yorkshire. If they do this, it uses none of our energy and does not break the Accords."

"I understand, Master."

"And do you understand why I offered them your painter?"

Fionn tensed. He bit his tongue hard to stop the hiss that wanted to shriek from between his teeth. Not trusting himself to speak, he shook his head.

"Did you think I was ignorant of you running to him in your sleep, little Zero? I allowed it for a time as it seemed to make you happy, and I do wish you to be happy. However, it became dangerous. You were risking your life and mine by meeting this man in the wakening. You were distracted from your vital work here. He was taking you from me. You must refocus where your folk need you. You are selfish. I have freed you of your own foolishness."

"You were at the manor?" Fionn said shakily. "It was you that I couldn't see?"

"It was. I needed to make sure the magic worked. He didn't have the gene required for the spell and so it was a gamble that your association with him would leave him open to it. A gamble that paid off."

Except it didn't, because he's free of that spell. Fionn buried the thought. He'd already brought unimaginable harm to Dayo. He wouldn't let his selfishness cause more.

"The Venetians' spell worked?" he asked, despite himself. *Is Harper okay? If her death is tied to yours, she must be alive.*

"It worked in part. Though less successful than I wished, there is a narrow well there. You and I shall be able to exploit that. You have a great destiny for such a small cat."

"Thank you for choosing me, Master, and allowing me to stay by your side even though I'm selfish."

"I love you, Zero. Lessons must be learnt, and they will be, but you will always have a place here. I believe you are starting to understand the errors of your ways. However, there is one more lesson you need to see with your own eyes."

"Yes, Master. Anything you wish." Fionn bowed, forehead to the floor. His nails, sharp as claws, dug into his wrists.

"You will visit the painter in this form, and cleanse your conscience through confession. You shall understand that what you pursued was never more than a dream."

Ringing in Fionn's head juddered through his body. He wanted to keep the memory of the garden, of staring into each other's eyes. The thought of that soft glow shifting to disgust and condemnation widened the deep crack through his heart.

"Go now, then return to the Great Hall. We have much to do to fix the problems you caused by helping the witch disrupt the spell."

"Yes, Master."

"I'm not without charity, Zero." His master cupped his chin, raising Fionn's eyes to meet zirs. "As long as you stay away from the painter, I shall ensure he is protected. He is already released and back home on my orders. Also, I shall allow you to speak to the witch. I wanted you away from her so you wouldn't have to fret over divided loyalties. I believed One could watch and contain the Seer's interference. I overestimated One's abilities. She will learn her own lessons."

Though Fionn couldn't stand the hare, a shiver of pity rippled over his skin.

"You shall return to guarding the witch. I release you from my command that she and her household not perceive you. New commands shall be placed when you return. England cannot afford for you to fall prey to your selfishness again, Zero."

"Thank you, Master." Relief washed through Fionn, even with the dread of facing Dayo.

"Go." His master released him. Fionn stood, bowed, and portalled away. He didn't go straight to Dayo, not wanting his dreamer's inevitable report to the Guard to mention the silvery portal. Its unusual appearance might be traced back to the castle and his master. Instead, he emerged in Harper's attic. Harper wasn't home, adding to his worry for her, but he could sense both AJ and Saqib downstairs. He wanted to dash down and glomp his friends, but putting off Dayo's inevitable rejection would anger his master further.

Shaking from head to toe, Fionn knocked a portal to Dayo's apartment, specifying that it was allowed to connect even if Dayo would observe it, so long as no one else could. He was gutted when it opened, his last excuse to avoid hurting his friend, gone. He stepped through.

The sight on the other side shredded the tattered ribbons of his heart. Dayo lay on his bed, staring listlessly at the ceiling. Stubble accentuated his stiff jaw. His only movement was an angry flick of one finger against something spinning in his hand. The plates in the corner were fuzzy, and a general smell of neglect permeated the air. Art lay everywhere, some broken into pieces. The stool where Fionn had sat lay on its side, one leg dangling. His own eyes stared up at him, hanging tattered from a slashed canvas next to a toppled easel.

"What happened?" He stared at the destruction in horror.

"Fi?" Dayo bolted upright. Dark circles hollowed out his eyes.

Fionn took a step towards him without thinking, then recoiled as a frown creased Dayo's forehead and he stared at Fionn's tail.

"What …? Why are you dressed up like a cat?"

"I'm … not." Fionn battled the acidic lump in his throat. He wasn't entitled to sadness. He owed Dayo the truth. "This is me. I'm … what you drew. These are my real eyes. I used … I used magic to hide my ears and tail." He hugged his tail tight to his chest. Fingernails dug through his fur. Pain was fair. Pain was grounding.

"I don't understand." Dayo took a step towards him.

Fionn backed away, almost putting his foot through a painting of tropical flowers. "I'm not … I'm not human."

Tears flowed freely, whether he was allowed them or not. Every part of his body ached to reach out. He scrunched his fist into his shirt as though it could stop the way his heart was bleeding all over the floor.

"I … lied. I changed my appearance so you'd think I was human and I … I'm the reason you were cursed."

"You …? Fi …? Slow down." Dayo rubbed his head, swaying, as he dropped back onto the bed. "Please, sit here and explain …"

"I can't. Dayo look at me. I'm. Not. Human. I'm a cat. The cat you met at the ruined abbey, that's me. The one you based your dream kitty painting on, that's me. The cat in your dreams for the last year and a bit, that's *me*. The man you kissed is a lie. He doesn't exist."

"No. That can't … You *cursed* me?"

"I didn't." Fionn sank to his knees. Breathing was almost impossible. He blinked back tears so he could have one last look at his dreamer, even if that look brought Dayo's loathing. "You were cursed *because* of me. I didn't realise. I thought our friendship was a secret. But because I'd been in your dreams, they could reach you. I didn't know it was possible. I made you vulnerable, because I was selfish and I loved your dreams. I … love *you*. Which is why you should know the truth, and you should hate me because I'm the cause of all the horrible things, and I *lied* to you, and I'm so, so sorry. I'm sorry." Fionn knocked behind him, unable to take the look of hurt confusion in Dayo's eyes any longer. "You'll never see me again."

"Fi, wait—"

As Dayo lunged for him, Fionn tumbled backwards through the portal into Harper's attic. The blackness of the void cut off Dayo's wide-eyed horror. The portal snapped shut before the artist could recklessly pursue and get lost in the bend of space.

Nothing had ever hurt so much in Fionn's life. His claws dug deep into his arms, dripping blood on the attic beams as he gasped for air. He wanted Harper, but she wasn't here, and when he tried to open a portal to her, nothing happened. Wherever she was, she was with people who mustn't see magic.

Fionn knocked three times, and fell through the portal into the waiting embrace of the one person he trusted to always take care of him. His master.

Chapter Thirty-Nine

Waking Up

The twin scents of antiseptic and coffee were the first to breach Harper's senses, followed by the sound of rubber-soled shoes and hushed, gentle voices. A page rustled at her side. Square, white tiles swam into view as she pried open sticky eyes. They were replaced a moment later by Grace's warm smile. Red lipstick. Amber eyeshadow. Clean hair.

"Hey, sleepyhead." Despite Grace's joking words, there was an edge of worry to her voice. "You're in hospital. Again."

Harper's lips cracked with a tiny smile. They probably had a rep in A&E.

"Here's some ice." Grace pressed a small piece to her lips. "Before you ask, because of course this is the most important thing, Theo dropped by. You know, the nurse you completely failed to date last year? I didn't tell him you might be seeing someone else, because it's none of his business."

Am I seeing someone else? Harper closed her eyes again. Her swollen tongue resisted as she forced it to form thick words. "It's nice he's still friendly with us." She appreciated Grace finding something light-hearted to talk about. It wasn't the right time or place for any of her million questions.

Words that might have been memory and might have been imagination swished in and out of her head. Dorian's voice. She'd Heard Dorian's voice. Old memories replaying, triggered by her dreamlike state. Only memories. *They couldn't be anything other than distant past. I can't have reached out to him across fifteen years and maybe hundreds of miles. I'm not a dreamwalker like Fionn. It must have been memory.*

By the time the hospital deemed her strong enough to leave, anxiety was growing as rapidly under her skin as the thorned plants trapping Sleeping Beauty. Saqib, Archbishop Marshall, and even AJ stopped by to visit and keep her occupied, but all she really wanted was to be home with her sister.

When they got there, Grace fussed around her bed like a mother hen. Heresy slithered into her lap. Flecks of gold glittered between the ashen particles of his body, and his bright grin was absent. He splayed out on the blanket.

Harper stroked him like she would a cat, her fingers passing through and leaving with a static tingle. "How are you?"

"Itchy." He fluffed, then settled again. "You do not need to remind me not to shield you again because I, unlike you, learn from my mistakes. Which are admittedly rare in occurrence."

Actions spoke louder than words, as the snarky illusion spirit wrapped a tentacle around her arm.

"Don't worry, I don't intend to get back into that situation anytime soon." Harper shot Grace an anxious look. *Right? Serenità isn't going to be back in a week?*

"I don't intend to let you, either." Grace sat on a corner of the bed, toying with the buttons on Harper's duvet cover. "There's been no sign of Serenità. Godfather has people hunting. I'm sorry I didn't protect you."

"Oh, Gray. I'm sorry *I* couldn't protect *you.*" Harper almost squished Heresy diving across the bed to hug her sister. "I thought we were prepared and we weren't, and it was all my fault for trusting my magic."

"Don't lose faith in yourself, Harp." Grace stroked her hair, their heads resting against each other. "We all misinterpret things, with or without magic and ... well ... they did have an unfair advantage. Even though you and I couldn't directly stop it doesn't mean we lost. You reached Porta and got zir to stop Serenità."

"Where is Porta?"

"At Bishopthorpe with Gabriel." Grace hesitated. "Miguel's there too. Porta is human and Gabriel's claimed ze was under Serenità's spell, so ze hasn't been arrested. Do you know who he ... ze ... claims to be?"

The pronoun slip was strange for Grace and Harper frowned. "No. I ..." She sat back, pulling her messy hair around to twiddle with the ends. "Before I passed out, I thought I heard something ..." *But that was a dream. A concussion or lingering effects of the curse. It wasn't real.*

"Harper …" Grace took Harper's icy fingers in her warm hands. "You know whatever happens with your birth family, you're always *my* sister, right?"

Harper swallowed tears. "I know. I never doubted you, Grace. Why … what happened that you're telling me that. Did Gabriel …?"

"No. He's not asked me though I can see the questions in his eyes like a brewing storm." Grace huffed a sigh. "I heard what Porta said to you. Ze won't confirm or deny it, but … What do you feel to be true?"

"What do I …?" Harper closed her eyes and breathed deep. Porta's words echoed in her mind. *'Because I failed to protect you when we were children. I couldn't let you die now.'* But that couldn't mean ze was … "Porta is … Dorian?"

Her mind baulked at the idea. Her brother hadn't been a dreamwalker. He couldn't have disappeared from England and ended up in Venice of all places. He wouldn't have returned to curse people. Not the sweet, caring boy she was starting to remember. Yet even reluctant acceptance opened a floodgate.

Grace held her silently as tears flowed and heartbreak clashed with the joy she wanted to experience at finding him. For a long time, Harper sat in bed and clung to her sister. Her only constant. A source of unconditional love.

When tears ran dry, she rubbed raw, itchy eyes and sat back. "When can I talk to him? Zir. I … I don't know what to think, what to feel. Ze's a stranger."

Grace curled up next to her and began the familiar ritual of brushing and plaiting Harper's hair, just as she'd done when nightmares thrashed Harper's locks into a rat's nest as a teen. "There's no 'should' for something like this. Whatever you feel is valid, even if it's all murky soup at the moment."

"Thanks, Gray. I love you."

"Love you, too, sis."

Harper rested her head on her knees. Fionn's soft lullaby hummed in the back of her mind, cooling her racing thoughts. Grace's fingers twined through her hair, and Heresy slithered up to sneak around her neck. Both were comforting, in their own way.

She looked out the mist-covered window, eyes unfocussed.

Swirling in the depths, a figure looked back. Words fell from the void where a mouth should be, Heard through magic.

Welcome home, Harper.

It's time to feast.

Acknowledgements

I am deeply grateful for my family and all the support they give my writing career. Sometimes writing is a solitary task, and sometimes it's an incessant chatter of semi-contextualised world building and plotting. My husband, Chris, handles both extremes with grace and love. My parents have let me take over their home office during school holidays so that I can meet deadlines while they play with their grandchild. Thanks, Dad, for being much better at marketing my books than I am, and Mom for always being the most eager to read them. Much love to my sister for always being on the other end of the phone when I need to chat.

Thank you to my wide network of writing friends, including (but not limited to) Team Tea and Books, the Secret Scribes, the Instant Cuppa, the British Fantasy Society, and my incredible street team, the Knights of the Theaverse (I did not pick that name!). Special thanks to my chaos co-writers, Sarah Fletcher and P. S. C. Willis, and to Mel Reynard for all their help with beta reading, plotting, and character development. Thanks also to Kim who is not a writer but now knows more about publishing than she probably ever wanted to.

Extra Special Thanks to P. S. C. Willis for something that needs a bit of explaining. You see, Dayo is not solely my character. As part of a weekly character development exercise, P and I thought it would be cute to introduce their cat-loving artist, Ash, to my art-loving cat, Fionn. This was a huge success. So much so that the characters started dating six weeks later. Knowing I would put him through hell, Fionn refused to go back to his own storyline unless he could keep his boyfriend. Huge thanks to P for giving their blessing to use Ash as a basis for Dayo, and for being alright with the characteristics I changed. At the time of me writing this, they are querying the book in which Ash is a side character. Keep an eye on @pscwillis on social media and pscwillis.com for updates. In the meantime, check out their queer YA fantasy meet-cute *Crying Out for Magic*.

There are several people who have given invaluable feedback and support so that this book could reflect real life diversity. Thank you to

Shereen for chatting with me about Saqib's responses to situations and the relevant prayers he might use, to Brent Lambert for his sensitivity read of Dayo, and to Carolina Lio (and another who declined to be mentioned by name) for the Venetian translations. Also to Mom for her Christian theology. As a practising Christian, it's something I have a reasonable handle on, but her knowledge and faith takes it to another level.

As always, many thanks to my editor, M. J. Pankey. It's always a pleasure working with you. Also, thanks to Stephanie Ellis for proofreading and formatting, and to Alison Flannery for the amazing cover art. Thanks as well to Steve and Heather at Brigids Gate for taking a chance on Harper and the gang, and for continuing to support them.

Lastly, my eternal love to my child, Sprite. Thank you for coming with me on working trips to York and Manchester, for your enthusiasm for books, and for taking naps. Thanks, too, for loving Fionn almost as much as P and I do, though I'd like to know where you hid my little glass cat.

About the Author

Alethea (ze/she) is an indie SFF author. Zir published works include the supernatural dark fantasy *Seer of York* series, published by Brigids Gate Press. Her short stories can be found in a variety of publications. Ze has a particular love for science-fantasy, dark fantasy, dystopias, and folklore. She also has soft spots for found family, hopeless romances, magi-tech, and non-human characters.

Alethea lives in Manchester, UK with zir husband, little Sprite, a cacophony of stringed instruments, and more tea than ze can drink in a lifetime.

Social Media, bonus content, and purchase options are all available via https://linktr.ee/alethearlyons.

If you enjoy any of Alethea's stories, please consider leaving a review.

About the Artist

Alison Flannery is a slightly feral artist who lives and works in Denver, Colorado. Her work is inspired by nature and she works primarily in oil paint and paper collage, sometimes both at the same time. Alison's work can be seen on her website: www.AlisonFlannery.com

Content Warnings

- Blood
- Death/dying
- Possession
- Violence
- Weapons
- Religion
- Memories of losing family
- Homophobia
- Injury to an animal (who is a shapeshifter with human level intelligence)
- Domestic abuse/gaslighting (towards said shifter)
- Aquaphobia/feeling like drowning
- Self-harm

More From Brigids Gate Press

The Wolf and the Favour

Catherine McCarthy

Ten-year-old Hannah has Down syndrome and oodles of courage, but should she trust the alluring tree creature who smells of Mamma's perfume or the blue-eyed wolf who warns her not to enter the woods under any circumstance?

The Wolf and the Favour is a tale of love, trust, and courage. A tale that champions the neurodivergent voice and proves the true power of a person's strength lies within themselves.

Fallen Destiny

Yolanda Sfetsos

Destiny isn't human and she has the horns to prove it. She's also damned good at blending into the human world.

That, along with her powers, has helped her forge a career out of locating **supernatural beings** and objects.

Got **demon** troubles? Need a mystical artifact found? Destiny's the one for the job.

All goes well for her until the day she's hired by a mysterious **nun,** and for the first time, Destiny's stumped.

How exactly does a demon hired by a nun find an **angel**?

The Seething

Ben Monroe

A family's relocation looked like a chance to relax and regroup—but as they settle into their new home, teenage Kimmie Barnes' special senses make her the target of something primordial, evil, and utterly malign.

Darkness...

Golden Oaks, California is a sleepy town on the shores of Oro Lake, and the residents have no idea what horrors lurk below the glittering waters.

Beneath the waves...

One by one, as people begin to disappear, the once quiet town is soon in the grips of a waking nightmare. An unimaginable horror consuming everything before it.

Hungry...

All while echoes of an ancient evil spread out like malignant spider webs, like dead hands reaching, grasping...

SEETHING...

A Man In Winter

Katie Marie

A mesmerizing psychological mystery from an author who brings a refreshing new voice to horror. This is a quick read, but one that keeps the reader thoroughly intrigued and entertained from beginning to end.

—Catherine Cavendish, author of *In Darkness, Shadows Breathe* and *Dark Observatio*

Arthur, whose life was devastated by the brutal murder of his wife, must come to terms with his diagnosis of dementia. He moves into a new home at a retirement community, and shortly after, has his life turned upside down again when his wife's ghost visits him and sends him on a quest to find her killer so her spirit can move on. With his family and his doctor concerned that his dementia is advancing, will he be able to solve the murder before his independence is permanently restricted?

A Man in Winter examines the horrors of isolation, dementia, loss, and the ghosts that come back to haunt us.

Visit our website at: www.brigidsgatepress.com

www.ingramcontent.com/pod-product-compliance
Lightning Source LLC
LaVergne TN
LVHW040133080526
838202LV00042B/2896